"IF IT'S WITCHCRAFT YOU WANTED, IT'S WITCHCRAFT YOU'RE GOING TO GET," SHE WHISPERED . . .

The woman riding in the wagon closest to Margaret, who had apparently overheard her, gave her a surprised look.

"My familiar's name is Vengeance," Margaret said softly.

The woman smiled bitterly. "Then give it to them."

The snake manifested in the midst of the crowd and screams filled the air.

"It's poisonous!" someone screamed. "Run!"

The crowd scattered.

"It's witchcraft!" someone else yelled.

"It's after the magistrate!"

He danced a sort of jig in an attempt to evade the copperhead, but he was unsuccessful. His screams of fear and agony filled the air as the fangs injected their poison in his leg.

"Will he die?" Margaret's companion asked.

"I leave that to the gods to decide," Margaret said.

The High Sheriff was undaunted by the diversion. He soothed the startled horses and led the wagon to the giant oak tree. Three nooses were already in place. The hanging was about to begin . . .

Books by Devin O'Branagan

Spirit Warriors
Witch Hunt

Published by POCKET BOOKS

WITCH HUNT

DEVIN O'BRANAGAN

POCKET BOOKS

New York   London   Toronto   Sydney   Tokyo   Singapore

An *Original* Publication of POCKET BOOKS

POCKET BOOKS, a division of Simon & Schuster Inc.
1230 Avenue of the Americas, New York, NY 10020

ISBN: 0-671-68455-8

First Pocket Books printing October 1990

10 9 8 7 6 5 4 3 2 1

POCKET and colophon are registered trademarks of
Simon & Schuster Inc.

Printed in the U.S.A.

This novel is dedicated to all those souls who have been, and continue to be, persecuted in the name of religion.

Acknowledgments

The author would like to thank Steve Kowit—who took a very bad poem and made it very good—and Garry, who continues to believe.

First Witch: When shall we three meet again,
In thunder, lightning or in rain?

Second Witch: When the hurlyburly's done,
When the battle's lost and won.

—Shakespeare, *Macbeth,* Act I, scene 1

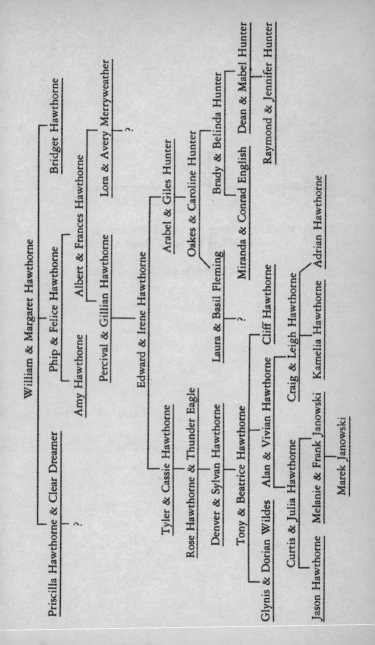

WITCH
HUNT

Prologue

Midsummer 1992
Montvue, Colorado

Preacher Alexander Cody was afraid. He hadn't been afraid since that horrible time in Nicaragua when he was a control agent with the CIA. But God had claimed him in his moment of fear, and, from that time on, he had never been weak of spirit again—until now, on this airplane.

His wife, Rachel, sat in the aisle seat next to him, holding their baby daughter, Eden, in the crook of her left arm. She sneaked her right hand into his, and it wasn't long before the sweat from their palms became intimate. Embarrassed by his own evidence of fear, Cody stared fixedly out the window and tried to avoid her gaze, but once she managed to capture it in the glass's reflection and give him a wan smile. As hard as he tried, he couldn't return her attempt at solace. Instead he averted his eyes and prayed, promising God the sacrifice of anything—even his delicious lust for Rachel—if only He wouldn't let the plane crash.

The small jet recoiled from the fury of the wind with another explosive shudder, and the cabin lights blinked, then failed. Cody gasped at the sudden darkness while muffled screams filled the air.

1

There were sixteen passengers on the short red-eye commuter flight which had originated in Colorado Springs. Because the airline serviced mostly business travelers, the seats were arranged in groups of four to facilitate small in-flight meetings. Cody and Rachel, who were returning home from visiting her mother in the Springs, were seated across from Alan and Curtis Hawthorne. Cody knew the men to be father and son, both of Montvue's most prestigious law firm, Hawthorne and Hunter. Cody was glad that the darkness now shielded his haunted face from the view of the important Montvue citizens who sat across from him. He had a reputation to protect. It was his reputation that had allowed him to reach so many people and spread the Lord's truth.

Alexander Cody had been in the Special Forces during the Vietnam War. His record had been heroic. Then, in the final months of the war, he had been caught in a VC napalm attack. He had survived, but just barely. It had taken years of skin grafts, plastic surgery, physical therapy, and, most of all, pain before he recovered enough to function in a normal fashion. Then, because of his record and connections, he was recruited by the CIA to be a control, or "mother" agent. His "babies" were field operatives, and his primary duties involved the coordination of their activities. It was five years ago when he had gone to Nicaragua to locate one of his missing babies, who was believed to be in the hands of the Sandinistas. There, in the first field action he had seen since Vietnam, he had frozen with terror. Cody had once felt invincible and had rudely discovered he wasn't, and with that knowledge had come fear. In that moment of inner blackness in the Nicaraguan jungle, he had, for the first time in his life, reached out to a higher power, and it had claimed him. He had been filled by a blinding light which lent him strength and courage, and he had successfully rescued the kidnapped agent. When he returned to the States, he submitted his resignation to the Agency and returned to his hometown, a small mining community in the Rocky Mountains. There he pursued his spiritual calling and was ordained as a minister by the local fundamentalist Christian church to which his parents belonged.

Then he wrote the book that launched him into the public eye. It was a book about the end times, called *Doomsday*. What made it unique was his military and espionage background, coupled with his burning-bush experience. In his public appearances to promote *Doomsday*, the media discovered that he was a dynamic presence with all the components necessary for celebrity status: charm, good looks, sex appeal, and charisma. An astute, entrepreneurial independent video producer named Max Malone had contacted Cody and proposed a pilot for a prime-time evening television series called "Preacher Cody." Max hauled his equipment to the ranch Cody had bought outside of Montvue and filmed a half-hour of taped discussion with the compelling preacher and his young bride, who possessed a fresh, Madonna-like innocence and beauty. He edited in dramatic footage which emphasized the evils of the world that the preacher discussed and added a slick musical soundtrack, and, when he was done, the finished product was captivating. The pilot sold immediately. Cody's message attracted the religious fundamentalists, his image attracted the right-wing conservatives, his age and good looks attracted the young, and the creative, polished nature of the production attracted most everyone else. Even those who didn't agree with his views listened to them anyway and used the material to fuel lively debates. In its Sunday-night time slot, Cody's television show shot to the top of the ratings, garnering a position as one of the most popular religious talk shows in history by its third week on the air.

Cody was startled out of his reverie by the captain's voice on the plane's loudspeaker.

"Ladies and gentlemen, Captain Cassel again." His voice sounded hearty and reassuring. "Don't panic, we're doing just fine. There's no denying it's a hell of a storm— these Rocky Mountain showers tend to hit unexpectedly and be a bit rugged—but I've flown through worse, no problem. We'll be landing at Montvue in about five minutes. Sorry there aren't any lights for you ladies to fix your faces by. Captain out."

The tension relaxed somewhat.

Generally peeved by the whole situation, Cody decided to file a formal complaint with the airline about the captain's use of profanity.

The cabin lit up from without. The flash of lightning illuminated the face of the man who sat across from Cody. Curtis Hawthorne gazed out the window with an impassive expression, and Cody felt a twinge of jealousy. That kind of courage was the ultimate evidence of faith. How could this man—whom Cody had heard wasn't the slightest bit religious—not be as frightened as he?

Darkness returned.

"Aunt Glynis told me at breakfast that she dreamed of the Salazar curse," Curtis Hawthorne said quietly.

There was a moment of silence.

Alan Hawthorne replied in a gruff voice. "Glynis is imaginative."

"Dad?"

"Yes."

"I love you."

The plane began to descend.

The lights of the landing field were blurred by sheets of rain, but Cody felt a wave of relief when he saw them. There was no need to advise the passengers to buckle their seat belts for landing; they had been told to strap themselves in when they encountered the storm. For the first time in fifteen minutes, Cody turned to Rachel and smiled, an overture she eagerly reciprocated.

Cody returned his gaze to the lights below. They were fast approaching.

Another streak of lightning appeared out of the night, and Cody watched in stunned horror as it struck the right wing of the plane. The jet trembled from the blow as a crash of thunder drowned out the sound of the engines, and then the plane began to rock. Bile rose in Cody's throat, and adrenaline began to surge through his body. A sense of unreality flooded him, and his world began to move in slow motion. "God, this can't be happening," he muttered. Shrill cries filled the cabin.

The rocking became more pronounced, and Cody felt one of the wings hit the ground. The jet casually flipped over.

Secured to his seat, he clawed with frenzy at the air in a vain effort to halt events. The whine of the engines and the sickening sound of crunching metal filled his ears. Hand luggage began to fly. The runway lights filled the cabin with an eerie glow, and he watched as Curtis's head slammed up against the cabin wall and dark blood began to flow. Next to him, Alan's seat buckled, and Cody imagined he could hear the old man's back snap as his body twisted. Rachel, her face glistening with tears as she clutched the baby tightly to her bosom, kept yelling Cody's name, but he didn't even hear her.

The inverted jet skidded down the runway shrouded in a veil of sparks.

After what seemed like an eternity, the plane's movement ceased. There was a moment of silence within the cabin, and then it was filled with chaos. Cody unhooked himself from his seat and dropped to the ceiling beneath him.

"Help us!" Rachel yelled, unable to release herself because she was clinging to Eden. But Cody didn't care. He just wanted to get out before the fire started. He could already imagine the imminent flames devouring his body. The other passengers watched him in obvious disgust as he pushed an old man out of his way and dodged for the emergency exit across the aisle, which now rested under the wing of the plane. Another man was already there, trying to open it, and Cody pushed him out of his way as well. He tried the latch, but it was jammed.

"Alex!" Rachel cried in a voice of disbelief. "Help us!"

Ignoring her, Cody made his way to the front of the plane and tried the door to the cockpit, but it was locked from the inside, and the pilot did not respond to his knocking.

He raced back to Rachel's seat. She had brought a small, hard carry-on suitcase on board. He reached up underneath her seat and fished for the case.

"Why won't you help us?" she screamed at him, struggling to open the seat belt with one hand while trying to hold on to the squirming baby with the other.

He found the case and slammed it against the window. He heard something crack and grew hopeful but then realized it was the suitcase, not the glass, that had broken. He began to sob.

Curtis, apparently dazed from his head wound, released himself from his seat and lowered himself to the floor. His father's chair dangled in the air, and Curtis made a move to release him.

"Don't try and get me down. My back's broken." Alan paused. "The plane's going to explode, son."

Cody spun around and looked out the window, following Alan's gaze. *Fire!* His sobs intensified when he saw the flaming engines.

"Help us," Rachel whimpered.

Curtis moved to her and opened her seat belt. He guided her and Eden down, then sank to the floor. "Dad . . . my head . . . I don't know how long I can stay conscious, but I'll keep the flames at bay. Can you help?"

"I'll try," Alan said.

Even in the midst of his terror, Cody registered their strange exchange. He crouched down and hugged himself as Curtis and Alan began to chant strange, unintelligible words. His sobs quieted as he quickly became mesmerized by the sound of their two voices. He looked up and saw that Rachel, too, was captivated by their chanting. He glanced out the window and saw that the flames of the engine fire were ebbing.

Cody began to feel as if he were floating. The noise and commotion of the other passengers seemed to fade away. He wondered if he were dying. He felt a strong presence of warmth and love, a sense of comfort and reassurance. "I love you, too, Mommy," he whispered, then he lost track of time.

Suddenly he was startled by a loud pounding outside the hull. Someone had arrived to help. He jumped to his feet. He could see no rescue vehicles yet, but there were people who had driven out from the small terminal. He rushed past Rachel and Eden and ran to the emergency exit door. "It's jammed!" he yelled at them through the glass. "The door is jammed!"

One of the men outside ran back to the car and removed a tire iron from its trunk. He returned and began to pry at the door from the outside.

Cody looked around. Curtis was now chanting alone— his father seemed to be dead—and the blood flow from his head had increased. As his voice became noticeably weaker, the flames outside began to spread. The correlation struck Cody, and a different kind of fear filled him. Curtis and Alan had actually been controlling the fire. How could anyone do such a thing? What were these men? They could only be in league with the Devil, he quickly decided. No normal, God-fearing human being could perform such a feat. Satan's servants, using his vile powers in an attempt to save themselves. His breath came in labored gasps.

He thought about his own pitiful behavior. Why had he been such a coward? Had these people cast a spell over him and stolen his faith? That would explain it. Rachel saw and heard their sorcery. She would understand what they had done to him. He began to hyperventilate. He had to escape this place.

The Hawthornes seemed to be in the possession of some infernal, supernatural abilities. Their powers were more than human beings had the right to possess. The angel Lucifer had been damned to hell because of his willful imitation of God; how much more heinous a crime to be a mere human being daring to do the same!

In that moment Cody made a vow to God that, if he survived, he would uncover the truth behind the Hawthornes' sorcery and reveal it to the world. He would be able to do that, too. God had given him the power.

The emergency door opened. Before Cody fled, he looked back and saw Curtis slump into unconsciousness. The flames instantly billowed up into the night air.

Eleven passengers managed to escape the wreckage before the plane exploded.

_____ *Chapter One* _____

June 1992

1

Thirty-one-year-old Leigh Hawthorne had left behind the horror of the past and created for herself the perfect life. But, as the Boeing 747 chased the sun across the sky, she fought a growing fear that her fairy-tale existence was coming to an end. Things beyond her control had begun to go wrong and had caused her old insecurities to resurface.

It had started with what her five-year-old son, Adrian, had seen. Then the telegram reporting the deaths of her husband's father and brother—the mysterious relatives about whom Craig never spoke. And now they were heading toward his old hometown in Colorado, a place that held the secret of the Hawthornes. Even though Leigh had spent the past ten years wanting to know what Craig had fled from, now the impending knowledge filled her with dread.

To relieve her anxiety, Leigh listened to the score of the musical *Razzmatazz* through the headphones of her Walkman. The music was dynamic and would work well with her acrobatic style of choreography, the uniqueness of which had been responsible for landing her the plum job with the show. It had been years since she had worked outside the home, having been long content with the creative demands of marriage and motherhood. But the urge had recently returned and she had pursued it with success.

Against the backdrop of her closed eyelids, Leigh imagined the athletic poetry in motion that was her trademark—dramatic leaps and kicks, flashy pirouettes, and what Craig called her hot-to-trot T-and-A sexery—and was pleased with the progress of her work on the opening number. However, she was dismayed to see the form of Crista Corrigan change into her own and had a momentary struggle to change the image. Crista was the star of *Razzmatazz*. She didn't have the incapacitating stage fright that had cut short Leigh's own career as a performer.

Leigh's passion for the theater had begun when as a young child she'd been desperate for some form of escape. It had grown during an apprenticeship with dance master Andre Beauchard. It had climaxed with winning the ingenue role in the Broadway musical *Hooligans*. And it had shriveled on opening night. Small audiences were painful for her, but she could nonetheless perform; large audiences were too great a hurdle for her stage fright to overcome. So she had taken her mother's advice and got married.

Leigh's eyes opened to slits, and she studied Craig, who sat across the aisle from her. It was the only good advice her mother had ever given her.

Craig sat with their nine-year-old daughter, Kamelia, both poring over a batch of medical journals. Like father, like daughter. Leigh sighed. The daughter was definitely not going to follow in the mother's dance steps. From the progress Kamelia was making, Leigh guessed that she would probably be awarded the Nobel prize for medicine after performing the first successful brain transplant by the time she was eighteen years old. Leigh grinned at the thought.

"What's so funny?" Adrian demanded.

Leigh opened her eyes and pulled the earphones from her head. "Did you say something, honey?"

Her son nodded. "I'm mighty bored."

Leigh gave him a weak smile. "You could take a nap."

Adrian crossed his arms and shook his head.

"I'll rub your back."

That served to weaken his resolve.

They lifted up the arm of the seat that divided them. Adrian lay down with his head in her lap, and Leigh began to give him a gentle back rub.

"Can we tell Daddy 'bout our secret now?" Adrian asked.

Leigh's stomach tensed with anxiety. "We must never tell him, Adrian. Okay?"

"Why?"

"Because."

"Oh."

Someday she'd have to offer him some real answers, but for now *because* would have to do.

Leigh's thoughts turned to her other major concern— the Montvue Hawthornes.

All Leigh knew was that Craig had left Colorado immediately upon graduating high school. He had gone to New York, where he had worked his way through college and medical school. Afterward he had gone on to develop a successful practice in obstetrics and gynecology in Greenwich Village. He had not contacted his family in twenty years. From the telegram that had arrived, however, it was evident the Hawthornes had known exactly where to find him.

"What's going on inside that pretty blond head?" Craig asked.

Leigh was surprised by his sudden attention. "I was thinking about your family. What are they like?"

"Capitalistic slimeballs."

"Mmmm. Sorry I asked."

"Don't waste energy worrying about it. We're in there for the funerals and then, like the wind, we're gone." He blew her a kiss and turned back to his reading.

Leigh liked Craig's style. It was . . .well, it was weird. Upon their first meeting, after he had inserted the specu-

10

lum, he had looked into her and said, "Far out." She had changed doctors but found a husband.

"It's a mighty long ride," Adrian said. *Mighty* was his newest word.

Leigh looked down into his face and resisted the urge to smother it with kisses. She thought him terribly cute. Just like his father. Kamelia, on the other hand, had inherited Leigh's grace and classic beauty. Somehow, in the baby-making, the genes had become strangely spliced. Kamelia had Leigh's looks and Craig's mind, and Adrian had Craig's looks and her creativity. It was that imagination that had caused Adrian to see what he had seen, she told herself for the umpteenth time. That's all there was to it. What else could it have been? She replaced the headphones and once again became lost in *Razzmatazz*.

2

It was nearing dark when the small plane they had chartered at Denver's Stapleton Airport finally landed in Montvue. They were met at the airport's tiny terminal by a middle-aged man with graying temples and troubled eyes. He did a double take when he first saw Craig; the shaggy collar-length hair, wire-rimmed glasses, baggy pants, and oversized shirt—Leigh called it Craig's mad professor look—obviously weren't what the man in the expensive tailored suit had expected. However, he quickly offered Craig his hand. "My condolences."

Craig shook his hand. "Ray." He nodded toward Leigh and the children. "My ball and chain and the two little anchors."

Ray looked uncomfortable.

Leigh smiled. "We keep him from floating away. I'm Leigh. Our children, Kamelia and Adrian."

"Ray Hunter. Partner in Craig's father's law firm."

"You're some kinda family, too. Right?" Craig asked.

"Some kind," Ray said, then chuckled. "Whatever have you become, Craig?"

"Free," Craig said.

Shaking his head, Ray took two suitcases in hand and led them to his Cadillac.

Montvue was a town of twenty-five thousand people, built where the foothills of the Rocky Mountains met the rich farmlands of the eastern prairie in northern Colorado. Even in twilight, Leigh was impressed with its picturesque beauty. On the outskirts of town were sprawling farms set against the backdrop of the blue snow-capped mountain range. As they entered Montvue itself, they were greeted by wide, clean streets lined with a variety of shade trees; old, mostly Victorian-style homes; spacious, well-kept lawns; colorful flowers and bird baths dotting the landscape; and old-fashioned lemonade stands abandoned for the day. Leigh felt a strange wrenching in her stomach. This was the kind of hometown she had longed for in her childhood. An unwelcome mixture of emotions welled up as she compared Craig's comfortable, upper-class roots to her own seedy background. Leigh looked at her husband with surprise. She would never have imagined him in such a wholesome, all-American setting. Did she really know him at all? She felt her insecurities surge, and her face became hot.

Without looking at her, Craig reached across the seat and took her hand. "Boring towns breed boring people," he said casually.

Did he know what I was feeling? she wondered. "You're not boring," she said.

"Yeah, well, I did a lot of LSD after I split."

Leigh at least knew him well enough to know that wasn't true. From Ray's sidelong glance in Craig's direction, it seemed he wasn't so sure.

"So, how's the old witch doin'?" Craig asked.

"If you're referring to your mother, as well as might be expected," Ray said evenly. "But you certainly seem to be taking this tragedy quite well."

Craig took off his glasses and began to clean them with his rainbow-colored tie. "I loved Dad and Curt. If I didn't, I wouldn't be here. I'm sorry my grief isn't evident enough to please you."

The car pulled into a cobblestone driveway, and they passed through an open wrought-iron gate. A gold-lettered sign on the tall, spiked fence said "Hawthorne Manor." The grounds through which they slowly drove were so unusual that Leigh found herself gawking open-mouthed at the sight. Beneath the ancient beauty of several towering oak and maple trees was an expanse of formal Roman gardens. A large fountain flowed lazily, the water dark in the dim light. Statues of Roman gods and goddesses dressed in green ivy were scattered throughout the yard. Classically designed sandstone benches were set among the multitude of flower beds, and blazing torches were perched on a variety of stands.

When they turned a bend in the drive and Leigh caught her first sight of the mansion, she gasped aloud. It was a three-story Queen Anne–style house with steep-pitched gabled bays, ornate wooden balconies, and prism-cut leaded glass windows. Ray parked at the foot of the stairs, which led to a large porch that curved around the house, encircling half of the first floor. The front door was open, and, as Ray unloaded suitcases from the trunk, Craig led his family into his childhood home.

The foyer was overflowing with sympathy wreaths and flower bouquets, but the room itself was dominated by a large statue of a winged Mercury. In front of it a lit brass oil lamp hung from the ceiling by three delicate chains. The oak parquet floor, polished to a dazzling sheen, reflected the flickering of the flame.

An arched inner doorway was made of cherrywood pillars and had a transom of stained glass. It opened into the parlor, which was brightly furnished with antique rugs and furniture and colorful Tiffany lamps. Bas-relief baroque moldings made intricate designs on the walls and ceiling, and water flowed in a small marble fountain which stood before a large mirror. The fireplace, distinguished by a delicately carved mahogany mantel, was alive with fire. A baby grand piano occupied one corner of the room.

"Wow," Kamelia said.

"Pretentious, isn't it?" Craig said.

Leigh shook her head. "It's wonderful."

A woman appeared beneath an arched doorway that led into the depths of the house. She was a small woman

13

in her sixties who had a regal bearing. Her strawberry-blond hair was streaked with gray, and she wore it in a short, elegant style. Her face, obviously once beautiful, was—with the exception of the red, puffy eyes of grief—still attractive.

"Craig." Her voice, which had a cultured English accent, was hard.

"Mother."

"Thank you for coming."

"Sorry I had to."

"Of course."

Leigh, embarrassed by the coldness of their exchange, tuned it out and studied the older woman. Her fair coloring indicated that Craig had got his dark looks from his father's side of the family. She glanced around, hoping to see a picture of Alan Hawthorne, but there were no photographs in evidence.

There was a loud commotion, and suddenly the room filled with people. A bent, elderly woman shuffled over to Craig and threw her arms around him. Craig didn't hesitate to return her embrace with affection.

"Oh, Craig. Craig," she said, weepily.

"Aunt Glynis." He patted her back. "It'll be okay."

An electric wheelchair rolled toward Craig, and the old man in it extended his hand. "My boy."

Craig shook it warmly. "Uncle Dori."

A teenage boy and girl stood in the corner and regarded the visitors coolly.

Ray deposited his load of suitcases in front of the fireplace. "Don't know where you want these."

"I'll take care of them," Craig said.

There was an awkward silence as everyone studied one another.

"It seems there's a lot of people here who don't know each other," Glynis said at last.

Craig cleared his throat. "The big beautiful blonde is Leigh. The little beautiful blonde is Kammi . . . Kamelia. The one who looks like me, only neater, is Adrian. I call him Slugger."

No one said anything. Leigh took a deep breath to steady herself.

"My mother's name is Vivian," Craig continued. "And, from the fond hellos, I'm sure you've figured out that Glynis and Dorian are my aunt and uncle."

"How do you do?" Leigh said politely, and then felt an instant regret. She knew how they were doing, and it wasn't very well. She wished she had just said hello. Besides, she found herself worrying that her Brooklyn accent was still too pronounced despite all her years of trying to rid herself of it.

No one responded to her anyway.

Adrian scrutinized his grandmother carefully. "Are you the old witch?"

A slight smile played at the woman's lips. "I imagine so."

"Mighty big hi," he said.

Vivian studied Adrian for a few moments with a bittersweet expression—Leigh wondered if she were recalling another little boy whom he resembled—before responding. "Hi," she said softly.

Glynis pointed to the teenagers. "That's Jason and Melanie, Curtis's children. He's seventeen. She's sixteen. They're orphans now. Did you know that Julia passed over?"

"I didn't know," Craig said. "I'm sorry. Julia was special." He looked at the teenagers. "I'm your wayward uncle."

"We've heard about you," Jason said.

"Yeah, I'm sure you have."

"Is Leigh . . . well, you know?" Melanie asked.

"Nope," Craig said, and six pairs of stony eyes turned to stare at her.

She didn't know what she wasn't, but Leigh suddenly wished she were somewhere else.

"And the children?" Vivian asked.

"Yeah, Mother, they are," Craig said, his voice weary.

"We are what?" Kamelia asked.

"Nothing that matters," Craig said pointedly.

A gasp, en masse, escaped the Montvue Hawthornes.

"When are the funerals?" Craig asked.

"What?" Vivian asked, her fair face even more pale than it had been before.

"Funerals," Craig repeated.

"Oh . . . tomorrow."

"What rooms should we take?"

"Those in the east wing."

Craig moved to retrieve their suitcases.

"Dinner will be served at seven," Vivian said.

"We ate on the plane. Our inner clocks are ticking to a different metronome. We're going to crash."

Vivian seemed startled. "Well . . . then breakfast is at seven in the morning."

"We'll be there with bells on," Craig said, then led Leigh and the children from the room.

3

"Am I what?" Leigh demanded when they were alone in their room.

"It doesn't matter," Craig said.

"It sure seems to matter to them."

"I don't give a flying rat's ass what matters to them."

"At first I thought they wanted to know if I was monied or something. But that doesn't make sense when applied to the kids."

"Nope."

"Well?"

He winced. "God, Leigh, I shouldn't have brought you. I can tell already it's going to be like taking sweet Alice on a tour through an ultra-bizarre wonderland."

That quieted Leigh. She didn't want him to regret her presence. And she knew that Craig hadn't kept his secrets for ten years only to suddenly bare his soul to her. She was good at patience. She was content to watch and wait.

Kamelia opened the door and glided into their room, unannounced. "Well, Dad, I'm impressed. Hawthorne Manor sure beats the loft."

"You should knock before entering your parents' bedroom," Leigh said.

"I always listen first, Mom. Didn't hear any sex."

16

"You don't always hear sex, dear," Leigh said. "Someday you're going to embarrass yourself."

Kamelia flashed her pretty smile. "I don't embarrass easily."

"Craig, I really think all those anatomy books you've given her have warped her sensibilities."

Craig pushed his glasses higher up onto his nose and regarded them both with a serious expression. "Actually, my strategy is to make her so sophisticated and worldly wise that she'll scare the piss out of any boy who might want to come on to her." He shrugged. "Then I'll never have to worry about those things that fathers of girls worry about."

"Take note of that, Kamelia," Leigh said. "It's all a diabolical plan."

"I'll take my chances." She gave them each a kiss. "I promise not to return tonight," she said, then winked at them and shut the door behind her.

"Well, it seems that we have permission," Craig said.

"For what?"

He stuck his hands deep into the pockets of his trousers and hung his head sheepishly. "You know, the effword."

Leigh laughed. "God, you're so . . . irreverent."

He looked up at her, his eyes brimming with love. "About God, maybe. About you, never."

And that was true.

He pulled her dress up over her head, then unhooked her bra, letting it fall to the floor. Momentarily, he captured a nipple in his mouth and suckled. Leigh felt her knees grow weak as pleasure coursed through her. Slowly, he began to kiss his way down her body, removing her nylons and panties as he descended. When she was completely undressed, he picked her up and carried her to the bed, where he gently laid her down.

He was out of his own clothes and on top of her almost immediately. Tenderly, reverently, he began to explore her body with his eyes, hands, and lips. She began to respond with a need to reciprocate, but, surprisingly, he restrained her. "It's Midsummer's. It's my day to worship at the gorgeous, green-eyed, blond altar of womanhood," he whispered. "So let me do my thing, okay?"

It wasn't the first time he had made such an unusual request. She surrendered to his wishes and lay back submissively, allowing him to make her feel good. He did it well, she mused as her nipples tightened with pleasure, her thighs began to quiver, and an intense heat invaded her pelvis. It wasn't long before she could no longer think and was floating on a sea of sensual delight.

He slid himself slowly into her body. "Your womb is the cauldron of life, where magic is born," she heard him say, but she was too lost in the world of pure sensation to respond.

He moved inside her with erotic precision while his hands caressed her artfully. As her passion began to peak, she had to resist the urge to wrap her legs around him and draw him deeper into her body, because he wanted her to be passive in receiving his adoration.

And there were times when she was afraid to be anything other than what he wanted her to be.

Afterward, they fell asleep.

4

"I love you, Daddy. Please don't cry."

"Your mother is a cunt. If she hadn't tricked me into marrying her by getting herself knocked up with you, I would be a success. Instead . . ." Grief overcame him again, and he shook with renewed sobs.

The little girl began to cry, too. "I'm sorry, Daddy. You want me to go away?"

"Naw. It's too late for that now." He guzzled the remaining whiskey and threw the bottle against the wall, where it shattered.

The little girl jumped, and her tears flowed harder. "I'll clean it up. It'll be okay." She scrambled to pick up the glass and, in her haste, cut her finger. The cut was deep and began to bleed. She was worried he would see and be mad and so tried to hide her hand in the pocket of her smock, but the blood soon soaked through

*the light cotton. She scooted across the floor and tried
to make herself inconspicuous in the corner, but a fat
rat was trying to do the same, and the two collided. She
screamed, which brought her mother stumbling out of
the kitchen. Soon she was hovering over the little girl,
breathing sour, wine-scented breath into her face.*

*"Whatsa matter, little Leigh?" She saw the blood on
her smock and croaked with horror. "What did you do
to my little girl, you bastard?"*

"No, Mommy! Daddy didn't do it!"

*Her mother grasped the broken neck of the whiskey
bottle and, with an animal cry, staggered toward the
couch. Her father tried unsuccessfully to dodge the
weapon—he was even more drunk than his attacker.
The sound of tearing flesh struck her little ears even
before she heard her father's screams.*

"No! Mommy! Daddy! No!"

"No! Mommy! Daddy!"

The yells were coming from the children's room. Leigh
forced herself to consciousness and made her way across
the hall. She opened the door and pushed the old-
fashioned wall button that turned on the light. Adrian
was thrashing about in his bed, whimpering and talking
incoherently.

"Mom?" Kamelia said sleepily from the other bed.

Leigh moved to Adrian and gathered him into her
arms, closing her eyes to the assault of tiny fists that
lashed out at her face.

"Hush, baby. It's okay. Mommy's here."

Adrian's struggles quieted, and he opened his eyes,
not slowly and sleepily but wide with sudden alarm.
"They're going to kill us all. All of us. Everywhere." His
voice sounded strangely mature, like it had been that
other time.

"Oh, God, it can't be happening again," Leigh
whispered.

"Who, son?" Craig asked. Leigh hadn't heard him
come in. Her heart sank.

Adrian looked around frantically, as if searching for
the enemy. "Them. The ones who have always been
afraid of us."

Craig sat down on the bed. "When?"

"Soon."

An involuntary sob escaped Leigh.

"Where?" Craig asked.

"Everywhere. It'll start here, but it'll spread. There will be no place that will be safe. It'll be worse than the last time. It'll even be worse than the time before that."

"Can we stop it?" Craig asked.

"Perhaps," Adrian said, and then he went limp in her arms.

"Adrian!" Leigh began to shake him.

Slowly Adrian opened sleepy eyes. "Mommy?" he asked, his voice small and confused.

She clutched him protectively to her bosom. "It's okay now."

Craig gave her a hard look. "This has happened before?"

Tears filled Leigh's eyes. Without really understanding why, she had been afraid of his finding out. But it was too late now. She nodded.

"The same vision?"

She shook her head. "He saw the plane crash. He saw your father and brother die. He spoke their names. He had never even heard their names before." She moaned. "Maybe this time it was just a dream?" she asked hopefully.

"Let's hope so." He paused for a moment. "You should have told me about this sooner, Leigh," he said, and then he left the room.

She tried to read Craig's face and tone of voice but couldn't decipher it. She could only tell that he was disturbed . . . with her, with Adrian, with the message Adrian had delivered, she couldn't tell. The hollow presence of dark dread took root in the pit of her stomach, where it was to remain for a long time to come.

This time it probably was just a nightmare, she told herself.

As Leigh gently rocked Adrian in her arms, she glanced at the old scar on her finger and thought about nightmares—those that were only dreams, and those that came true.

The dining room was no less impressive than any other corner of the mansion. The table and sideboard were solid oak, with heavy claw feet, and the shelf on the sideboard was poised on two small wooden griffins. A matching china cabinet was filled with an impressive collection of chinaware. The bronze and crystal chandelier held a dozen wax candles. When Leigh and her family arrived for breakfast, the maid, a striking woman not much older than Leigh, was serving coffee. She smiled at Leigh, who returned the smile gratefully—it was the first gesture of warmth anyone had offered her since her arrival.

Vivian, Dori, Glynis, Melanie, and Jason were already seated.

"You may serve now, Helena," Vivian said.

"Yes, madam," the maid replied. She spoke with a thick Polish accent.

"My significant others here know nothing about our family . . . history," Craig announced suddenly. "I like it that way."

"As you wish," Vivian said. She passed a chilled decanter of orange juice around the table. "Since we're now all together, perhaps we could toast to Alan and Curtis."

Everyone filled, then raised their glasses.

"Will you propose the toast, Craig?" Vivian asked.

A tense silence filled the room. Leigh held her breath. She imagined he would say something like, "Now that you're in the know, guys, tell us, is Elvis *really* dead?" But he surprised them all.

"To Dad and Curt. I'm sorry I never said good-bye, but even in absentia, our ties were strong. We'll meet again."

"To Alan and Curtis," voices said.

Glasses clinked.

Adrian dropped his glass and flooded the table with juice.

"You little klutz!" Melanie shouted as she jumped up to avoid the orange stream.

Leigh stemmed its flow with her linen napkin. Adrian began to cry, and she tousled his hair playfully. " 'Sokay."

Melanie glared at her.

Leigh sighed and sopped up the rest of the flood with Adrian's napkin.

Helena served strawberry ice, garnished with fresh mint sprigs.

"You're a doctor now," Glynis said.

Craig nodded.

"Good work for someone like you."

"If you've got it, flaunt it."

"What about your children?" Vivian asked. "What kind of special gifts do they have?"

"Kammi's going to take after me and be a healer." He paused and looked at Leigh. "And it seems that Slugger's got the Sight."

Vivian looked pleased. "Is that true?" she asked Kamelia.

"I'm going to be a doctor just like Dad," Kamelia said proudly.

A special gift. Maybe he's not mad after all, Leigh thought.

"So, how did you two meet?" Melanie asked Leigh.

"I was one of his first patients."

"Kinky," Melanie commented.

"Isn't that sort of unethical or something?" Jason asked.

"Hippocrates be damned," Craig said.

Leigh was glad Helena chose that moment to serve the plates of quiche and melon wedges.

Light, insignificant chatter ensued, and Leigh was relieved. She studied Melanie and Jason. The teenagers' eyes weren't reddened from tears, and they seemed quite self-possessed. She thought it was odd for children to be so unaffected by their father's death.

Melanie caught Leigh looking at her. "What's your trip?" she asked harshly.

"I was thinking how sorry I am for your loss," Leigh said.

Melanie shrugged. "We're used to it." Her voice was dull.

"That's too bad," Leigh said.

"Now that your father and brother have passed over, I assume you'll move back home, Craig," Vivian said.

Craig shook his head. "No way."

"But you're the man of the family now. You must come back. We need you."

"No fuckin' way."

"But—"

Craig stood up abruptly, knocking his chair over. His anger was more evident in his trembling finger as he pointed at her than in his tightly controlled voice. "Stay out of my life, Mother. I claimed it, it's mine, and you can't have it." He righted his chair and left the room.

Seemingly unmoved, Vivian took a sip of coffee and looked at Leigh. "I'm sure you're very sweet, dear, but you must understand that you're never going to be a part of this family."

Leigh was stunned. She wasn't good at assertiveness, but, for the sake of Kamelia and Adrian—who were staring at her with mouths agape—she managed to say, "It's a little late for that now, Vivian. Like it or not."

The Hawthorne family finished their breakfast in silence.

6

It was a hot day to be wearing black, Leigh thought as she stood beneath the white glare of the sun.

There had been no cool funeral home reserved for the family and friends of the deceased to pay their final respects. Instead they had gathered together under the open sky in the local cemetery for a graveside service.

The graveyard was packed with guests, curious townspeople, and local reporters. The deaths of such wealthy and important men had attracted considerable attention.

After it appeared most of the notable guests had arrived, Vivian nodded toward Ray. Standing at a small podium with a built-in public address system, he began the eulogy. He spoke for half an hour, beginning with the tale of the Hawthorne family's arrival in Montvue in the 1800s and the part they had played in the town's development, and ending with praise about the high caliber of Alan's and Curtis's characters and the many selfless contributions they had made to the lives of the people in their orbit of influence.

Afterward, the family threw flowers into the open graves and then arranged themselves into a receiving line. Despite a disapproving look from Vivian, Leigh took her place beside Craig and their children.

Dozens of people filed past them, offering kind words and occasional tears. Leigh felt strange accepting condolences for two men she had never met, but she tried to handle herself as gracefully as possible.

Helena and her family moved down the line. Leigh was pleased to see a friendly, familiar face.

"How are you this afternoon?" Helena asked.

"Better than this morning," Leigh said.

"I don't envy you," she whispered, then put her arm around the ruggedly handsome man at her side. "This is my husband, Marek Janowski. He works for the Hawthornes, too, as groundsman."

"Hello, Marek. I'm Leigh." She offered him her hand. He surprised her by kissing it.

Two teenaged boys stood next to him, fidgeting uneasily.

"My sons, Frank and Gil," Helena said.

Leigh nodded to them warmly. "You have a good-looking family."

"I know," Helena said proudly, then gave Leigh a gentle chuck under her chin. "Keep it up, okay?"

"Thanks, I will."

The Janowskis moved on and were replaced in line by a tall, distinguished-looking woman with silver-gray hair.

"Vivian," she said curtly. Her mask of grief rivaled Vivian's own.

"Katherine."

Leigh was shocked by the hostility in the women's voices.

"I'm surprised you came," Vivian said.

"I didn't come for you. I came for him . . . and for me." Her voice broke, but she recovered herself. "I share in your sorrow."

"Well, I'm touched," Vivian said sarcastically.

"Romantic rivals," Craig whispered in Leigh's ear. "The witch won."

Katherine dropped her head and began to leave.

Leigh grasped her arm as she walked by, and the older woman looked up at her, startled.

"Please accept my condolences," Leigh said gently.

Katherine's bright blue eyes welled with tears. "Thank you." With head raised a little higher, she walked away.

Suddenly, the microphone whined loudly.

"What the . . ." Craig said.

Leigh looked up to see that a very familiar-looking man had ascended the podium and was adjusting the microphone. "Attention! May I please have your attention!"

"Mom," Kamelia said, a breathy tone to her voice, and Leigh instantly knew who the stranger was. Kamelia and her girlfriends had nicknamed him the Incredible Hunk. He was Preacher Cody.

The crowd quieted, and the people who had been preparing to leave stopped.

"I'm Preacher Cody, and there are a few things I want to say."

"What the hell is he doing?" Vivian asked.

Craig shrugged.

"I want to point out something to you good people of Montvue. Did you notice someone missing here today at this funeral?" Cody asked. "God. It is God who is missing. I heard no prayers and noticed no clergy participating in this burial. I find that strange, don't you?" He paused, and the reporters began to move foward. "Well, it doesn't surprise me that there were no religious aspects to this burial, because the Hawthornes are not a religious family. As a matter of fact, there is no history of this illustrious family ever, in their hundred-year reign in Montvue, *ever* having attended a single religious service of any kind. For members of a God-fearing, Christian society, I find that strange. Don't you?"

"Craig?" Vivian's voice betrayed her fear.

Craig stepped forward. "Hey, preacher man! Knock it off!"

Cody looked at him, confused.

"You're out of line!"

Cody laughed. "Me? Out of line? No, I'd say it's you and your entire Devil-worshiping family who's out of line."

A startled gasp passed through the crowd, and the air was filled with the sound of camera shutters clicking.

"I think you've let that Hollywood stuff go to your head and you've rocketed straight into fantasyland," Craig shouted.

"I was there," Cody said quietly, and the crowd hushed itself. "I was there!" he shouted, and the crowd started. "I was on that plane that crashed, and I survived! I survived because God wanted me to live and tell the truth about what happened on that plane! I sat across from the men who now lie in those coffins. I heard them chant their spells. In their moment of panic, in a desperate act to stay alive, their respectable facades vanished and they called out to Satan! I heard them! So did Rachel!" He pointed to the beautiful young woman who stood next to the podium. He lowered his voice again. "And—knowing I was God's servant—they cast their spell on me and, for a moment, I forgot God and was afraid. For that, I am truly repentant. But I am here today to tell the truth. To tell God's truth. These people whom you so revere are witches and Satan worshipers, and we cannot tolerate that in our midst." He paused, and with final dramatic flair he yelled, "We cannot tolerate that in our midst!"

A moment of stunned silence filled the graveyard.

"Diane Fox, with the *Post-Dispatch*," a reporter said, announcing herself to Cody. "I tend to agree with Dr. Hawthorne. Don't you think that your actions here today are somewhat out of line, Preacher Cody?"

"I am being bold, that's true. But one must stand on conviction, not convention."

"If something significant happened during that plane

crash, I'd be interested in the details," Diane Fox said. "But this is neither the time nor the place."

Cody nodded. "You'll have your wish, Miss Fox. In the meantime, I want you Hawthornes to stand ready to be exposed for what you really are. Our American forefathers had the faith and courage to deal with those of your kind. And, as it happens, so do I."

"It's begun again," Craig muttered, then wiped the sweat away from his tearing eyes. "Damn. It's begun again."

_____ *Chapter Two* _____

1692
Salem Village, Massachusetts

1

It was shortly after dawn and the air was frigid. Margaret and William Hawthorne walked through the fields of their farm looking for the first sign of spring. They found it in the green buds of a lilac bush. Margaret felt a rush of delight. The earth's body was awakening from the long sleep, and Margaret's own body trembled in response. She fell to the ground, pulling her husband down to join her. They lay together on the cold, hard earth in tight embrace. She buried her face in the crook of his neck and breathed deeply, enjoying his smell. His heart beat loudly against her chest, and she experienced an exquisite pain; it was as if her heart were rending itself to open to his. When she could stand the pain no longer, she disentangled herself and gently pushed William onto his back. She straddled him, and beneath the privacy of her long skirt, she removed his turgid organ from his breeches. She stroked it for a time, enjoying the feel of its rigid eagerness for her, before—naked beneath her petticoat—she mounted him and began to ride.

He filled her completely. She closed her eyes and allowed the definitions of her personal consciousness to fade. She knew William had done the same, because soon their minds were flying together on the wind of chaos, their direction led by no will, their pleasure beyond any control. Their bodies coupled of their own volition while their souls celebrated the joy of union.

The thunder of their blood and the lightning of their consummate lust returned them to earth.

Later Margaret reached inside herself and claimed the mingled creative essence of their two beings. She used the clear fluid to draw a crescent moon on William's forehead. He, in turn, reached inside her, took the elixir, and blessed her. Then Margaret sat for a time bare to the earth and offered it libation directly from her body.

It was in such a manner that the Hawthornes of Salem Village performed their Spring Rite.

2

Margaret removed the small basket from storage. The "spring basket" had been prepared in September for the family's celebration of spring's first morning.

The basket contained dried apples, pears, and plums as well as a wax-sealed earthenware crock filled with berries—strawberries, blueberries, raspberries, and blackberries—preserved in a light sugar syrup. She served the treats as breakfast to her children, along with their customary pewter bowls filled with hasty pudding and molasses.

Margaret was thirty years old, a year younger than her husband. She was a big, strong country woman, filled with an honest and open lust for life. Her handsome face was creased with lines which were a testament to easy laughter. Her blue eyes reflected a natural humor, and she carried herself with an air of confidence that was uncommon among the women of her village. But she served the women as midwife and so avoided the rancor her free spirit might have otherwise elicited. She and William ran a successful farm on the outskirts of the village and, because of the relative privacy of their lives, were able to maintain the secret practices of their family religion. Margaret and William Hawthorne were loyal to the old religion of their ancient English ancestors. They had no interest in the Christian religion, particularly as it was practiced by their Puritan neighbors.

Twelve-year-old Bridget produced a book from the bench on which she was sitting and handed it to Margaret, who sat across the table from her. "Sarah Bradford gave me this yesterday. She said that with all the witches appearing in the village, I had better repent and save my soul or they—the witches—might capture it."

The book was a leather-bound volume of *Day of Doom* by the Reverend Michael Wigglesworth. It had been selling well among the colonists, and Margaret had heard about it. She flipped through its pages. "So, the Kingdom of God is at hand and we should all repent and be saved, I see," Margaret said, her contempt undisguised. She slammed the book shut. "I don't believe in living in fear and I don't consider myself"—she paused, reached across the breakfast feast, and gently pinched Bridget's cheek—"or you, either, a sinner in need of salvation. We love each other, the earth, the gods, and our fellows. That's all any God could expect from us."

"So, what do I do with the book?"

Margaret glanced at the exuberant fire in the massive fireplace and thought about what she'd like to do with the book, then sighed. "Return it to Sarah and thank her very much for her concern over your soul."

"Are we witches, Mother?" four-year-old Phip asked.

Margaret choked on her cornmeal mush and, unable to catch her breath, bore the assault of William's beating on her back.

Priscilla, only two years older than Phip but a great deal wiser, shook her finger at her brother. "Don't ever say anything like that again."

"Why?" Phip asked.

"Because," Priscilla explained, her tone superior.

"The witches those teenage girls have called out upon do bad things, like torture and murder children, and share communion with the Devil," William said, still pounding on Margaret. "We don't do things like that,

30

and we don't want people to think we do. Do you understand?''

Phip nodded solemnly. "What's the Devil?"

William shrugged his shoulders. "Some invention of Christianity, best I can figure."

"Why?" Phip asked.

Margaret stopped choking and forced the answer from her raspy throat. "Because they need something besides themselves to blame their faults on. Their horned and cloven-hoofed Devil is their scapegoat."

"Are there witches like they say?" Phip asked.

Margaret shrugged. "I don't know. For the most part, I think that the girls who claim to be having all these visions ate some kind of poison herb—there are some that will make a person see things and suffer seizures like I've heard they are—and that's the source of all the trouble."

"Well, there was Tituba, too," William said. Tituba was the local minister's Barbados slave who had entertained his children with harmless voodoo tricks and thus inspired their imaginations. It was the minister's daughter and niece who had instigated the frenzy that was spreading throughout the village.

"Yes, and there's Tituba. She hasn't helped matters. If she hadn't confessed to everything they accused her of, and embellished it all to make herself seem important, I believe the whole matter would be over," Margaret said. She downed a cup of cider to soothe her throat. "But she claimed that she read nine names in the Devil's book, and so now the magistrates are determined to ferret out each and every one of 'God's offenders.' "

"I heard that Tituba confessed because Reverend Parris thrashed her until she did," Bridget said quietly.

An uncomfortable silence fell over those at the table.

"If that's so, I'm sorry for her," Margaret said at last.

Catch, the family's dog, padded up to the table in search of treats.

"Can I give him something?" Phip asked.

William nodded.

Phip scrambled off the bench and, with great effort, lifted his bowl down, added a splash of berry syrup and the rest of his milk to the remainder of the hasty pudding, then set it on the floor. The dog quickly lapped it up.

Margaret studied the shaggy mutt and shook her head. "What a sorry sight that dog is. I think we should find ourselves one more handsome."

"Catch helps me hunt!" William protested.

"We love him!" the children cried in unison.

Margaret grinned. "Just wanted to get your blood flowing."

"You are an evil one, Margaret," William chided. "Are you sure your name isn't in the bad old Devil's book?"

3

The birth had been a hard one. Blood and sweat flowed, and Margaret felt a pang of helplessness when she saw the dim light with which the child was born. She could tell it was one of those babies not destined to live long. She had seen it before, but it was something no one else could see, and so she was unable to warn the mother. Instead she offered her hearty smile to Susanna Weston, the pale and exhausted mother of this child, and said, "You have a beautiful daughter."

The pain in Susanna's eyes was replaced with relief. "She's well?"

"All fingers and toes in place."

Susanna reached out to claim the child.

Margaret lightly sponged blood off the crying baby, wrapped her in a tiny blanket, and handed her to the waiting arms.

"Have you a name picked for her?" Margaret asked.

"Grace. She's God's grace to me. I thought I'd never have a child."

Margaret felt a growing sorrow. Her mind raced for the possibility of something, anything, that might help Grace survive. She had always before just accepted the observance of a newborn's dim light as an irreversible death sentence. She fumbled in her satchel of herbs. "It was a hard birth, Susanna, and both you and Grace are weak from it. I'm going to prepare a blend of herbs I want you to brew. Drink a cupful of the tisane every morning yourself, and give the baby a spoonful as well. It'll make you both strong.''

Susanna frowned. "The baby, too?"

"It won't hurt."

Susanna nodded. "Whatever you say. All the women in the village say you're the best midwife in all of Massachusetts.''

Margaret frowned. "Only in Massachusetts? I'm offended.''

Susanna laughed and placed Grace's mouth to her already dripping breast.

4

Margaret's home was a fine dwelling. She and William had built it themselves when, as newlyweds, they had moved to Salem Village from their home in England. The oak building was constructed around a massive brick fireplace. Downstairs were two rooms: the kitchen and the parlor. Up a short staircase were two bed chambers. The pine floors were always swept clean, and the small window panes were covered with colorful woolen curtains. Cooking pots of food habitually hung from the andirons in the central fireplace, and breads were usually baking in the brick oven which was attached to the chimney. The house always smelled of simmering stew, beans or succotash, baking rye and Injun bread or meat pies, and roasting pork, beef, mutton, or wild game. The family's fields kept them rich in vegetables, and their cows provided their milk and butter. Margaret loved her kitchen. She enjoyed cooking for her family, tending her small indoor herb garden, spinning thread and weaving cloth with her daughters next to the warmth of the fire, and teaching her children the knowledge of the old brain.

It would be another year before she would begin giving Phip instruction—he was still too young to be trusted to silence—but Bridget and Priscilla were both already apt students.

Knowledge of herbs was an ongoing lesson with the girls—there was so much to learn—but that morning Margaret chose to teach them instead about magical protection. It seemed a dangerous time to be without protection.

William, Phip, and Catch were out plowing the fields for the spring plant, and the women were alone. Bridget and Priscilla sat obediently at the kitchen table while Margaret drew the curtains over the windows to shut out the light of day, then lit a tallow candle which she placed before the girls. The flames of the fire in the hearth threw shadows while Margaret removed the loose brick from the chimney and withdrew the tiny box of deadly nightshade. She took two berries from the box and ground them with her mortar and pestle to a fine powder. She mixed the powder with a cup of hard cider and then administered the concoction to the girls by spoonfuls until she was convinced each had received the proper amount for her body weight. She placed a few drops of scented oil—a mixture of lilac and violet—in the flame of the candle to scent the air with a pleasant aroma. All the while she hummed an old English lullaby she had often sung to the girls while they were in their cradles. Before too long, the drug took effect, and the girls, their eyes slightly dilated and their lips curved in crooked grins, became relaxed and euphoric.

"How do you feel?" Margaret asked.

"I'm floating," Bridget said.

"Happy," Priscilla said.

"Good, because we're going on a journey together."

"Where?" Priscilla asked.

"Hush. Listen to me, and speak only if I ask you to."

"Yes, Mother," Priscilla said.

"She said hush!" Bridget said.

Margaret grinned and waited for them to settle down.

"Now, close your eyes and listen to what I have to say."

The girls obeyed.

Margaret spoke slowly and carefully. "Inside each of us is a new brain and an old brain. The new brain is a fairly recent gift from the gods. Because of it, people can read and figure sums and create marvelous inventions like muskets and gunpowder. The old brain, however, has existed in human beings ever since they first found form in the world. It's the same brain that animals have. It possesses the instinct, the natural knowledge of how to survive and live with the earth successfully. It's that brain from which we learn our magic. Do you understand?"

The girls, now more relaxed, merely mumbled and nodded.

"In that brain, owing to the roots of our human evolution, there's an unwavering link with a member of the animal kingdom. For each of us there is a special kind of animal with which our old brains have an affinity; this animal is like a brother or a sister. Once we discover the animal, our power increases, because we tap an internal spring of knowledge and strength. Today we're going to undertake a journey into our old brain to try and find this animal. Are you ready to explore?"

Bridget nodded, but Priscilla didn't. Concerned, Margaret took Priscilla's hand and felt the blood pulse at the wrist, but it was strong. She hadn't given the child too powerful a dose of the herb. She released her hand and continued.

"In your imagination I want you to picture a cave. It doesn't matter what kind of cave it is; it can be a dark, mysterious cave or a bright cave full of crystal rock and dancing light. But you must find a cave and enter it."

She gave them a few minutes to follow her instructions.

"Now, inside your cave, find a staircase and begin to walk down it, and keep walking further and further down into the earth until you can go no further."

She paused again. She noted that both girls' closed eyes were fluttering and moving about. That told her their journeys were proceeding well.

"When you've reached the bottom, look around for an entranceway into the inner world, then pass through it. When you've gone through, look around at the wondrous scenery." She paused. "Look for the animal wait-

35

ing there to greet you." She paused again. "Talk to it.
Pet it. Hug it. Ask its name."

Margaret gave them time to befriend their animals
before calling them back home.

A loud voice brought Bridget around, but Margaret
had to shake Priscilla awake. She wanted them to revive
and remember before they forgot.

"It was an owl, Mother," Bridget said sleepily. "A
beautiful owl with bright eyes and huge wings. I climbed
on its back, and it took me flying over the trees. It was
so wonderful."

"What was its name?"

"Moonlight."

"And yours, Prissy? What was your animal?" Margaret asked.

Priscilla couldn't quite keep her eyes open, but she
managed to answer. "It was a little doe. We ran together in the field. She was sweet and pretty."

"What did she call herself?"

"Samara."

"Good. You both did well, but there are some rules
about your animals that you must follow. First, you
must never tell anyone else—anyone except your father,
of course—what your animal is, or that you even have
an animal. Do you understand?"

"Yes," they said in unison.

"Second, you won't need the herb to visit that world
again. Now you can go there simply by imagining your
cave and the stairs and climbing down into your mind.
After a time, you won't even need to journey there, you
can just close your eyes and be there. Will you practice
and practice until you can go there easily?"

"Yes."

"And finally, I want you to practice calling your
animal—Moonlight and Samara—to you. Make it come
into your world to be here for you. There may come a
time when you'll need its help."

"You mean Moonlight will appear and fly around
here?" Bridget asked.

"Yes, but it's likely that only you will see it. Sometimes a very powerful animal can manifest to others, but

most likely if it does, it'll be in the form of one of its counterparts already in this world."

"Like the owl in the barn?" Bridget asked.

Margaret nodded. "The owl in the barn may let Moonlight enter it to help you in some fashion."

"Like how?" Bridget asked.

"Well, it can act as messenger for you. Or protect you."

Bridget's excitement grew. "Oh, that would be wonderful."

"You must never harm any of your animal's reflections in this world," Margaret said. "And you, Prissy, can never eat venison again. Otherwise you'll offend your animal and it will desert you."

"How do I call Samara?" Priscilla asked.

"Silently. You always call out silently," Margaret said.

"Oh, what fun," Priscilla murmured.

Margaret looked at her daughters with compassion. What seemed like a new toy could well turn into a deadly game someday. That was the lot of every person with true power who lived in a world that didn't understand. She hoped her daughters would never have to find that out for themselves, but she feared otherwise.

Margaret helped her daughters upstairs to their beds so they could sleep away the effects of the narcotic.

"Do you have an animal?" Bridget asked as she was being tucked in beneath the covers.

Margaret nodded. "A snake."

"What's its name?"

Her snake had a name she couldn't repeat to the girls. It would not be wise. She kissed Bridget and then Priscilla, who was already fast asleep by her side.

Before leaving, Margaret removed two specially prepared pieces of cheesecloth from her pocket and tied one on each of the posts at the head of the bed. As the cloth strained food in her kitchen, so it would now act as a sieve for the children's dreams. It was time their nonsensical dreams gave way to dreams of the old knowledge. "Rest well, my daughters, and dream ancient dreams of power," she said softly before returning alone to her kitchen.

5

The constable came for Margaret in late April.

Cherry blossoms had burst forth in white splendor, violets and cowslips dotted the grassy yard with color, and robins, redwing blackbirds, and bobolinks danced and sang together in celebration of the renewal of life as the constable's wagon pulled up in front of the Hawthornes' house.

Margaret and her daughters were planting seeds in the outdoor herb garden which was beside the house. William, Phip, and Catch had just come in from the fields for dinner—their midday meal—and were washing away the dirt from their labor in a bucket of water drawn from the well. Margaret felt the anxiety that had been inexplicably growing in her stomach for days explode.

"Goodwife Hawthorne?" the constable asked as he stepped down off the wagon.

"Yes."

He approached her and grabbed her roughly by the arm. "I have a warrant for your arrest." He yanked her into motion. "Come on, then."

William stepped forward. "On what charge do you arrest my wife?"

"The charge of witchcraft."

William began to lunge for the constable.

"No!" Margaret screamed. "Don't be a fool, man."

"Mother!" Phip yelled, and began to run to her.

William stepped in front of him and swept him up into his arms.

"Mother!" Phip yelled again, and he reached out lamely toward her.

Catch began to growl at the constable.

"Oh, no," Bridget said desolately, and then began to cry.

"Let her go, you bad man!" Priscilla said. She stamped her foot.

The constable bound Margaret's hands with leather straps and then shoved her up into the back of the wagon.

"Don't go away, Mother," Phip pleaded. He started to scream and struggle in William's arms.

Catch ran to the wagon and began to bark and snap at the constable. The constable scrambled for the wagon seat, but Catch managed to nip his leg. The constable grabbed a length of rope from the seat next to him and lashed out at the dog with it.

"You devil dog! You vile witch animal!"

Catch became more riled for the whipping.

Too late, Margaret realized what was going to happen. "Get Catch!" she yelled to the girls.

Bridget raced to the animal, quickly restrained him, and started to lead him away.

"No you don't, little girl. Bring that devil dog here."

Trembling, Bridget looked to her mother.

Margaret feared for her children. She nodded.

Reluctantly, Bridget returned Catch to the constable. He made a noose out of the rope he held and slipped it over the dog's head. Catch began to growl again until the constable pulled the noose tight. Catch yelped, and the constable laughed, looking around for the nearest sturdy tree limb. He found it on a nearby maple tree. He dragged the yelping dog to the tree, threw the rope over the limb, and then began to pull on it, lifting the dog off the ground.

Priscilla screamed. "No! Stop!" She started to run to her beloved pet.

Horror filled Margaret. "Stop her, Bridget!" she yelled.

Bridget grabbed Priscilla and tried to hold her, but Priscilla squirmed out of her grasp.

The dog, hanging three feet above the ground by its neck, made desperate gurgling sounds and thrashed about in the air helplessly. The constable snickered. "We hang witch dogs just like we hang witch bitches." He turned and gave Margaret a look of triumph. "It just takes a little longer to get the likes of you to the noose, that's all."

Margaret saw Priscilla descend on the constable. "Don't, Prissy!" she yelled helplessly.

Priscilla ran up to the constable and kicked him. He grunted and looked down at her angrily. "Ah, so you're one, too, huh?" With his free hand, he reached out and grabbed her; with his other hand, he yanked down hard on the rope and broke the dog's neck, then let the rope go slack. Catch fell to the earth in a lifeless heap. The constable threw Priscilla roughly to the ground and bound her still kicking feet as well as her hands, then tossed her into the back of the wagon alongside Margaret as if he were tossing a sack of flour.

Margaret gave a cry of anguish.

The wagon began to move beneath her.

6

Baby Grace Weston had died in her cradle of no apparent cause, as Margaret had known she would. In the witchcraft hysteria that had seized Salem Village, the death was not as easily dismissed as it would have been in another time. Susanna blamed the herbal brew that Margaret had prescribed and she had administered. The young girls of the village whose "visions" were the basis for most of the witchcraft arrests found their imaginations primed by Susanna's plight. They "called out" on Margaret and she was quickly arrested.

Margaret and Priscilla were taken to jail in the nearby town of Ipswich, where they were held until they could be examined and officially charged with their crimes.

Margaret and Priscilla's preliminary hearing was scheduled for the Monday following their arrest. It was held in the large meetinghouse in Salem Village. Samuel Sheldon was the magistrate assigned to conduct the hearings. There was a bar of justice at which the accused would stand to face their accusers. The accusers were a row of teenage girls who sat on a bench in the front of the auditorium. The room itself was filled to capacity by throngs of people eager to enjoy the scandal in their midst.

William left Phip at home in the care of Bridget and went to the meetinghouse to stand with his wife and daughter. It frightened him to expose himself to the accusers, but it frightened him more not to stand with his family. He had always been their guardian and protector.

Dressed in his best blue cloth suit, a black hat, and black shoes, he walked into the meetinghouse as confidently as he was able. The room was already filled, and upon his arrival an excited buzz of voices spread among the spectators. He closed his mind to their ridicule. His jaw tightened, and his lips drew thin. He fought back his anger. How many of these women's babies had Margaret brought into the world? How many of the mothers would have died in the birthing without Margaret's expertise? Where was their gratitude and respect? He stood in the back of the room waiting for the proceedings to begin. When the hearing was called to order and the first prisoner, Priscilla, was brought to the bar, William strode forward to be with her.

"Father!" Priscilla's pale face lit up when she saw him.

The knot in the pit of William's stomach tightened when he saw her dirty and disheveled condition, but he smiled at her, walked to her side, and took her tiny hand in his.

"I'm William Hawthorne," he told the magistrate. "I believe my wife and daughter to be innocent of the crimes they've been accused of, and I'm here to stand with them during this examination."

Sheldon nodded curtly. "That's your right." He looked down at the papers on the table before him. "We have before us now the examination of six-year-old Priscilla Hawthorne. She's accused of the abomination of witchcraft." He looked across the bar at the small girl.

"So, are you a witch?"

Priscilla thrust out her chin and said defiantly, "I am not."

The magistrate cleared his throat. "My notes here

41

indicate that you're not a churchgoing Christian. Is that true?''

"I don't go to church.''

"Why?''

"It's too far to come into town every week. We live on a farm.''

"Other farm people come into town to attend church.''

"Ours is the farthest farm from town. It's very far.''

"If you haven't been instructed in the faith, how do you know that you aren't a witch?'' Sheldon asked.

"Because I heard that witches do bad things and kill people and play with someone called the Devil, and I don't do any of that.''

"Does anyone in your family do those things?''

"No.''

William felt Priscilla's fingers tighten on his. He gently squeezed her hand in return.

"Why did you kick Constable Stone?'' Sheldon asked.

"Because he was hurting Catch. My dog.''

"Your dog was attempting to prevent the arrest of an accused witch. Only a devil dog would do such a thing. The constable's action—the hanging of that beast—was appropriate to the circumstance. Why did you try to prevent it?''

Priscilla's face reddened and her eyes filled with tears. Her composure faded as she whispered, "I loved him.''

Sheldon gave her a hard stare and then turned to the six young girls who sat primly on the bench before the bar. "What say you, God's mouthpieces?''

On that cue, four of the girls began to writhe and moan. Then two of them fell onto the floor in convulsions.

"She pinches me!'' the girl named Elizabeth cried, holding out her arm for everyone to see the tiny spot of blood. "Her shape is here and is *pinching me!*''

William squinted his eyes and strained to see the marks.

"Get away, little witch! Leave me alone!'' Elizabeth shouted as she flailed the air around her at the unseen specter and continued to develop new wounds.

Then William saw the tiny flash of reflected light. Elizabeth had a needle in the palm of one hand and was surreptitiously poking herself with it! William's mouth fell open with surprise. He looked to Sheldon, but the magistrate had apparently not seen.

The clamor the girls were making was increasing in volume. William had never seen or heard such commotion. Was this show performed at every hearing? How could grown men take such things seriously? One of the girls who had been on the floor convulsing jumped to her feet and began to run around the room, flapping her arms. "She's trying to make me fly! Oh, make her stop!"

Another girl began to run around the floor on all fours, barking.

Elizabeth pointed to her. "See! The devil dog has come back to be with his mistress."

The dog-girl stopped in front of the bar, squatted and urinated a huge puddle, then scampered back to the bench and the other girls.

The crowd gasped their horror.

"I've seen enough!" Sheldon shouted. "Take the little witch away to Boston where she'll be held over for trial."

"Father!" Priscilla turned and threw her arms around William's waist.

Rage filled William. He pointed at Elizabeth. "She was sticking herself with a needle. I saw it."

Sheldon appraised him coolly. "If you saw something, I'm sure it was the witch's doing."

"Search her. See for yourself," William said.

Sheldon hesitated a moment and furrowed his eyebrows. He shook his head slowly. "If there's a needle on her person, I'm certain it was placed there by the witch."

"But she was sticking *herself*," William pressed.

Sheldon sighed with exasperation. "Then the Devil, or this young witch, made her do it."

William's mind raced. "She cried."

"What?" Sheldon asked.

"I've been told witches don't cry." William turned Priscilla's tear-soaked face toward the magistrate.

"I see the Devil pouring water into her eyes," Elizabeth shouted, the venom in her voice more pronounced than it had been before William's attempt to discredit her.

"There you have it," Sheldon said. He waved his hand in a gesture of dismissal. "Take her away."

Priscilla was pried out of her father's arms and led away.

William's head spun.

Margaret was brought into the room and led to the bar. Relief crossed her face when she saw William, but she shook her head to tell him that he shouldn't have come.

"Margaret Hawthorne, you've been brought to this hearing on the charge of witchcraft," Sheldon said. "Are you a witch?"

"If a witch is one who harms the innocent and cavorts with the Devil, no, I am not," Margaret said calmly.

"Did you deliver a baby girl, named Grace, to Susanna Weston on March twenty-eighth?"

"Yes, I did. I'm a midwife."

"Did you devise a blend of herbs for Goodwife Weston to give to her newborn?"

"And to take herself. Yes."

"Why did you do that?"

"It was a hard birth. Goody Weston lost a lot of blood. She was weak. The child had taken a long time to be born, and she, too, was weak. I gave them herbs to strengthen their hearts and enrich their blood. I've given it to other mothers and babies in the past."

"What were the herbs you gave Goodwife Weston?" Sheldon asked.

"A blend of hawthorn berries, shepherd's purse, and comfrey. They're quite common herbs, your honor."

"And you are aware that baby Grace Weston died this Wednesday past?"

"I didn't know until my arrest, but yes, I'm now aware of that."

"Did the herbs you forced on Goodwife Weston kill baby Grace?"

Margaret almost grinned at his ludicrous statement. "I

did not *force* anything upon Goody Weston, and no, I'm sure they didn't harm the baby at all."

Sheldon paused and studied his notes. "Where did you obtain your knowledge of herbs?"

Margaret searched her thoughts for a safe answer. "I read books."

"What books? You mean the Devil's books?"

"I mean books. Books you can get at the market."

Sheldon leaned across his table and gave Margaret a significant look. "Have you signed the Devil's book?"

Before Margaret could reply, the girls on the accuser's bench once again began their hysterics. Two fell immediately onto the floor to writhe, while Elizabeth shouted accusations.

"She appeared to me one night while I slept and forced me to drink a potion. I burned with fever for days afterward."

Sheldon looked behind the row of accusers at a matronly woman who sat behind Elizabeth. She nodded her head as if to confirm Elizabeth's dread illness.

Sheldon turned to face Margaret. "Did you poison this innocent child?"

Once again, the absurdity of the accusations almost brought Margaret to laughter. "No, I did not," she replied.

Elizabeth then shocked the entire room to silence. She pointed at William and said, "And he was with her. He held me while she poured the potion down my throat."

Margaret felt her heart break. William was filled with terror.

Sheldon looked at them both with a contemptuous expression. "Well, so we have a witch and a wizard, too. I should have known." He waved the constables forward. "Arrest this man on a charge of witchcraft. Take the rampant hag to Boston, along with the little witch. These hearings are adjourned."

Margaret did not know anything about devils, but demons were familiar to her. The Boston jailhouse seethed with demons.

The horror that permeated the building was generated by those it housed. Very few true criminals had passed through its bars. For the most part, it had hosted victims.

As the jailer shoved Margaret and Priscilla forward into their new cell, Margaret gagged from the stench—the two slop pots in the huge cell were overflowing. Eight pairs of desolate eyes stared at the Hawthornes dully as they were locked into leg chains. Margaret fought back tears as she watched Priscilla's tiny ankles taken captive. She wondered if they had forged the miniature restraints just for the occasion or if they were accustomed to arresting children in Boston.

"The examiners will be in soon," the jailer said gruffly.

"Examiners?" Margaret asked.

The man turned away without responding and hurried out of the cage.

Margaret looked around at where she and her daughter would be housed for the months ahead—she had heard that the trials would not even begin until summer. There was a bucket of water and a bucket of corn gruel, apparently the day's meal. Mounds of old straw were scattered throughout the cell, and most had women perched upon them. Margaret led Priscilla to one of the piles, and they sat down while Margaret tried to ignore the bugs that already had possession of the straw.

Priscilla, exhausted from the difficult trip to Boston, curled up in a ball, her head in Margaret's lap.

"I hate them," Priscilla mumbled.

Margaret stroked her hair. "Who?"

"The Christians."

"Don't hate, Prissy. You only hurt yourself with hate."

"They treat us like animals."

"Does Samara hate people?" Margaret asked, keeping her voice low.

Priscilla thought about it. "No. But she's afraid sometimes."

"Fear can be a tool of survival. Hate is another matter altogether."

"I wish I could be free, like Samara."

"Why don't you visit with her, then?"

A slight smile played at Priscilla's lips. "All right," she said, and was quickly asleep.

Margaret heard the feeble cry of a baby and looked around, startled. Two straw piles away, she saw the telltale bundle squirming listlessly in its mother's arms. Gently, she extricated herself from Priscilla's sleeping form and went to investigate.

The pale mother watched her approach with a wary expression, clutching the baby to her bosom protectively.

Margaret smiled. "How is it that you have a baby here with you? Was it charged as a witch, too?"

"I birthed it three days ago."

Margaret looked at the bloodied straw on which the woman sat and was aghast. These were not fit conditions for delivering babies. "I'm a midwife. May I see?"

The woman clutched the baby more tightly. "The midwife-witch that murders babies?" she asked with alarm.

Margaret sighed and sat down on the floor a few feet from the woman. "So they say. But you must know that they lie. I'm no more a witch—by their standards—than you."

She paused for a time to allow the woman to think about her words.

"My name's Margaret," she said at last. "And who are you?"

The woman's apparent fear seemed less pronounced but not altogether relieved. "Rebekah."

"And your baby?"

A welling of tears filled Rebekah's eyes, and she shrugged. "I've not named him."

"Not named him? After three days? Why do you delay?"

Rebekah shrugged again. "He's not going to live."

Margaret approached Rebekah and gently took the baby from her arms. When she unwrapped the dirty and bloodied petticoat that served as the child's swaddling clothes, she gasped aloud with horror. The infant's eyes were running with yellow pus, and his tiny face was dotted with inflamed sores. He was nearly dead already, it was true.

"What happened?" Margaret asked.

Rebekah's voice was expressionless. "It's not so clean here. The bugs bite him. I have little milk . . ." Her voice died off.

"What of your husband? Your family? Why don't they come for him?"

Rebekah looked at Margaret and uttered a brief, bitter laugh. "Because I'm a witch, of course."

"The authorities will do nothing?"

Rebekah shook her head.

Margaret set her jaw firmly and injected strength into her voice. "Well, then. We'll just have to see to the situation, won't we? When my daughter Bridget comes to visit me next, I'll ask her to brew us some herbs. A golden seal wash will clear up his little eyes, and a chamomile poultice will soothe those bites. Pennyroyal oil will keep the bugs from biting him, and marshmallow will increase your milk flow. You'll see. It'll be fine."

Rebekah's eyes lit up with hope. "You think it'll be all right if I name him?"

"What would you have named him, if things had been different?"

"Daniel."

Margaret smiled. "Daniel is a fine name."

"Daniel," Rebekah said softly.

There was a loud commotion at the cell gate, and the examiners came for Margaret and Priscilla.

Six women entered. Several of them quickly placed handkerchiefs to their faces, protecting their noses from the room's stench, but the others seemed unmoved by the odor. Margaret immediately noted their hard expressions as they scanned the room for their prey.

The oldest woman, who seemed to be in charge— Margaret guessed her age to be around fifty—pointed a finger at Priscilla's sleeping form. "There's the one."

Margaret stood up and moved to her daughter. "What do you want?"

"Ah, and there's the other."

The six women moved in to surround Margaret and Priscilla. "We're the jury sent to examine you," the eldest woman said. "Rouse your little witch, and the two of you strip yourselves."

Margaret was stunned. "What?"

"Are you deaf? Strip your clothes. We're here to look for teats and devil's marks. On with it."

Margaret knew she had no choice but to comply. She shook Priscilla awake. "Get undressed, Prissy. These women are here to examine us."

Priscilla rubbed her eyes awake as she sat up. "Examine?"

"Yes, dear. Do as I say."

Priscilla began to remove her dress.

Margaret, too, began to strip away her clothing. Although she knew no shame for her own body, she cringed under the jurors' eager and greedy appraisal of her growing nakedness.

Margaret looked over the heads of the women who surrounded her and could see the lasciviousness in the face of the jailer as he strained to catch a glimpse of flesh. Margaret could feel herself flush with embarrassment.

"What exactly are teats and devil marks?" Margaret asked, surprised to hear the quivering of her own voice.

The spokeswoman put her hands on her hips. "Well, if you're a witch, you know. If you're not—which I very much doubt, from what I've heard—I'll tell you that they're marks left by the Devil's incubus where familiar spirits are given to suck. The teats feel no pain." Margaret stared in mute horror as the woman pulled out a long, sharp needle. "So, let's get on with the pricking."

Each of the six women withdrew needles of various types and sizes and poised ready for attack.

"Mother?" Priscilla said, a note of hysteria in her voice.

Margaret felt her own rising panic. She could easily bewitch Priscilla so she would feel no pain, but that would damn them both as witches. She realized that she had no option but to let them torture her daughter. "Don't fight them, Prissy."

Six pairs of eyes and hands began to probe Margaret and Priscilla's bodies. The jury immediately zeroed in on a birthmark above Margaret's right nipple. She closed her eyes as a needle punctured her flesh, and she did not even attempt to mask the pain it produced. Tears came to her eyes, unbidden, as the hand holding the needle jerked to pierce her nipple as well. She glanced at the woman who was holding the offending needle and wasn't surprised to see a slight look of triumph on her face. Margaret had never understood the nature of the mind that enjoyed inflicting pain on others. She swallowed her bile as she felt the blood began to trickle down her body.

Shrill screams pierced the air as a needle slid into a small mole on Priscilla's arm. "Mother!"

"The pain will pass, Prissy." Margaret's tears began to flow harder.

A needle ripped a freckle on Margaret's back. She winced, noticeably, she hoped.

"Mother!" A needle found a reddened flea bite Priscilla had gotten while asleep on the pile of straw.

"Bend over," a voice demanded of Margaret.

Margaret was filled with revulsion as the women began to probe her anus and vagina, looking for suspicious marks.

A finger prodded an area behind her vaginal opening. "There. Look at that."

"It's a scar caused by childbirth," Margaret said lamely, but the jurors were unconvinced. The darning needle plunged into the scar.

"Mother! Mother! Make them stop!"

One of the jurors began to laugh.

Bent over as she was, her head began to swim. Priscilla's cries grew more frantic and filled Margaret with an overwhelming sense of helplessness. The jurors' laughter rang obscenely in her ears, and the needle tore into her again, off target, and stabbed her urethra.

With the echo of her own screams following her into the blessed darkness, Margaret fainted.

8

Bridget watched helplessly as the sheriff seized the goods of the family.

"But don't you have to wait until the trial? And then only if they're found guilty?" Bridget asked in as authoritative a voice as she could muster. Phip was hiding behind her skirt.

The sheriff chuckled. "Merely a technicality."

He continued to heap the Hawthornes' pewter, furniture, lamps, clothing, cooking utensils, foodstuffs, and tools onto the bed of his wagon. He tied two cows and three horses to the back and topped off his load with three cages of chickens.

"How will Phip and I live?" Bridget asked fearfully.

"By your wits, child. By your wits."

The sheriff drove away in a cloud of dust, and Bridget resisted the urge to hurl rocks after him.

"What are we going to do?" Phip asked, his voice small.

Bridget's anger, overshadowing her fear, gave her the edge of defiance she needed. "We'll show them . . . we'll survive."

"I'm hungry," Phip said.

"Get used to it," Bridget returned.

When Bridget had come home from Boston to find the sheriff gathering together the livestock and loading his wagon with the family belongings, she had stopped a distance from the house, unmounted her horse, Silver, and slapped him hard to cause him to run. It took five days of searching the countryside on foot before Bridget found Silver in a distant meadow, courting a beautiful filly. As a result, Bridget did not make it back to Boston in time to deliver the herbs designed to save baby Daniel's life.

The despair that filled the cage that contained her mother and sister was so thick that Bridget began to tremble. "I'm sorry I didn't get here in time."

Sadness reflected from Margaret's face. "You did your

51

best. Don't fret about it.'' She paused. ''So, they took it all?''

''We still have the house and land. I still have Silver.'' Bridget passed a small basket of dried herbs through the bars. ''Here, I gathered these. There's kelp, dandelion, and alfalfa. You always said that combination gave you all the body needed to stay healthy. I guess you'll just have to eat them. I'm sorry I couldn't brew them for you, but . . . I don't have a pot.''

Margaret's shock grew as the harsh reality of Bridget's and Phip's situation became clearer. She forced herself to examine the basket she held. ''You made this?''

Bridget nodded.

''It's a fine basket.''

''Thank you.''

''If you make a real tight weave—tight enough to hold water—you can heat water in it by dropping in hot rocks.''

''That's good to know.''

''Have you seen your father?''

''Yes. He sends his love to you and Prissy.''

They glanced over at where Priscilla sat, hollow-eyed, staring vacantly into space.

''She looks awful,'' Bridget said.

''They keep coming back to hurt her,'' Margaret said.

''Will she be all right?''

''I'm trying to get her to visit Samara more often.'' Margaret raised the basket. ''This'll help, too.''

''I wish I could have brought you other things to make it easier for you, but . . .'' It was unnecessary for Bridget to finish the sentence.

''I love you.''

Their fingers embraced through the bars.

''I love you, too, Mother.''

9

There were far fewer men than women arrested by Salem authorities for witchcraft. As a result, the conditions the accused wizards enjoyed were, if not more luxurious than those of their female counterparts, at least less cramped.

The cellmate William had been sharing his small cage with since his arrest—an irascible old man who had the unfortunately damning habit of talking to himself—died of the hardships of his imprisonment. He was replaced by an irascible young man named Jansen Van Carel.

"Damned self-righteous, sexually inhibited, Puritan clowns!" Jansen said to William in greeting.

William grinned. "Well, for a society that can have twelve to fourteen children per family, I'd say they really aren't *that* sexually inhibited."

Jansen grunted. "So, are you one of them that stepped out of line or what?"

"I'm not one of them."

Jansen waited for William to explain, but after a considerable period of silence passed, he shrugged and said, "I'm Jansen—call me Jan—Van Carel. Out of New York City."

"William Hawthorne. What did you do to get yourself damned by Salem's fine folk?"

"My ship ran into trouble, and I dropped anchor in their port. While I was waiting on repairs, I came ashore to conduct some business, and . . . well, I have an affliction . . . and it attracted the wrong sort of attention, and here I am."

"You're a ship's captain?"

"I own a shipping and trading company. Caribbean Cache. Heard of it?"

William shook his head apologetically. He studied the other man's rich apparel and jewelry. Caribbean Cache was an apparently lucrative venture. "Has your ship got a load on it?"

"Sure. Why?"

"What became of your ship?"

Jansen's animated face assumed an exaggeratedly grim expression. "They've seized it while awaiting the outcome of the trial."

William sighed. "Then prepare yourself to meet the gallows, man, because they want your cargo."

Jansen's face reflected his instant outrage. "Those

greedy bastards! Those filthy, *oversexed*, greedy bastards!''

William smiled. "I haven't heard such colorful language since leaving England. It's rather refreshing, actually.''

Jansen looked around at the straw piles and, with obvious distaste, chose the neater of the two and sat down on it. William easily relinquished his own bed to the other man and took the recently vacated roost.

"Well, we Dutchmen aren't so prissy as the Puritans. The society we created in the New World is a lot more relaxed than theirs.''

"Wish I'd known that sooner," William said.

Jansen studied his companion. "Yes, I'm sure that's true." He removed a pipe and tobacco pouch from his shirt pocket, packed the pipe, and then lit it. "What was your sin?''

"Telling the truth.''

Jansen puffed smoke into the room. "That's the true original sin, sure enough," he said dismally.

William decided he liked Jansen Van Carel.

10

Bridget, Phip, and Silver searched the sandy beaches for crabs and sea vegetables. They found large sea shells to use as cups and bowls and dragged home huge bundles of driftwood to add to their growing store of firewood. Although it was only summer, they were already preparing for the winter that lay ahead. The sheriff had taken their axes, and they had no other means to create fuel but to scavenge the land and seashore.

They worked their fields by hand, trying to produce as large a crop as they could without tools. They wandered the countryside gathering berries, fruit, and birds' eggs. They harvested herbs from the tiny herb garden next to the house. They set simple traps and caught rabbits and squirrels. They dried the meat and tanned the skins, with which they planned to make furs to stave off the looming winter cold.

Bridget learned to heat water in tightly woven baskets.

None of the Hawthornes' former friends or neighbors offered to help them. No one would associate with the children of accused witches.

Bridget made weekly trips to Boston to share her meager bounty with her family and to help keep hope alive.

Bridget and Phip closed off all the rooms of the house with the exception of the kitchen, and the kitchen became their home. They made their beds of bales of straw and cuddled together on cool nights to keep warm. Bridget discovered a creative gift she had not known she possessed and became a consummate storyteller. Her gift helped her and Phip get through the long, dark nights.

In July, Bridget quietly celebrated her thirteenth birthday.

11

William stood in the darkness of his cell and looked out the barred window, studying the sky. When the bright sliver of moon finally appeared in his sight, he bowed reverently to greet her. Every month of his life, from his earliest childhood, he had greeted the night lady's return in such a manner. Life was like the moon, he mused. It began slight and fragile, grew in might until it shone with glory, then started its decline until it disappeared from sight altogether. However, it always returned. He bowed a second time to the new moon. "Life does return," he whispered to the night. Sadness threatened to overtake him. In an effort to see the outcome of his family's situation, he had the day before, when the moon was dark, scryed. After Jansen had fallen asleep, William had taken a cup of water from the barrel and magically charged it. Then he had sat on his bed and gazed into it. He had not been surprised by the vision he had seen, but the reality of his own fate had finally been faced. He hoped he had the courage to see it through to the end. He sighed and, careful not to disturb his snoring cellmate, moved to his own bed, where he reclined.

He had not been allowed to see his wife, even if they were housed in the same building, since their incarceration in Boston. However, on every new moon they had visited each other.

William closed his eyes and fell asleep. Once in the dream state, he laid himself down on his bed of straw and fell asleep again. Then, in the dream's dream state, he made himself awaken and stand up. He looked around at the shimmering quality of his surroundings and knew he had passed from the material world into the world of stars—the name he gave to this other dimension he occasionally visited. His body of light passed through the jail wall and moved to the nearby grove which had previously hosted his monthly assignations with Margaret. She had not yet arrived, and he waited.

Soon a luminous figure glided into the clearing, and he saw the glorious form of his wife. As she neared, she spoke the name that was their password between the worlds, so he would know it wasn't an impostor. He returned the proper response, and they came together. They embraced and caressed each other tenderly. His emotions of love and sadness welled up with the extreme intensity that was characteristic of the star world, and he struggled for greater control.

Margaret wiped away crystalline tears from his face. "Don't cry. What happens happens. They can't separate us. We're bound for eternity. We're two halves of one whole."

"What becomes of our children?" William asked.

"Perhaps they'll change the world. Or perhaps their children will. We Hawthornes are a power to be reckoned with."

Her beauty overcame him, and he wished her form to be naked. His wish was granted, and, after he willed away his own diaphanous covering, they fell together in sexual embrace.

When William finally awoke in the state from which he had begun, his pants were wet with the earthly remains of his passion.

12

The arrival of Mirasaya not only added color to the grim cell of women prisoners, but also spirit. Mirasaya was spirited.

Mirasaya was West Indian, a slave whose nonconformist ways had labeled her a witch. She was bewitchingly beautiful, and that had been her first offense. The Puritan men with whom she came into contact found her desirable and, as that was strictly forbidden among their ranks, covered their "sin" by accusing her of haunting their sleeping forms in the guise of a succubus and forcing them into sexual relations. This charge came from more than a half-dozen devout Puritan men.

To make matters worse, she refused, despite repeated whippings by her master, to don the "ugly" dresses that were the required wear of Puritan ladies. Instead she made her own clothes, dying the drab cloth she had been given into a startling array of colors and sewing them into a style more pleasing to her tastes.

Her third sin was that she had developed a liking for the effects of tobacco and had taken to smoking a pipe. And, despite her life of slavery, Mirasaya was happy. That was the worst sin of all in the eyes of her oppressors. She was easily labeled a witch and shut away in prison so that she could be an example to other slaves who might be tempted toward independence of character.

When the public heard of this brazen, wanton witch, they hastened to Boston from all parts of Massachusetts to view her. The cells in the Boston jail had large, barred windows which opened to the street. Like animals in a zoo, the accused witches were gawked at and allowed no privacy.

The morning after Mirasaya's arrival, the crowd grew quickly. The dark-skinned beauty calmly lit her pipe and watched them watch her.

A young woman threw a hunk of animal dung at Mirasaya's feet. "Here, put this in your pipe and smoke it," she said.

Mirasaya smiled, picked up the dung, and threw it back at her. "Maybe you like it for supper?"

The crowd murmured disconcertedly at that but soon became quiet.

"You!" Mirasaya jumped to her feet and pointed at a man who had curled his lip at her in an exaggerated sneer. "You make face at Mirasaya! Mirasaya no like that!" Her voice dropped in timber and became menacing. "Tonight I come to your bed and make you sin. I take your little, tiny, wormlike man thing and I make it grow big . . . oh, so big that you don't even know it your own little worm . . . and I tickle it with my tongue until it explode with juice."

Horrified gasps and cries escaped the crowd, and they quickly scattered. For a time the women in the cell were alone.

Mirasaya looked at Margaret and gave her a delightful grin. "They want show. I give them."

Margaret smiled. "Pretty soon they'll start selling tickets."

"That man, he have messy dreams tonight," Mirasaya said mischievously.

Margaret laughed and looked around at the other women in the cell. They were amused. If they had been on the outside, they would have been as shocked as the others in the crowd. Prison was stripping them of the conventions of their former society. Inside, here, they were all just women, plain and simple.

Mirasaya sat back down on her perch and, between puffs on her pipe, began to sing an upbeat Caribbean song. Soon the women began to sway to the sound. Priscilla upturned the empty water bucket and began to beat an accompanying rhythm on its bottom. Mirasaya threw her head back and laughed, set aside her pipe, and started to clap. Margaret, filled with warmth and conviviality, felt the urge to dance and—despite the cumbersome weight of the heavy leg chains—didn't hesitate to do so. Rebekah—who until that moment had still been grieving for the loss of her son—was quickly by her side, imitating her unabashed movement. Soon Mirasaya stood and took the hands of the other two women, and they formed a small, undulating circle. Their cellmates began to stamp their feet, clap their hands, hoot, and whistle in encouragement. Margaret looked over at Priscilla and was overjoyed to see a smile on her wan face. Margaret silently thanked the gods—and Mirasaya—for that smile.

The moment was shattered by the arrival of the examiners. The women burst into the cell, seemingly aghast at the sight and sounds that confronted them.

"What witchery goes on here?" the leader of the examiners—Margaret had learned her name was Hannah—bellowed.

The music, dancing, and laughter came to an abrupt halt.

"That's better," Hannah said. She pointed at Priscilla. "We're here for the little witch again."

Margaret wanted to scream with rage but held her silence.

"No, Mother! Not the pricking *again!* No!"

The examiners moved toward where Priscilla sat, but Mirasaya stepped into their path. "You no more stick the little one with your pins."

Hannah looked at the dark woman in disbelief. "Who are you to be telling us what we'll do?"

Rebekah moved to Mirasaya's side. "You'll not stick Prissy anymore. She's been stuck enough to please any God, I'm sure," she said in a matter-of-fact tone.

Two more prisoners moved to stand with Mirasaya and Rebekah, their eyes blazing with defiance.

Hannah's mouth fell open, and she began to sputter.

Margaret felt her eyes sting with tears. Power had descended upon the small band of women, *and they were using it*. No longer afraid of the repercussions, she moved, as did the remaining prisoners, to guard Priscilla.

"We'll see about this!" Hannah shouted. Defeated, the jury of six women stormed out of the cage.

There was a moment of silence, and then Priscilla began her drumming anew. The women looked at one another, the pride of their accomplishment washing over their faces, until each of them was smiling. Mirasaya began to sing her song and clap her hands, and soon they were all dancing.

13

Jansen's fit roused William from sleep. At first the sounds in the cell mingled with William's dream.

He was in a huge butchering hall, and dozens of screeching chickens were being slaughtered in cruel and tortuous fashion. The scene passed from his mind, and he became aware of Jansen lying on the floor, screeching and convulsing. Dawn was upon the sky, and in the dim light William watched the fit in amazed fascination.

Jansen's eyes were open and bulging, but they seemed to be unseeing. Foamy spittle and blood from his gnashed tongue sprayed from his mouth. William had seen fits that accompanied high fevers and certain illnesses, but never before had he seen the strange contortions Jansen assumed or heard the sounds he made. William squinted his eyes and shifted into a seeing mode. The aura of light surrounding Jansen's body came into focus, and William saw the parasite that was attached there. A hideous, dark, claw-shaped shadow was attached to the body of light, around the area of the head. Only once before, as a young man in England, had he seen anything similar. It was on a sailor who had recently returned from the West Indies. It had been magically implanted on the sailor's person as a result of a tangle with voodoo. The sailor's family had called in Margaret—who even in her youth was highly regarded for her healing skills—to rid him of the curse. William struggled to remember what she had done to accomplish the task.

Soon Jansen's fit quieted, and, without coming to consciousness, he fell into a sound sleep. William picked him up and placed him back onto his bed, then waited patiently for him to awaken.

14

The first thing Jansen became aware of was the telltale soreness of his tongue. It had happened again! He wondered at times how he could bear to go on living with the affliction. As he became more aware of his surroundings, he decided that, as circumstances dictated, he might not have to go on living too much longer after all. Those damn Puritans, anyway. He opened his eyes to see William gazing at him, and embarrassment flooded him. Damn William, anyway. He could have been a gentleman about the whole matter and pretended it hadn't happened.

He pushed himself up into a sitting position and, despite his inflamed mouth, said, "So, now you know."

"Do you ship and trade in slaves?" William asked.

What kind of fool question was that, out of the blue? "In my youth—about a dozen years ago—I dabbled in the slave trade. It was distasteful to me. I don't do it anymore."

"How long have you had this affliction of yours?"

"Since . . ." The connection dawned on him for the first time. "Since about a dozen years ago." He looked up at William. "What are you getting at?"

"Island magic. Voodoo."

Jansen waved his hand in a gesture of dismissal. "Superstitious shit, all of it."

"I know of . . . an old folk remedy to deal with such things, if you'd like me to try it on you." William shrugged casually. "I mean, you're right that it's probably all just shit, but it couldn't hurt, could it?"

It was obvious that William was choosing his words carefully and deliberately trying to be nonchalant about the matter. Could he really be a wizard? Could there truly be such things? Hell, what could it hurt, indeed?

Jansen shrugged. "It would give us something to do with our miserable time, at least."

The men's drinking water was stored in a large wooden barrel, and the water level was low. They emptied the remainder of the water and kicked the bottom of it out.

After William chanted some strange words over it, they laid it on its side. With a few handfuls of straw, William made a small poppet, which he hung from a short rope made of woven straw on one end of the barrel. William stood back proudly, surveying their creation. "Well, there it is."

Jansen looked at the scene with amusement. "All right. So, there what is?"

"The place for your passing through."

"All right," Jansen repeated, his skepticism growing. Now he'd have to slip the guard a handsome bribe to get another water barrel. What had he got himself into, anyway?

"See, if you pass through a specially prepared hole—although usually it's in a tree or a rock, but this'll do in a pinch—then the parasite will be pried loose and take refuge in the poppet that's hanging there."

"Ask me if I believe you," Jansen said.

William shook his head impatiently. "It doesn't matter if you believe."

Jansen was slightly touched by William's sincere desire to help. He sighed. Well, if it would make him feel useful, he'd humor him. "So, I just crawl through, huh?"

"Yes, but you must be naked, of course."

"What? Are you daft? What if the guard comes along?"

William thought about it for a minute and then smiled. "We'll tell him you were trying to take a bath."

Jansen looked at the open-ended barrel and burst out laughing. "Hell, I'll do it just so I can see the guard's expression when we make such a ludicrous explanation."

Jansen stripped his clothes and, feeling like the village idiot, crawled into the barrel and out the other end, beneath the hanging poppet. Once Jansen had passed through, William quickly snatched the poppet and set a flame to it.

"There," William said, a broad grin on his face. He ground the ashes beneath his feet. "It's gone."

Jansen sat on the cold floor, naked, looking at William

with his triumphant foot on a pile of ashes, and felt like a total ass.

"I can see how you managed to get yourself arrested for witchcraft," he said sullenly, and proceeded to get dressed.

15

Jansen's wife and son were finally notified of his plight, and they visited him. Alida Van Carel was a comely woman, with dusky blond hair like Jansen's own, and gray eyes which mirrored some deep, unexpressed pain. Or at least that's how William read her eyes. But he was quite good at discerning such things, as a rule. Peter Van Carel was a friendly and open fourteen-year-old. William enjoyed their visit nearly as much as Jansen seemed to.

It wasn't an affectionate reunion of husband and wife, but it was friendly. Alida passed a small satchel through the bars to Jansen. "A pipe and tobacco, some fruit, a change of clothes."

"I appreciate it," Jansen said. He rifled through the bag and pulled out the pipe and a measure of the tobacco. He offered it to William. "Since I already have one, would you like to use this?"

William was grateful. "I would. Thank you."

"William performed an old folk remedy to rid me of my affliction," Jansen said, and winked at Peter. "I owe him."

"Did it work?" Peter asked.

"Too soon to tell," Jansen said solemnly. He handed William two apples and two pears. "Here, these'll make you feel better."

William took them reluctantly. He looked at Alida. "I . . . I don't want to be rude, but do you think that maybe you could take these to my wife and daughter? They're here, in this prison . . . if you wouldn't find it too much trouble . . ."

Alida studied him with her haunted eyes. "You keep those. I'll be happy to take them some fruit of their own."

William smiled. "Thank you. Thank you very much. Margaret and Prissy Hawthorne."

"I'll do it this afternoon."

"Thank you," William said again. Had he ever thought it possible he would be so terribly grateful for a few pieces of fruit? He moved to a far corner of the cell to allow the family some relative privacy and to savor the gifts of their generosity.

16

"I've arranged to escape on the way to the trial," Jansen quietly announced to William the day before they were to be taken back to Salem for their hearings. "The transport will be waylaid by some of my men. There's a boat waiting in the harbor. Will you come with me?"

The offer was tempting. "My wife and children?"

Jansen shook his head. "I thought about it, but there's no way it can be arranged."

William shrugged.

Jansen nodded. "Of course." He paused. "So, do you have a strategy? I've heard if you plead guilty they won't hang you, at least."

"I'm not going to plead at all," William said softly.

"Not plead? But they'll force you to plead."

"They can try."

"I don't understand."

"If I don't plead, they can't take my land from me. I have nothing else to leave my children. They'll have no future otherwise."

"But . . ." Jansen's voice died off as the full measure of what William had said settled into his mind. He felt a wave of respect for the other man. "God, William, you're a better man than I." He took a piece of paper and pen from Alida's latest package and scribbled his name and address on it. "Here. Whoever of your family survives this should come to New York, and I'll do what I can."

William took the paper. "I'll give it to Bridget. Expect at least her and Phip."

Jansen nodded. Unfamiliar emotions flooded him, but he didn't know how to express them.

"I think your spell worked. It's been a month since I've had a fit. I don't seem to have the affliction anymore," he said at last.

17

Jansen's escape was successful, and William stood mute before the court.

The first of his family to be brought to trial in Salem, William steadfastly refused to plead. He was taken from the courtroom and interrogated by the magistrate in a holding cell.

"Why do you not plead?" Sheldon asked angrily.

For the first time in months, William felt a sense of control over his own fate. "If I don't plead, your honor, you can't seize my land. It's the law."

Sheldon, his chubby face already red, began to perspire. "You cannot refuse to plead to the charge."

"Yes, I can." William was filled with a sense of deep calm.

Sheldon began to rant. "We have ways to make you plead! You'll not get away with this. We'll break your fool's silence. You'll not embarrass this court!"

William smiled at the man's anger. It felt good to turn the tables of frustration and impotence. "Do what you must, because that's just what I intend to do."

Sheldon stormed from the cell as William began to prepare the deed that would convey his land to Bridget and Phip.

Bridget, who had come to the meetinghouse that morning for the beginning of William's trial, visited her father after he had been taken from the court. He gave her the deed.

"My land is yours now. They can't take it from you."

Bridget silently nodded. She didn't understand exactly what was happening, but it felt as if it were an ending, and she felt sad.

"You've been so strong and brave. I'm very proud of you."

Bridget did not know what to say.

"Did you bring the berries?"

Bridget handed him the small box of deadly nightshade, and he removed a fatal dose.

Bridget's mouth went dry. "Are you going to kill yourself?"

William looked into her fearful eyes. She was no longer a child. "No, they'll kill me." He held up the berries. "This'll make it quicker."

Bridget felt as if she would explode with grief.

"Tell your mother I'll wait for her on the other side. Take care of your brother and sister. Raise them well."

Bridget's stomach lurched. "Is Mother going to die, too?"

William inwardly recalled his vision. "I may be wrong, but I see you three together, without us."

"What will we do?"

"When the madness stops, sell the land and go away from here. This isn't a good place for people like us. Go to New York." He pressed Jansen's address into her palm. "Jan said he'd help. He says there's greater tolerance there. Try to find others like us to marry. Keep the blood alive. Don't lose the old ways."

"I promise, Father."

"Buried beneath the stones of the hearth in the parlor is a book. Don't uncover it until the day you leave this town. It has been handed down for generations. It has the secrets that your mother and I haven't had time to teach you children. Study it, and share its lessons with Prissy and Phip." His voice broke, and he paused to collect himself. "There's a lot we haven't had a chance to teach you."

Bridget began to cry.

William handed the tiny box back to her. "Take some of these to your mother, in the event that she'll need them, too."

She nodded.

"Go home. Don't stay in town today."

So, it will happen today, Bridget thought. "I'll always love you," she said.

He stroked her cheek. "Then we'll meet again."

That afternoon, William was taken to an open field on the edge of Salem Village. A large crowd turned out to watch. William was made to lie down, and the sheriff began to pile heavy rocks on his chest, one by one.

"Do you consent to plead?" Sheldon asked as the fourth rock was placed on William.

The pain was crushing. William's tongue toyed with the berries he had hidden in his cheek. It was still too early in the procedure to surrender to death. "More weight," he managed to say.

Some in the crowd began to cheer the sheriff on.

William felt the blood begin to flow from between his lips.

"Consent to give testimony and we shall remove the rocks," Sheldon said.

William could no longer speak.

"Give him more," Sheldon told the sheriff.

William bit into the berries.

Within moments he began to feel lighter. The drug—or was it his small victory?—made him feel happy. He could freely sense the emotions of those in his audience. He felt a few who were appalled by the "justice" of the court. Good, he thought. There was hope in that. His giddiness increased rapidly, and then suddenly the paralysis set in.

He was finally free.

18

"How long have you been a witch?" Sheldon asked Margaret.

"I don't understand your question," she replied.

"Were you born a witch, or did the Devil make you one?"

"I don't know what the Devil is."

"Did you poison Grace Weston?"

"No, I did not."

"Did you give a sickness potion to the girl Elizabeth?"

"I never saw her before my preliminary hearing."

"Who's the tall man of Boston that other witches have named in their testimony?"

"I've never heard of him."

"He's the leader of the witches, the keeper of the Devil's book. Who is he?"

"I don't know."

"How long have you practiced witchcraft?"

"I don't even believe in this thing that you call witchcraft."

Sheldon looked pleased with himself. "That in itself is damning evidence, you understand."

Margaret sighed wearily. She had no spirit to go on with this. William was dead. Priscilla, in her brief trial, had been convicted of witchcraft and had been sentenced to imprisonment of an undetermined length—the court was reluctant to condemn convicted child witches to death—but she could not possibly survive a long prison term, Margaret knew. However, for the sake of Bridget and Phip and their continued safety, she knew she should cooperate. She tried to think of a defense; accused witches were not allowed the benefit of counsel. She knew from the results of other trials that if she were to confess to the crime, they would not execute her. But that would put Bridget and Phip at peril. She did not know what to say.

"I have enough evidence to easily find you guilty of the crime with which you are charged, Margaret Hawthorne," Sheldon said imperiously. "I condemn you to death by hanging on Gallows Hill this Tuesday next."

19

Margaret meditated over the berries. She briefly considered poisoning Priscilla—it would be more merciful than leaving her alone in the hell to which she had been condemned. But Margaret believed that with life there was hope.

She decided against taking a fatal dose herself. It

would be best for her children if the authorities believed they had been the executioners. It was a fact they found to be a great source of religious pride. Instead, she took merely enough to elevate her spirits. She would rather leave this world happy than sad.

She thought about her life. It had been good. She thanked the gods for the gifts they had given her. She prayed to them to protect and keep her children.

She thought about distant relatives, three hundred years before, who had died in the European witch hunts. She thought about distant relatives three hundred years hence and hoped they would not face the same thing. She wondered if humanity would ever learn from their mistakes.

She held Priscilla as tightly as she could until they came for her. They had to pry the girl from her arms.

Two other women rode in the wagon with Margaret to their death that morning. Margaret was not frightened, but—despite the drug she had taken—she was angry. She had admonished Priscilla not to hate and was surprised to meet the face of her own demon of hatred. As the wagon neared Gallows Hill, she was sickened by the blood lust that rose in waves from the crowd. She thought of her familiar spirit, and the corners of her lips curled slightly. "If it's witchcraft you wanted, it's witchcraft you're going to get," she whispered.

The woman riding closest to Margaret, who had apparently overheard her, gave her a surprised look.

"My familiar's name is Vengeance," Margaret said softly.

The woman smiled bitterly. "Then give it to them."

The snake manifested in the midst of the crowd, and screams filled the air.

"It's poisonous!" someone screamed.

"Run!"

The crowd scattered.

"It's witchcraft!" someone else yelled.

"It's after the magistrate!"

Sheldon danced a sort of jig in an attempt to evade the copperhead, but he was unsuccessful. His screams of fear and agony filled the air as the fangs injected their poison into his leg.

"Will he die?" Margaret's companion asked.

"I leave that to the gods to decide," Margaret said.

The high sheriff was undaunted by the diversion. He soothed the startled horses and led the wagon to the giant oak tree.

Three nooses were already in place.

As the wagon stopped beneath the tree, Margaret looked up to see the owl circling overhead. She smiled. "Tell Bridget I love her, too, Moonlight," she whispered.

The noose was hooked around Margaret's neck.

"I'm coming to you, William."

She heard the whip as it struck the horses and felt the wagon move from beneath her. She felt a sudden jerk, a wrenching pain accompanied by the loud noise of breaking bone—then Margaret escaped the world that had turned on her.

20

Bridget, using a sharp stick as an awl and dried sinew as thread, made three fur capes from the small pelts she had been collecting all summer and fall. She delivered Priscilla's to her before the first snow fell.

Rebekah and Mirasaya had, on Margaret's advice, both pleaded guilty to the charge of witchcraft. They had been spared the gallows but, like Priscilla, sentenced to remain in prison. Without their warmth and love— and the inner escape that Samara continued to provide— Bridget knew that Priscilla would have lost her mind.

Bridget braved the difficult winter travel and continued her weekly visits to Boston to take Priscilla, Rebekah, and Mirasaya food. Her food store was meager, but she rationed it carefully and kept the five of them alive through the darkest months of their lives.

Spring came, and using their bare hands and sharpened sticks, Bridget and Phip began to prepare the fields for planting. They had managed to save enough seed to sow two fields. Wearily, they did their best.

In May, sanity returned to Massachusetts, and the governor issued a general pardon for all condemned witches and ordered their release from prison. However, according to law, all prisoners had to pay the jailer for their keep from the time of their arrest. The fee was two shillings and sixpence a week. Priscilla had been imprisoned for more than a year. Bridget couldn't claim her sister until she had sold the farm.

"What about you?" Bridget asked Rebekah and Mirasaya as she finally completed negotiations to secure Priscilla's release.

Rebekah shrugged hopelessly. "There's no one who wants us. No one to pay the prison fee."

Bridget was confused. "So?"

"So, we're here for life, it seems."

Shock filled Bridget. She thought about the money she had received for the farm. After paying off their debts, there was little left. There was enough to buy freedom for one of them. But whom could she leave behind? "I . . . I can help one of you. That's all I've got the money for."

Hope lit up both their faces, but Mirasaya's expression was quickly replaced by one more cryptic. "I no want freedom from witchcraft prison paid for by witch family. Bad luck," she said quietly. "You take fragile one here."

Bridget was stunned. "You know we're witches?" she whispered.

Mirasaya put her hands on her hips. "What, you think we stupid or something?"

We? They both knew? Bridget looked at Rebekah, who shrugged. "It's all right with me. I . . . I love you."

So it was decided.

As they prepared to leave, Bridget hesitated. She looked into Mirasaya's eyes, and for a moment their souls touched. She realized that Mirasaya wasn't at all concerned by the fact that the Hawthornes were witches. She had performed a supreme act of charity, and Bridget was overcome by emotion. She threw her arms around the older woman. She wanted to make her promises of an ultimate rescue, but she couldn't be sure. She didn't want to give her false hope. "You're very special, Mirasaya," she said instead. "I'll always carry you in my heart."

Mirasaya hugged Bridget tightly. "I remember you 'til I die, and even after. You good girl, strong and brave."

Not as strong and brave as you, Bridget thought, before she scurried from the Boston jail and the tragedy that remained within its walls.

Outside, Bridget lifted Priscilla onto Silver. With Phip and Rebekah walking beside her, they began the long trek south to New York. As they left Salem behind, Bridget thought about the Puritans, their religion and their law, and—despite all the loss and suffering she had endured—she was very glad she was of the blood of witches.

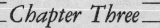

Chapter Three

June 1992

1

Leigh was trembling. She hadn't stopped trembling since Preacher Cody had made his startling appearance at the Hawthorne funeral. But she held her questions until she and Craig were alone in their room.

"Witches and Satan worshipers?"

Craig snapped the strap of his zebra-striped suspenders and sighed. "Not Satan worshipers."

"What then, witches?"

He nodded, stuck his hands deep in the pockets of his baggy black trousers, and began to pace.

Leigh sat down on the edge of the bed and laughed nervously. "But there is no such thing."

"Don't be naive, Leigh."

His words and tone made Leigh feel as if he had slapped her across the face. To take her mind off the affront, her thoughts returned to the words of Preacher Cody. "He said something about the Hawthornes not being religious. . . ."

Craig chuckled. "Oh, my family's got religion. That *old* time religion, to be exact." He stopped pacing and looked at her. "That's what witchcraft is. It's the old

73

religion. It goes back to tribal society, to the individuals who had extraordinary powers which they used to benefit the tribe. They were the shamans—or medicine men and women—who could heal, help their people with visions of future events, charm the wild animals into not harming the tribe or, conversely, becoming the evening's dinner, or hex the tribe's enemies and thus protect their own. Some of those bloodlines have been preserved, along with the knowledge those individuals possessed. The Hawthornes are hereditary witches."

They looked at each other for a long time in silence.

Inside Leigh a storm was raging.

She tried to understand the concept of witchcraft as Craig had described it. She held it up against all the models her mind had: the Wicked Witch of the West in *The Wizard of Oz*; the sultry Kim Novak's Gillian in the movie *Bell, Book and Candle*; the suburban Samantha Stephens and her bizarre relatives on "Bewitched"; the assorted weird, self-proclaimed modern witches who had appeared with Phil Donahue and on the local news shows at Halloween; the Devil worshipers the Christians had always painted witches to be.

If Craig's witchcraft were hereditary, then not only Craig but the children, too, would be witches. She tried to see how that might apply.

Craig had an extraordinary ability to heal; even his colleagues had often commented on it. He had taken women who had lost baby after baby, and whom other physicians had given up on, and brought them through successful pregnancies with smooth births. His success with infertility cases was phenomenal, and he had practically developed a cult following in that regard over the past five years.

She remembered the time Kamelia had been holding a dying cat—one that had been hit by a car—and it had suddenly revived and leaped from her arms, completely well. Leigh had been so sure its back had been broken.

She thought about Adrian's visions.

A sob escaped her.

Then anger filled her, and she threw it at him. "Why didn't you tell me?"

"I should have."

"What's the truth behind your cutting yourself off from your family?"

"They became power trippers. I was afraid of losing the magic to the politics of power."

"How will we tell the children?"

"We don't have to. Didn't you see their faces when the preacher man called us witches?"

"No."

"They knew. They just needed to be reminded."

Leigh's anger melted into fear. "What he said about Satan worshipers . . ."

"They've always been afraid of us, so they've always made us out to be evil. It isn't the power that's good or bad, it's how the individual uses it that matters. It's the same with them. There have been powerful Christians who have misused their power, just as there have been evil witches who have done the same. That's just part of the human picture."

"We've got to get the children away from here before something comes of Preacher Cody's accusations. I mean, things could get crazy and someone could get hurt."

Craig burst out laughing. "Oh, Leigh. My dear, naive Leigh. Yes, that could happen."

Leigh felt again as if she had been slapped, and she began to cry. "Don't be condescending to me. I'm more than a little overwhelmed."

Craig sat down and slipped his arm around her. "I'm not laughing at you. I'm . . . it's so much more serious than you understand, that's all. Think about the things Slugger said last night. Try and remember."

They're going to kill us all. All of us. Everywhere. It'll start here, but it'll spread. There will be no place that will be safe. It'll be worse than the last time. It'll even be worse than the time before that.

"Oh, my God," Leigh whispered as Adrian's words echoed in her mind.

Craig began to gently stroke her hair. "The last time was the Salem witch hunt. The Christians killed about twenty people, two of them Hawthornes. The time before that was the Inquisition, what we call the burning

75

times. Somewhere between a half-million and nine million people—estimates vary depending on their source—were killed as heretics. Many were witches. Now, how many really were witches and how many were simply random victims of the Christian witch mania is also debatable. The Hawthornes were nearly wiped out during that time. Slugger said that this new killing spree would be even worse than the burning times. Do you realize what that means?''

"It couldn't happen today. We're more enlightened. We've got civil rights.''

"We've also got mass media and a world that's terrified of extinction. Fear looks for scapegoats. And fear breeds hate. Look at history—the Inquisition, Salem, Nazi Germany. Charismatic and powerful people can sway the masses to support the most heinous of crimes against their fellow man. And unfortunately, the preacher man has what it takes.''

"What can we do?" Leigh's voice was tremulous.

"Slugger said that perhaps we could stop it. The stakes are high. We've got to try.''

"Can we send the children away, at least?" Leigh asked.

"Where do we send them? To your folks?''

Leigh thought about their alcoholism and how advanced it was. "No.''

"Besides, like Slugger said, there isn't any place that will be safe.''

2

Cody sat at the desk in his study across from Diane Fox, the aggressive reporter from the *Montvue Post-Dispatch*. He had chosen her to conduct the interview because she had a reputation for hard-line journalism, and he felt she wouldn't soft-sell the information he had to share. He also thought that, with her reputation—which had been established during her years with the *Rocky Mountain News*—his news would be taken more seriously than otherwise.

He had decided that at this point in time he didn't want to make his attack on the Hawthornes a national one. He wanted to vindicate himself among the locals who had heard of his cowardice during the plane crash, but he didn't want to bring undue attention to it among his national audience. However, his attack against witchcraft would begin on the very next episode of "Preacher Cody." It had already been filmed and was set to air. And it would be just the beginning of many more such shows. God had shown him what his next mission was to be. If the Christians were to survive the end times, their faith had to be protected from those who would seek to capture it. And the witches seemed to be the most powerful agents of the Devil in that regard.

Cody studied Diane as she studied her notes. She was blond and beautiful like his wife and, he had noticed earlier, like the wife of the witch Craig Hawthorne—his sources said she was named Leigh. However, they were three distinct types of women. Whereas Rachel's beauty was chaste, Leigh's was sexy, and Diane's was hard. He found it uncomfortable to be around a woman such as Diane, with her painted face, her masculine clothes, and the heavy cloud of perfume she exuded. He thought it a terrible travesty against what true femininity should be.

"So," Diane said, interrupting his mental condemnation of her, "you claim that two of the Hawthornes' ancestors were tried and condemned for witchcraft during the Salem witch trials. Another one was also arrested for the crime but died before he could plead. Throughout the family's history there have been repeated rumors and suspicion leveled against them for unusual, supposedly supernatural behavior and activity. They have never been publicly associated with any established religion. And the two Hawthorne men buried today, Alan and Curtis, were heard to be chanting some kind of spell after the commuter airplane crashed which seemed to control the spread of fire within that plane." She started to say something else, then sighed in exasperation. "How can you expect an intelligent, well-educated public to buy this kind of stuff?"

"It's the truth."

"How can you be so sure of what you saw and heard on that plane? You yourself admitted that you panicked."

"I wasn't the only witness to their acts."

"Mass hysteria could account for that."

"Those are straws you're clutching at, Miss Fox."

She tapped her pencil on the edge of the desk. "Okay, okay. Let's just say it happened your way. Doesn't your charge imply that—if it's true—these Hawthorne men saved lives during that crash, yours included?"

"God saved our lives. If you notice, the two witches are dead."

She smiled and shook her head. "I'm sorry, Preacher, but I think this all really is bunk. I mean, witches simply aren't real. They're Grimm's fairy tales."

"Like creation is Darwinism instead of divine? I think that the well-educated public can be greatly misled about reality. It's the sad fact of worshiping the mind as God. The Bible warns us about that. It also warns us about witches and tells us what our stand should be. Old Testament, Deuteronomy, King James Bible: 'When thou art come into the land which the Lord thy God giveth thee, thou shalt not learn to do after the abominations of these nations. There shall not be found among you any one that maketh his son or his daughter to pass through the fire, or that useth divination, or an observer of times'— that would be an astrologer—'or an enchanter, or *witch*, or a charmer, or a consulter with familiar spirits, or a wizard, or a necromancer, for all that do these things are an abomination unto the Lord: and because of these abominations the Lord thy God doth drive them out from before thee. Thou shalt be perfect with the Lord thy God.' Are you calling God's word bunk, Miss Fox?"

"Well, I for one am not at all sure that the books of the Bible haven't been altered somewhat by man over time. As a matter of fact, in college, my lit professor showed us that, indeed, the Bible had been changed a number of times to reflect the values of the times. The common man didn't have access to the Bible until relatively recently. The church held it captive, and the church, we all know, was a greatly political entity."

Cody felt his anger but willed it away. "I'll not get into an argument with you over the verity of God's word as reflected in the Holy Bible. Now, you're a reporter—an excellent reporter, from all I've heard—and I expect you see that the good, Christian community of Montvue will be interested in the facts that I've provided you. That's what news is all about, isn't it?"

"How did you dig up this stuff on the Hawthornes?"

"I have connections."

"Through your CIA involvement?"

"The CIA doesn't deal with domestic concerns."

Diane smiled again. "Yes. Of course."

"It is my spiritual duty to confront the Hawthornes and ask them to repent. It is my mission to save souls, you understand. I plan to go to their home Sunday night, after my show is broadcast, and inform them of God's grace and mercy."

Diane's eyes widened with surprise. "I see. Do the Hawthornes know about this?"

"No, but I expect they will after your article is printed. And I expect the Christians in Montvue will, too. Any who care to accompany me in a show of God's force will be welcome to stand with me."

Diane stuck her pencil up behind her ear and shook her head. "That's a terribly explosive situation you're proposing. I don't think I want to be party to lighting that fuse."

"Well, then, Miss Fox, I'll find a reporter who does."

3

Leigh found her children in their room. Adrian, exhausted from the ordeal of the funeral, was asleep on his bed, his thumb securely tucked away in his mouth. *Dangerous-looking witch there,* she thought as she took his shoes off and pulled the side of the bedspread up to cover him. Kamelia was lying on her bed, staring pensively at the ceiling.

"Can we talk?" Leigh asked.

"Sure, Mom."

Leigh sat down on the edge of the bed and brushed a stray wisp of hair out of her daughter's face. "So, tell me what you're feeling."

"Like a lot of the pieces of my life were finally put in place today. You know, there've been things about myself that I've never understood, that just never fit anywhere."

"Such as?"

Kamelia took her glasses off and rubbed her eyes in a manner characteristic of her father. "Well, I know that the Christians burned the witches. I know that there's a great big problem between religion and this thing that's called witchcraft." She paused and fumbled to put her thoughts into words. "I . . . I've never had much interest in religion. I mean, you and Dad didn't raise us with religion, but you never stopped me from doing it, either. And when the Incredible Hunk hit the air, boy, did I try. Most of my friends managed to find religion real quick, but it just didn't feel right, you know?"

Leigh nodded.

"On the other hand, I always felt that something—something powerful—was there taking care of me and that everything was just fine, that I was protected and safe. It was like I knew God, or whatever, without having to go looking."

Leigh had never known that her daughter entertained such thoughts. She wanted to ask questions but thought it best to just let her talk.

"And so often I just know things. Things I shouldn't know. Like, I can walk into your bedroom and know you're not doing sex, not because I listen at the door—I just made that up—but because I *know* that you're not. And"—she rubbed her palms together—"my hands get so hot, and I touch things and stuff happens. Like Cindy's cat. You remember Cindy's cat?"

Leigh nodded.

"Well, stuff like that happens with my friends, too. Like, Tara and Heather and I would be doing something we shouldn't, and Tara—the klutzoid—would get hurt." She rubbed her hands together again. "I could make it better so her mom and dad wouldn't know."

"Did you ever tell Dad?"

"Yeah. And all he would say is that it was a gift I inherited from him. That it was cool and not to worry."

Leigh felt a twinge of resentment. Why hadn't anyone told her?

"Why didn't Dad tell me about the witch thing?"

"I don't know, honey." Leigh's anger returned, but she pushed it back. "Tell me, Kammi, do you believe you're a witch?"

A look of wonderment crossed Kamelia's face. "Yeah. It doesn't seem weird, or space-cadet time, or anything. I sort of understand, and it feels okay."

"What about Adrian? Has he said anything?"

"Not really. Well, before he fell asleep he looked at me and said, 'I didn't like preachers in my last life either.' "

Leigh experienced a wave of gooseflesh. She felt like a stranger to her family, an outsider. "I'm not . . . a witch. You understand that, don't you?"

"Did you know Dad was?"

Leigh shook her head.

"That wasn't real fair of him, was it? Kinda like poor Darrin on 'Bewitched.' "

Leigh forced a smile. "Kinda like."

Kamelia sat up and hugged her mother. "Well, for a mortal, you're real cool by me."

Leigh clung to Kamelia and basked for a moment in her love. Then she disentangled herself and gave her daughter a serious look. "This isn't a sitcom. Your Incredible Hunk's going to cause trouble."

"Yeah, I got that impression."

"Your dad thinks it'll be real bad trouble."

"Are we going to fight or run?"

Leigh didn't like the concept of fighting. "We're going to stay here and try and stop Preacher Cody."

Kamelia nodded. "Sounds like a cool plan."

Leigh tousled her daughter's hair affectionately. "You sound more like your father every day."

Kamelia shrugged. "Well, I am a Hawthorne, after all."

4

Diane Fox picked up her three-year-old daughter, Tiffany, at the Montvue Heights Preschool and Day-Care Center on her way home from Preacher Cody's ranch.

Tiffany was the result of a two-year affair Diane had had with a married coworker at her previous job as a reporter for Denver's *Rocky Mountain News*. When she had discovered her pregnancy, Diane quit the man, quit the job, and quit Denver.

Determined career woman that she was, it had shocked her to discover the power of her maternal instincts. Even though the child was unexpected, she discovered that she wanted the baby more than she would ever have imagined possible. Diane, big-city born and bred, had wanted her child to grow up in a world that was more gentle than the one she had known, and so she chose Montvue as their new home.

It wasn't easy for Diane to find a place for herself in a conservative town like Montvue. The *Post-Dispatch* had been reluctant to hire her because they couldn't come close to matching the salary she had had at the *News*, but she ultimately convinced them that she would be content with what they could offer. Then, because of her skill and reputation, she had been a threat to many on the paper. For months, her only assignments had been of the bottom-of-the-barrel variety. During that time, she saw enough dog shows, cat shows, horse shows, doll shows, antique shows, and the like to last her a lifetime. When she happened to be covering preparations for the annual Policeman's Ball and was at the right place at the right time to get the scoop on the arrest of the mayor's son on drug charges, she wrote up the story and submitted it to the city editor. It was an arrest that, in Montvue, would have otherwise been kept from the media—out of respect for the mayor—and in a bold move the *Post-Dispatch* ran the story. The reaction from the public was positive, and, the precedent having been set, she began to get more juicy assignments. Soon she was the paper's lead reporter.

But her pregnancy had become obvious, and her status as a single woman threatened to make her the scandal of the town.

She had remained undaunted and eventually carved out a comfortable niche for herself and her daughter. Diane wasn't the most popular woman among Montvue's citizenry, but she had earned their respect in her four years of life there. With Tiffany she found an emotional fulfillment that kept her from being so keenly aware of her loneliness.

"Momma's got a hard decision to make," Diane told Tiffany as she strapped her into her car seat. "There's this crazy man who believes in witches. Like in 'Hansel and Gretel.' You remember Hansel and Gretel?"

Tiffany nodded solemnly.

"Well"—Diane slid in behind the wheel and strapped herself into her own seat—"this crazy man wants me to tell everyone that these certain people are witches and that witches are bad because this book he has says they are." Diane started the engine and pulled out into the flow of late-afternoon traffic.

"Now, this man, a regular gospel shouter he is, is planning to do some shouting at these witch people and wants lots of other people to be there to back him up. He wants—you want a burger, honey?"

Tiffany giggled. "Want a burger," she said happily.

Diane pulled into Wendy's and got their dinner at the drive-through window, then headed home to eat it.

"Burger!" Tiffany yelled, straining for the aromatic bag that was just out of her reach.

"You're too messy an eater, honey. We'll be home soon. Anyway, this crazy man—who's this odd version of Rambo-gets-religion—wants me to write the story about the witch family and announce this rally at their home Sunday night. If I don't do the report, he'll get someone else to."

"French fries?" Tiffany asked hopefully.

"In just a minute. However, I think if I keep the story, and write it in a manner that shows both sides, it would be better than giving it to Joe or Paula or some other twirpy reporter at the *Post* who's gaga over this crazy man. I mean, they'd write whatever he wants them to, because they think he's just so terrific. So, I think I'll keep the story and do it with objectivity. What do you think?''

"Cherry Coke," Tiffany said.

Diane grinned. "Thanks for your input, honey. Don't know what I'd do without you."

5

The Sunday-morning issue of the *Post-Dispatch* carried Diane's story about Preacher Cody, the Hawthornes, and witchcraft.

The Hawthornes passed the newspaper around the breakfast table.

"It says they'll be here at eight tonight," Melanie said.

"What are we going to do, Craig?" Vivian asked. Her composure had deteriorated in the few days since her husband's and son's funeral. Dark circles shadowed her eyes, and her voice quavered with fear. She had also begun to bite her fingernails.

"We could secure the gates and not let them in. Wish we had some alligators for the moat."

"What's a moat?" Adrian asked.

"A ditch dug all around a castle and filled with water," Kamelia said.

"We got a moat?" Adrian asked.

"No, silly," Kamelia answered.

Adrian nodded and popped a strawberry into his mouth. "Okey-doke." *Okey-doke* was his latest word.

"Maybe you should call and talk to the police," Leigh suggested.

Craig nodded. "It wouldn't hurt."

"Some protection magic wouldn't hurt, either," Jason said.

Melanie peeked over the top of the newspaper. "I'll help you with that."

"Can I come?" Kamelia asked.

Everyone looked at Leigh.

Leigh cleared her throat nervously. "I . . . I don't know . . ."

"Go for it, Kammi," Craig said. "Now the covers are pulled, you'd better not keep sleeping in the buff."

"Thanks, Dad."

Dorian began to cough and couldn't seem to catch his breath.

Glynis slapped his back a few times. "He's not well today. I think it's the stress of it all."

"Put him to bed after chow time. Kammi and I will be by later to give him a look-see," Craig said.

"Can't eat," Dorian said, his voice raw. "I'll go now."

Craig nodded.

Dorian maneuvered his electric wheelchair away from the table and out the terrace doors onto the path that led to the small guest cottage that was his and Glynis's home.

"He's scared," Glynis said.

"We're all scared," Vivian said as she gave more attention to her fingernails than to the food on her plate.

"I'd like to discuss why everyone's so scared," Leigh said.

"What's to discuss?" Jason asked.

Leigh ignored the harshness of his tone. "Well, I went to the library yesterday and did some research on modern witchcraft. I didn't realize it before—guess I just never paid attention—but these days it seems to be pretty well accepted. I mean, *Books in Print* lists all kinds of how-to books on the subject. I ran down some major magazine articles that spoke of it as being a folk religion. In England it's officially been declared legal, and witches are even unionized. There are people who claim to be witches doing the talk-show circuit, and they aren't being persecuted. Why, besides Adrian's vision, is everyone here so scared?"

"The talk-show witches usually dress like ghouls, with black robes and eye shadow, and act strange," Craig said. "They aren't threatening to Joe Public because of how unbelievable they come across. America's got free speech, and you're going to find books about all kinds of weird stuff on the shelves. People are used to it, and, for the most part, they just ignore what they can't use them-selves. Some scholars and intellectuals understand the reality of it all and write wonderful articles in an attempt to dispel the myths. But they're only going to appeal to other scholars and intellectuals, and those folk aren't the problem. Okay . . . are you with me?"

Leigh nodded.

"Okay, the average Englishman is—no offense to my fellow countrymen—more sophisticated about such things than the average American, so witchcraft is much more accepted there than here. Look at America's roots—fundamental Christianity. I mean, it's what we were built on. We're talking deep-seated psychological blue-printing. Because of this, even if a person isn't a practic-ing fundamentalist, it doesn't mean that—on some level—he's not influenced by it. And fundamentalism is a to-tally prejudicial system. Hell, to a fundamentalist, a Catholic isn't even considered a Christian. They're so damned narrow-minded!"

He paused and took a deep breath, obviously trying to calm down. "Narrow-minded people tend to be threat-ened by what doesn't fit into their own specific niche, because if anything else is right, then they've got to be wrong. That's why they're so vocal—they're always trying to justify themselves. Add to all this a charismatic leader like the preacher man, his labeling of us as satanists—a heady subject these days everywhere—small-town mentality like Montvue's, a seemingly respectable and powerful family such as ours, and you have a major *kaboom* waiting to happen."

"And don't forget about our ancestors who were killed for witchcraft," Glynis said. "If for no other reason, we're scared because it's happened to us before."

"Then there's this," Jason said, shaking the newspaper noisily.

"Well, at least the killer dyke didn't defend the en-emy," Melanie said. "She is actually making an attempt at reason in the article."

"Killer dyke?" Leigh asked.

Melanie nodded. "Diane Fox, the reporter. As a re-porter, she tends to go for the jugular, and, well, everyone knows she's a dyke. I mean, she dresses like a guy, and she doesn't date or anything. I think her kid just must have been a case of rape or artificial insemination or something.''

Leigh sighed. "Sorry I asked.''

Helena came in with a fresh pot of coffee.

"What's with the phone ringing off the hook this morning?" Jason asked her.

Helena shook her head. "You don't want to know.'' She began to refill cups. "But I will say it's amazing how well some of those Christians out there can swear. I've heard more vulgarity today than you could get at a . . . well, a Charlie Bronson film festival.''

Leigh had been meaning to ask her but hadn't had a chance. "What do you think of all this, Helena?"

"All what?''

"The fact that you work for a family of accused witches.''

"Well, it's no surprise to me.''

"Oh, you knew, then?''

Helena smiled a beautiful, slow smile "Well, very often it takes one to know one.''

6

Sergeant Tom Cosworth of the Montvue Police Department wasn't surprised when the phone call came in. He had read the morning newspaper.

"Is this the head honcho, the biggest cheese?" a man's voice asked when Cosworth picked up the phone.

Cosworth scratched his ample belly and relit his tired cigar. "Well, Lieutenant Brody is the watch commander, but he's unavailable right now. I'm Sergeant Cosworth. What do you want?''

"This is Dr. Craig Hawthorne of the Hawthorne Witch Club. I assume you've heard of our respected organization.''

Cosworth chuckled. "Yep, your PR department's done a bang-up job.''

"So, would you understand it if I said that our teeth are chattering and our knees are knocking?''

Cosworth chewed on his cigar butt. "Yep, I would."

"Can the distinguished men—and women, of course—in blue, or whatever color you're wearing these days, make like the cavalry?"

"Well, Dr. Hawthorne, there's not a whole lot we can do at this stage of the game."

"Does the preacher man have a permit?"

"Doesn't need one."

"Doesn't need one? You need a permit to take a piss in this goddamn country! What do you mean, doesn't need one?"

Cosworth sighed. "If he doesn't block free travel into and around your home, he doesn't need one."

"Isn't there a law prohibiting this sort of ballyhoo in front of a man's private castle?"

Cosworth tapped an ash into the pot of the plant on his desk. "Well, they can't carry picket signs and they can't tell the neighborhood kids things like you murder babies, but, yep, they can gather to save your soul."

"My goddamn soul is just fine, thank you!"

Cosworth really didn't blame the doctor for giving him an earache. "You could all just go somewhere else tonight. Not be there."

"Would you turn tail and run?"

"Not me. This is America."

"Says it all, doesn't it?"

The phone receiver went dead in Cosworth's ear.

"Poor bastard," he muttered, and then he relit the dying ember on the end of his cigar.

7

The guest cottage that served as Dorian's and Glynis's home was located just inside the south gate of Hawthorne Manor. It was small but cozy, and Craig had always been more comfortable there than in the big house. With its bright chintz curtains, simple overstuffed furniture, and scattering of homey knickknacks, it was a warm and inviting place. The only telling influence of the Hawthornes' wealth was the original

Norman Rockwell painting that hung on the living-room wall.

"I think part of it is his allergies and asthma," Glynis said as she slowly led Craig and Kamelia into the bedroom where Dorian lay. "When he gets excited or nervous he has troubles. I've put the house plants back outside, and I've been keeping the windows closed. I even had Marek put a new filter in the air conditioner. But still, it's pretty bad this time."

"How ya doing, you old fart?" Craig asked as he sat down on the edge of Dorian's bed.

Dorian, his aged face a mass of leathery wrinkles, grinned. "Don't like being old."

"It's a bitch, ain't it?" Craig said. He pulled his stethoscope out of his bag. He placed it to Dorian's chest and listened to his noisy bronchi. "Rock, rattle, and roll," he commented. He took Dorian's temperature and examined his glands and throat. "Aunt Glynis's diagnosis hits the nail on the head. Best thing you can do is rest. Try and sleep."

"Sleep?" Dorian asked, his voice croaky. "With that crazy preacher breathing down our throats? He'll be here in just a few hours. How can I sleep?"

Kamelia pulled some small blue cloth bags out of her pocket and handed one to Dorian. "Here's an amulet. Melanie, Jason, and I made them. It'll help protect you."

Dorian took it and immediately began to sneeze and cough. He thrust it back at her. "Herbs in it. Can't handle it right now."

Kamelia's face reddened, and she stuffed them back into her jeans. "I . . . I didn't think. Sorry."

Craig grasped Kamelia's hands and gave them a comforting squeeze, then placed them on Dorian's solar plexus. He put his own hands on his uncle's head, and within moments he could feel the connection of his and Kamelia's energies as they coursed through Dorian's body.

Dorian tensed at first, then began to relax. "Oh, yes. Nice."

"This'll mellow you out and start the fences mending," Craig said. He watched Dorian's face as it became more smooth, and a smile came to his own lips. He loved and respected the old man who had given his all for love. It was a story he had heard as a small boy from his grandmother, Beatrice, during one of her many wine-sotted tirades. The story of Glynis's and Dorian's romance, and the violence his grandfather had used to try and thwart it, had been one of the many reasons Craig had chosen to go his own way in life.

"Will he be better now?" Glynis asked as her arthritic fingers struggled to tuck a stray lock back up into the hairnet that held her silver hair.

Craig nodded. "He needs some Z's. Let's make back to the land of Oz for now and leave him be."

"Yes, the Wicked Witch of the West is waiting," Glynis said conspiratorially, dissolving into giggles, her hand hiding her mouth shyly.

Craig stood up and put an arm around her frail shoulders. "Oh, dear, I see I'm having a nasty influence on the home front."

"You're like a breath of fresh air, Craig. A breath of fresh air."

Together, Craig, Glynis, and Kamelia walked back to the mansion. On the way, Craig held Glynis's hand and sent healing energy into her arthritic joints.

8

Preacher Cody's handsome face stared out at the Hawthornes from their television set.

"And Paul warned of this when he told the Galatians, 'This I say then, Walk in the Spirit, and ye shall not fulfill the lust of the flesh. For the flesh lusteth against the Spirit: and these are contrary the one to the other: so that ye cannot do the things that ye would. But if ye be led of the Spirit, ye are not under the law.

" 'Now the works of the flesh are manifest, which are these: Adultery, fornication, uncleanliness, lasciviousness.' " As Cody spoke these lines from the Bible, the television screen cut to a visual collage of sexual images backed by a pulsing, rhythmic musical score—" 'Idolatry, *witchcraft*, hatred, emulations, wrath, strife, seditions, heresies' "—the screen flashed to brutal photographs of a black mass and ritual murder with a heavy metal music background—" 'envyings, murders, drunkenness, revelings, and such like' "—scenes of ghetto street violence, backed by a black rap song—" 'of the which I tell you before, as I have also told you in time past, that they which do such things shall not inherit the kingdom of God.' "

Preacher Cody returned to the screen, this time in an outdoor setting. He was dressed in blue jeans, a western-style shirt, a cowboy hat, and boots. He stood in a grassy field with a beautiful white mare and her newborn foal. His piercing blue eyes looked directly into the camera. "God has spoken to me again, my friends. The first time He spoke to me was in the jungles of Nicaragua, when He told me to speak to His people of the end times. That I have done. Then He spoke to me again last week, very near to the place I'm now standing, in a plane crash that should have taken my life. But He saved me so that I could warn you people about one of the sins of the flesh that threatens to insinuate itself into our Christian lives and steal from us our faith and ultimate salvation." The screen returned to the scenes of the black mass and its heavy metal musical accompaniment. "Witchcraft. The abomination of witchcraft." Suddenly the photographs of the black mass became animate, and the gore and horror of the ritual sacrifice being played out came to life, replete with horrified screams from the young children who were sacrificial victims and devilish laughter of the perpetrators. "Ah, but these witches are subtle," Cody continued. "They've tried to whitewash our thinking so that most of us, in our twentieth-century sophistication, don't even believe in them." Cuts of childish, fairy-tale versions of cartoon witches became interspersed with the shots of ritual murder. The alternating scenes began to speed up until, with a loud crescendo of heavy metal noise, they merged. The final scene was an overlay: the pretty, blue-eyed blond child character, Tabitha, from the television show "Bewitched" had conjured up the Tooth Fairy, while, in the overlay, a little blond girl, whose throat was cut, was having her teeth pulled out for use as charms by members of a satanic coven.

The camera returned to Cody, who had been joined by his angelic-looking wife and baby daughter, both dressed in flowing white dresses that moved gently in the wind. The lilting sounds of a flute, with a soft bongo backbeat, filled the airwaves.

"We need to protect ourselves, and our loved ones, from the growing menace of evil that these witches pose. The signs of their presence are all around us." The song "Age of Aquarius" from the rock musical *Hair* accented a photographic montage of newspaper astrology columns, Tarot card readers, occult shops, and New Age publications.

"Eradicating these obvious satanic influences from our Christian society is only the first step. Because then it gets more subtle. Beware the false prophets!" Eerie chanting began, and pictures of East Indian gurus flashed on the screen.

"And last of all are the witches who lurk in our midst in disguise." The lovely Samantha Stephens and the theme song from "Bewitched" played. Preacher Cody's voice became soft and seductive. "Beware the witches who might be your next door neighbors . . ."

The sun set over the mountains as Preacher Cody and his wife and daughter basked in the bright love of God and each other.

Then the screen faded to black.

"And so it begins again," Melanie mumbled.

"You might as well kiss your liberty, and probably your sweet ass, for that matter, good-bye," Craig said.

9

The people began to congregate outside the south gate of Hawthorne Manor at eight o'clock.

"What are we going to do, Craig?" Vivian asked as she began to cry.

"Play hide-and-seek or show-and-tell." He put on his

favorite golf cap and snapped the strap of his polka-dot suspenders. "After giving it some more thought, I think show-and-tell might be more productive. If we ignore them, the problem isn't going to go away. Adrian said that the worldwide persecutions he saw could possibly be prevented. I want to give reason a try."

"You're not going out there?" Vivian asked.

"Unless you have a magic wand that'll make the preacher man and his followers disappear in a *poof*."

"You know I don't," she said.

"No, we witches are so terrifyingly powerful, such a horrible threat to them, and yet we can't even keep them from persecuting us. Makes a whole lot of sense, don't it?"

"We're going with you," Jason said. Melanie stood defiantly by his side.

Craig nodded. So far, he had seen them only as a sullen sixteen-year-old girl and an angry seventeen-year-old boy. It was good to see that they had some redeeming features to their personalities. "Okey-doke."

"Okey-doke," Adrian echoed.

"Me, too," Kamelia said.

"Nope."

"But, Dad."

"Nope. You're going to stay inside the castle with the drawbridge raised."

"I'm coming," Leigh said.

Craig shook his head. "It's not your fight."

"The hell it's not."

Craig was surprised by the tone of her voice. He shrugged. "You stand with us, you'll damn yourself."

"Any way you look at it, it seems I'm damned anyway."

He grinned. "Lovely commentary on the situation, don't you think? Well"—he snapped his suspenders again—"shall we, boys and girls?"

The four of them went out into the night to meet the gathering crowd.

They walked slowly through the grounds, not anxious for the confrontation. Lighted torches on a myriad of stands illumined their path.

"I'm sorry I never told you about the witchcraft," Craig said to Leigh. "I guess I hoped it would never come up . . . that we could be kinda like Rob and Laura Petrie."

"That's bullshit," Leigh said, the initial anger of her discovery still evident in her voice. "You go to great lengths to ensure that our family isn't of the normal all-American variety."

Craig sighed. "You don't understand. If I were concerned with being a witch, I'd go to great lengths to act normal—so no one would be suspicious. Look around you. That's how my family is. It was because I felt free that I could be . . . well . . . odd. Can't you see?"

Leigh maintained a stony silence.

"If I had told you, then I would've been a 'witch' again, and I couldn't have been free just to be."

It was Leigh's turn to sigh. "Well, it's a moot point now."

"Ain't it the truth."

They neared the gate.

"I don't think you should open it," Leigh said.

"Then they'll know we're scared of them," Craig replied. "We've got to show them we have nothing to be scared of, that we have nothing to hide."

"What if . . . well, something happens?" Leigh asked.

"Then at least we've tried. It's better than cowering with fear and letting evil have its way."

Leigh looked at him curiously. "Evil? I've never heard you use that word before."

"Doc Hawthorne's dictionary defines it as that which stifles life, creativity, and joy. People like the preacher man, who spread hate and inflict guilt, they're the evil ones."

Preacher Cody stood outside the gate with fifty or so supporters. Craig recognized few of the faces in the crowd, but the torchlight fell on one person he remembered well. James Bradshaw, the President of the Montvue First National Bank—which held the Hawthorne millions —stood with the preacher.

Cody smiled in greeting. "I didn't think you'd face us, Dr. Hawthorne."

"I'm not going to be intimidated by the likes of you."

"Is that why you won't open your gate to me?"

Craig opened the gate wide.

"Did you watch my broadcast this evening?" Cody asked.

"Yeah, and I'd like to say that your facts are for shit."

"Oh, and how is that?"

"You showed a bunch of satanists doing a black mass. That has nothing to do with witchcraft."

Cody smiled. "Do tell."

"Satanism is a deliberate perversion of Christianity by demented, rebellious individuals. Witchcraft is just the folk religion the Europeans practiced before the advent of Christianity. Witches don't even believe in the Devil, let alone serve him."

"Well, Dr. Hawthorne, I'm impressed by your familiarity with the subject. How is it that you know these things? Are you a witch?"

Craig was not about to admit to Cody that he was a witch, not when the preacher had such a perverted concept of what that meant.

"I'm familiar with the facts because I'm a well-educated man. If you were well-educated, then you'd know the facts, too."

Cody threw his head back and met Craig's attack in turn. "I am well-educated in the ways of the Lord. Can you say the same?"

"I have no interest in your religion, preacher man. That's my constitutional right."

"And it is these people's God-given right to oppose you!"

Craig heard Leigh utter a small gasp as Cody's powerful voice rose and shook the night air.

"We've come here tonight to tell you of God's forgiveness for your sins, if you'll repent and ask for it! We have come here tonight to show you that our God is one of mercy and grace!"

Cody's followers punctuated his words with shouts of "Amen" and "Glory be," and in their excitement they began to surge forward.

"God's word says that you are an abomination! If you accept Jesus Christ as your savior and leave behind the ways of the flesh that taint your soul, you can be saved! It doesn't matter that you were born into a family of vile witches, or that you, Mrs. Hawthorne, married a witch and bore witch children, because your true birthright is divine! All you need do is claim it!"

Before Craig could react, the crowd swarmed in around them and pushed them back farther onto their property, off the cobblestone driveway, and toward the guest cottage. As they moved farther into the shadows, people began grabbing the flaming torches from their stands in order to light their way.

"Craig!" Leigh shouted, but the mass of bodies bearing down on him kept him from moving to her side.

"And you children," Cody shouted, "perverted by the sins of your elders, you, too, can find God! It isn't too late!"

"Get the fuck away from us, you creep!" Jason yelled as he tried to push the preacher backward while shielding Melanie from his grasping hands.

"The end times are at hand. All who don't find salvation beforehand will have to suffer the wrath of God's retribution as the world is punished for its grievous sins!"

The body of people stopped moving when they reached the cottage.

Craig, straining to see Leigh among the crowd, noticed James Bradshaw standing with a flaming torch held high above his head. The flames of the torch were licking at the wooden shingles that extended from the cottage's roof.

"Bradshaw!" Craig yelled, pointing at the roof. "Look up!"

The banker's attention—as well as that of everyone else in the crowd of believers—was on Cody, who took Craig's verbal cue.

"Yes, look up to heaven and see the hosts of angels waiting to welcome the righteous into eternal paradise!"

The wind gusted, and the shingles accepted the flame.

"Fire!" Craig became frantic.

"Yes, the flames of hell fire and damnation await those who deny the Lord thy God!" Cody, trancelike in his exhortation, seemed oblivious to the events occurring around him.

Craig unsuccessfully tried to plow his way through the crowd to reach the cottage. "You goddamn bastards, you've started a fire!"

"And the fire of truth will burn away the dross material of our mortal beings, and our souls shall be free!"

Craig lunged for Cody and grabbed him by his shirt. He roughly drew his face toward his own. "Your people have started my uncle's cottage on fire, and he's in there, crippled and bedridden!"

Cody's cloudy eyes cleared, and he focused on Craig's. Shock registered, and he strained to look in the direction Craig was pointing. "Oh, Lord." He pushed Craig away and tried to clear a path through the mass of people. The crowd, no longer mesmerized by their leader's words, noticed the flaming roof and began to scream and scatter. James Bradshaw, jostled by those around him, inadvertently dropped the torch. It landed on the ledge of the closed window behind him, breaking the glass. Before he managed to retrieve it, the flames ignited the inside curtains.

"No! Uncle Dori!" Melanie shouted.

Craig, Cody, Melanie, Jason, and Leigh all moved closer to the small frame building which was quickly being engulfed by the fire.

When they were near enough to feel the heat from the flames, Cody froze, a look of stark terror crossing his face. "Oh, God, not fire," he whispered, then slowly began to back away.

Craig didn't pause to weigh the risks or consider the probabilities as he left his family's side and raced toward the front of the cottage. He heard Leigh call to him but didn't turn back. He didn't want his resolve to weaken. He had to try and save Dorian. He couldn't leave the old man alone to die such a terrible death.

He ran up the wheelchair ramp and burst into the house through the front door. "Uncle Dori!" he shouted, and then began to choke as the smoke filled his lungs.

He raced down the hall to the bedroom. As he entered the room, he drew back in horror—Dorian's body, showered by flaming ceiling boards, was on fire, his shrieks of agony filling the air. Craig reached for the quilt that was draped over a chair and headed to smother the flames, when a great billow of fire raced down the hallway to claim him. The searing pain he felt before losing consciousness reminded him of another, similar death he had suffered at the hands of Christians in the distant past.

It was like a bad dream, replaying itself again and again.

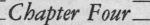

Chapter Four

1840
Ireland

1

Cassie ni Callaghan awoke with a start, her straw bed damp with her own sweat, the stink of the putrid fields crossing over from the dream world and filling her nose with a rancid smell of decay. She moaned her disgust and fumbled in the darkness for the flower sachet she had made when the dreams had begun. "Shit," she mumbled in frustration.

"Cassie?" Angus, her father, asked sleepily.

"Go back to sleep, Da. 'Twas the dream again."

"Seems the gods are tryin' to tell you somethin', lass."

"To be sure." Cassie's hand found the small linen bag and rushed it to her face. She breathed deeply of the delicate bouquet, and, despite the gnawing stomach pain that always accompanied the recurring nightmare, she slowly began to relax.

"Morrigan, be my strength," Cassie prayed to the ancestral warrior goddess whom she worshiped—a goddess who, according to legend, bestowed upon her devotees the gifts of ferocity and fearlessness. Cassie was never afraid. But she was determined to get out of Ireland before the land began to die.

2

Tyler Hawthorne shifted uncomfortably in the saddle, his crotch burning with discomfort.

Sir Cedric eyed him astutely. "The rot?"

Tyler shook his head and winced as his horse slowed to a more jarring trot. "Too much attention. There was a young lady on the crossing who was . . . lively."

"Well, it's a good thing you're wife hunting. You don't want it to fall off from wear. That's something you won't have to worry about with a wife."

"Depends on the woman in question, I should think."

"Don't hold any illusions, son. Take it from an old man. Get married, and your pecker'll never get sore again. Unless you stray from home, of course."

"Since it's your daughter I'm here to court, I'll leave that one alone."

Sir Cedric's eyes twinkled their amusement. "Yes, I'd think that wise."

Tyler grinned. He had come a long way in search of a wife, and this was the end of the road. Unless Miss Gwendolyn Walkins was a real toad, he would ask for her. He liked Cedric, and the dowry wouldn't be wanting; Sir Cedric Walkins was one of the wealthiest landlords in Ireland. Most important of all, the Walkinses were of the old blood. Despite the problems finding a spouse had often created, the Hawthornes had never married outside their religion.

The path they were riding was boggy and difficult for the horses to traverse, which kept Tyler alert with pain. Sir Cedric made a visible effort to stay his amusement.

"I hope you don't mind the scenic route through my lands, son. Didn't anticipate your, ah, situation."

"No problem," Tyler assured him.

The two horses drew up at the river, and Sir Cedric urged his horse onto a narrow path that ran along the shoreline. "There's a crossing downstream."

Tyler followed him onto the path, and when they rounded a bend in the river, he was startled to see a naked young woman, standing calf-deep in the water.

"Nice scenery," he commented as he took note of her plump breasts and rounded buttocks. The angular beauty of her face and the shimmering quality of her long ebony hair were noted as an afterthought. His was a more lusty than aesthetic nature.

Sir Cedric chuckled. "Black Irish, but one of us."

"Us?"

"Old blood. I have a lot of them on my lands. It's become their haven from Catholic oppression, which they claim is worse than English oppression. We have a Catholic church, but I've been able to manage its tyranny in these parts. I control their coffers, so they don't fuss with me too much. About the pagans, I like them here for reasons of my own. I have the most productive farmland of any of the other landholders in the country. We still—in a circumspect manner, of course—practice the old fertility festivals. It's a good life."

They rode up alongside the naked woman.

"Yes, I can see that," Tyler said.

"Mornin', Sir Cedric," the woman said, not making any attempt to hide her nakedness.

Sir Cedric tipped his hat in passing. "Cassie, dear. You're looking lovely today."

She flashed a bright smile and threw her shoulders back slightly. "Thanks for noticin'."

Tyler laughed at her boldness and nodded a greeting to her.

After they had rounded another bend in the river, Cedric said, "Speaking of fertility rituals, Cassie's the only one who's been able to get my horn to fill—if you get my meaning—in recent years."

"Mmmm. Yes, her talents did seem worthy," Tyler said, and squirmed uncomfortably in his saddle.

3

Tyler openly studied Gwendolyn. He took note, with disappointment, that her breasts were small and her middle was rather thick, but she had a pleasant face, with a big mouth—which he could teach her to use to pleasure him if all else failed to arouse his desire. She looked to be good breeding stock, which is what he wanted most in a wife. So, in his own mind, it was settled.

Gwendolyn raised an eyebrow and gave him a cool look. "Well, do I pass inspection?"

He was startled by her tone. He didn't really wish to be ungentlemanly about the whole matter. "I apologize for my rudeness. Ah, yes, you do."

"Good. Now, let's hope you pass mine." She brushed past him, her full silk skirt and petticoats rustling loudly as she disappeared out the front door.

Sir Cedric took Tyler's hat from him and hung it next to his on a rack. "I should have warned you. Gwendolyn doesn't think too highly of Americans. She has an idea they're coarse and uncultured."

"She's right."

"Well, I think it's a good match. It just might take a little doing to convince her."

Tyler laughed. "And here I thought I was such a catch there'd be no holding her back."

"Women can be a humbling experience, son. Take it from an old man."

4

"Da, he's beautiful. Like Lugh himself, his yellow hair bright like the sun. I want him." Cassie and Angus sat by the turf fire in their one-room cottage, eating a meal of boiled potatoes and buttermilk.

"A sun god, eh?" Angus paused to slurp the milk. "I heard he's a rich American, of the old blood, here to marry Miss Gwen."

"Sure, and they're not married yet."

Angus's long tongue reached up and wiped away his buttermilk mustache. "And how are you fixin' to make off with him? You goin' to sashay up to the big house and charm his breeches off? I imagine he's done all the sightseein' he's goin' to do. There won't be another festival for a month. The only kind of gatherin's that leaves are weddin's and wakes, and no one's been about marryin' or dyin' of late."

Dying. The smells of her nightmares came back to gag her, and she choked on her food.

"All right, lass?"

Her heart began to beat louder, and for a moment she thought she heard the sound of wings beating the air around her. "You're wrong."

"What's your blathering?"

Cassie felt exhilaration creep up in her blood. The wings returned, seemingly louder. She got the vague impression that they were the strong wings of a raven. She felt a dark shadow fall on her. Then she understood. It was Morrigan's raven! Surely it was the harbinger of the goddess's presence. Legend told how it was. She looked around anxiously but could see nothing.

Angus had stopped eating and was watching Cassie's odd behavior. "Lass?"

Cassie dropped her cup and bowl, and her breath came in gasps. She felt a surge of might, and she was seized by a sense of being invincible. The blight to come became clear in her mind, as did her route of escape. She fixed her cloudy eyes on her father.

Angus began to tremble. "Lass, I don't know what's come over you, but it makes me feel mighty queer."

"I was about to tell you that you were wrong, Da."

"I don't like the mean in your voice, Cassie."

"I heard the banshee last night. Right outside our window. The one closest to your bed, Da."

"Put the knife down, lass."

Cassie looked down into her hand and saw the firelight reflecting off the blade. She hadn't even realized she had picked it up. "It's not me. It's the goddess, Da. She's come for you."

Angus struggled against age and fear to rise, but he was too slow. The knife tore into his gut.

"I need to have a wake so the bright American will come and let me bewitch him."

"Lass." Angus's strangled voice was sad. " 'Tis not the goddess. You're daft, child."

"You've lived long enough, Da. You'll serve me better dead."

"Daft," Angus murmured, and then slumped forward onto her.

She pushed his dead weight off her and looked down to see the stain on her hands and the front of her dress. She rubbed her fingers together, feeling the stickiness of the blood, and then put her fingers to her mouth in wonderment. The taste and smell elated her.

"Oh, Da. Sure, and I belong to the goddess now."

5

Eleanor Walkins was a fat woman who talked too much. Tyler became transfixed by the gaping maw of her mouth as it rambled virtually nonstop. With dismay, he realized that the daughter's mouth was much more likely to follow in the direction of the mother's mouth than be trained by him to coax and pleasure.

"What's the name of your shipping line again?" Eleanor asked.

"Van Carel and—"

"Hawthorne. Of course. And you and the Van Carels go back quite a long time, I understand?"

"Since the late—"

"Sixteen-nineties. Yes, I've heard. And you live in New York City with . . ."

"My mother and—"

"Your sister and her husband. I know. It's a shame that your father died last year. His heart, wasn't it? But I guess that's what prompted your deciding to take a bride—to ensure the name is carried on." She smiled, popped a slice of sausage roll into her mouth, and began to chew. "We've checked into you, as you can see."

Tyler looked away from the unsightly mush that slithered around in her mouth while she talked and gazed into the warm gold of brandy that filled the snifter he held.

"We're not going to surrender our daughter to just anyone, even though you do come highly recommended, of course. Ever since the persecutions, we've had to be so careful"—another slice of roll was popped into the maw—"lest spies infiltrate our ranks and learn our secrets. We can't afford another massacre, or the old ways might be stamped out for good. Of course, the persecutions I refer to were hundreds of years ago, but I understand you lost family less than a hundred and fifty years ago."

"Yes, my great-great-grand—"

"Parents, I know. They died during that awful time in Salem. Nasty thing, that was. Shows us that we can never be too careful. Never too careful."

Their fireside chat was interrupted by the servant girl. "Excuse me, Sir Cedric, but there's a young boy from the village here to see you."

Cedric looked relieved, and Tyler suppressed a grin. No wonder Sir Cedric could only get it up with that country girl. Well, Tyler thought, he would have Sheila for diversion.

"Send him in," Sir Cedric said.

"Cedric!" the maw bellowed. "We're entertaining!"

"Now, my dear, I would think that at this late hour it must be important, or the child wouldn't have come all this way in the dark."

A tiny boy tentatively walked into the parlor, his hands nervously clutching a small hat in front of him, his eyes—bright from the reflection of the fireplace light— wide with fascination.

"All the way in, boy," Cedric urged.

The visitor inched his way deeper into the room, toward the large easy chair in which Sir Cedric sat.

"Never been to the big house before, son?" Sir Cedric asked.

"Nae."

"What do they call you?"

"Phelim."

"Well, Phelim, what's your business?"

"Miss Cassie sent me to say that her da, Angus McCleary, he's up and died, sir. There's a wake in the makin'."

Sir Cedric's face fell. "Old Angus, eh? He was a good man."

"Aye, sir, he was that, true enough."

The intense sincerity in the tiny boy's manner touched Tyler, and, despite the solemnity of the moment, he smiled.

Sir Cedric bent toward the heavily laden platter of appetizers and scooped some treats onto a linen napkin which he handed to Phelim. "Here's for your trouble, son. Tell Miss Cassie that I'll be by to pay my respects."

Phelim stuffed the napkin into his shirt and offered an awkward bow toward the women, then turned and hurried from the room.

"You're not going there tonight?" Gwendolyn asked, her tone harsh.

Tyler cringed.

Sir Cedric downed his brandy in one gulp. "Angus was one of us. Of course, I'll go to see him off. Want to come, Tyler?"

"Take a guest to see a dead man?" Eleanor asked, appalled.

These women gave fresh meaning to the word *witch*, Tyler thought as he politely excused himself and accompanied Sir Cedric.

6

Angus was laid out on a board that rested on his old bed frame—the straw that had been the mattress having immediately been burned to ward off any inclination Angus's spirit might have had to linger in the comfort of it. A white sheet draped the body, making it appear wraithlike, and two smooth stones were laid on his closed eyes to keep them that way. A rack of stag horns was laid at his head, and a large seashell full of seawater rested at his feet. A dozen candles were alight in the small cottage, and the big black pot in the fireplace simmered with stew. Never had Cassie enjoyed the slaughtering of lambs before the way she had on that evening. However, she disguised the elation she was feeling; it wouldn't have seemed fitting for the occasion.

A dozen people were already crammed into the small cottage when Sir Cedric and Tyler arrived. Cassie, dressed in a simple dark blue dress, greeted them at the door and ushered them in.

Sir Cedric handed her a bottle of quality whiskey. "It was Angus's favorite."

She clutched it to her bosom. "Aye, he'd be pleased."

"Cassie, you remember my companion here from the river? This is Tyler Hawthorne, a visitor from America."

She made a slight curtsy. "Sir."

Tyler removed his hat and was startled by how perfectly the color of her eyes matched the dress she wore. "Miss McCleary."

" 'Tis Miss Callaghan. I carry my mother's name. An ancient tradition. But I'm Cassie to folks."

"Too bad about Angus," Sir Cedric said, moving gingerly toward the body. "How did it happen?"

"He was helpin' me fix supper, and he tripped, poor old fool. Fell on the butcher knife. 'Twas a sorry way to go, to be sure."

Tyler recognized the symbolism of the horns at Angus's head—they represented the god of death come to claim the soul of the departed—but didn't understand the seashell. He gestured to it, questioningly.

" 'Tis there to lure Manannan, god of the sea," Cassie explained. "He drives his chariot 'cross the tops of the waves to ferry the souls of the faithful from death to Mag Mell, the land of happiness."

"Ah, like our Summerland," Tyler commented, referring to the name his own English tradition gave to the Elysium.

The guests had begun to gather in a circle around Angus's body. Solemn greetings were shared among the tenants and their landlord, and Sir Cedric introduced Tyler to Angus and then his mourners.

"Cassie, darlin'. I was goin' to pass the cup full of my poteen here"—an elderly man raised a jug of homemade liquor—"but I see you have somethin' much more fittin'. Don't you think it would do better in our bellies than keeping your pretty tits warm?''

Cassie looked down to see she was still clutching the whiskey to her chest. "Oh, to be sure, Murphy. Hand me the cup.''

The cup was, in actuality, a ritual goblet. Tyler recognized it as such, even though he had never seen one exactly like it. The stem was made of gold and fashioned in the shape of a phallus, and the cup was silver and womblike. Theirs was, of course, a fertility religion, and their deity a father/mother god worshiped in a variety of guises. Suddenly, Tyler felt a sense of utter unity with these people. Even though they were strangers and of a different nationality, they were of the old blood . . . his blood.

Cassie filled the goblet with whiskey and raised it to Angus. "The greatest blessin' the gods can give us in this world is to be born again among our own. We pray you find us again, Da." She took a sip and passed the cup. All drank reverently—and lustily, requiring that the cup be refilled repeatedly—until the cup had passed around the circle and was once again in Cassie's hands.

There was a loud commotion at the door, and Father O'Donnell stumbled through the doorway, tripping over the form of Phelim, who had apparently tried to stop his entry. "You damnable little runt!" the good father cursed as he went sprawling.

"Ah, father, you've come to pay your respects," Cassie said with calm bemusement.

Father O'Donnell stood up and brushed himself off, his pudgy face red from anger and embarrassment. "It's sorry I am for your father's passin'. Thought I'd come and offer him a blessin'. It's never too late, you know."

"Thanks for your concern over his soul, father, but we've already offered his blessin'." She handed him the goblet. "You're welcome to join in the toast.''

He shrugged. "Aye, I'll toast to old Angus." He took the cup and was raising it to his lips when he froze, his eyes fixed upon the golden phallus he held. "Jaysus Christ!" He let go of the cup, and Phelim dove to catch it. "Heathen sinners!" His eyes fell on Sir Cedric, and he pointed at him with a shaking hand. "You! Are you one of them?"

"Father O'Donnell, I'm their landlord, you're their priest. The Almighty is the only one with the right to pass judgment—read your own Bible. Now, I realize you're relatively new to these parts, but unless you learn to dwell in harmony with these people, I'm afraid I'll have to request your transfer to another parish." He reached down, took the goblet from Phelim, and refilled it with the last of the whiskey. "Now, I've got a pecker, you've got a pecker, and I understand old Angus here had a pretty good pecker himself. If you're going to be put off by the simple facts of life, you're never going to get these people to listen to your diademic oratory; and if they shut their ears, your hopes for converts are right out the window." He thrust the cup at the priest. "So, are you going to toast to old Angus?"

Father O'Donnell, looking properly chagrined, took the goblet. "May God bless your heathen soul, Angus McCleary," he whispered, and then he drained the cup.

7

Father O'Donnell stayed long enough to partake of Cassie's stew and potato bread, then made his escape.

"Thanks be that the father didn't preach too much," Murphy said as he uncorked the jug of poteen and started it on its rounds.

"Aye, but he got in his digs," Cassie said as she removed Angus's good pipe and smoking tobacco from a shelf and offered it to Sir Cedric.

He declined, pulling his own pipe and pouch from his coat pocket. "Tyler, perhaps?"

Tyler accepted the smoke, and while several of the women took up keening by Angus's body, the men began to share stories of Angus's life. After a time, with the loud wailing and storytelling vying for supremacy, the air become a raucous din, and Tyler stepped outside to relax his aching head. After a few minutes, Cassie followed. She found him sitting on the low stone fence that surrounded the cottage.

"Might I sit with you, sir?" Cassie asked.

Tyler laughed. "It's your fence, and I'm not a sir. Call me by my given." He gave her a sideways glance. "So, how are you feeling?"

"It's anticipatin' the lonely I'm about right now."

"Your mother?"

"She died at my birthin'. Both Ma and Da were well on in years when they made me. She was too old to tough it out."

"You're what, about twenty?"

"That I am."

Tyler, well aware of her ripeness, spoke the obvious. "Why don't you marry?"

Cassie chuckled. "Were you lookin' about that room tonight? There's no man in this village, of the old ways, who's less than twice my age—unless you count little Phelim, but that's a wee bit young for my needs." She paused and gave him a coy look. "And you, what age are you bein'?"

"About half again your age."

"Sure, and that's better than twice."

There was a long pause.

"I've come here to marry Gwendolyn Walkins."

"Miss Gwen is a loud cow . . . but I'm sure she'll be bringin' a fat dowry."

Tyler felt both amused and defensive about Cassie's observations.

"I'm rich enough that I don't need the dowry," he said.

"Then whyever would a man such as yourself be wantin' to marry a loud cow?"

Tyler sucked in a breath as Cassie's words struck a raw nerve inside him. The primary ambition of his intercontinental quest had been to find a wife of the old religion. Gwendolyn's wealth and position had merely sweetened the pot. But did it sweeten it enough to overlook the truth of her undesirability as a woman?

Cassie grabbed his hand, hopped off the fence, and urged him to follow her. "Come on, then. A walk through the sweet heather on a summer night with an Irish lass might be somethin' to remember on those cold American nights spent with Miss Gwen.''

The raw discomfort of his groin which he had been nursing all day instantly melted away and was replaced by a quickening throb. Tyler didn't resist her invitation.

They walked silently through the high heather, hand in hand, the crescent moon shedding its slight light on them. Tyler allowed her to lead the way, content to begin the process of surrender to his senses. He inhaled the rich, loamy aroma of earth until he felt his lungs would burst. It was the smell of the Mother that he found most erotic, for it evoked from him the response of primitive instincts. The woman whose soft hand he held had held the ritual goblet with authority. Was she the priestess of the village's rituals? Tyler began to caress her palm lightly as he considered. If so, then she was most likely able to draw down the moon—or goddess energy—into her form. There had only been one occasion when he had made love to a woman of the old religion, and nothing had ever compared. His heart began to race with anticipation, and the surge of energy that coursed through his body made him want to run and shout with happiness.

Cassie sensed Tyler's mood, and in response she let go of his hand. "Catch me and I'm yours," she urged, and then she ran into the night.

Tyler didn't hesitate to take chase. He quickly lost sight of her in the dim light but relied on intuition to guide him.

They ran through the fields swiftly, laughing and punctuating the night with loud, frenzied whoops. And they both sensed the feral overshadowing of Tyler that occurred when, possessed by a wild energy, he overcame and tackled her.

They rolled together on the soft earth, ripping and tearing at each other's clothes until they were both laid bare. Tyler entered her body without preliminaries, and she responded with passion of an intensity she didn't know was possible. From within the deepest recesses of her being, she felt the birth of an overpowering need to merge, to become one with her lover. She strained to receive him even more deeply into her body, she wrapped her legs around him as a vise, she locked his lips in an impassioned kiss. He struggled to meet her unspoken need and plunged into her with all the ferocity possible to him. He surrendered himself to her completely, driven only to fulfill her desire. The stroke of his organ urged the heightening of her pleasure, and when she achieved her peak of union, he saw it in his mind as an explosion of light that illumined her empty womb. With a cry of exultation, he surrendered his essence to her so that she could be filled.

8

The shreds of clothing with which they returned to the wake declared their mutual passion.

"Ah, so the discomfort passed, I see," Sir Cedric said to Tyler in greeting.

The obvious edge to Sir Cedric's voice disconcerted Tyler. He hadn't planned for this to happen, particularly with the woman Sir Cedric had been rolling. Not to mention the issue of Gwendolyn.

Tyler grinned sheepishly. "Would you believe that I was overcome by grief and wasn't responsible for my actions?"

Sir Cedric shook his head solemnly.

"Would you believe that I've decided I want to marry her?"

A hush fell over the room except, Cassie was sure, for the sound of her startled heart. He had said nothing about marriage, but then that had been her plan all along. Was her magic now so powerful? She smiled with the knowledge of her secret.

Cedric looked from one disheveled lover to the other and laughed. "That I can believe."

Tyler took his response to mean acceptance but was still feeling contrite. "I'm sorry, old boy. I didn't mean to usurp anything, or offend your family."

"Well"—Cedric took a long draw on his pipe—"I'm

going to miss the bed sports, that's true. And there'll be no living with the Walkins women for a time, but the hurt pride will pass.'' He shrugged. ''Who am I to argue with young lust?''

Cassie threw her arms around him and squeezed tightly. ''Aye, and you're a great one, Sir Cedric Walkins.''

He gave her a wet kiss. ''And you're just full of surprises, Cassie ni Callaghan.''

9

Angus was buried next to the body of his wife in an ancient graveyard hidden high in the hills. Despite protestations by Sir Cedric, Eleanor and Gwendolyn threw Tyler out of the house.

Tyler was taken in by Murphy and his grandson, Phelim, and the wedding plans were expedited, as Tyler was anxious to make the journey home before the weather turned.

Cassie, according to custom, kept away from the groom while making her bridal preparations.

On the eve of her marriage, Cassie was packing her meager belongings when, his arms laden with packages, Sir Cedric burst in the front door of her cottage.

''Sure, and what have you got there?'' she asked as he dumped his load onto her bed.

''It's your trousseau. No self-respecting lady can get married without one.''

Cassie was confused. ''Trousseau?''

''A new wardrobe. One fitting your new rank as Mrs. Tyler Hawthorne, of the shipping line of Van Carel and Hawthorne, of the very rich American Hawthorne family.'' He pulled a bottle of brandy out of one of the packages. ''And this is for me.'' Sir Cedric rummaged in the cupboard for a cup and poured himself a drink.

Cassie was speechless.

''I bought most of it on my last trip to London—for Gwendolyn's trousseau—but it seems that since you won the husband . . . well, I had that seamstress, Finola, alter them to fit you.''

"You're a grand man," Cassie said at last.

Sir Cedric waved his cup at the bed. "Well, aren't you in the least bit curious?"

She began tearing into the packages. There were colorful skirts, lace blouses, bright bonnets, black leather boots, shawls with long fringe, fur muffs, embroidered petticoats, silk stockings, and various items she couldn't identify. These she held up questioningly.

"Corsets, my dear," Sir Cedric explained. "They're a must in decent society."

"But what do you do with them?"

"Strip yourself and I'll show you."

Cassie took off her dress and drawers and stood before Sir Cedric in the buff.

He winced at the sight of her flesh. "By the gods, woman, what a sight you are."

She held the corset up. "To business, Sir Cedric."

He sighed. "To business." Pausing only to playfully nibble a nipple, he helped her into a corset, placing his boot to her backside in order to pull the laces tightly enough to imprison her. Then he stood back and admired his handiwork. "There you are. That's what you do with a corset."

"But I can't breathe."

"That's all right, they don't expect you to." He gave her a sympathetic look, then poured her a glass of brandy. "My dear, there are some things you need to know about what's expected of a lady in today's society. For instance"—he pinched her cheek—"you look too healthy. You need to increase your pallor."

Cassie sipped at her drink. "Aye, and how do I do that?"

"Well, Gwendolyn drinks vinegar and eats chalk."

Cassie burst out laughing. "You're jokin', to be sure."

"No. Explains a lot, doesn't it?"

She nodded.

"Yes, ladies are expected to be fragile and delicate, obedient and doting to the gentlemen, and, of course, they faint a lot."

Cassie tried, without success, to take a deep breath. "Aye, I can see why."

"Rich ladies, more particularly, are expected to be idle. If you're wealthy, you must never *do* anything."

"Seems a mighty price to pay," Cassie murmured. She began to realize how little she knew about the world she had chosen, and she felt an emotion she had never before experienced. It was insecurity. Impulsively, she threw herself into Sir Cedric's arms, and they enfolded her.

"What's this?"

"Will they like me?" she asked, her voice small.

Sir Cedric thought about it. "Don't hold any illusions. It's not going to be easy for you. But Tyler's mad about you, so hold on to that." His hand moved down to caress her buttocks and he winced again. "Oh, Cassie dear. Take me on one last time?"

Cassie, unable to bend, slid down Sir Cedric's body until she was on her knees. Then she removed his hopeful organ from his breeches and put it to her mouth.

10

It was shortly after dawn when Tyler, in the company of Murphy and Phelim, rode to claim his bride. Dressed in his most expensive suit, he dismounted his horse and knocked at the door of her cottage. Sir Cedric startled him by answering it.

"Oh . . . Sir Cedric . . . I'm here to take Cassie to be wed."

Sir Cedric gave him a hard look and then cleared his throat. "I've decided to keep her for myself. Bad luck, son." With that, he slammed the door in Tyler's face.

Tyler's head reeled, and his anger surged. "The dirty bastard," he muttered. "Damned dirty bastard!" he yelled, then kicked the door. He tore off his jacket, throwing it back over his shoulder, and then rolled up his sleeves. "We'll see about this!" His anger mounted. "I'll bash your head in, Sir Cedric Walkins, you can count on it!" He backed up a few feet and then gave a running kick to the door.

"Nae, won't do any good to bust in the door, sir,"

Phelim said, pointing off into the distance. "Seems they've gone out the back way and are ridin' off."

Tyler spun around in time to see Sir Cedric's and Cassie's horses disappearing over the ridge to the west of the house.

"Damn him!" Tyler leaped onto his horse and slapped it into a gallop.

Murphy and Phelim quickly joined in the adventure.

The horses kicked up the soft earth as their riders drove them mercilessly. Sweat poured from the animals and men alike as they pursued Tyler's kidnapped bride. As they rode, other pagans—who had been on their way to the marriage site—saw the action and joined in the chase. Soon there were a dozen horses tearing up the ground, bearing down on Sir Cedric and Cassie.

When Tyler and his party reached the river, they slowed and negotiated the narrow path that led to the shallow site where they could cross. Once on the other side, they tracked the bride and her abductor until, once again, they were within sight.

Tyler's rage peaked. With a carnal yell, he kicked his horse's ribs and closed in on his rival. His riders joined in with hoots and hollers, cries and screams, and, closely resembling an American Indian war party, they descended upon the enemy.

Tyler came up alongside Cedric, and he grabbed for him. Together, they tumbled to the ground. "She's mine!" Tyler yelled as they rolled clear of the horse's hooves. "I'll kill you!" Tyler pinned Sir Cedric down and had pulled his fist back as far as he could manage to gain enough momentum to smash in the other man's face, when he was suddenly restrained by three of his own men. He looked up to see Phelim's tiny face staring down into his.

" 'Tis only a game. You mustn't kill Sir Cedric," Phelim said solemnly.

"A game?" Tyler was dizzy with anger and exertion. "A fucking game?"

"Ah, yes, son," Sir Cedric said, his voice strained. "A challenge, actually. See, we take the concept of winning the bride quite literally in these parts."

There was a moment of uneasy silence while all awaited Tyler's reaction.

Tyler looked from Sir Cedric, to Phelim, and, finally, to Cassie. She stood by her horse, in her beautiful white dress, with her hands on her hips and a wide grin on her face. She mouthed the words, *My hero*.

He rolled off Sir Cedric and, overcome by the absurdity of it all, burst out laughing.

Everyone else issued a mass sigh of relief.

Tyler laughed so hard he couldn't catch his breath. "How . . . how many . . . people . . . die . . . doing this?"

Sir Cedric rubbed the back of his neck tenderly. "I had a friend break both his legs in an attempt to recapture his bride. Made for a sorrowful wedding night."

Tyler propped himself up on his elbow and wiped away the sweat from his brow. "I think I may be a bit . . . out of sorts . . . for my own wedding night."

"Nae, Tyler Hawthorne," Cassie said. "I've got a powerful magic way about me. Sure, and you'll never be . . . out of sorts . . . again."

11

Triumphantly, Tyler lifted his bride onto his horse and rode her to the wedding site—the beach of a concealed cove along the rugged Atlantic shoreline.

The sun was nearly overhead when the ceremony began.

Cassie and Tyler stood holding hands, facing Sir Cedric, while those gathered to witness the rite formed a circle around them.

"There's magic to be done here, the magic of love," Sir Cedric began. "This place is calling to you, O Lady of the Moon, Eternal Woman, Mistress of Magic, Virgin, Mother, and Lady of Death!

"This place is calling to you, O Horned God, Eternal Man, Keeper of Rough Magic, Sexual Stag, Shepherd of Wild Things, Divine Sacrifice!

"Come and witness the forming of this alliance between our sister and brother!"

Sir Cedric then addressed the bride and groom. "Do you two consent to the ancient rite of handfasting?"

"Aye," Cassie said.

"Yes," Tyler said.

Sir Cedric bound together their wrists with a cord made of red satin and silver threads, then held their hands up for all to see.

A cheer rose from those gathered.

Sir Cedric offered the ritual goblet to Cassie, who tasted the wine, then to Tyler, who drained the cup.

"Now—for the sake of your assured fertility—leap the broom," Sir Cedric said.

Phelim moved into the circle, carrying the broom, and held it while Cassie and Tyler jumped over it.

Sir Cedric kissed them both. "May the high gods protect and keep you, Tyler and Cassie Hawthorne."

Cheers erupted once more, and the celebration began.

The feast was laid out on blankets, and jugs of wine and ale were passed around. The musicians among them began to play the old songs on their crude instruments, and Cassie and Tyler had their wedding dance.

Then a committee was formed to present the wedding gift.

Phelim handed the velvet bag to them, and Murphy made the speech. "Our circle has had it for generations, and then some," he said. "But we wanted you to take it into the New World with you . . . to keep alive the old ways."

Tyler opened the bag and removed the ritual goblet. Understanding the sacrifice it represented, he was moved beyond words.

Cassie wasn't moved in the slightest. She had planned to steal the goblet when she left anyway.

12

The *Carina*, a Van Carel and Hawthorne ship carrying a load of textiles—woolens from England and linens from Ireland—and a half-dozen passengers, docked in New York City after a forty-day sea voyage. Tyler and

Cassie Hawthorne were greeted on the wharf by Tyler's family.

Tyler's mother was a tall, slender woman with silver-gray hair and a graceful manner. She embraced Tyler and bent to hug Cassie. Cassie, taking note of her elegance and style, felt diminutive in the other woman's presence—from more than the disparity of their respective heights.

"Mother, this is my wife. Cassie, my mother, Irene," Tyler said in greeting.

Cassie nodded. "Top o' the mornin, ma'am."

At the sound of Cassie's accent, Irene's smile wavered slightly. "Please, call me Mother."

Cassie, never having called anyone Mother, felt awkward. "Mother."

Irene's faint eyebrows knitted themselves together. "So, Cassie, are you an Eldon, Carlyle, or Walkins?" she asked, referring to the three families Tyler had gone to England, Scotland, and Ireland to visit in his search for a bride.

" 'Tis a Callaghan I am, Mother," Cassie said evenly.

Irene gave Tyler a startled look.

"The ladies in question were all toads or cows," he said. "Cassie shares our religion, and she's not a toad or cow."

Irene's smile vanished altogether, and she sighed. "I see."

"Mother?" Tyler said, a sound of warning in his voice.

Irene looked at him and shrugged. "I'm sorry." She took Cassie's arm. "Well, you're a Hawthorne now, dear. So, let's introduce you to your new family."

She led them to a nearby carriage.

A pretty young woman jumped from her seat and hugged Tyler enthusiastically. "Oh, Tyler! I'm so happy you've finally found a wife." She regarded Cassie warmly.

"Cassie, this is my sister, Arabel Hunter."

Arabel grasped both of Cassie's hands. "You're simply lovely! We've waited so long for Tyler to marry."

Cassie, grateful for Arabel's kindness, knew it wouldn't last when she discovered her to be low-born. So she decided to just get it over with. "Aye, but 'tis an

Irishwoman he's gone and married, so I don't fancy I'm too welcome."

Arabel dropped Cassie's hands and turned on Tyler. "So! You've told her we're snobs, have you? Well—" She gave Cassie a gentle push toward the man and small boy who stood loading baggage into the carriage. "I'm a romantic, and if my brother loves you, that's all that matters to me. Come meet my husband and son."

Cassie was introduced to Arabel's boyish-looking husband, Giles, and their nine-year-old son, Oakes. Then, the baggage securely in place, everyone piled into the carriage. Giles slapped the reins, and the four horses pulled the large carriage into motion.

Cassie sat spellbound, watching the sights of America's largest city. The traffic of horse-drawn vehicles of every description was heavy, the street vendors were loud, and the pigs that acted as refuse collectors were everywhere.

"Was your crossing smooth?" Arabel asked.

"No, Cassie and I kept the boat rocking."

Arabel giggled. "Sounds like your honeymoon was as energetic as ours was."

"So, are the Callaghans happy about this match?" Irene asked.

"I've no livin' family, Mother."

"I'm sorry," Irene murmured.

"Despite that sad fact, Cassie didn't come entirely without a dowry," Tyler said. "Her circle gave us an ancient goblet to add to our family's ritual tools. It's quite priceless, actually."

"That was very nice of them," Irene said.

"Sure, and it was," Cassie replied. A terrible longing for that circle of people suddenly overcame her. She felt the tears threatening.

Oakes tugged at her sleeve. She looked down at him, and he thrust a small package at her. "This is for my new aunt," he said, an impish grin on his face.

She took the brightly wrapped gift hesitantly. She was sure it had been meant for an aunt who was an Eldon, Carlyle, or Walkins, not an aunt who was a dirt-poor orphaned Irish waif.

"Go on," Arabel urged.

Cassie took a deep breath and forced a smile. " 'Tis kind of you, to be sure." She unwrapped the small crystal bottle of amber perfume.

"It's called patchouli," Arabel said. "It's all the rage now."

Cassie opened the bottle and inhaled the pungent odor. It was strong. *Strong*. That word reverberated in her mind with great force, like the thunder that follows the flash of lighting. She caught her breath. She also had the ability to be strong. What had she been thinking? She was a priestess of Morrigan. She was invincible. She shook her head in an effort to clear away the weakness and insecurity that had taken possession of her. Then she smiled and applied the scent. "Nice," she commented.

"We also have a dressmaker lined up to make you a special gown for your reception," Arabel said.

"Reception?" Tyler asked.

"Your wedding reception. A party to present your new wife to New York society," Irene said, her voice straining to be cheerful.

"Cassie's such a beauty, the men will all be envious and the women jealous," Arabel said.

"A party?" Cassie said, her returning confidence washing over her like a flood. "Aye, and won't that be grand!"

13

The Hawthorne mansion was located in the fashionable Bowling Green district. It was more impressive than any home Cassie had ever before seen—the big house that the Walkins lived in didn't even come close to comparing in grandeur.

A large Negro woman met them at the door and took their wraps.

"We'll take tea in the drawing room, Odelia," Irene said. "And assemble the servants to meet the new Mrs. Hawthorne."

"Yes, ma'am," Odelia said, giving Cassie a curious once-over with her bright, brown eyes.

"I didn't know it was slaves you were ownin', Tyler," Cassie whispered.

"I don't. All of our help get wages, board, and lodging."

Sir Cedric had painted an entirely different picture of America. She had so much to learn . . . and unlearn, it seemed.

The drawing room was plushly outfitted, with brightly colored floral carpeting, heavy satin drapes, French wallpaper, and rosewood furniture with opulent upholstery. Cassie sat down in a chair by the fire and closed her eyes. She had never even imagined such luxury could be hers. If the Walkinses could see her now, she thought, a smile betraying her satisfaction.

Tyler sat down on the arm of the chair and startled her with a kiss. "You look happy," he said.

"Sure, and I'm a princess now."

His magnetic eyes captured hers, and she felt his magic—the magic of his powerful sexuality—as it stirred her deep inside. As she gazed into his eyes—blue like the sky—set in a bright face surrounded by his golden hair, the warmth grew within her. She was sure that he, indeed, embodied the energy of the great sun god. Nothing less could make her feel the way he could.

With great flurry, the servants piled into the room, then quickly arranged themselves in a line a few feet from where Cassie and Tyler were sitting. Tyler's attention was caught by the only Caucasian member of the staff, a very pregnant young woman. The woman smiled at Tyler and made a subtle gesture toward her belly. Anxiety filled Cassie when she saw Tyler raise his eyebrows in surprise and burst into a mischievous grin in response.

Odelia set a tray, laden with a silver tea service, on a low table and then took her place at the head of the line of servants.

Irene made the introductions. "Cassie, you've met Odelia. She's in charge of keeping the downstairs. Her husband, Fuzzy"—a fuzzy-headed black man next to her nodded respectfully—"is our groundskeeper. Clem"

—another Negro man—"runs our stables. His wife, Magnolia—we call her Maggie—is our cook. And Sugar—Clem and Maggie's daughter—and Sheila are chambermaids."

Sheila was the woman with the big belly.

"This is Cassie Hawthorne, the master's new wife."

"Missus Hawthorne," the servants said in a chorus.

Cassie didn't know how she was expected to respond. So she said what was on her mind. "I see you're about to drop, Sheila."

"Aye, missus, it should be born within the month." She paused and brushed a wandering strand of red hair back in place. "Is it the same accent I'm hearing from you, missus?"

"Aye."

Sheila's freckled face lit up with a broad, toothy smile. "Sure, and it is I'm happy for you, missus."

"I'm touched," Cassie said sarcastically, and was pleased to see Sheila's teeth disappear.

"You're dismissed," Irene said quickly, and the servants filed out.

"You didn't need to be rude to Sheila," Tyler said.

"Nae? And was it my imagination, or is that your baby she's carryin', Tyler Hawthorne?" Cassie didn't care that the rest of the family was listening.

"It's mine. What, do you think I wasn't a man before I met you?"

Cassie sighed in exasperation. "So, what is it you're plannin' to do with the girl and her bastard now that it's me you're married to?"

"I don't plan on laying with her anymore, if that's what concerns you. And the child, well, we'll care for it in an honorable way."

Cassie patted her own slightly rounded belly, which contained the child she and Tyler had conceived their first time together. "And what about our wee one? Whose baby will have first claim as your heir, mine or that little whore's?"

Tyler gave her a hard slap across the face, which served to shock Cassie to silence.

Tyler's anger was dark but controlled. "Don't ever

call Sheila a whore again. She pleasured me well for a long time, as a man needs to be pleasured. We're not of Puritan stock in this family. We aren't ashamed of our needs. You, if anyone, should understand that. The Hawthornes are an honorable family, and we'll not ignore the fact of that child. But you needn't worry about your baby's claim on me—it'll take precedence. Now"—he paused and looked around the room at his family, who were pretending to ignore the altercation—"I think you should take tea in your room. It'll give you some time to think about things. Arabel, show her the way."

Her face burning from humiliation and the slap of Tyler's hand, Cassie meekly followed Arabel.

"Sure, and I could use a jigger of whiskey right now," Cassie said when they were out of earshot of the others.

Arabel gave her a sympathetic look. "I'm sorry, Cassie, but in America ladies don't drink liquor."

"Right now, bein' a lady in America seems to be as appealing as sleepin' in a pile of horseshit," Cassie said, disregarding Arabel's shocked, ladylike little gasp.

14

"Well, his chances for a political career have been shot to hell," Cassie overheard a man named Chamberlain say to a man named Morehead. She was on her way to refill her crystal cup at the punchbowl—the ladies' punchbowl—when she heard the hushed tone of their conversation. She unobtrusively positioned herself behind a large, free-standing oval mirror and listened.

"She's truly ravishing, but a paddy without manners or breeding . . ." Morehead said.

"It seems his need to dip his wick overpowered his reason on this one. To support a man like that would be foolhardy anyway," Chamberlain said.

"I can't see anyone agreeing to finance his campaign under these circumstances."

"It's a shame."

Cassie left her hiding place and casually walked up to

the two men. "Mr. Chamberlain. Mr. Morehead," she said warmly.

Chamberlain appeared flustered. "Ah, Mrs. Hawthorne, you certainly have a good head for names."

"Sure, and I wouldn't be forgettin' the names of such worthy gentlemen as yourselves." Inwardly she was working her magic.

"It's a nice reception," Chamberlain said.

"Aye, the Hawthornes know how to put on a party."

"How do you like America so far?" Morehead asked.

" 'Tis a grand country." The air around them was getting extremely warm.

Chamberlain was beginning to sweat. "We've known the Hawthornes for many years. They're good people."

Cassie smiled a slow, languid smile. "That's true enough."

"Our trading company has shipped exclusively with Van Carel and Hawthorne since we established ourselves." Morehead's voice was strained.

Cassie's furtive glance assured her that both men had achieved gigantic erections. "Tyler certainly knows the value of prize goods," she said pointedly, then excused herself.

She had worked the same spell once before and knew their erections wouldn't subside, even for a moment, until the time of the next new moon, which wouldn't arrive for a week. "Let's see if your need to dip your wicks doesn't queer your reason, gentlemen," she said under her breath.

She hadn't known that Tyler was anticipating a career in politics. There was power in politics in America, Cassie had learned in her two short weeks spent in the young country. That power was of a kind she found exciting. Perhaps, instead of being a hindrance to Tyler's ambitions, she could use her powers to help him.

A small group of women was huddled around the punchbowl.

"Well, my sister dragged me with her to a meeting of the spiritualist group that Madame Michelle heads," a woman by the name of Lilian Austin was saying. "You know, I'd heard all about her when I was in Paris last year. Well, she moved to New York this past spring and opened a branch of her Society for Psychic Studies here. Let me tell you, it was the most entertaining evening I'd spent in a while. She went into a trance and called up the spirit of Paulette DeBow's dead uncle, George. I thought I'd die myself when we heard that whistling— you know that little song he was always whistling. Then someone broke the circle—we were all holding hands— and we lost him. But I'm seriously thinking of going to another seance next month. When Richard goes on those endless business trips, I simply have to find something to occupy myself, you know. And—'' She noticed Cassie's presence. "Oh, lovely reception, Mrs. Hawthorne."

"Thanks, but sure, and you can call me Cassie, Mrs. Austin."

"Cassie," Lilian returned, not extending a similar invitation.

"I heard you talkin' about callin' up spirits. Is it ghosts you're meanin'?" Cassie asked.

"Yes, the spiritualist movement is making headway in America right now," Lilian said.

"Well, if it's a ghost caller you're wantin', I could oblige you," Cassie said.

Lilian exchanged looks of surprise and skepticism with her friends. "Oh, so you're a medium?"

"It's not exactly sure that I am about what you're callin' it, but, aye, I've got the gift. All the women in my clan's had it. There's a tale that the ma of my great-great-grandma was a changelin'—the fairies took her and left one of their own, you see—and the Callaghans have had the gift ever since."

Lilian only partly suppressed her amusement. "What a simply delightful story, Cassie dear. We'll have to get together sometime for coffee and discuss it further."

Cassie smiled. "Aye, that would be grand."

Tyler appeared at Cassie's side. "Cassie, the Van Carels have finally arrived. I'd like you to come meet them."

"Your wife is very . . . sweet," Lilian said to Tyler.

"Sweet isn't exactly how I'd describe her," Tyler

said good-naturedly. "Gorgeous, outrageous, exciting perhaps. But sweet, never."

Lilian looked slightly embarrassed. "Yes, perhaps your description is more to the point." She extended her hand to Cassie. "Honestly, dear, let's have that coffee and talk again."

"I'll be waitin' for your invite, Mrs. Austin."

Tyler took Cassie by her elbow and led her across the room to where the Van Carels were gathered.

"Cassie, this is my business partner, Marten Van Carel," Tyler said.

Cassie's hand was kissed by an extremely debonair gentleman in his late forties. "You are a vision, Mrs. Hawthorne."

"Of what?" Cassie asked, not understanding why everyone around them began to laugh.

"A wit, too. How lucky you are, Tyler," Marten said. He put his arm around the woman at his side. "This is my wife, Nicole, and"—he gestured to the three young women beside her—"our daughters, Juliana, Carina, and Francina."

Cassie greeted everyone in kind.

"Nicole and I have mixed feelings about your marriage," Marten continued. "We had hoped to marry one of our daughters to Tyler, but, on the other hand, he is like a son to us, so that might have been a little incestuous, don't you think?"

Cassie didn't really understand the question, but she understood that the three Van Carel girls were beauties, and she decided that she didn't like them, or Marten either. "I think, Mr. Van Carel, that since I've come to America I've been hearin' a lot about the way proper folk should act, and I'm thinkin' that you tellin' me what you're tellin' me ain't quite proper." Cassie began to lightly scratch her cheek, while mentally chanting the spell.

Marten scrunched the muscles in his forehead until it was a mass of wrinkles. "I'm sorry if I've offended you, Mrs. Hawthorne. Tyler never did court any of my girls, so please don't feel as if they were in any way serious competition for his affections."

Cassie's fingers moved down to her chin, and then she casually ran them across her brow. "Nae, Mr. Van Carel, it's not a trio of pimply faced girls I'm thinkin' to be competition."

Nicole looked at her daughters in confusion, and her piercing scream brought the rest of the room to silence. As the girls looked to one another and explored their own faces with curious fingertips, the screaming intensified.

"Oh, God," Juliana moaned. "Is it the pox?"

Cassie leaned toward her thoughtfully. "Nae, looks like a bunch of pussy old pimples to me, lass."

"Take me home!" Francina wailed as she tried to cover her face with the shawl she wore.

Carina began to sob uncontrollably.

"Jesus, Tyler, I think we'd best get the girls home," Marten said.

"Perhaps it was something they ate," Tyler said comfortingly.

"I'm sure there's a simple explanation." Marten shook Tyler's hand. "Well, my boy, she's beautiful, as well as being outspoken. I'm sure she'll keep you hopping." He gave Cassie a wary look. "Nice to meet you, Mrs. Hawthorne." With that, he ushered his frantic women out of the room.

Tyler put his arm around Cassie and drew her roughly to him. "None of that nonsense again, do you hear?" he whispered.

"I didn't like him," she said.

"Well, he didn't like you, either."

"Good, it's even we are," she said, and pulled free of his grasp. Then she went to check on the progress Chamberlain and Morehead were making in their attempts at civil conversation.

15

"So, is it politics you're wantin' to do?" Cassie asked Tyler when they were finally alone in their room.

Tyler was stripping himself of clothes. "At one point I was considering running for mayor in the next election. Now I don't think it's something to pursue."

Cassie, already naked and in bed, said, "Because you married me?"

Tyler stopped and looked at her for a long moment. "It wouldn't be feasible now."

"Because you married me?"

Tyler sighed. "Yes. You're wonderful, and I love you, but you're not the material political wives are made of, Cassie."

"Why? The common folk would warm to me."

"That's true. But it's the uncommon folk who invest in political campaigns, and they won't now."

"You're rich. Invest in yourself."

Tyler threw off the last of his clothing and slid into bed beside Cassie. "My money's already invested . . . in Van Carel and Hawthorne. It's tied up. I'm not liquid."

Cassie frowned, not understanding his words, but she got his meaning. "What about the banks? Didn't you tell me they be lendin' people money?"

Tyler began kissing her neck and massaging her plump breasts. "No banker would lend me money for a campaign, given the circumstances. It would be a bad risk."

"You could sell something."

"Like what?"

"Like your half of Van Carel and Hawthorne."

Tyler laughed. "You're crazy . . . but you're luscious." He moved his mouth to her nipple and began to suck.

"What if Marten up and died? What would happen to the business?"

Distracted, Tyler replied while moving his mouth to her other breast. "Mmmm, his family would inherit his interest."

"What family?"

It was a few minutes before Tyler replied. "His immediate family. Why all the questions?"

"I'm trying to understand your world." She rolled him over and climbed on top of him. "What if Marten, Nicole, and the pimply triplets all piled off a cliff. Who'd get it then?"

"Our partnership agreement states that the company

would revert entirely to the Hawthornes," Tyler said as he positioned his penis at her opening. "Any more questions, Mrs. Hawthorne?"

"Aye, Mr. Hawthorne. Are you goin' to fuck me or fritter away the night gabbin'?"

16

It had taken Cassie a while to gather all the items she needed to cast the spell, and her clandestine quest had taken her into depths of New York City's seamy underbelly, but she had been successful. On the first new moon after her arrival in America, she worked her first serious act of magic.

After Tyler and the rest of the household were asleep, Cassie got dressed in dark clothing and quietly made her way to the stables, where she picked out a feisty stallion. She murmured the soothing words her father had taught her to use and shared her breath with the animal until his spirit was calm. Then she straddled him, bareback, and urged him into the night.

She rode him at full gallop, using her body language to guide him in the right direction, confident of his instinct to steer them clear of obstacles. Riding had always thrilled Cassie, and when they were a fair distance from the mansion, she emitted a shrill cry of ebullience. A slow smile of self-satisfaction crept across her face when she realized that the cry echoed the battle call of Morrigan, as described by legend.

They rode until Cassie saw the faint shadow of the giant oak tree she had claimed as her own. She halted the horse and dismounted him, then soothed him until she was sure he wouldn't wander away.

From the pocket of her coat she removed a candle and matches. She stuck the candle into the ground beneath the tree and put a light to it. Then, using a large spoon taken from her pocket, she dug up the special objects she had so carefully obtained and hidden beneath the tree. Finally, she spread out a red cloth on the ground and used it as the altar upon which she cast her spell.

In a small brass censer, Cassie lighted a pile of tobacco leaves and powdered ginger root. It was a makeshift blend of incense designed to attract the attention of the warrior goddess.

Then she carefully laid the mandrake root on the altar. The root was the first of its kind she had ever handled—although she had heard tales of its magical properties from her teachers. It had a short stem topped with small purple flowers and a thick, forked root. The overall effect was that the plant resembled a human form with legs, torso, and head. She took the three strands of red hair that she had taken from the victim's hairbrush and wove them around the stem. Then she uncorked the small jar that contained the mixture of baby fat and powdered hellebore, and, using a small stick, she smeared the concoction over the mandrake. Finally, she tied a length of black string around the plant and chanted the verse she had composed:

> "Morrigan, dark lady of the night,
> Sure and your daughter's ready to fight.
> Oh, great queen of destruction and death,
> Take from the bastard all life and breath.
> As I wrap the cord 'round the poppet,
> Let no power be there to stop it."

The hex properly complete, Cassie wrapped the poppet in the red cloth and buried it deep among the roots of the giant oak.

17

The labor pains awoke Sheila from a deep, and strangely unsettling, sleep. Good, she thought, ready to get the birth behind her. She needed to summon Odelia and Maggie to help her, but when she started to roll onto her side so that she could sit up, she realized she couldn't move. There was no moon that night, and the room was in complete darkness. If she hadn't known better, she would have believed there was someone there holding her down on the bed. Irrationally, she waved her arms in the air all about her to verify what she already knew—there wasn't anyone else in the room. So why couldn't she move? "It must be the nerves I've got a case of," she whispered, and she relaxed and took a few deep breaths.

A flood of water gushed from between her legs, and a stronger pain seized her. The birth was coming fast—strangely fast. Everyone had told her to expect a long, hard first birth. She needed to get help.

She made yet another effort to move, without success.

Well, she thought, Sugar's room was right next to hers; she'd yell and awaken her.

She opened her mouth to shout . . . but no words would come. She repeatedly renewed her effort, but all that emerged from her constricted throat were a few croaking sounds. The illness was worsening by the minute, she decided, because she had been able to talk only moments before.

The pains began to come faster and harder, and Sheila started to panic. She croaked and flailed her arms around in an effort to reach the lamp on her bedtable. If she could knock it down, the noise of it crashing to the floor would certainly bring someone to her aid. But the lamp was just beyond her reach.

Then the birth began.

The pain and terror nearly drove Sheila mad. Mentally, she steeled herself, and, finding that her legs would spread open some, she began to push at the baby with her belly muscles and silently pray.

Hail Mary, full of grace; the Lord is with thee.

OH GOD, IT HURTS!

Blessed is the fruit of thy womb, Jesus.

Holy Mary, Mother of God, pray for us sinners.

OH, ODELIA, SURE AND YOU WERE RIGHT! IT DOES FEEL LIKE SHITTIN' A WATERMELON!

Now and at the hour of our death.

She issued a final shove and heard the squall of new life.

Amen.

Then the baby's cries were choked by a strangling sound. And there was silence.

Sheila's screams shattered the night.

18

The mood that evening at dinner was somber. Nevertheless, Cassie piled her plate high with steak, fried potatoes, corn on the cob, and big chunks of bread and butter.

"Odelia said the child strangled on its own cord," Irene said softly as she ignored her plate and sipped at a cup of coffee.

"What I don't understand is why Sheila didn't get help," Arabel said.

"She told me she couldn't move or cry out," Tyler said, giving Cassie the same quizzical look he had been giving her all day.

"Back in the old country, sometimes a fright would make people be that way," Cassie said helpfully. "Could be when the birthin' commenced she got feared."

"Could be," Tyler said.

"Sugar said it was a boy," Oakes said.

"I'm sorry for you, Tyler," Giles offered.

Tyler nodded somberly. "Sheila's beside herself. I think we'll loan her out to the Johnsons as a wet-nurse. I know they've been looking for one. It would do well to get her away from here for a while, and caring for a child might help her deal with her loss better."

Irene slammed down her cup, the coffee spilling over the edge and staining the white tablecloth. "How can you eat so heartily, Cassie? There has been a death in this home today!"

Cassie swallowed the mouthful she had been chewing and washed it down with some beer. " 'Tis sorry I am that I'm not in dire mournin', Mother." She patted the swelling evidence of her own pregnancy. "Is it such a dreadful thing, my wantin' to give my husband his firstborn?"

Irene's eyes narrowed. "Did you have anything to do with what happened here this morning?"

"Now, whatever could I have done to make a birthin' go sour?"

"Oh, don't play me for a fool, Cassie. The same kind of thing you did to Van Carel's daughters and to the unfortunate Misters Chamberlain and Morehead."

Cassie giggled. "You know about the fellas?"

"What did she do to Steven and Percy?" Tyler asked.

"Jane Chamberlain confided in me about a peculiar condition Steven had which was . . . well, it was making it hard for Jane to walk for a time," Irene said. "She said it came upon him—and she had heard from Percy's wife that it had come upon him, too—at your wedding reception."

Cassie opened her eyes wide and batted her lashes innocently. "Well, they were deservin' of it. They said some unflatterin' things about my Tyler."

Irene's fist hit the table. "We don't hex people in this family, Cassie."

"Ever?" Cassie asked, not believing people with powers wouldn't use them to their own advantage.

"Not unless we were in a life or death situation would a member of our family ever use his or her powers to hurt another. And for better or worse, you are a Hawthorne now. You'll abide by our rules." Irene's trembling hand reached for her coffee. "So, did you hex Sheila's baby?"

"No."

"Well, maybe you could call his spirit up at some seance and see if he points his tiny finger at you in accusation," Arabel said sarcastically.

"What?" Tyler asked.

"The tongues of the ladies' club I belong to are wagging over your pretty wife's claim that she's a medium. She said she'd do seances for Lilian Austin," Arabel said.

Tyler's eyes grew wide with alarm. "Cassie! Is that true?"

Cassie shrugged. "What's your fussin' about?"

"Cassie, we don't advertise our abilities. This world

is one which doesn't treat kindly those who possess power. You've heard of the burning times? You've heard of the Salem witch trials? We lost family in both, Cassie. It could happen again at any time. We have to be circumspect . . . careful, Cassie. We must all be careful."

Cassie sighed. "If it's secret you want me to be, sure enough, and I can oblige you." She pointed to the dessert tray. "Could someone hand me a piece of pie? I've a powerful hunger about me this evenin'."

19

The sub-zero temperature kept Cassie, who was in her final month of pregnancy, away from the mass funeral held for the Van Carel family. Marten, Nicole, Juliana, Carina, and Francina had all succumbed to the influenza within the same three-week period. The Hawthornes and Hunters had gone to the late-afternoon burial services.

Cassie, alone in her room, lay on her bed and distractedly fondled the melted remains of the five red candles. She had made each candle herself, at appropriate phases of the moon, carefully combining the bits of hair, nails, and clothing—surreptitiously taken from the Van Carels during her months of courting their friendship—with the wax that formed them. Unable to make any more midnight rides because of her condition, she had burned the candles and quietly chanted her verses in stolen moments alone. It had been her greatest challenge, but she had been successful. Now there was only one more phase of her magic left to be accomplished. Then her husband would be free to enter politics. Who was to know? Maybe he would even someday be president of the United States.

Self-satisfied, Cassie got to her feet and threw the remnants of her spell into the flames of the fireplace. Then she sat down on a stool in front of the fire and began to conjure Morrigan.

20

Clancy O'Connell was the night watchman at the Van Carel and Hawthorne docks. It was already dark when he came on shift at five o'clock. He had come straight from the Van Carel funeral, and he had had to resist the strong urge to stop for a bottle of whiskey on the way. His sadness for the passing of Mr. Van Carel was a special one, for he had been Clancy's benefactor. When his heavy drinking had got Clancy fired from his previous position, Marten Van Carel had given him that chance he needed to pull his life together. Clancy had parlayed his good fortune into a decent home and a fine family and hadn't felt the need for a drop of liquor in more than ten years . . . until now.

He relieved the day watchman and stood for a time by the small pot-bellied stove that warmed his tiny office. He rubbed his hands together to warm his arthritic fingers, and—the good Irishman he was—he gave vent to the tears of sorrow he felt for the mister and his beautiful women. " 'Tis a powerful loss," he moaned, and then paused to blow his snotty nose. "Aye, the Devil's a cruel one," he murmured, then filled his coffee cup from the pot that rested on the stove.

He was finishing up the last of the thick, black brew when he was startled by a shrill, keening cry.

"Holy Mother, have mercy!" he exclaimed, dropping the tin cup to the floor. He inched his way toward the window and peeked out into the black night. He jumped when he heard the cry again. " 'Tis the call of the banshee, to be sure," he whispered, then crossed himself. "But the mister's already croaked. What does the banshee want here?"

Clancy swallowed his fear and, grabbing a lantern, went outside to investigate.

The wind was beginning to blow with bitter fury. The ships on the dock were rocking violently in the water, and debris that had been littering the wharf was flying wildly about in the air.

Then Clancy heard the cry a third time. It seemed

to be coming from the main warehouse. He said a special abridged version of the Our Father prayer that he used in cases of emergency and made his way to the cavernous building, hesitating only for a moment before entering.

The light he held threw oddly shaped shadows, and Clancy, spooked as he was, imagined he was seeing all sorts of strange creatures amid the crates of goods stored in the building. As he went deeper into the warehouse, he began to hear the sound of wings beating above him. Within minutes, the air all around him seemed to vibrate with the sound of wings. His heart began to pound hard in his chest, and he felt short of breath. It was as if the beating wings were sucking the air away from him, and his hand flew to his neck, where he loosened the knot of the scarf he wore.

When he turned to flee, he felt the dizziness. It was a strangely familiar sensation. It was the dizzy of drunkenness. As a giddy feeling began to grow within him, he surrendered his fear to mirth. His laughter echoed in the rafters, joining the wings of the raven. Yes, he could now tell that the bird was a raven—huge and ferocious. He thought it might be amusing to see if he could fly up to meet it. He dropped the lantern and flapped his arms wildly. He was oblivious to the fact that the flame of the lantern had set his pant leg on fire.

21

The effort Cassie made to cast the fire spell brought on an early labor. She did not want to call Odelia or any of the other servants to help her; she decided to wait for Irene and Arabel to come home. She wanted her baby delivered by someone with power. If anything were to go wrong with the birthing, Irene and Arabel's skill superseded even that of the local physicians. Facilitating births had been the domain of witches since the dawn of mankind.

However, it wasn't until midnight that the Hawthornes and Hunters returned to the mansion. The pains were coming fast when Cassie left her bed and made her way downstairs.

She found the family sitting together in the drawing room. A hot fire burned in the large fireplace. Oakes was asleep on the ottoman, with his head in Arabel's lap; Giles sat next to her, holding her hand while she softly wept. Irene and Tyler were sitting in chairs. Everyone looked pale and drawn. When Cassie entered the room, she noticed that they all were holding snifters of brandy—even the women.

"I thought ladies didn't drink liquor in America," she said in greeting from the doorway.

Everyone looked at her, but no one replied.

Cassie doubled over as another pain struck. "Sure, and I'm goin' to have a baby."

Tyler got up and helped her to a chair.

"How soon?" Irene asked, the weariness she felt evident in her voice.

"I don't feel it beginnin' to crawl yet," she said.

Irene nodded and downed the contents of the snifter she held. "We'll go up in a few minutes."

"Sure, and it was a long buryin'. Did they have a wake?"

Tyler cleared his throat. "Ah, no, Cassie. We were delayed by . . . there was a great fire at the docks. Clancy was killed. We . . . we lost everything. The ships—all but two were in port—the warehouses, and all the cargo contained in both. It was horrible . . . horrible. We're financially ruined."

"Ruined? But what about your insurance? You told me you had insurance to pay in case of fire." That was why Cassie had made the fire. She had believed they would give him money for his losses, and all the money would be his because the Van Carels were dead, and he would be liquid at last. Then he could finance his own political campaign and become a man who was powerful in a worldly way. She grabbed his arm and clenched it between tight fingers. "You said they'd give you money!"

Tyler looked at her with piercing eyes, and she realized that he knew.

She heard Irene's words as if they came from a long distance. "Our lawyer informed us this evening that the insurance company was a fraud. They don't have the means to settle with us. We've lost everything. What we have left—including the house, of course—will have to be sold to pay the trading companies who lost their goods tonight."

"Cassie," Tyler said in a terrible voice. "Oh, Cassie."

"Aye, but I thought . . ."

"Cassie?" Irene asked.

Cassie's head began to spin. She stood to bolt from the room when another contraction seized her. The pain and dizziness overcame her, and she fainted.

22

Cassie came to in her bed as the worst pain yet tore through her. Tyler, Irene, and Arabel were standing together at the foot of her bed talking about her, so she didn't respond to the pain. She lay quietly and listened.

"When you first brought her home, we were shocked by her lack of breeding, but we tried to welcome her into the family," Irene was saying. "However, it didn't take long for her behavior to sour even Arabel's acceptance of her. I think she's evil, Tyler. Since she's been with us, Sheila's baby died under extremely strange circumstances, then the Van Carels, and tonight old Clancy. You believe that she was responsible for the fire. If you're right, that makes her Clancy's murderer for sure. I always had a feeling she had something to do with Sheila's tragedy, too. And if she devised the Van Carels' deaths . . . well, what can I say? The gods only know what all she's done. She has more power than anyone has had in our family for generations, but she seems to use it in a terrible way. You know, it's not the knife, it's whether the one wielding it is of a mind to carve a piece of art or murder a child with it. Personally, I think she's insane."

'Tis not the goddess. You're daft, child—old Angus's words replayed in Cassie's mind. Her father had also

thought she was insane. She had an urge to hex Irene on
the spot, but she was too weak from her condition to
focus her energies.

"What are you going to do with her?" Arabel asked
Tyler.

"After the baby's born, I'm going to divorce her. I'll
send her back to Ireland. We'll keep the baby, of course.
We'll get Sheila back from the Johnsons to nurse it. It's
the least we can do for poor Sheila."

Cassie couldn't take it anymore. "Divorce me, my
ass! And I'll be bloody damned if you'll take my baby
from me and give it to that whore!" She started to get
up off the bed.

Startled, the trio at her feet went into action.

Arabel and Tyler moved to hold her down, while
Irene yanked the sashes free from the curtains and began to tie her to the bed. Cassie struggled against them,
until she grew too weak. Sweating and cursing, she
succumbed to the baby's urgent need to be born.

"Damn you all," she whimpered as the child began to
tear at her insides.

"What about the baby, Mother?" Arabel asked. "Will
it be evil, too?"

Irene shrugged. "It'll be powerful, there's no doubt
about that. But I've always had a good feeling about this
little one. You know, a rose has a dangerous stem, but
the flower is fragrant. We'll see."

"I hate you," Cassie whispered, gasping as another
sensation of being torn apart ripped through her body.
"Aye, and I hate you, too, you little bitch."

Positioned between Cassie's legs, Irene and Arabel
gave each other surprised looks. "So, it'll be a girl,"
Irene said. "Rose would be a pretty name, don't you
think?"

Arabel nodded. "Oh, I can see her head, Mother."

Cassie looked across the room to where Tyler stood
watching her impassively. "I was a good wife to you,"
she said through clenched teeth.

"You don't have the ability to be a good anything,"
Tyler said sadly.

With a great sense of relief, Cassie felt the baby free

itself from her body. She closed her eyes as Rose Hawthorne made her loud presence known in the world. *Aye, and the Hawthornes only think they're ruined,* Cassie thought. *When I get my strength back, I'll show them what ruined really can be.*

"Cassie's hemorrhaging, Mother," Arabel said.

Cassie's eyes flew open, and she struggled against her restraints to see how badly she was bleeding. A muffled scream escaped her when she saw the pool of blood between her legs. For the first time in her life, she was truly scared.

"Do something," she whispered to Irene. She knew Irene could stop it. She could have stopped it herself, if she hadn't been so weak.

Irene gave her a cold stare. "No. No, I don't think so." She took the baby from Arabel's hands and quietly left the room.

Arabel looked startled. "Tyler? Do you want me—"

"Go with Mother," Tyler said softly.

"Nae!" Cassie shrieked.

Tyler followed Arabel from the room and closed the door behind them.

"Nae!"

Terror flooded Cassie. She began to feel cold and clammy. She tried to yell again but was too weak. She closed her eyes. She was so tired.

"Morrigan?" she whispered. "Sure, and you'll come and take me to Mag Mell?"

'Tis not the goddess. You're daft, child.

"'Tis the goddess, Da," she murmured.

It wasn't very long before the wings began to beat above the bed. Cassie knew She would come for her. She smiled and opened her eyes to greet the Lady.

A large raven hovered over the bed, only it didn't have the fierce, proud warrior presence that was Morrigan's, as described by legend.

Horror filled Cassie as the hideous monster swooped down to devour her.

Chapter Five

June 1992

1

It was a cold dawn. Leigh sat on a sandstone bench staring vacantly at the charred, wooden skeleton of the cottage. The burned remains of Craig and Dorian had been removed hours before, but Leigh couldn't bring herself to leave.

Leigh, who for most of her life had lived on the verge of tears, couldn't cry. She felt hollow and empty, as if there were no part of her left to shed in the venting of grief.

Two thoughts kept running through her mind. One was that the whole thing was a bad dream and, surely, she would soon awaken and all would be as it should. The second was that she had been angry with him. She had been angry with him for days about the fact that he had kept such an important secret from her. She hadn't been warm or loving, and now he was dead; now it was too late.

And now, without Craig in it, the world seemed to be a totally different place.

The emotions that had filled the night echoed in the stillness of the creeping dawn. The children's tears, the

teenagers' anger, Glynis's hysterics, and Vivian's cata-
tonia all melded together in the throbbing gloom of the
new day. Someone—Leigh thought it was Melanie—had
eventually led Kamelia and Adrian away and put them
to bed. Leigh felt a detached regret that she hadn't been
more attentive to the children's grief, but she had never
before known such pain, and it held her captive.

Someone put a coat around her shoulders, and she
looked up to see Marek standing behind her.

"We came as soon as we heard," he said. "Helena's
gone up to the house to see to the family."

Leigh nodded.

"This is the beginning of bad times," he said.

Leigh thought of Craig's intentions. "Maybe we can
stop it from going any further."

Marek shrugged. "Look at the holy wars in India and
the Middle East. Look at Northern Ireland. Religious
persecution knows no bounds."

"Maybe we can stop it from going any further," Leigh
repeated. She had to believe there was hope.

He sighed. "Maybe."

"What about you? Do people know you're witches?"

"They might infer it now."

"So, are you going to leave us?"

"No." He sat down on the bench next to Leigh and lit
a cigarette. "Helena and I left Poland to give our sons a
better chance. It wasn't easy for us to leave; I held an
important position in the local government. Our escape
was complex and dangerous. But we made it, and through
the underground of families who practice the old ways,
we found the Hawthornes and a place for ourselves in
this country. There are times when I feel regret that I
didn't stay in Poland and work to change the status quo.
I think my days of running from oppression are over."

"And your wife and children?"

"Helena chose to be a witch. She knew the risks. My
sons, well, they're old enough that if they want to run,
they may."

Leigh was confused. "What do you mean, Helena
chose to be a witch?"

143

"I made her a witch, after we fell in love. I initiated her into the old ways."

"That's possible? I thought a witch was born."

"Not necessarily. There's a magical way to awaken power in another."

"Oh." Leigh still had so much to learn.

"You said maybe *we* can stop it. Does that mean you're not going to run?"

Leigh took a moment to think about it. Of course she wanted to take her children and run. But Craig had lost his life in an effort to alter the course of events. Could she respond to his sacrifice by making no further attempt? On the other hand, what could she do to change things? She was a pitiful example of a warrior; she was timid and weak and emotionally fragile. But who else would try if she didn't? What kind of world would her children grow up in—if they lived to grow up at all—if no one tried?

What else could she do?

"If it comes to it and there's no other way to survive, I'll run. But for now, I'll stay and fight."

2

Sergeant Cosworth's coffee was bitter. He sipped it as he read the morning report that detailed the tragedy at the Hawthorne estate. He knew he shouldn't feel a sense of guilt; there truly was nothing he could have legally done to prevent what happened. But nevertheless, he did. What made him feel even worse was that there wasn't much he could do now, either. Dr. Hawthorne had opened the gate to the preacher and his followers, they hadn't stormed it. And all accounts agreed that the fire had been started accidentally. There was no one who was criminally culpable for the deaths. But it sure as hell wasn't right.

Cosworth had what he called "old cop gut." And his gut told him that the dying wasn't over yet.

He downed the dregs of his coffee, picked up the phone, and dialed the Hawthornes' number. The least he could do was see that they could bury these two dead men in peace. If last week's funeral was any indication, this next one would be a circus.

A heavily accented woman's voice answered the phone. "Hawthorne residence."

"Hello, ah, this is Sergeant Cosworth of the Montvue PD. I'd like to offer the services of my men to help ensure the privacy of the burial service for Dr. Hawthorne and Mr. Wildes."

There was a moment's hesitation on the line. "Why?"

"Because, ma'am, it's the best I can do."

3

The sun was high overhead when Leigh finally returned to the mansion. The house was quiet, and Leigh wandered about aimlessly for a time on the main floor. She was exhausted but didn't want to surrender to sleep just yet.

"Mrs. Hawthorne?" It was Helena.

"Leigh. I'm Leigh."

"Leigh. May I fix you something to eat or drink?"

She thought about it. "Coffee?"

Helena smiled comfortingly. "I just made a fresh pot."

Leigh followed the other woman into the kitchen and sat down at the colorful tile-top table. The room was bright and cheerful, and the air was rich with the smell of coffee. When Helena set the steaming cup down in front of her, Leigh uncharacteristically heaped it full of cream and sugar. A part of her knew that she needed to pamper herself a little, rather than fret and worry about the million calories the brew now contained.

"Where is everyone?" Leigh asked.

"In bed. I had to give Mrs. Wildes some valerian root to calm her down. Then Mrs. Hawthorne, well, she's awake, but she's not there. I mean, her mind seems to have shut off. Can't really blame her for wanting to escape, with all she's been through in such a short time. And Miss Melanie was throwing up all morning, but I

145

fixed her some alfalfa and red raspberry tea, and she was finally able to fall asleep.''

"You're very kind, Helena.''

Helena sat down at the table and gently brushed a streak of ash off Leigh's cheek. Helena's warmth and natural radiance made Leigh feel a little less desolate. She studied the other woman for a time, taking note of her luminescent brown eyes, her long mahogany-colored hair, and her strong face.

"You're beautiful,'' Leigh said.

Helena smiled her easy smile and put her hand over Leigh's. "So are you.''

Leigh wasn't self-conscious about their exchange, as she might normally have been. On the contrary, it seemed comfortable and natural. Leigh wondered if this was how it felt to have a sister.

"You going to be okay?'' Helena asked.

"I think so.''

"A Sergeant Cosworth, from the police, offered to keep people away from the funeral. He wants me to let him know when it's going to be.''

"Funeral?'' Leigh asked, her mind fuzzy. *Didn't we just do that?* she thought.

"I think you should try and get some sleep. If Mrs. Hawthorne doesn't snap out of it soon, you're going to have to get some of these things taken care of.''

"Yes, of course.''

"I'm sorry for you,'' Helena said gently.

Leigh shrugged and managed a weak smile. "I'm sorry for me, too.''

The doorbell interrupted them. Helena went to answer it and returned to summon Leigh.

"It's a Miss Diane Fox, a reporter with the *Post-Dispatch*.''

Diane Fox, the killer dyke. "No, I don't want to talk with any reporters right now.''

"She said she didn't come as a reporter.''

The coffee had revived Leigh somewhat, and she was curious. Besides, she was also angry with this Diane Fox. Would Craig be dead if it weren't for the story she wrote? She steeled herself and went to meet her.

Leigh was surprised by Diane's appearance. She wasn't in the least like Melanie had described her. She was extremely chic, with short, smartly styled platinum-blond hair, dramatic makeup, and a slight figure made to look imposing by an expensive tailored suit. She looked like a model.

"What do you want?" Leigh asked, startled by the harshness in her own voice.

Diane's pale blue eyes didn't flinch. "I came to offer my condolences. I . . . I feel badly about what occurred here last night."

"Well, you should. You set the whole thing up quite nicely."

Diane shook her head. "That wasn't my intention. He said he'd get another reporter to write the story if I didn't. I thought I'd keep it and try and write it responsibly."

Melanie had said she had done that, too. Leigh softened. "So, what kind of follow-up are you planning?"

"It'll be a condemnation of Preacher Cody and his followers, an examination of prejudice and mob violence."

Leigh uttered a harsh and bitter laugh. "In that case, if I were you, I'd stock up on fire extinguishers."

"Pardon me?"

"You defend us and you become one of us. That's the way the game's always been played, Miss Fox."

4

As Cody crossed the bridge from sleep to wakefulness, a horrible feeling of dread descended upon him. Vainly, he tried to recapture the blessed comfort of his dreams. He didn't want to return to the world and face what had happened—what he, inadvertent as it was, had caused to happen.

The bright sun streamed in through the bedroom window and stung his eyes as they opened. He glanced at the clock by his bed. It was one o'clock. It had been almost dawn before he had been able to shut his mind off long enough to fall asleep. He sat up and stretched, then rang the bell that was designed to summon his wife. Within minutes, she arrived, making her normally graceful entry, and set the tray down on his lap. She gave him a soft kiss and gently sat on the edge of the bed.

"Good morning," she said in her endearing, little-girl voice.

Cody took a sip of his orange juice. "Afternoon, actually."

"You okay?"

He shook his head. "Oh, Rachel. I didn't want anyone to get hurt. I . . . I was just trying to . . ."

"I know." She took his free hand and held it.

He began to feel better; Rachel had a soothing presence. He started to nibble at his toast.

"Maybe it was God's will," she offered.

He thought about it. God's will *was* often harsh. He reflected upon the deaths that Alan and Curtis Hawthorne had suffered in the plane crash, and those of Craig Hawthorne and Dorian Wildes last night. Then the words of Exodus 22:18 popped into his head, and he felt as if a lamp were suddenly lit in the midst of his guilt, dispelling the shadows. Of course! It hadn't been his fault at all. It was divine law that had caused the deaths. As he considered further, a moment's anger touched him. It wasn't fair of God to make him the instrument for the fulfillment of His laws. But then, he had chosen the ministry. If the punishments were severe, that wasn't his own responsibility. A sense of heavy oppression filled him. "Lord, thy will is hard," he mumbled.

"Amen," Rachel said dutifully.

"Exodus twenty-two, verse eighteen," Cody said.

Rachel lifted the Bible from the bedstand and opened it. Her china-blue eyes grew large as she read aloud in her breathy voice, " 'Thou shalt not suffer a witch to live.' "

5

Leigh checked on her children and found them both asleep together, locked in each other's arms. A soft whimpering came from Kamelia, and Leigh considered awakening her but knew that the reality was as bad as the nightmare and declined to do so. She gave them each a gentle kiss and then went to her own room.

A renewed wave of grief assaulted her when she entered the room she and Craig had shared and saw the reminders of him. Polka-dot and rainbow-colored ties, zebra-striped and bright paisley suspenders, American flag and zodiac-inspired golfing caps all lay scattered on furniture in the room. She picked up the bed pillow he had been using and buried her face in it, inhaling the scent of his musky aftershave. She hugged the pillow tightly, aching for his embrace, and crawled into bed.

It was then that the tears, which she did not think were in her, began to flow.

6

Helena returned to the kitchen with the untouched tray of food. "Mrs. Hawthorne wouldn't eat again. She hasn't touched a bite since it happened."

Leigh, Melanie, and Kamelia were sitting at the kitchen table nibbling from a tray laden with fruit and freshly baked muffins. In the two days since the latest tragedy had befallen them, the family had been gravitating more and more to the warmth of the kitchen. As none of their appetites was good, Helena had been keeping a ready supply of food on the table for them to consume as they could. Vivian, however, hadn't left her room since the fire.

"Maybe we should call a doctor to come see her," Leigh said.

"No." Melanie's voice was hard. "We don't use doctors."

"Oh? What do you do when you're sick?"

"Grandpa was the healer. Now . . . I don't know. Helena's good with herbs. Jennifer Hunter, Ray's wife, she heals. But I don't know . . ."

Leigh added an extra spoonful of sugar to her coffee. She was beginning to like it sweeter than ever. "Is there a problem?"

"I don't know. I tried to call Uncle Ray yesterday. He was funny . . . strange. I think he's scared. He didn't offer any help, like he did when Dad and Grandpa died."

Leigh nodded. "That's a human reaction."

Melanie's anger surged. "Yeah, but he's one of us! It's not right that he should turn his back on us now!"

"Well, I think that we're going to be surprised by who stands with us and who doesn't," Leigh said. "It would probably be best if we don't entertain any expectations."

Melanie slammed her butter knife down and glared at Leigh.

Leigh was beginning to get used to Hawthorne hostility, so she didn't let herself get too upset by Melanie's. "I don't understand a whole lot yet about the way all this works, but I do know that Kammi's a healer." She leaned across the table and chucked Kamelia gently under the chin. "Will you go try and do something for your grandma?"

Kamelia, whose despondency had been growing worse each day since her father's death, shook her head. "No."

"Why?" Leigh asked gently.

"I don't want to be a witch."

"Why?"

"It's too much responsibility."

"What do you mean?"

Kamelia began to cry, but Leigh resisted the urge to bundle her up in a comforting embrace. She waited patiently for her to regain control.

"It's my fault Dad died."

"I don't understand."

Kamelia pulled four small blue cloth bags out of her pocket, laid them on the table, and stared at them, her bottom lip still quivering.

"The protection charms," Leigh said. She, out of deference to her daughter's wishes, still carried hers.

"I forgot to give Dad his. I . . . I tried to give Uncle Dori one, and he couldn't take it because of his allergy. I was embarrassed, and I forgot to give any more out."

Oh, my poor baby, Leigh thought. "I see you've got four."

"One's mine. The other one was supposed to be Aunt Glynis's."

"Well, see. Glynis didn't die. You can't blame yourself for what happened to your father or uncle."

"But you said yourself that you don't understand how all this works. How can you say it wasn't my fault?"

Leigh's mind groped, and she took a chance. "Melanie will agree with me, won't you?"

Melanie's eyes met Leigh's and they stared at each other. Leigh held her breath and silently pleaded with the girl to be gracious.

Melanie surprised her.

"The charms help, but they aren't infallible. Even with the charms, it's likely it all would've come down the same."

Leigh let out her breath and smiled.

"You think so?" Kamelia sat up a little straighter, and the air seemed washed with relief.

"Yeah," Melanie said.

"So, will you go sit with your grandma awhile?" Leigh asked.

"Sure, I'll see what I can do," Kamelia said, and, without any further hesitation, she left on her mission.

"Thank you," Leigh said to Melanie.

"I did it for her, not you."

"I realize that."

Leigh studied Melanie. Her shoulder-length hair, which was a warm, russet color, was crimped in the latest fashion, and her skin was a tawny tan. Her eyes, which always seemed so cold, were an unusual amber color, and her figure was attractive. If it weren't for the perpetually sullen downturn to her lips and the lack of animation in her face, Leigh thought she would be quite stunning.

"Take a picture," Melanie said harshly.

"I would, if you'd ever smile."

"Oh, fuck you."

Leigh sighed. "I went ahead and made funeral arrangements. We'll bury them tomorrow morning. Everyone who's going to go will meet here at nine o'clock, and we'll have a police escort to the graveyard."

"Where were they when we needed them?"

Better late than never, Leigh thought ruefully. "I don't know who'll be attending. Perhaps you could phone the Hunters, and whoever else might want to be there, and let them know the time. I've asked the mortuary not to issue a press release."

"Who put you in charge?"

"Necessity."

"You aren't one of us. You've no right to insinuate yourself into our lives."

"Listen to yourself, Melanie. You and your family are as bigoted as Preacher Cody and his followers are."

Melanie's eyes grew wide with shock, then she threw her balled-up napkin at Leigh. "Go to hell!" she shouted as she stormed from the room.

Leigh had to fight back the recurring urge to tears. She felt so alone. "I'm already there, Melanie," she whispered, and added another teaspoon of sugar to her coffee.

7

Melanie dialed the law firm of Hawthorne and Hunter. In her mind, Raymond Hunter was the last semblance of a man of the family left. If only she could gain her uncle's cooperation, she thought she could keep the overbearing Leigh from taking over completely.

"Law offices of Raymond Hunter," the woman's voice said in greeting, instead of the usual "Hawthorne and Hunter."

Melanie was startled. "Ah, Mr. Hunter, please. This is his niece calling."

"I'm sorry, but Mr. Hunter doesn't have a niece."

Melanie chuckled. "Excuse me, but may I speak with Susan?" Susan was the receptionist who had been with the firm for five years.

"Susan is no longer with us. This is Barbara, her replacement."

Melanie felt her face begin to burn. "Would you please tell Mr. Hunter that Melanie Hawthorne is on the phone?"

"Hold a moment."

A few minutes later, Ray's voice came over the line. It was strained. "What is it, Melanie?"

"What the hell did she mean, 'Mr. Hunter doesn't have a niece'? And who the hell gave you the right to change the firm's name?"

"First of all, according to my partnership agreement with your father and grandfather, if there ever came a time when there was no Hawthorne practicing law, the rights of ownership of the firm would revert to me. And vice versa, if there were no practicing Hunters. Now, you needn't worry about the firm's assets. Your family will be getting what's due. The figures are being drawn up now. And as to your status as my niece . . . well, you aren't my niece, you know. 'Uncle' is often used as a polite way to refer to an older male who is a distant relative." Ray's words began to sound rehearsed. "A Hunter married a Hawthorne woman sometime in the first half of the nineteenth century. That hardly makes us close blood kin."

"You goddamn, chicken-livered bastard!" Melanie shouted.

"I think, young lady, that you've just terminated this conversation."

The phone line abruptly went dead in Melanie's ear, and she was filled with an overwhelming sense of shock and betrayal. She had always loved Ray and had been close with his family. Jennifer Hunter had nursed her through all her childhood illnesses. Aunt Jenny had, in many ways, filled the gap left by the death of Melanie's mother, who had been killed in a car accident shortly after her birth. And now they were not only keeping their distance, they were actually publicly disavowing the Hawthornes.

A sob escaped her, and she rubbed her belly, where there was still no visible evidence of the growing fetus. In her life, she had come to rely on the strength of the men around her. And now there were no men left. She felt that there was only one hope remaining for her and her baby. She had been a fool to put it off so long. She grabbed her purse and headed out into the bright afternoon.

8

Frank Janowski had a favorite fishing hole. It was outside of town, in a small inlet that connected two lakes. The fish would often become trapped in the stream by the myriad of beaver dams that obstructed their path, and this made the sport an easy one, which was good, because Frank wasn't terribly ambitious. But he was cute, and that's why Melanie had pursued him so avidly. She parked up the road from the inlet and walked in to where Frank spent most every summer afternoon, then stood behind a cottonwood tree and watched him as he sat holding his pole above the water, eating candy and tapping his foot to the rock music that blared from his portable cassette player. He was sixteen, two years younger than his brother, Gil. Gil had inherited Marek's rugged good looks, whereas Frank had a shadow of Helena's beauty. He wore his dark hair long and wild and had large brown eyes made more emphatic by thick lashes. His smile was quick and electric and set off deep dimples that Melanie thought were sexy. As a matter of fact, there wasn't anything about Frank that Melanie didn't think was sexy. She emerged from her hiding place.

"Hi, Frankie. Thought you'd be here."

He turned and grinned, and Melanie felt her knees weaken. He patted the ground next to him. "Have a seat, honeybuns. Ain't it a great day?"

Melanie shrugged and sat down. "Well . . ."

His dimples vanished, and he seemed contrite. "Didn't mean to sound . . . you know. How are you doin'?"

"Not so good."

"I know. It's a bitch, ain't it? I'm thinking of taking off. My Dad said I could if I wanted. Could be a blast."

Melanie felt her hopes begin to collapse. She struggled to keep her voice steady. "How would you make it?"

"Oh, I dunno. Take my axe with me, maybe join up with a rock band in LA or something. But I'm not in any rush about it. I'll wait 'til things start to close in on me a little more. Know what I mean? I'm having a laid-back summer. No need to give up on it too soon."

"Right." Melanie didn't know how to broach the subject now, so she just decided to forgo tact. "I'm pregnant."

Frank looked at her with surprise. "No shit? Whose is it?"

Melanie caught her breath. She didn't know what she had expected, but it certainly wasn't what she got. "Yours, of course."

Frank popped another Hershey's Kiss in his mouth and looked away. "So, how'd it happen?"

"How it usually happens."

"You know what I mean."

Melanie shrugged. "I decided against the birth control we talked about. I . . . I guess I wanted your baby."

Frank's jaw tensed, and his eyes narrowed. He began to reel in his line. "Thanks for asking me how I felt."

"I'm sorry." She paused. "How *do* you feel?"

He stood up and began packing his things. "Like you're a selfish bitch and like I want no part of you or the kid."

"I'm sorry," she repeated. She felt bereft. It seemed as if she had now lost every single thing of importance in her life.

"Sorry, huh? Well, tell it to the fishes," he said as he threw his gear into the back of his Volkswagen and drove away.

9

The funeral procession was pathetically small. Besides the police escort, it consisted only of the two hearses and two stretched limousines, carrying the Hawthornes and the Janowskis.

"I'm glad you're feeling better, Vivian," Leigh said as they rode to the cemetery.

"I want to die," Vivian said.

Jason chortled. "Well, you just might get that chance, Grandma."

"Don't talk like that," Leigh said.

155

He glared at her. "Who are you, my mother?"

"I'm concerned about Vivian, that's all."

"Well, that's infinitely precious," Vivian said sarcastically.

Leigh sighed.

"Don't worry, Grandma," Jason said. "Gil and me, we've got a plan. We're not going to be like the Jews who meekly went to their deaths in the Nazi death camps. Or like all the witches who went to the stakes without hexing their executioners. This time we're going to fight back. They want a war, they'll get a good one."

Vivian's face paled. "No, Jason. Don't cause trouble."

"Don't cause trouble?"

"Jason!" Leigh said, reprimanding.

Jason thrust a trembling finger in her face. "I told you, you're not my mother!" He turned back to Vivian. "They're the ones that started the trouble. Gil and me, we're just going to finish it."

Just then, as the limousine slowed to turn a corner, the side window was splattered by a juicy tomato. Jason lunged across Leigh's lap and opened the window.

"You want trouble, you sons of bitches?" he shouted at the youngsters who had thrown the tomato. "You're going to get more than you ever bargained for!"

"Jason, sit down!" Leigh ordered.

"Go fuck yourself," he murmured as he settled back down in his seat.

When Leigh went to raise her window again, she glanced back at the young rowdies and was surprised to see that Preacher Cody had stepped out of a doorway behind them. He looked at her, and for just a moment, their eyes met.

It took hours for Leigh to dispel the feeling of cold dread that glance had given her.

10

That night, after the rest of the household was asleep, Leigh called a cab and directed it to take her to the nearest Catholic church. Leigh had never been religious, but she had been christened Catholic, and it was the only religion to which she had any ties. She was disconsolate, and the funeral had only added to her despair. There had been no minister to offer placating homilies, and this time there hadn't even been a eulogy offered. The family had merely wept and cursed and said goodbye to two boxes of burnt human remains. She didn't know what comfort it would bring her to visit an anonymous church in the dead of night, but she was desperate enough to try anything.

She asked the cabbie to wait until she was sure that the church doors were open, and, after determining that they were, she sent him on his way.

The church was small—Montvue apparently didn't have a large Catholic populace—and Leigh was grateful for that. It made it easier for her to make the bold move of entering such a foreign and, to her, forbidding place.

It was dark inside except for a bright altar of flickering candles at the front of the church. The room was silent, and so she tiptoed up the aisle to the first row of pews, where she sat down. The ghost of incense haunted the night air and added to the supernatural quality of the room. In a strange way, it served to help Leigh relax.

She looked up at the rows of votive candles that burned in glass holders and saw that they were overseen by a radiant statue of the Madonna. As an artist, she appreciated the creative genius that had made the fine statue. As a woman, something stirred deep within her soul at the sight of the woman from whom God had supposedly been born. Carl Jung had said there was an archetypical feminine, or Great Mother, which had an undeniable impact on the human psyche. Leigh realized in that instant that, whether she was historical or mythical in nature, the Virgin Mary was a symbol of that archetype, and it was a symbol with which she could readily identify. If divine reality existed or not, there was something implicitly metaphysical about the creation of a human being within the womb of woman.

But that insight didn't shed any light on the nature of God, the reality of death, the survival of the soul, or the reasons why.

"Do you need some help?"

Leigh started at the man's voice. She looked around and saw the young priest standing in the shadows.

"I . . . I was just thinking."

"Would you like to talk?"

She shrugged. "Okay."

He moved closer and sat on the pew near her. Now that she could see him better, she was surprised to see he was even younger than she. It made her feel a loss of confidence in his ability to provide answers.

"Oh, I recognize you," he said, once he'd got a closer look at her. "Aren't you one of the Hawthornes?" She had been in the pictures the newspaper had run of Alan's and Curtis's funeral.

Leigh began to feel frightened. How stupid it had been for her to come, of all places, to a Catholic church. Wasn't it the Catholics who had been responsible for the Inquisition? What had she been thinking? She stood up. "I think I'd better go."

He smiled and shook his head. "Don't be afraid. I won't burn you."

There was something in the tone of his voice, a self-mocking gentleness, that calmed her. She looked at him for a long moment, then sat back down.

"Are you Catholic?" he asked.

"Sort of . . . not really."

His eyes twinkled mischievously in the dim light. "Are you a witch?"

"No." She paused. "What if I were?"

"Well, I'd probably be compelled to give you a blessing."

"I'm scared."

"I would be, too."

She looked at him quizzically. "Your church killed thousands for the same reason."

"My church has been known to be wrong."

"Isn't that a radical stand?"

He grinned, then changed the subject. "What brought you here? What are you looking for?"

"Truth. Answers to the same age-old questions."

"Well, there are a lot of truths. The Bible is full of them, and many contradict one another, and many are subject to interpretation. But me, I kind of settled on one theme. To me, it simplifies the whole mystery of life."

"Oh? And what's that?"

He quoted Christ. " 'You shall love the Lord your God with all your heart, and with all your soul, and with all your mind, and with all your strength.' And, 'You shall love your neighbor as yourself. There is no other commandment greater than these.' "

She thought about it. "But that implies a belief in God. I don't know . . ."

"All I know is that the whole of creation is simply too miraculous to be accidental. There's an intelligence about it that's undeniable."

"So, you love this undeniable intelligence, and you love your fellow man, and, for you, that's the truth."

He grinned again. "The whole truth, and nothing but the truth, so help me God."

"What about the tragedies?"

"I personally don't believe that I understand the whole picture well enough to judge the tragedies."

"Isn't that a cop-out?"

He shrugged. "Not wasting time on things I can't do anything about leaves me more time and energy with which to love."

He was somewhat amazing, she thought. "Why aren't you in some third-world country sacrificing your all for your fellow man? I mean, why are you in Montvue, Colorado, of all places?"

He threw his head back and laughed, the warm sound reverberating in the empty room. "That's one of those inexplicable tragedies over which I try not to waste time and energy."

An hour later, Leigh left Montvue's Sacred Heart Catholic Church. Her conversation with the young Father Shaw had given her a great deal of food for thought.

She felt the stirrings of the beginning of faith. But what form it would take remained a mystery to her.

She walked to the corner, where she had earlier seen a phone booth. She called for a taxi and went outside to wait. A minute later, a Ford van pulled up to the curb. Before she could react, the side doors slid open and two men yanked her inside.

Chapter Six

1858
Nebraska Territory

1

Rose Hawthorne wore bloomers, much to the shock and dismay of many of the ladies on the wagon train. She had a wide array of the colorful outfits consisting of knee-length skirt, loose trousers fastened at the ankles, and the customary matching wide-brimmed hat. To Rose, it seemed the only logical way for a woman to travel across the plains.

The trip had been Rose's idea. When the eastern newspapers began to carry stories of the rumored gold finds in what they were now calling the Pike's Peak Gold Region in the Kansas Territory Rockies, Rose knew it was a probable solution to her family's problem. Her family had never recovered from their loss of wealth and status caused by the misdeeds of Cassie ni Callaghan Hawthorne. Rose felt confident in their ability to find the rich yellow veins. Even if the gods had other ideas about their finances, Rose knew the adventure of it all would liven up a rather dismal crew of people. It had already begun to do that, at least.

The family had sold all of their remaining possessions to finance the trip. They had three wagons. Rose,

Tyler, and his longtime companion, Sheila, drove one. Giles and Arabel had the second. Oakes, his wife Caroline, and their children, Laura and Brady—who were four and six years old, respectively—had the third. A team of four oxen pulled each wagon, and they had between them three good horses. They also had brought along a solemn-eyed cow named Ambrosia to provide them with fresh milk.

Rose sat under the darkening August sky on a three-legged stool and drained Ambrosia's teats into a bucket while she watched the men try to set up the tent in the late-afternoon windstorm. The uncooperative fourteen-foot-square canvas tent provided the greatest challenge Tyler, Giles, or Oakes had had in a great many years, and Rose laughed out loud at their struggle. She glanced up at the high wall of dark clouds the wind was blowing toward them and shook her head. "Well, Ambrosia, it seems we're going to get wet tonight; our men are still such greenhorns. But have you noticed the new sparkle in their eyes? It makes it worth even a drenching."

Ambrosia mooed her agreement.

The bucket full, Rose went to where the women were setting up the kitchen. Sheila and Arabel were hunched over the sheet-iron stove, trying to build a fire in it.

Finally, Arabel threw her hands up in disgust. "Oh, this wind. It looks like we'll be having milk and dried fruit for supper." She looked up at Rose and grinned. "Unless . . ."

Rose set down the bucket and rolled up her sleeves. "Just keep an eye out for a curious audience."

Caroline joined the other two women in keeping guard while Rose used her magic to light the buffalo chips. Fire was one of her strongest gifts.

"Sweet Jaysus," Sheila mumbled and crossed herself. In the eighteen years since she had become privy to the secret of the Hawthornes' witchery, she had never quite accustomed herself to the fact of it.

Caroline, a black-haired, blue-eyed beauty from French witch stock, laughed. "Do you talk to priests about all this in the confessional, Sheila?"

"Nae. And it's sure to damn me to hell."

"Then why don't you confess?" Caroline asked.

"Because it's entertainin', lass. And that's a sight more than I can say for those sotted priests and all their blatherin'. Truth is, I'm more afear'd of a dull life than a hot death, if you get my meanin'."

Soon the coffee was boiling and the food was cooking.

For supper, the women fixed large amounts of creamed dried beef, fried potatoes, and fresh biscuits. Because of the anticipated storm, they also baked bread which, with the berries they had picked that day on the trail and a share of Ambrosia's milk, would be tomorrow's breakfast.

"Mother, Laura did bad," Brady said as he returned to camp from visiting the children who were traveling in the wagon behind the Hawthorne and Hunter party. He was practically dragging his younger sister by her arm.

A look of apprehension crossed Caroline's face. With young children, there was always the fear of loose talk of witchcraft. She knelt down in the tall grass and faced her son and daughter.

"What did she do?"

"She told Mrs. Stewart that Sheila wasn't married to Uncle Tyler."

Caroline groaned. "Oh, Laura, why?"

Laura twisted her pigtails nervously, scrunched up her freckled face, and began to cry. "I dunno."

"As good a reason as any, I guess." Caroline looked at Sheila. "I'm sorry."

Sheila shrugged. "Ah, never fear. To be sure, we've got worse secrets in this family than that."

"Damn! Blast! And bother, too!" Tyler's colorful language announced the defeat of the men. "There'll be no tent tonight, ladies. We've gone and given up the struggle."

"We'll probably survive," Arabel said. "At least, if we get this food down before the storm hits. Come on, then. It's ready."

Sheila, Arabel, and Caroline served their men, while Rose saw to the children.

"And what did you cook, dear?" Giles asked Arabel solicitously.

163

"I made the entree. Do you like it?"

Giles shoveled a spoonful of the creamed mixture into his mouth and chewed, making appreciative smacking noises. "Mmmm. You're the best cook, Arabel."

Their evening ritual thus complete, Giles and Arabel sat down together to finish their supper.

Rose smiled. Poor Arabel. When the Hawthornes had found themselves thrust from the ranks of the rich and pampered, Irene and Arabel had, as the story went, been totally lost in the domestic arena. Sheila, who in the position of wet-nurse was the only one of the servants to have stayed with the family, had taught the Hawthorne women how to cook, clean, and do laundry. From that point on, they had always needed constant reassurance. And Irene hadn't done well under the strain. She had died of a heart attack when Rose was five years old.

"You know you're causing quite a stir among the single men on this train, Rose," Tyler said.

She laughed. "It must be the bloomers."

Tyler took a swig of coffee. "No, I think it's your spunk."

"Could be her vivacity," Arabel suggested.

"It's probably my glorious beauty," Rose said sarcastically. She had inherited a stray Irish gene that had lent her a bright cherry-red head of hair, her eyes were hazel, and Cassie's angular features had combined with the Hawthorne lankiness to produce in Rose an overall horsey effect. The result was generally considered unattractive. But Rose wasn't self-conscious about herself in the slightest. She laughed and threw up her hands. "Let's face it, it's because I'm the only eligible woman on the train."

"All of the above," Giles said, settling the matter.

"Well, let them be stirred," Rose said. "I'm not looking to get married."

Tyler winced.

Rose sighed; it was an ongoing debate between them. "Papa, it's not like you need me to marry to carry on your name or anything. The Hawthorne name ends with me. That's just the way of it. And there's so much I want to do before settling down."

"Like what?" Tyler asked, even though they had covered the same ground before many times.

"I want adventure. Everyone takes life so seriously. It's really a marvelous game to be enjoyed. Shakespeare talked about the world being a stage upon which we act out roles. Mine is as an adventurer, pioneer woman, lady gold miner, witch extraordinaire. I think Shakespeare was one of us, you know."

"You're changing the subject," Tyler said.

She smiled. "Exactly."

"Someone's coming," Arabel whispered.

A small group of people, including Mr. and Mrs. Stewart, approached their camp. Reverend Dix led the pack.

"May I help you?" Tyler asked.

"We've come to talk to you about your ungodlike ways," Reverend Dix said, his voice trembling with outrage.

Tyler held his tin plate up for his inspection. "We're eating our supper. I don't suppose this can wait?"

"The delay could prove fatal."

"To what?"

"To the souls of the decent people on this train."

Tyler furrowed his brows, and his eyes swept the others in his family, looking for a sign of what had happened. Rose made a subtle gesture toward Sheila and then touched the ring finger on her left hand.

Tyler cleared his throat and returned his attention to Dix. "Well, I wouldn't want to be the cause for the ruination of anyone's soul. Speak your mind."

Reverend Dix thrust an accusing finger at Sheila. "This woman is a harlot with whom you're living in sin."

"This woman—her name is Sheila Rooney, by the way—is my daughter's nanny."

The Reverend looked at Rose. "Your daughter seems a mite big to be needing a nanny."

"Rose is fragile. She needs constant care."

"Your daughter is anything but fragile. Which brings me to her unladylike conduct. She wears unfeminine clothes and rides with the men and straddles her horse.

We're trying to maintain some semblance of civilization in this wilderness God has moved us to traverse."

Tyler snickered. "Oh, God has moved you to go west in search of gold, has he?"

"That, sir, is none of your business."

"So, what the hell gives you the right to butt into mine?"

Dix waved his finger in front of Tyler's face. "And your language is another matter. It's a bit rough for our women's ears."

"Oh, fuck off," Tyler said, and grinned mischievously when the women in Dix's party gasped in shock.

"You'd better leave this train. Tonight couldn't be soon enough, Mr. Hawthorne." With that commandment made, Reverend Dix and his small flock scattered.

"My, my, but we're a controversial family," Rose commented as she bit into a warm biscuit.

"Always have been, always will be," Tyler said.

"So, are we going to leave?" Caroline asked.

Tyler shook his head. "Not now. I spoke with Captain Parker a while ago, ran into him when I was watering the horses at the river. His scout had just come back from checking out the trail ahead. Seems a train that went through here four days ago had a run-in with the Cheyenne. Some fool-headed bastard on the train came upon some squaws washing at the river and shot them. Just up and shot them for the hell of it. The Cheyenne took exception to the matter and demanded that the murderer be turned over to them for punishment. The captain of the train had no option, so he did it. They skinned the fellow alive, I understand, which was probably better than he deserved for his crime. However, the scout reported hearing the sound of war drums while on the trail last night. He thinks the Cheyenne might be planning to get some restitution for their losses." He paused. "We're not going to leave the train just yet."

"Restitution?" Arabel asked, her eyes wide.

"For the loss of their women," Tyler said.

"Holy Mother, have mercy," Sheila whispered, then crossed herself twice.

2

Because of the news his scout had brought, the captain directed the thirty wagons of his train to be parked in a large circle for the night. With the windbreak it provided, Tyler, Giles, and Oakes were finally able to set up their tent. However, because of the threat of danger, only the women and children spent the night within its walls. The men armed themselves and stayed in the wagons.

The storm hit shortly after dark. The noise of the rain pelting the roof of the tent and the crashing of the thunder, as well as a healthy measure of fear about the Indians, kept Rose and her companions awake. Finally, they lit lanterns, and Caroline pulled a large, colorful book from her suitcase. It was a recently released volume of Grimm's fairy tales. Her voice straining above the noise of the storm, she began to read to the children.

Rose listened for a while, slightly amused by the Grimm brothers' view of the supernatural, but soon became bored and pulled a book from the carpet bag that she had been keeping by her side every night they had spent on the road. It was the Hawthorne Book of Shadows—the name by which witches called their spell books—and contained the magical knowledge that was her family's legacy.

The book was ancient. Its pages were parchment, bound in a heavy leather cover, and it contained the occult wisdom of generations of Hawthornes. It was a thick book, with many pages still blank, awaiting knowledge yet to be gained. Rose had heard that from the time of the Inquisition, many witch families had insisted that each person's book of spells be burned upon its owner's death. This was supposed to act as a protective measure to keep other family members from possible discovery. But Rose thought that tradition was silly. How much valuable information had been lost that way? And the Hawthorne book, by having been passed through so many gifted hands, practically trembled with power. The study of it never ceased to thrill her.

The early pages in the thick book were written in an archaic script, one she could not literally understand but, with the accompanying diagrams, one from which she could infer. She flipped through these front pages and then the middle section, until she came to a page near the end which she felt appropriate to the situation in which she found herself. It was a section devoted to the dispelling of fear. Little had happened in her life to cause her to have to deal with her own fear, until now. She was terribly afraid of the Indians.

Embrace your owne fearrs, as you wellcome your owne joys, for bothe are part of being in the humann condition. If you fight them, they gaine powwer. Feare is rooted in the awareness of the selfe as separate from nature and other humann beings. Whereas instinct for survival is pressent in all living creatures, a humann being hass the power to goe beyond. Concentrate your thoughts in the centter of your chest and, in your imagination, picture a warme, golden ball of light. As the sunn in your heart gains strength, your fears will grow less. By doing this you will begin to melte into the worlde, until you are in complete harmmony with it. From that place nothing can truly harme you.

A little farther down on the page was an addendum.

And, in cases of extreme emergency when you are taken unnawares put your hande over your heart, fleshe against fleshe, envisione the golden ball of light, and rub three times from lefte to righte.

The bottom of the page was signed by its author, Bridget Hawthorne, and dated 1753.

Rose, who, like the others, had gone to bed fully dressed, unbuttoned her blouse and slipped her hand inside. She used her strongly developed imagination to visualize the golden ball of light in the area of her heart. As fire was her particular strength, the miniature sun leaped into instant life. She could feel the warmth and comfort quickly begin to spread through her body. She rubbed her chest as Bridget had suggested, and with each stroke the jitters her stomach had been entertaining relaxed. A profound sense of well-being filled her, and she felt herself to be a perfectly placed thread in the complex tapestry of the universe.

In that moment she realized that the intelligent force in charge of the loom wouldn't let anything happen to her that wasn't part of the grand design.

3

As the eastern sky turned purple with the promise of the sun's return, Thunder Eagle removed his clothes and put on his magical armor. While he drew the dazzling array of patterns and colors that comprised his war paint, he contemplated the significance of each design—for each one had been given him in dreams by his spirit-helpers for protection and to increase his skills as a warrior. He put the feathers that were his badges of honor into his hair. Lastly, he uncovered his shield, the sacred object that embodied his personal power. The symbols drawn on it represented his medicine, the universal forces from which he drew his strength. In the center of the thick, round buffalo-hide shield, a black eagle was painted. Above the eagle were dark thunder clouds and, beneath it, the ominous funnel cloud that held the tremendous ability to destroy. These powers revealed themselves to him when he had undertaken his first vision quest. And the symbolism had been an accurate representation of his special gifts. The black eagle manifested in his introspective nature that allowed him the insight to see things in a total way, as if he were truly high above, looking down. The storm clouds represented the intensity of his emotions, which he had learned could be used either constructively or destructively. And the tornado symbolized the magical affinity he had with the wind. The wind was the greatest of all his powers.

Thunder Eagle thought about the battle to come. The murderer of his wife and unborn child, as well as of the other three women, had been punished, and that was good. But was it enough? The white men, in their eagerness for the yellow rock that caused craziness, were fouling the Cheyenne streams with their garbage, spreading disease and decay among his people, using the fire-water to steal from the Cheyenne men their power, destroying the buffalo, the Cheyenne staff of life—and slaughtering their women and children for entertainment. When would it stop? In the battle that dawn, many whites would be killed. But it wouldn't be for entertainment. And maybe it might help to slow the destruction of the Cheyenne way of life.

As he tied the soft deerskin breechcloth around himself, he grabbed his testicles and held them. They were full of the seeds of past and future generations of Cheyenne. The white man had taken from him the fortunate seed that had taken root and begun to grow. The whites owed him another chance for his seed to find form. He had decided that he would take one of their women as his new wife and plant his future in her.

4

At dawn, the leader of the small war party gave the signal, and the Cheyenne warriors left their own horses in their camp with forelegs loosely tied to prevent straying and crossed the river on foot to silently infiltrate the sleeping wagon train.

The man who was on guard duty was the first to feel the sharp blade of the Cheyenne knife. With the advantage of surprise, the warriors were able to kill many of the whites in their sleep before another man awakened and sounded an alarm. The white men responded with the force of their rifles, and Thunder Eagle's friends Walking Coyote and White Lion were the first of the Cheyenne to fall.

Thunder Eagle chose to avenge the death of Walking Coyote, and, taking advantage of the killer's need to reload his weapon, sprinted toward then tackled the tall, thin white man who had been responsible. He knocked the rifle from his hands, and they tumbled to the ground, where they struggled. The older man put up a formidable fight, but Thunder Eagle managed to overpower him and plunge his knife into his enemy's heart. To capture his spirit and prevent his ghost from pursuing its own vengeance, Thunder Eagle took the man's scalp. He grabbed the graying yellow hair in one hand and cut a circle around it with his bloody knife. Then he yanked it free from his head and stuck it into the belt of his breechcloth.

The high-pitched scream of a woman overrode the other sounds of battle. Thunder Eagle turned to see an ugly white woman with hair the color of blood running toward him, making hysterical noises. She lunged at him, but he rolled to avoid her. She collapsed onto the dead body of the man he had just killed and hugged him tightly, weeping and seemingly trying to urge him back to life. Impatient with her outburst, Thunder Eagle grabbed her hair and pulled her to her feet, then shoved her toward the small group of women and children who were huddling together fearfully near a flaming tent.

Thunder Eagle's attention was immediately grabbed by the young woman who had black hair and eyes the color of the sky at midday. She was beautiful, for a white woman, and she could bear him beautiful children who might also be blessed with such eyes. He decided to take her. He grasped her hand and started to pull her from the arms of the two children who were clinging to her, when the ugly woman with hair the color of blood reached out and touched his arm. An intense heat issued from her fingertips and burned his skin, startling him. He let go of the black-haired woman for a moment, then reached for her again. The ugly woman didn't hesitate to burn him again. He looked at her, surprised, and she glared back at him with a wild ferocity. He had never known anyone before who could wield such power. He studied her more closely. Her appearance was so odd, but her courage was great. And her powers seemed extraordinary. He hesitated only a moment before deciding that he'd rather have mighty children than beautiful ones.

Crazy Mule and Sleeping Rabbit came up to where Thunder Eagle was standing with the women and children.

"All the white men are dead," Crazy Mule announced.

"Have you chosen one?" Sleeping Rabbit asked.

Thunder Eagle nodded. "The ugly one with hair the color of blood."

Crazy Mule and Sleeping Rabbit looked at him as if he were insane, then shrugged.

"Then I'll take the dark-haired one," Crazy Mule said.

"What about the others?" Sleeping Rabbit asked him.

"We can give the children to Owl Woman. The older women will do us little good. We might as well kill them."

"Let me tie this one up first," Thunder Eagle said, and, ignoring his friends' bewilderment, he threw a rope he found on the ground around the ugly woman so that her arms were tightly secured by her side. Then he gave the signal for the others to proceed.

As the warriors raised their tomahawks to fell the two old women, one stretched out her arm and pointed to the woman in restraints. She shouted something that caused Thunder Eagle's prisoner to become silent and hang her head.

Before leading her away, the ugly woman with hair the color of blood made an attempt to grab a small carpet bag that lay on the ground.

Thunder Eagle ignored her effort. "You won't need any more of the white women's things."

She shook her head, and her piercing eyes bored into him, and he felt her mind connect with his. Then he understood. It was her medicine bundle. He picked it up and handed it to her. Every person of power had a right to possess his or her items of power.

"If I can get used to the way you look, we might have an interesting history together," he said before taking her home.

5

This trip was your idea! You're as evil as your mother was! Arabel's final words haunted Rose more than anything else that had happened. A part of her wondered if Arabel had been right. Had Cassie reached through her from beyond the grave in a final effort to destroy the Hawthornes? Had Cassie somehow managed to influence her mind to urge the family to undertake the fatal trip? For the first time in her life, Rose was filled with self-doubt.

Rose and the other prisoners, all young women and children, were sitting together under the night sky in the Cheyenne home camp. They had been herded up and driven like cattle from the wreckage of their train to this, their new home. They had been directed to sit together in a group out in the open, while the hot afternoon sun beat down upon them unmercifully. The Cheyenne had offered them water but no food, and the children had grown increasingly restless. Their mothers struggled to keep them quiet and well-behaved for fear that the Indians would otherwise intervene. As night had fallen, the camp had become active with obvious preparations for a victory celebration. Now, to the horror of the prisoners, it had begun. The Cheyenne women were dancing around a huge bonfire, singing and waving high on long sticks the scalps of the fallen whites.

The prisoners had not spoken much among themselves. All of them had lost husbands or fathers and were still in a state of shock. Rose herself was numb. Caroline, true to her gentle nature, had tried to remove the sting of Arabel's final words.

"She didn't mean it," Caroline had told Rose earlier. "No one in your family ever thought there was any of your mother's badness in you. She was just scared. Don't pay any attention."

Although it didn't assuage her guilt, Rose had been grateful for Caroline's support. Caroline, Brady, and Laura were all the family she had left.

Unlike the other prisoners, Rose wasn't scared. She had found an effective way to deal with fear. She somehow understood that the Indian who had killed her father had claimed her as his own. Was he one of the braves who had lost a wife to the senseless brutality of that man from the earlier wagon train? Would she be his new wife, or, more likely from what she knew of the Indians, would she become his slave? Why had he decided to choose her instead of Caroline, to whom he had obviously been attracted? Was it the powers she had exhibited? Was he a man of power himself? She had sensed something exceedingly dynamic about his presence, and that had been confirmed when she had mentally communicated to him her need for the Hawthorne magical treasures. She had heard tales of Native American shamans, or medicine men—*medicine* being the concept they used to describe magical power. Was he one of them? If so, maybe there was a purpose for her in this camp. Just the night before, she had been filled with the certainty that nothing happened arbitrarily, without design. Maybe the life work of Tyler, Sheila, Giles, Arabel, and Oakes had been completed and the gods had worked through the Cheyenne to free their souls for what was yet to come. Maybe the gods had brought her to this place so she could fulfill her own life work. Maybe it really was all a plan, and perhaps this magic man who had claimed her would somehow be the instrument of her personal transformation.

Whether it was true or not, it was what Rose chose to believe.

6

With the actions of the war party's raid now completely accounted to the tribe's elders and the Hair-Kill Dance well under way, the Indians began to divide up the spoils. The horses and cattle were given to the parents of the Cheyenne women who had been murdered, the goods that had been seized were divided up among the families of Walking Coyote, White Lion, and Proud Hawk, who had been killed in that day's battle, and, lastly, the prisoners were claimed.

Owl Woman, who had lost her children the previous summer to the spotted disease the white man had introduced to the tribe, came late to collect her new wards.

She tried unsuccessfully to pry them loose from the arms of the black-haired, blue-eyed white woman who seemed to be their mother. "Don't be afraid, little ones," she urged. "I'm going to adopt you. I'll be your new mother."

Steadfastly, they clung to Caroline.

Thunder Eagle, who was overseeing the assignment of prisoners, pulled them roughly from the woman's arms and pushed them toward Owl Woman, then stood in their way so they couldn't return.

Owl Woman pulled a cake of pemmican from her dress and held it out to the children. "Are you hungry? I have good food in my lodge. Come on, and we'll eat together."

Lured by the food, the hungry children followed Owl Woman to her tipi.

Crazy Mule claimed the woman Thunder Eagle had rejected. "I will call her Sky Eyes," Crazy Mule announced as he wiped away the tears that filled them and lifted her chin so all could admire their beauty.

"It's a good name," Thunder Eagle said, a bit wistfully.

"What will you call yours?" Crazy Mule asked.

He thought about it. The Ugly Woman with Hair the Color of Blood was appropriate, but he didn't want a wife with such an epithet. Also, it said nothing of the power she had. "Red Fire Woman," Thunder Eagle announced after a few minutes of consideration.

"Truly?" Crazy Mule scratched his chin thoughtfully. "It, too, is a good name. We've done well today."

Thunder Eagle sighed. No white woman, even one with great medicine, could ever replace Morning Star in his heart and in his sleeping robes. But still it was something. "Yes, we've done well today," he said, then led Red Fire Woman to her new lodge.

7

Inside Thunder Eagle's tipi, a small fire burned which illumined the dwelling and, he hoped, made Red Fire Woman feel welcome. He gestured for her to sit down on the sleeping robes that had belonged to Morning Star, then offered her a hunk of buffalo roast he had scrounged from the wife of Sleeping Rabbit. She ate with zest, and

Thunder Eagle was pleased. Afterward, he pulled her to her feet, handed her one of Morning Star's beautifully quilled white deerskin dresses, and urged her to put it on. She responded by shaking her head and saying something in the language he couldn't understand. Becoming impatient, he ripped her clothes away from her body. Seemingly startled, she didn't fight him too hard, which was good. But she did try to cover her nakedness from his sight, which wouldn't do at all. He quickly moved to pin her arms at her sides so that he could examine her more carefully. Her breasts and nipples were large, which would benefit their children; he himself had no interest in them as objects of pleasure, for that would be unmanly. He was amused to see that her short hair was as red as her long hair, and he had a strong urge to touch it but couldn't do so and hold her arms pinned at the same time. He didn't dare let her strike out at him with her hands of fire. Instead he let her go, stepped quickly backward, and pointed to the dress that lay at her feet. She sighed, bent over to retrieve it, and tried to put it on. It was then that he understood what she had been trying to tell him. It was far too small for her large size. She wasn't fat, but she was tall and big-boned. He shrugged and decided she could make a dress to fit herself in the morning. For now, he would forgo the preliminaries and just go ahead and take her.

He bent down and pulled her feet out from underneath her, which caused her to flop down hard onto the sleeping robes. He quickly climbed on top of her, bearing the painful assault of hot hands until he could release himself from the breechcloth he still wore. Then he struggled to restrain her, all the while thinking of Morning Star in order to make his organ eager to enter the woman who lay beneath him. When he was ready, he parted her legs with his strong thighs and pushed himself into her opening. He was surprised when his organ met with resistance and her cries of protest turned into those of pain. He stopped himself and pulled back. It dawned on him that she had never lain with a man before. She was one who had never married. Well, with her looks, it was no wonder, he decided.

He pondered on how best to proceed. He felt no tenderness for Red Fire Woman and, thus, no real desire to give her pleasure. But if he wanted her to be a wife, he couldn't allow her to dread union with him, either. He took the long rawhide thong from his breechcloth and tied her wrists together, securing them to the lodge pole above her head. Then, able to relax more and take his time, he bent to explore the folds between her legs.

Her woman smell was strong but not unpleasant, and he soon moved from caressing her with his hands to tasting her with his tongue. It wasn't long before the rigidity of her thighs began to give way to a gentle trembling. Soon afterward her breath began to come in soft gasps, and she began to utter small woman noises. He felt his organ begin to respond to her signs of enjoyment, and by the time he felt her spasms—signaling that she had achieved her pleasure—he was ready to enter her without having to exercise his memories. He moved into her gently and pierced the blood skin, then began to move to meet his own needs.

In the mindless moment when he filled her body with his seed, he called out Morning Star's name, and the loss of his beloved wife washed over him like freshly spilled blood. Abashed, he felt the tears he had not yet shed for Morning Star make their need known. He reached up and cut Red Fire Woman's hands free, then rolled off her and turned his back while he vented his grief.

For just a moment, he felt the tentative touch of his new wife's hands on his arm and, for the first time, they didn't burn him.

8

In the weeks that followed, Rose quickly adjusted to her new life. She decided to call the man to whom she now belonged Magic Man. She had heard others of his tribe call him by his proper name, but the words meant nothing to her, and so she made up her own name for him. She assumed, because of the respect with which the other Cheyenne treated her, that she was now his wife.

She thought it ironic that, despite her best efforts to remain single, she had become married nevertheless.

Magic Man was young, virile, and handsome, and he had awakened Rose's sexuality. As a result, she felt a strong bond with him. But she did not believe she belonged with his people. She had heard that it had worked for a distant relative of hers—Priscilla Hawthorne, of the Salem Hawthornes, had married an Iroquois shaman and lived with him until her death. But family tradition said that Priscilla's mind had escaped from reality during her year of imprisonment, and the shaman was the only person with whom she could ever again truly communicate. Rose, on the other hand, still had aspirations beyond domestic chores and the bearing of children, and those she could not pursue if she remained with the Cheyenne.

From Magic Man's behavior, she understood that, indeed, his wife had been one of the murdered women. Also, from the partially constructed cradle board she had found among his wife's belongings, Rose inferred that she had been pregnant. Although Rose did not feel that the Cheyenne attack on the wagon train was a forgivable offense, she had an understanding of the grief and anger that had motivated it.

Rose was treated well, and from what she could tell, Laura and Brady were thriving in their new home. Caroline, however, had been taken as a slave and was withering from the strain. Her beauty had already begun to fade, and there was a deeply haunted look in her eyes. Rose was afraid that she was being passed around among her owner's friends for sexual purposes as well, but she wouldn't shame Caroline by asking her about it. Caroline's magic had always been slight, and Rose knew that she had no significant powers to draw upon to aid her survival. All Rose could think to do was sneak extra food to her whenever possible and hope it would help to keep up her strength until they were rescued or could escape.

One day in mid-September, the smell of smoke in the air brought the tribe to a near panic. The women began to run around the camp shrieking excitedly, the young children started to cry, and the men formed a very serious-looking delegation that visited Magic Man's lodge.

Magic Man admitted them into his home, and together the seven men passed around the ceremonial red stone pipe that they always seemed to use at solemn occasions. Rose watched and listened to them converse from where she sat on her sleeping robes. Finally, after the pipe had been smoked by each of the men, they all filed outside, and Magic Man gestured for Rose to follow him. She obeyed, and together they went out into the bright afternoon sun. Taking two of his horses, they rode toward a high bluff.

Rose thrilled to the ride. It was the first time she had been on a horse since before the wagon train had been attacked. She was surprised that he had allowed her a mount of her own. Magic Man seemed to treat her with more deference than most of the other men treated their wives.

When they reached the top of the bluff, they dismounted, and Rose could see what had caused all of the excitement. A massive wall of prairie fire was being blown in their direction.

Magic Man pointed to the fire, and Rose nodded. He closed his eyes, began to sing and perform an odd dance. His actions made Rose begin to feel strange, as if she couldn't catch her breath. She thought she might swoon, so she sat down on the ground near where he continued his ritual. Soon she was swaying to the rhythm of his feet as they struck the ground in a purposeful manner. Before long, Rose began to notice a change in the air around them. The wind, which was blowing the fire toward them, had turned on itself and formed a small whirlwind; Rose saw she and Magic Man were at its center. Abruptly, Magic Man ceased his dance and pointed the index fingers of both his hands at the fire. In that moment, the wind literally turned around completely and began to blow in the opposite direction, away from them. The wall of fire started to move away from the Cheyenne village and back toward the river, where, presumably, it would extinguish itself.

Rose was stunned. She had known that Magic Man

had power but until now hadn't seen its manifestation. She looked up to see him staring down at her with a haughty expression. He had brought her along so that she could witness his particular medicine in action.

"So, you think that's something? Let me show you what I can do," she said, seeing in his expression a hint of challenge.

She rubbed her hands together for a moment, then held them over a dry clump of prairie grass in front of her. With the use of a specially devised pattern of breaths—long and short, then panted, and long again—she invoked into herself the element of fire with which she felt such close affinity. Through her powers of concentration she channeled the fire out through her hands, and within minutes the telltale wisps of smoke began to rise from the grass.

She looked up expecting to see Magic Man's expression of repect and awe but was shocked to see instead a face darkened with anger. He jumped forward to stamp the fire out, yanked her to her feet by her hair, and slapped her across the face. He shouted something at her and pushed her toward the horses, where he whipped hers into motion before she could mount. He pointed to the ground beside his own horse and conveyed the order for her to walk back to camp beside him.

With a sinking feeling, Rose realized that she had insulted his need to impress his wife by turning it into a competition. A chill passed through her as she realized that their horns were now locked in a bitter contest that neither might survive.

9

Thunder Eagle was sullen. He had understood the nature of Red Fire Woman's medicine. Why did she have to steal his glory by flaunting it at him? It showed him that she didn't respect him as much as he respected her. Otherwise, she would not have humiliated him. Ever since he had taken her as his wife, he had never humiliated her—until he had struck her and made her walk back to camp.

For days, Thunder Eagle brooded over the situation and how best to handle it. Finally, he accepted the fact that he could not allow her to feel she had an equal status with him in the realm of the medicine powers. It was not proper. He would simply have to prove to her that he had the greater medicine.

He found her outside their lodge using stones to pound the wild cherries that, mixed with buffalo meat and fat, would become cakes of pemmican. He appreciated how quickly she was learning to be a Cheyenne woman, but now that was not enough to satisfy him. He yanked her to her feet and took her inside the tipi, where he began to gather the items they would need for their vision quest. He piled together a smoke-blackened buffalo robe, a bunch of slender greenwood poles, a satchel of special rocks, two blankets to keep them warm through the long nights ahead, a paunch full of water, both of their medicine bundles, and his medicine shield. He urged Red Fire Woman to take a share of the load and follow him as he led the way on foot toward the high butte that was his power spot.

Red Fire Woman followed him obediently and quietly, both traits that were unusual to her. Thunder Eagle knew that she felt badly about their hostile encounter and sensed that she was aware of her misdeed, but that wasn't enough to right what had gone wrong.

When they arrived at the top of the butte, Thunder Eagle cleared a space of land and began to construct the sweat lodge. He sank the pliant poles he had brought with him into the ground and then bent them together at the top, securing them with a strip of rawhide. Within the frame, he dug the fire pit, filling it with tinder and various forms of fuel he could gather from the surroundings. He stooped to start the fire, when it occurred to him that the sweat would most likely be more purifying if the heat of it was started by one of the medicine powers. He pantomimed his desire to Red Fire Woman, and, hesitantly, she fulfilled it.

When the fire was hot, Thunder Eagle placed rocks into the pit and covered the small frame with the buffalo robe. He took off his clothes and urged Red Fire Woman to do the same. He was dismayed to see her naked form, because it made his organ stiff and he could not allow himself to become distracted by pleasures. He turned away from her and thought about the last buffalo hunt he had participated in until, finally, his desire drooped. Steadfastly avoiding her gaze, he opened the flap of the sweat lodge, and together they crawled in.

The fire had become a bed of orange coals, and in the darkness of the lodge, the rocks possessed a bright glow. The smell of spent smoke hung in the air until Thunder Eagle threw a handful of sweet grass onto the rocks. It momentarily lit up the lodge as it flared with fire, then became transformed into thin wisps of fragrant smoke that softly scented the lodge. When it had finished burning, he opened the paunch and poured water onto the rocks. The air hissed, and a blast of steam assaulted them. He could hear Red Fire Woman gasp and then begin to cough, while he felt the scorching heat burn his own face and lungs. His skin became damp from steam and sweat, and a sense of suffocation threatened to overcome him. Red Fire Woman made words of protest, and Thunder Eagle thought she might try to leave, so he blindly groped for her arm. Finding it, he jerked it downward to indicate he wanted her to stay. She didn't complain again.

After the purification process was complete, Thunder Eagle threw open the lodge's flap, and they tumbled out into the bright afternoon sunshine. Red Fire Woman lay sprawled out on a soft bed of prairie grass, panting and looking somewhat ridiculous, he thought, with her normally pink skin shriveled and now possessing a hue very much like that of her hair. Out of respect for the solemnity of the occasion, he tried not to laugh too hard.

He laid their blankets on the ground and sat down on one, facing the direction of the sun's rising. He gestured for her to sit on the other, and she obeyed. He unrolled his medicine bundle and removed a long, red stone pipe. He had never before smoked with a woman, but these were unusual circumstances. He packed the bowl full of tobacco and lit it in the traditional manner—he didn't want Red Fire Woman's strange power to touch one of his personal power objects. The pipe had been handed down through his ancestors and was exceedingly special to him. He said a silent prayer to Heamavihio, the great spirit who was called the Breath of Wisdom, and made a request that their vision quest would be successful. He puffed on the pipe and trusted that his petition would be carried to Heamavihio by the smoke. He handed the pipe to his wife, who mimicked his actions. They shared it back and forth until the tobacco was spent. Thunder Eagle gave the ashes to the earth, along with a pinch of fresh tobacco as an offering.

When he returned his pipe to his medicine bundle, he didn't roll it back up. Instead, he spread out the sacred items for her to see, and he pointed to her bundle and urged her to do the same. She opened the brightly colored bag and began to lay out the items for his inspection.

His attention was immediately captured by the shiny vessel that had a stem shaped like a man's organ, complete even to the last detail, including the seed sacs at the base. He looked at her quizzically, wondering what powers it held. Then his eyes returned to their examination of the contents of her bundle. There were two large squares of dark leather that contained between them many sheets of animal skin. He had seen other, similar objects in the wreckage of white man's belongings. They usually had pictures and symbols in them that comprised a written form of their language. There were oddly shaped and beautiful stones, as there were in his own bundle. There was a black-handled knife which had two sharp edges, a pointed tip, and unusual markings scratched into it, as well as a rather ordinary-looking white-handled knife. And the most startling of all her objects was a large, round, flat thing that reflected the sun. He leaned over it to get a closer look and was startled when he saw his face in it; he had only seen his face before in the still water of a lake. With a quick movement, he jerked away. That had to be the most powerful of her objects if it was able to capture the essence of others. He noticed that there were symbols painted on it—the symbols of the night sky easily recognizable to him, the others too foreign for him to know. It was round, like his shield, and was painted, like his shield.

"Your shield is a good one," he told her. He held his out and pointed to hers, so she could see that he wanted her to use hers as he would his.

She shook her head and made words of protest, but he was firm in his directive. If they were to force a confrontation of powers, they needed to have a similar focus.

Finally, she relented and returned everything but her shield to her medicine bundle. He in turn rolled up his, and then the contest began.

10

Rose understood that she and Magic Man were performing a ritual of some kind which undoubtedly had to do with her insulting him the day of the prairie fire. He probably wanted to prove who was more powerful. She knew she should let him flaunt his ability and do nothing to upstage him, but on the other hand, she had believed from the beginning of her time with the Cheyenne that the gods had provided her this experience as an opportunity for personal transformation. What should she do, play it safe and deny her powers, or accept his challenge and accept the consequences? The choice was, for her, an obvious one.

She did wish, however, that he hadn't chosen the star mirror for her to work with. It was something she had always been afraid to use. The mirror, like the spirit blade—the black-handled knife—had come from distant ancestors in England, and both intimidated her. The blade was used to harness energy and direct it to create force fields which were often used in rituals. The mirror was used as a doorway through which the mind could enter the next dimension, called the star world by her ancestors, the astral plane by occultists, and heaven and hell (heaven being the upper levels and hell being the lower levels) by the Christians. It was a world much like this one but subject to experiences far more intense. Depending on one's state of mind, inner nature, and

colored stones. They worked at breakneck speed, using one another as step stools to gain the height necessary to construct the upper half of the arch. The building materials they employed seemed to be a vast array of precious stones, including diamonds, rubies, emeralds, and sapphires, and—with the interplay of the luminous light of which the star world was composed—the end result was a dazzling prismatic display that delighted Rose. Upon completion of their work, one of the star beings entered the archway and looked out at her, and she found herself in eye contact with it. Her smile faded, and she became quite disconcerted. She wasn't really afraid; she was more self-conscious than anything else. However, when the star being gestured for her to come into the mirror, she resisted. She had no wish to relinquish her body to visit another dimension. It was far too scary a concept for her to pursue. She shook her head and held her ground. The shiny eyes of the creature blinked in seeming confusion, and his face took on a vague semblance of frustration. He was quickly replaced by another being who also tried to lure Rose into the archway. When he failed to coerce her, another creature replaced the second one.

The star beings were tireless in their efforts, and it was in such a manner that the second night passed.

On the third day, Rose's resistance failed. Her hunger had passed, but her thirst was unbearable. She felt weak and dizzy and was afraid she was going to die. The need for sleep was urgent, and she began to experience a strange feeling of disassociation from mind and body which disoriented her. The scorching heat of the sun became an enemy, and she could no longer imagine the sun in her heart and garner any sense of comfort from it, so the fear she felt began to expand and threatened to overpower her sensibilities. Finally, around noon, Rose decided to abandon the ritual and acknowledge Magic Man as being more powerful. She stood and began to gather up her things.

"I quit. You win. Let's go home," she said, her throat parched and raspy.

Magic Man grabbed her wrist and pulled her back down beside him.

"Please? Please let me go home." She began to cry.

Magic Man shook his head, and in her own language, in her own mind, she heard his thoughts. *You have great power, but you lack harmony with the earth. You'll never be truly great until the earth becomes your friend and not your enemy.*

Startled, she ceased crying.

You must gain balance, his mind continued to tell hers. *Don't fight the pain. Surrender it to the earth, and you'll free yourself of its bondage and become its friend.*

Rose had experienced psychic moments but never one such as this. She presumed that the fragile thread that now connected her to life had broken down the normal mental barriers that provided resistance. *How do I do that?* her mind asked.

Thank the earth for the pain because it's a gift you can use to go beyond.

She tried to feel thankful for her suffering.

If we never knew pain in this world, we would never seek to explore the other one, he told her. *Therefore, it's a great gift which we must learn to use.*

Rose thought about the world in her mirror. *Tell me what you know of the other world.*

It's the world of causes. This world is the effect. You become intimate with the other one, and you have tremendous power here because you can manipulate the cause.

Rose sucked in her breath as his thoughts clarified hers. She now understood the nature of reality and what it was her witchcraft was designed to do. She wondered how many of her ancestors had truly understood the mechanics of how their magic had worked.

She silently thanked the gods, and Magic Man, for the insight, and she settled down to continue the ritual. She attempted to conjure an attitude of gratitude for her misery, and it wasn't long before she began to relax. The pain was there, the exhaustion was there, the thirst was there, but it didn't seem to upset her equilibrium any longer, and she felt her mind and body attain a comforting sense of harmony. The remainder of the day passed quickly.

That night, when the star beings summoned her, she went. As soon as one of them appeared in the archway and beckoned to her, her mind agreed that it was all right to go, and her consciousness fled from the slumping body, entering the archway into the star world.

She found herself in a world that was resplendent with light and color. Her senses seemed heightened, and her emotions were intense. She felt an onrush of giddiness fill her as she realized that she had indeed passed into another reality. She looked down to see that her body was naked, but a bright, pulsating mist seemed to envelop her. The star being who greeted her in the doorway stood only to the height of her waist. He—she didn't know why, but he seemed to her to be a male—took her hand and led her through the arch and into the waiting arms of the other star people. As if she were weightless, the group of six lifted her up, and, holding her above their heads, they began to fly through the foggy air. The sensation of flight was exciting to Rose, and she began to laugh with sheer joy. She had never felt so light and so free, and she was intoxicated by the experience. All too soon they put her down, and she found herself at the feet of an old woman. The woman, completely human in appearance, was dressed in a flowing black gown and had bright gray eyes which perfectly matched a bright gray head of hair. She smiled at Rose, and, as it had been earlier with Magic Man, she heard the woman's words in her mind.

Welcome to reality, my daughter.

Is this the ultimate reality? Rose asked.

The old woman laughed. *Mercy, no. Just reality as it directly applies to your own world.*

Who are you?

One of your teachers.

What do you have to teach me?

The old woman handed Rose a small box made of gold. It resembled a round jewelry box and had an image of the sun engraved on its lid. *This is your gift. It's time you truly exercised it.*

Rose opened the box and was blinded by the bright fire it contained. She tried to avert her stinging eyes from its ferocity but couldn't do so. Then, as if she were a moth being irresistibly drawn to the flame, she entered and became one with the fire.

The old lady and the box were suddenly gone, and Rose was a billowing ball of fire.

The previous definitions of her body were gone, and she felt herself to be an undefinable mass composed of heat, light, and energy in combustion. The choleric nature of the element threatened to overpower her, and she successfully fought back the anger and irritation that arose. Courage and enthusiasm replaced the disagreeable emotions, and for the first time in her life, Rose experienced her power with passion.

For an undeterminable period of time, Rose reveled in her element. Then she felt the cooling wind begin to blow on her. In a startled flash of comprehension, she knew that Magic Man had found her.

At first she didn't know how to react to the confrontation. How could fire destroy air? She tried to resist his efforts. She concentrated on intensifying her own nature to counteract the calming effect of his, but he seemed to be the stronger force. In a moment of inspiration, she realized that she could destroy him by consuming him. Her attitude changed, and she began to devour the air and use it to fuel her own fury. Within a space of time that seemed like moments, her might became so intense that it literally exploded upon itself. She felt the fireball self-destruct, and in the wake of its demise she found herself back on the high bluff where her journey had begun. Only she wasn't in material form. She stood by the sweat lodge and observed the bodies of Magic Man and herself slumped together on their blankets, both still unconscious. However, the form of Magic Man had a luminescence about it that hers did not have. She assumed that the body of energy that housed consciousness had returned to his form, while hers, obviously, had not. She thought about what he had told her earlier regarding the nature of the other world. Her mind was still conscious in the world of causes—perhaps because of her victory—and his was not. Perhaps the reward for her success was the possibility of engineering an escape. She glanced up at the location of the moon and judged it was still the middle of the night. Urged on by instinct, she approached his body and wished for something to tie him up with. Instantly, a glowing length of energy rope appeared in her hands, and she used it to bind him.

Then she wished herself to be where Caroline was, and her consciousness was transported to where a small bonfire was burning out on the prairie not far from the Cheyenne village. Caroline was lying on a buffalo robe while an Indian whom Rose knew was called Wolf Tooth—although how she knew his name was a mystery to her—was engaged in sexual intercourse with her. Startled, Rose didn't know at first how to proceed. However, she soon reasoned that she could bind him as well, even given the circumstances. When she wrapped the glowing rope around him, he stopped his movement and became rigid. Rose could feel Caroline's confusion as she pushed the stiff, unconscious body off her and began to pull on her clothes.

Good. I hope you're dying, you drunken bastard, were the thoughts Rose heard from Caroline before she wished herself to be with Brady and Laura.

She found the children asleep in their lodge on robes near where their adoptive mother was sleeping. Rose bound the woman and her husband, who was asleep in his own robes. Then Rose wished herself back into her body.

With a start, she awoke. She carefully eased herself away from Magic Man, but her caution wasn't necessary. She realized that his slumber was sound and would remain so for quite a while. She knew that, with his power, he would eventually be able to overcome his bonds and awaken, but she hoped it wouldn't be until she and her family were safely away. And she knew that after he revived, he would also be able to bring the other three around. She stood over him for a time. In his way, he had been kind to her, and she had learned a great deal during her short time with him. She put her hand on her belly, where, unbeknownst to him, his child was

191

growing. She wondered, with the mingled essence of their respective powers, what kind of child she would bear. Before she turned away, she bent and gave him a tender kiss.

11

Her ordeal had changed Caroline into an exceedingly nervous, high-strung person.

"Why did we have to bring these cows?" she asked Rose as they crossed the Platte River on horseback, urging on their three stolen cows—cows that had originally been stolen from their own wagon train by the Cheyenne.

"Because we're going to need a stake when we get to the end of the line. I doubt if milk, cheese, and butter are readily available in the mining camps."

"But they'll slow us down, and the Indians will find us." Caroline started to cry. "They'll kill us."

"They'll kill us if they can catch up with us, but I started that fire to sidetrack their energies." Rose looked back to the shore of the river from which they had just come and noted with approval the progress of the fire she had made. The wind was taking it toward the Cheyenne camp. When Magic Man awoke, his priorities would be clear. He wouldn't sacrifice his village to follow her.

"How do you know where we're going?" Caroline asked.

"We follow the river south, and it'll lead us to the gold camps."

"Why don't we just turn around and go home?"

Rose sighed. "Because the Rockies are closer, and besides, we don't have any home left to go back to."

The children were quiet. Laura rode with Rose, and Brady rode with his mother. Rose didn't sense that they were necessarily pleased to have been rescued from the Cheyenne. They had found happiness in the lodge of the cheerful, fat squaw who had adopted them. Now they were once again facing the unknown.

Rose had only taken two horses to minimize the Indian's anger. Since buffalo was more highly prized by them than cattle, she hoped the missing cows wouldn't incite them too terribly much, either. She hadn't wanted to create a situation that was unbearable for them to ignore with honor. She hoped that as a warrior people, they would respect the fact that some of their prisoners had managed escape. She thought that Magic Man probably wouldn't feel a desperate need to retrieve her; her power had defeated his, and it was doubtful he would want a wife who was stronger than he. At least, that was what she hoped.

As they rode, Rose nibbled on one of the many cakes of pemmican she had brought along and sipped the water the paunch contained. She had taken enough provisions to see them through until they reached their destination.

"Women alone. We'll be raped by the men in the camps," Caroline said, her voice beginning to grate on Rose's nerves.

Rose answered patiently. "I've heard that the men in the camps, for the most part, have good moral character. We'll be all right."

"So, what are we going to do, start a dairy?"

"To begin with. And I'm going to look for gold."

"Gold?" Caroline spat the word. "That's what got us in this mess in the first place."

"And that's what's going to get us out of it, too."

That was something Rose didn't doubt in the slightest.

12

At the junction of the South Platte River and Cherry Creek was the small settlement of Denver City. A half a day's ride east of the Rockies, it was a tiny frontier town consisting of little more than a crude gathering of tents and hastily built cabins. The wagon train that the Hawthornes and Hunters had been on represented one of the few groups of people who had responded early to rumors of discovery of gold in the vicinity, and so the population in the area was still light. When Rose, Caroline, Brady, and Laura arrived, it was already well into the month of October.

"This is pitiful," Caroline said upon seeing the scrawny town that was, for them, the end of the road.

"If the rumors are true, it'll grow," Rose responded.

A look of panic crossed Caroline's face. "If the rumors are true? Oh, dear gods, what if they're not?"

"Then, come spring, we'll head for California and open a dairy farm or something. Ambrosia and Velvet Eyes are pregnant; could be one's got a young bull in the oven, so we could eventually breed." Rose's patience was wearing thin. "Please, try not to think the worst. The worst is over. Now's the time to muster some enthusiasm for our new beginning; if nothing else, do it for the sake of the children."

Caroline started to protest but pursed her lips and stopped herself.

Rose issued a sigh of relief.

A small contingent of men met the travelers as they stopped on the edge of town to water their horses and cattle. They eyed the newcomers, all dressed in Indian garb, with confusion.

"Howdy, ma'am," a tall, skinny man said in greeting, a toothless grin gracing his mouth. "I'm called Zach. We don't see many women in these parts." He scratched his unkempt head of hair. "Ah, you look white, but you're dressed red."

"I'm Rose Hawthorne. This is my sister-in-law, Caroline Hunter, and her children. We survived an Indian attack on our wagon train. The Cheyenne took us, but we managed to escape."

"Jeez, you the only ones who made it?"

"Any of the others who lived through the raid are still prisoners of the Cheyenne."

Another, more distinguished-looking man spoke up. "I'm Edwin Walker, the proprietor of the Cherry Creek Saloon. Sorry for your loss, ladies. What are your plans?" He gave Caroline—who, even with what she had endured, was still a great deal more attractive than Rose—a lurid look.

"Not what you're hoping," Rose said, her tone hard. "We're decent ladies, and we expect to be treated with respect. We lost all our family and have no home to return to. With these milk cows, we're thinking of opening a small dairy operation. Do you have a problem with that, Mr. Walker?''

Appearing appropriately contrite, Edwin Walker shook his head. ''No, ma'am.''

''Tell me, are the rumors of gold true?'' Rose asked.

''The Cherry Crik's got it,'' Zach said. ''And there's some who swear that there's a shit-load—excuse my cussin'—up on the mountain in the Clear Crik, but nobody's staked a claim just yet.''

''Good. Then why don't you gentlemen tell us where we can have a small piece of this town to call our own. It seems as if we'll be staying.''

13

After Thunder Eagle discovered that Red Fire Woman had finished making the cradle board Morning Star had begun, he went on a solitary vision quest. If he had known that his white wife was pregnant, he would have immediately sought her out and brought her back. Surprised by the unexpected victory of her medicine over his, he had decided to let her go. She had won the right. But the fact of the child changed the matter entirely.

It was winter on the plains, and as he sat on the high bluff wrapped in a buffalo robe, the bitter wind buffeted him and threatened to extinguish his fire. He found the irony amusing.

He asked his medicine to give him the sight to find his child and the strength to claim it. Instead, his medicine gave him a vision of what atrocities were to befall his people in the short years ahead. He saw that if he were to return his child—he saw it would be a son—to his tribe, the boy would not live to become a man. He also saw that their paths would cross again, although the images didn't reveal in what fashion.

He contemplated the facts as he had seen them and battled with his pride to allow his boy to be born and remain among the whites. A dead Cheyenne was better than a live white. However, unlike most whites he had encountered, Red Fire Woman had the power to raise the child with correct knowledge. Perhaps he should let it be so.

Thunder Eagle lit the tobacco in his red stone pipe and asked Heamavihio to grant him the gift of patience.

14

"What are you going to name him?" Caroline asked as she placed Rose's newborn son in her arms.

Rose had given it a great deal of thought. She had been tempted to name her baby after her father, but that was the past. She wanted her baby to be of the future. "Denver's a nice name for a boy."

Caroline raised her eyebrows. "Well, it's different. But it is rather fitting, I suppose."

Rose, exhausted from the birth but grateful for its success, put Denver Hawthorne to her breast for the first time and then took Caroline's hand. "Thanks for your help."

Caroline shrugged and sat down on the bed next to them. "It's spring. Soon they'll be arriving in droves."

"Soon I'll be climbing the mountain right along with them," Rose said.

"You can't be serious! Not with Denver to care for."

"I'll wean him onto cow's milk as soon as I can and ask you to take care of him. You know the little bit of gold we've recovered from the creek isn't the windfall I'd hoped for. I've got a feeling about what's up in the mountains."

Caroline squeezed Rose's hand, and Rose could feel her fear. "But there are grizzly bears up there. And there'll be lots of wild men. It won't be safe. Then, if you find gold, there are claim jumpers. Rose, I just don't know what I'd do without you. Our life's not so bad as it is. We've got this nice little cabin, our livestock's got a snug barn, our business is good and getting better. We might even find husbands among all the men headed this way. Why don't you just chase off this gold fever?"

"Because I've got it bad. Don't know any herbal remedies to cure it. Do you?"

"Oh, Rose." Caroline issued a rare laugh. "Not a one. Not a single one."

15

The Hawthorne family's Book of Shadows had an entry about water witchery. It said that the art could be used to dowse for any natural resource . . . including gold.

There was still snow on the peaks when Rose packed camping gear on her horse's back and headed up into the mountains alone.

A part of everything that exists in the world is in you. Therefore, you have a kinship with all life, animate and inanimate, the Book of Shadows had said. *Because of this law, nothing shall remain unknown to you if you seek it with diligence.*

Rose followed the traces of the broken path that led to Clear Creek, where the Lawrence party had found gold and had begun to stake out claims. Not wanting to be conspicuous, she made her camp among the pine trees above the Creek and spent days exploring the mountainside, trying to make friends with the land.

Everything that exists is a form of energy. You must harmonize yourself with the nature of the energy you are seeking.

It wasn't the gold in the creek that Rose was interested in. Through the winter months, she had tired of panning for the precious metal. She wanted to find a lode that could be mined, and she believed that, using her powers, she could locate one.

To dowse effectively, you must possess a need. The earth doesn't easily grant her favors.

Rose's gold fever stemmed from a need to justify the deaths of so many members of her family. Before the tragedy, she hadn't much cared about the carrot of wealth that rumors had dangled before her. Now it meant something more to her than merely an accumulation of money.

This world has two natures, tangible and intangible.

Both are identical yet different. The key to dowsing is found in knowledge of the intangible world.

Magic Man had taught her about the subtle world of which the material world was but a shadow. Every night that Rose was on the mountain, she explored that causal world by venturing into it through her star mirror. She acquainted herself with the pockets of incorporeal gold that she discovered there. Even though she couldn't immediately pinpoint their material counterparts, she felt her encounter with them there would eventually result in a worldly encounter.

Unless the dowser knows harmony, success will be elusive.

Magic Man had also shown her the quality of harmony and the means to achieve it.

For days she roamed, her mind focused only on the object of her search, her emotions and body in equilibrium with each other and with the ground upon which she walked.

On the third day, her wandering seemed to have unconsciously narrowed to a specific area north of the creek. It was only then that she withdrew from her belt the long, forked stick that she had so carefully chosen before beginning her search.

Rose had never attempted dowsing before, but she felt confident that she possessed the gift. In truth, it never occurred to her that she might not.

Walk bare to the earth, so she can freely bestow upon your body her messages.

Rose removed her boots, and, thanking the earth for the discomfort of bare toes on the frigid ground, she began to dowse.

Grasp the forks, palms up, and rest your fists on your hips. Point the tip of the rod straight out ahead of you, holding it with the force necessary to keep it from drooping. Then begin to walk, slowly and with a neutral attitude.

Within minutes, Rose felt a slight tremor of muscle spasms shudder through her arms, and the point of the rod began to tug violently downward. The place the rod pointed at was a sharply sloped area thick with brush and bramble. Rose dropped the rod. With a giddy feeling of anticipation, she grabbed the small miner's pick that dangled from her sturdy belt and began to break up and toss aside the dense growth of bushes and shrubs. Behind the brush, she found the opening to a small cave. She lay down on her belly and tried to squirm her head and torso through the opening, but she was too large. She settled on sticking her arm in as far as it would go, and her fingers explored the sides of the rocky interior. Using her pick, she blindly chipped away some of the stone and withdrew a large hunk of quartz. She set it on a boulder and, using the side of the pick, split it. She gasped when she saw the sunlight reflect off the yellow veins that were revealed.

When the earth has presented you with her gift, don't forget to thank her.

Chapter Seven

July 1992

1

"Will you deny the Hawthornes and their witchery and accept Jesus as your savior?"

The man's voice was muffled, as if he spoke through a mask, but Leigh was sure it belonged to Preacher Cody. The disembodied voice had the same rhythm and inflection as his possessed.

She had lost track of time. Upon snatching her after she left the Catholic church, her captors had immediately blindfolded her. They had also bound her hands behind her back.

The place in which she was held smelled musty and mildewy, but the bed upon which she sat had clean bedding. She knew it was clean, because when she had broken down and cried, she had buried her face in the fresh-smelling pillow to wipe her nose.

"How can you expect me to deny my children?" she asked.

"You must save your own soul. Then perhaps, with my help—and God's, too, of course—we can save the souls of your children as well."

"What, you'll try and deprogram them with sadistic

brainwashing techniques like this? No. I don't think so."

"It's our understanding that you didn't know that your husband was a witch. But despite your initial innocence, you've been tainted by his evil. You must ask God to forgive you and ask Jesus to come into your heart. Only He can rescue you from the clutches of the Devil." The man's voice seemed infinitely patient.

Leigh felt the tears trying to be born once again. "Go to hell."

"Why won't you join Jesus's flock, and then work with me to try and salvage your children from their abominable legacy? Don't you care about their welfare? What kind of mother are you?"

"I'm tired. Please let me sleep." She allowed her head to fall over onto the pillow and tried once again to fall asleep, but the man slapped her across the face and pulled her back up into a sitting position.

"You didn't answer me. What kind of horrid mother are you that you don't care about the fact that your children are going to burn and writhe in eternal damnation?"

Despite all her best efforts to deny them, the tears came. "I'm a good mother. I've always been a good mother. Please, just let me sleep."

"*No!*" His voice made her jump. "We'll not sleep until you come with me into Jesus."

God, how her bladder hurt. As much as she knew she'd be humiliated again, she couldn't hold it any longer. "I've got to go to the bathroom."

"The pot's right here. I'll help you."

The man took her by the shoulders and guided her to the big pot that was on the floor next to the bed. He unhooked her jeans and opened the zipper, then pulled them—and her panties as well—down around her ankles. Her face was burning with embarrassment. He steadied her while she crouched down over the pot. She winced with shame at the sound of splattering urine and the odor of ammonia that wafted upward toward them.

"The Devil fucked that cunt," he said, his voice just inches from her ear. "Your husband served the Devil, and when he fucked you he acted as the Devil's servant.

You're unclean. Only Jesus can cleanse your body and your soul of the taint of corruption."

"And I suppose you'll be Jesus's agent in the cleansing of my cunt," she whispered, her voice registering the resignation she felt. She believed it was only a matter of time before he raped her in the name of Jesus.

"No. I wouldn't contaminate myself in such a manner," he said.

However, he did devote a great deal of attention to wiping her with the toilet paper before pulling her panties and jeans back into place.

Then he sat her back down on the bed.

Her stomach growled with insistent hunger.

"Do you want me to feed you something?" he asked.

"No." She was afraid if she ate she'd have to defecate, and she couldn't do that in front of him. "Some water?"

He held the glass up to her lips, and she drank, but it didn't assuage her discomfort or help her feel any stronger. "How long have I been here?" she asked.

"Not long enough."

"Please let me go."

"You aren't a good mother. Just like you haven't been a good daughter."

"What do you mean?"

"Well, just look at the conditions in which your parents have been living. In the slums of New York. Living hardly better than animals."

Leigh felt guilt wash over her like a flood. She had always felt somehow responsible for her parents' self-destruction. "They're alcoholics. They choose to live that way. I've tried to help them, but they—"

"Don't give me that crap. If you loved them, if you truly loved them, you could have helped them."

Leigh bit her lip to try and stop its quivering. "What do you know about it?"

"Because Preacher Cody loves them. And he was able to help them."

Confusion swam in Leigh's head.

She heard him walk across the wooden floor, and then she heard the sound of a lock turning. More footsteps and voices followed. She knew the voices. Her heart began to pound hard in her chest. The door closed, and the lock turned.

"Baby?" The woman's voice was tremulous.

Leigh thought she might be hallucinating. "Mom?"

"Yes, baby, it's me."

"Take her blindfold off," a familiar man's voice said. "Dad?"

Fragrant hands fumbled with the scarf around Leigh's head, while other hands untied the knot that held her wrists.

As the blindfold fell away, the sudden light stung her eyes, and she had to force them to stay open. But they grew wide with the surprise of what they beheld. Her mother and father, appearing as she had never before seen them, stood in the small room by her bed.

"We came as soon as we heard," Sam Lindsey said.

Stunned by their presence, she proceeded cautiously. "Heard what, Dad? Have you come to set me free?"

"Yes, Leigh. We want to help your soul to freedom."

Leigh felt the tentative rise in her hopes leveled by his words. She studied them for a moment. "You both . . . look different." They were nicely dressed, they seemed clean and well-groomed, and—more surprisingly than that—their eyes were clear. Neither regarded her with the clouded, vague look that was an undeniable testament to their disease. Beyond that, their faces reflected a serenity Leigh had never seen in their countenances.

"We are different, baby girl," Dorothy Lindsey said as she sat on the edge of the bed and took her daughter in a warm embrace.

Leigh sniffed for the sour telltale odor, and it wasn't there. She held on to her mother for a few extra moments. It was the first time they had ever shared a sober embrace. "What happened, Mom?"

"Preacher Cody."

Leigh drew back. "Preacher Cody?"

"He showed up at our place one night last week. This big TV star, this man of God, he came to our little cold-water dump to see us. He told us about your terrible plight—with that evil family—and he prayed for us. He sat right there on the floor with the bugs and the rats, and he took our hands and prayed for and with us. He said that God wanted us to be well, so we could help save you and Kamelia and Adrian.''

"It was a miracle, Leigh,'' Sam said. "It really was. He asked God to remove our sins and cleanse our bodies and . . . well, look at us. I've never felt better. Didn't go through any kind of withdrawal, either. And I don't want a drink. God, Leigh, I never thought I could put the bottle down.''

Leigh stared at them, her eyes vacillating between them as she struggled with her emotions. "Is Preacher Cody the one who kidnapped me?''

Dorothy gently took her hands. "Honey, baby doll, we hired someone to try and deprogram you.''

Leigh angrily reclaimed her hands. "You what?''

"Preacher Cody helped us, and now we want to help you,'' Sam said. "We know how you felt about Craig. But you can't let that influence you to side with those witches. Your very soul is at stake here. Don't you see that?''

Leigh shook her head. "That's no deprogrammer, that's Preacher Cody. And anyway, how the hell could you have the money to pay anyone for anything?''

"I sold the truck,'' Sam said. The truck was his livelihood.

That silenced Leigh. Even with all the years of drinking and struggle, he had steadfastly clung to his truck. Did they love her that much? She had never known. "Oh, Dad, you shouldn't have sold the truck.'' Suddenly, she felt like the little girl who was always trying to make sure her parents were going to be okay, who was always trying to make things right. Her stomach became wrenched with guilt. "You shouldn't have sold the truck for me.'' She began to cry.

Sam pulled Leigh to her feet and enfolded her in his big, burly arms. "You're our baby. We never did right by you. We're trying to do right now. Don't you see?''

Leigh clung to her father, and her tears became a flood. Emotions long buried surfaced, and she felt like a child of five. "Oh, Daddy, do you really love me that much?"

Tears began to stream down his face. "More than that. More than I could ever begin to show you."

"I love you, too. I know you think I deserted you and Mom, but I just didn't know what to do to help you anymore. They told me I had to stop enabling you, that if I cared about you, I had to practice tough love."

"And you were right to do what you did," Sam said, using his handkerchief to wipe Leigh's face. "And that's exactly what we're doing here for you. It's not for nothing that they call it tough."

Leigh disentangled herself from his arms and took his handkerchief to use to blow her nose. She struggled to steady her emotions. "Dad, this isn't right. It's not right to try and force religion on someone."

"It worked for us," Dorothy said. "I mean, look at the miracle—"

"But it won't work for me! I don't belong to any cult, and I don't need to be deprogrammed! I married into an unusual family—"

"Not unusual. Evil," Dorothy said.

"They're not evil! This is evil!" Leigh faced them defiantly, trembling from her outburst.

Sam and Dorothy exchanged meaningful looks, and before Leigh could react, her father grabbed her hands and retied them while her mother replaced the blindfold that plunged Leigh into bleak darkness once again.

2

Diane Fox studied the list of Associated Press wires that the satellite dish was pulling into the *Post-Dispatch*'s computer. The directory showed several that sparked her interest, and she called them up.

Los Angeles (AP)—*The Zen Buddhist Temple of Los Angeles was firebombed shortly after dawn today. One monk, whose name has not yet been released, was killed, and fourteen other people were seriously injured. Police say the incendiary device was a pipe bomb, and a fundamentalist Christian group calling themselves the Christian Purist League has taken responsibility. In a taped message delivered to the* Los Angeles Times *this morning, the League was quoted as saying, "We've just begun to fight."*

San Francisco (AP)—*A group of Hare Krishna chanters were assaulted on Market Street today. Witnesses report that the three men who attacked the six Hare Krishnas with tire irons were in their late twenties or early thirties and wore business suits. They were heard to shout that they were doing it for the sake of Jesus and the welfare of America. Two of the Krishnas remain hospitalized in critical condition.*

Hollywood (AP)—*NBC issued a press release this morning stating that their popular sitcom, "Freshman Year," has been canceled. Popular televangelist Preacher Cody threatened the show's sponsors National Mills, Pizza Giants, and Hot Rock Soda with a boycott unless they withdrew their advertising from "Freshman Year." The controversy stemmed from the airing of an episode which dealt with an astrological-oriented dating service. Despite the fact that the show has rated consistently in the top ten of the Nielson ratings since its second season, no other sponsors could be found to fill the advertising gap. In a related story, CBS announced the cancellation of their successful Saturday morning cartoon show "A Witch Called Wanda."*

Selma, Alabama (AP)—*Authorities are investigating the circumstances surrounding a house fire in which elderly recluse Melvina Jefferson died. Neighbors report that the eccentric woman had been rumored to be a witch. Following last evening's telecast episode of "Preacher Cody"—the second in a series denouncing witchcraft—a small contingent of Christians from the Watershed Baptist Church attempted to visit with the eighty-one-year-old Jefferson. The fire began shortly thereafter, and Selma Police Chief Dewey Chaney issued a statement that "its origin was suspicious in nature."*

Detroit (AP)—*The body of a three-day-old baby girl was found in a trash bin behind the Motor City Liquor Store this morning. Her throat had been cut. Police followed a blood trail to a nearby housing tenement and located the mother, an unwed teenager. She was reported as telling authorities that the father had "been into the occult" and she was afraid the child would be demonic. She confessed to killing the baby as an act of mercy.*

There was more, but Diane couldn't stomach it. Preacher Cody was getting what he had asked for . . . and more. The witch hunt, like a contagious disease, had begun to spread.

3

" 'For rebellion is as the sin of witchcraft, and stubbornness is as iniquity and idolatry. Because thou hast rejected the word of the Lord—' "

"Oh, shut up," Leigh said wearily. He had been quoting the Bible for so long, she was beginning to think in *thees* and *thous*.

The palm of his hand made sharp contact with the soft flesh of her cheek. "Don't ever tell me to shut up again."

She ignored the pain. "You had no right to involve my parents in this."

"Would you rather your parents were groveling in filth and disease?"

"Of course not. I . . . I appreciate that you were able to help them—"

"Preacher Cody helped them."

"—but you had no right to bring them into this."

"They hired me to help you."

"If they paid you money, it was to protect your ass. I'm not stupid. I've read the papers. If the parents hire you to deprogram their child—even if he or she is an adult—you can most likely get out of criminal prosecution for kidnapping. But I swear to God, I'll sue you in civil court."

"You don't even know who I am."

"I know who you are."

"So, can your witches cure people of alcoholism? Was your husband ever able to resurrect your parents' souls?"

"No." She hated to admit it, but as hard as he had tried in the early days of their marriage to help her parents, he had never been successful.

"So, how can you deny the power of Jesus, the living God?"

"I'm not denying the power of God . . . if there is one. But people have the right to choose for themselves what they want to believe."

"Would you let your children drink the bleach from under the kitchen sink because they have some inalienable right to choose to believe it won't hurt them?"

"Of course not."

"No. Because you know it would hurt them, and because you love them, you would slap their hands and take the bleach away. It's the same here, Leigh. I love you, and I see you as being a spiritual child. I'm not going to let you harm yourself because you claim the right to choose. And in turn, you must make the same choices for those children of yours that you profess to love."

Oh, my God, she thought sadly. *He's beginning to make sense.* "How do you know that these witches are bad?" she asked.

"Because . . . well, for instance, Preacher Cody told me that on that plane when he sat across from the Hawthornes, his faith—the faith that God had given him in his moment of enlightenment—was stolen away from him. No good power would have had such an effect on him."

"I've heard the story, Preacher Cody. Ever think that God took away your fear in Central America, and in a weak moment you merely took it back? Are you so perfect that you're incapable of backsliding all by yourself?"

"Preacher Cody has been blessed by the grace of God. His weakness did not come from within, it was imposed upon him from without." He sounded agitated. "I have to use the toilet. I'll be back."

"What, the pot I'm using isn't good enough for you to piss in, too?"

"No," he said, and then she heard him leave.

When her mother had taken the blindfold off her, she had seen that she was in a small room in what appeared to be a shed of some kind. A rusted horse harness and old hand plow had been lying in the corner on the dirty wooden floor. She had glanced out the window and seen that the area was farmland. It had been daylight then. She wondered if it was now. She struggled with her wrist bindings. If she could only free herself, she would be able to escape. She had to. Otherwise she had the feeling Preacher Cody might win. He had been in the CIA, and his brainwashing techniques were good; she didn't know how much longer she would be able to resist. If she had come into this with a firm foundation of belief, she felt she could have been stronger, but as it stood, his advantage was great.

From behind her, Leigh heard the tinkling of glass breaking and falling onto the bed. Then she heard the window slide open.

"What? Is someone there?"

"We've got to be quick." She immediately recognized the man's voice as Marek's.

Leigh felt her wrists released from their bonds by the slice of a blade. She reached up and pulled the blindfold off, then quietly followed Marek out the window and into the night.

4

"Are my children okay?" Leigh asked as soon as they were in Marek's truck and safely on the road into town.

"Physically they're fine." He paused, then cleared his throat. "Vivian told them that you had run off and deserted them because of the danger we're facing, because you're not one of us."

Leigh's face became hot, and the effects of instant rage seized her stomach. "That bitch. Did they believe her?"

"I don't think completely. But, well, they are children, and they've been through a lot lately. To be honest, I don't think they're quite sure of anything anymore."

"Did anyone ever notify the police I was missing?"

"No."

Leigh felt tears threatening. "How long did they have me?"

"It's been three days."

That was only three days? "It seemed like weeks."

"I can believe it." A small flame illumined his face for a moment as he lit a cigarette. "Did they get to you?"

"Almost, but not quite."

"I'm glad you were strong."

"How'd you find me?"

"Tracking is one of my gifts."

"Thanks."

"No problem."

"Did you see the man who was in there with me? Was it Preacher Cody?"

"He had some kind of surgical mask and a baseball cap on. It could have been. I'm not sure."

"Damn. That means he'll get away with it."

The orange tip of his cigarette became brighter as he took a deep drag. "Of all of us, I know you've got it the roughest; being in the middle, not belonging to either camp."

Leigh thought about it. It was indeed hard on her to be an outsider caught in the middle, but until now she hadn't realized what her remaining outside could do to the children. Whom, besides herself, did they have to rely on? Whom could they completely trust? And if she wasn't one of them, how could they truly relate to her in the manner necessary to sustain that trust? Something Marek had once said came back to her now. "You said that a witch could be made?"

"Yes."

"Explain that to me."

"Everyone has power, but in most it's latent. If a person's born into a family of witches, because of the fact power is awakened in his or her parents, it usually is in the child as well. Other people, because of past-life development, can be born with awakened power no matter what the circumstances of the birth. Some have power awakened through their own efforts—mystical devotion or involved meditative practices, for instance. Even Jesus—since I'm sure you've probably got him on the brain right now—told his disciples that they were capable of performing even greater miracles than he. The fact that man has a greater potential is generally accepted.

"Now, a witch can use his or her power to help awaken power in another. What form that power will take—what particular gifts it will bestow, for instance—depends entirely upon the makeup of the person in question. And of course, if it'll be used for good or evil also depends on the character of the individual involved."

"Craig said witchcraft was a folk religion."

"It has religious elements, a way of relating to the inner and outer worlds. The roots are found in some of the earliest imaginings of mankind. There was a pristine quality about the way our ancient ancestors viewed life. It was uncomplicated and to the point. Many of us acknowledge and incorporate the old religion into our lives. Others just play with the power without giving the spiritual laws much thought."

"What are the religious beliefs?"

"Well, to sum up, I guess that life is never-ending, it just changes form. Birth, life, death, and rebirth are the landmarks of existence that are celebrated. We believe ourselves to exist within a greater intelligence which is conceptualized, for the purpose of worship, as a myriad of gods and goddesses, each representing different aspects of the whole. By worshiping a 'god,' it's possible to tap into and possibly manifest the quality he represents: wisdom, healing, courage, creativity, fertility, and so forth."

Leigh thought about it for a while. "I like that. I really do. It makes sense."

"I think so."

Leigh knew she couldn't straddle the fence any longer. If Preacher Cody represented what the other side was, then she didn't want it for herself or her children. True, Cody had manifested a miracle in relation to her parents. But she had witnessed startling witchcraft miracles as well. Cody wasn't omnipotent any more than Craig had been omnipotent. As Marek had explained, different people manifested different gifts as a result of supernatural power. Cody's power worked with drunks. Craig's power had worked with more organic illnesses. Neither manifestation of power was superior. But Craig's character had certainly been superior to Cody's. On the other hand, the Hawthornes in general weren't the most wonderful people. Maybe that's what Craig had meant when he said that he had originally left home because he didn't want to lose the magic to the politics of power. Maybe the magic was an extension of the religion, whereas the power alone tended toward corruption. If so, her children did indeed need guidance if they were to develop their power in a more healthy direction. The responsibility fell to her.

"Can you . . . will you make me a witch?"

Marek took another bright drag on his cigarette. "Initiation is an extremely intimate affair. I would need to consult with Helena."

"Can we do that now? I don't want to waste any more time."

"You don't want to go home first?"

"No. When I return to that house, it'll be when I truly belong there."

5

Helena sat across the kitchen table from them and sipped a cup of coffee. It was two o'clock in the morning, and Leigh and Marek had awakened her.

The Janowski home was quite conservative and suburban. *Beware the witches that might be your next-door neighbors* replayed in Leigh's mind as she studied her surroundings. She shook her head in an effort to exorcise the preacher from her mind.

"If you're going to survive the days ahead, you're going to need power. I won't stand in the way of you getting it," Helena said at last.

"Thank you." Leigh didn't understand exactly what was about to happen to her, but she had the feeling it represented some sort of sacrifice on Helena's part.

"Ah, should I eat and sleep to regain my strength first, or what?" Leigh asked.

"No, actually the fact you haven't eaten or slept will be to your advantage," Marek said. "It helps to break down the obstacles your rational mind will try to impose."

"Then we can do it now?"

"Given the circumstances, we don't really have much choice."

The Janowskis' basement had been finished and made into a ritual room. When Leigh entered it, she was immediately soothed by its atmosphere. The floor was brightly polished oak parquet, the walls and ceiling paneled with rough-hewn woods of different varieties. In the middle of the room was a large circle made with stones: chunks of amethyst, quartz crystal, lapis lazuli, magnetite, tourmaline, onyx, jasper, and turquoise combined to make a beautiful design. In the center of the circle was a three-by-seven-foot altar draped with green silk. On the altar were two candlestick holders, one silver and one gold, containing candles of corresponding colors. Between them was a fresh bouquet of flowers. Along the north wall was a massive planter full of lush greenery with an ultraviolet growing light above it. From the ceiling at the east wall hung a large brass censer from which a trickle of incense smoke issued. On the south wall there was a lighted crystal oil lamp sitting on a marble stand. Against the west wall a fountain resembled a miniature waterfall.

To Leigh it all seemed so primitively evocative, except . . .

"A plant light?" she asked.

"Witchcraft in the nineteen-nineties."

"I assume it all has significance?"

"Earth, air, fire, and water—the four elements that comprise the universe," he explained, gesturing toward the items placed at the four directions. "The circle is that of Mokosh, the great Earth Goddess whom our people worship. The altar and candles represent the

Earth, Moon, and Sun. The Earth feeds our bodies, the Moon our souls, and the Sun our spirits."

"It's very lovely," Leigh said.

"I'm glad you're comfortable with it." He dimmed the overhead lights. "Now we've got to undress."

"Naked?"

He grinned. "I told you an initiation was an intimate affair."

"Of course." Self-consciously, Leigh began to strip away her clothes while Marek removed his. When they were finished, they turned toward each other and studied each other's body with frank appreciation. Leigh had been with only one man besides Craig—a fellow dance student during her days with Andre Beauchard's company —and the physical beauty of both of her former lovers paled in comparison to Marek's. He was tall, with impressive, well-developed muscles. His chest was darkened by hair that faded at his flat belly and reappeared farther down to cradle his massive organ. Leigh was fascinated by his ample endowment and found it difficult to avert her eyes.

"Your beauty is breathtaking," she heard him say.

"So's yours," she replied, trying to sound more casual than she felt. She was dismayed to feel herself respond with sexual stirrings to a man other than Craig. He had been dead only a little more than a week. "What's going to happen here?" Her voice was strained, her face hot.

"I'm going to make you a witch." He took her hand and led her into the circle of Mokosh, where they knelt side by side before the altar.

"In the old religion creation is seen as being a duality, masculine and feminine," Marek said, and then—with obvious reverence—he lit the silver candle. "The Goddess, or female aspect of creation, is responsible for giving life form, nurturing its development, and the dissolution of the forms that house it. She is viewed as a threefold goddess: the virgin, or receptacle; the mother, or nurturer; the crone, or destroyer." He paused and, in like manner, lit the gold candle. "The God, or male aspect, is the life that is born, dies, and is reborn through

214

the feminine. And since he is also the life that impregnates the womb of the universe, he is considered to be an empowerer. But, as guardian of life, in the realm of creation it is the Goddess who is the true wielder of power. As a result, the women in our religion have the dominant position. As a priest of the God, it is my purpose to empower the priestess of the Goddess.''

He gave her time to assimilate all he had said.

A female-dominant religion, Leigh thought. *No wonder the patriarchal church has done its best through the ages to try to destroy it.*

Marek took her by the hand and led her to the planter at the north. From a small iron cauldron within it, he withdrew a pinch of salt, which he sprinkled on her head. "Be purified by earth," he said before leading her to the east. There he cupped the incense smoke with his hand and, in a graceful movement, maneuvered it toward her face. It possessed a soft, sweet smell which Leigh inhaled appreciatively. "Be purified by air," he said, then led her to the south, where he took the crystal chimney off the lantern and passed her hand briefly through the flame. "Be purified by fire." Finally, he led her to the west, showered her with a handful of water, and said, "Be purified by water."

They returned to the altar. Marek put the flowers on the floor and moved the candles to one end, then took Leigh by the hand and urged her to lie down on the altar, her head immediately below where the candles now rested. She reclined on her back, the silk of the altar cloth strangely sensual against her skin.

It was then that she felt a wave of disappointment and a sense of betrayal. Was he simply going to mount her, and was that supposed to make her a witch? If that was true, then all her years of having sex with Craig should have made her one. Were Marek and Helena just into some sort of open-marriage type of life-style? Would Helena join them, and together they would all cavort for a time in a bizarrely staged ménage à trois? No, she needed to believe in someone. She tried to drive the doubts away.

Marek removed a clear vial of golden oil from beneath

the altar and thickly anointed an area on her lower belly, about two inches below her navel. He rubbed it gently, massaging the oil into her skin, as he spoke.

"Within you, at this place, lies your divine birthright. This is the center of your body, the inner altar where the fire of the spirit lies smoldering. When through initiation the golden embers are fanned into flame, power awakens, and the journey of transformation begins."

Leigh closed her eyes and surrendered to his words and ministration. The oil he was using smelled like cinnamon and myrrh, and it was making her skin feel warm.

"We all have this internal altar of golden embers within us, but as the human consciousness has evolved, so has our preoccupation with the power of our minds. We've neglected this more primal center of strength and creativity, and in most it's become dormant. Once it is awakened, it moves within us and we become greatly changed by it."

The heat of the oil—or was it the circular motion of his fingertips?—was beginning to penetrate her skin and move deep into her belly.

"Now I'm going to move on and in you to summon the presence of the Goddess. While I do this, try to maintain your concentration at your central altar."

He lifted the pressure he was placing on her belly, but the heat seemed to remain. Dutifully, with eyes still closed, Leigh rested her thoughts on that spot.

Marek moved to her feet and tenderly kissed each one. "Blessed be your feet that connect your body with the greater body of Mother Earth." Then he moved to her knees and kissed each of them. "Blessed be your knees that kneel at the sacred altar." Leigh lost her concentration when he moved to spread her legs and bent to kiss her. "Blessed be your sex, from which life is born." After saying the words, his kiss returned to her womanhood, then lingered, and his tongue moved to part her lips. His touch felt electrical, and a shudder escaped her, but then she struggled to return her attention to where it was supposed to be. She wondered if she was so sensitized because of her lack of sleep. Soon the heat of pleasure began to merge with the warmth of her belly, and she sighed her enjoyment. After a time he turned his attention to her breasts. "Blessed be your breasts, which nourish life." He kissed, then suckled, and finally gently nibbled at her nipples, while his fingers caressed the plump flesh around them.

Leigh's belly started to grow hot.

"Blessed be your lips, which shall speak the sacred words of the Goddess." When his mouth moved to meet hers, she responded hungrily, enjoying the masculine taste of tobacco on his tongue as it became entwined with hers and the rough feel of his face as his day-old stubble scratched her delicate skin. As they kissed, his body covered hers, and his rigid member found her opening. He entered her slowly, and Leigh savored every second of his entry. She could feel herself stretch to accept him, his enormous size filling her in a manner she had never before known.

Still, she tried to remember the special place in her belly.

When he made contact with her cervix, he continued to press himself into her, and much to her surprise, she opened to receive him further until she was able to accept his entire length and width. When they were completely united, his movement ceased, he lifted himself up slightly, and his fingers once again began their massaging of the golden oil.

"The time has come for you to claim your power," he whispered.

She lay with eyes closed, feeling the heat and seeing the flames of the fire he had awakened within her; behind her closed eyelids, her mind was bright with light. She felt a sudden onrush of joy, and an overwhelming exhilaration filled her. Then she became seized by a new might that sought instant expression. Forceably, with a strength she didn't know she possessed, she rolled a resistant Marek over onto his back and, holding him down beneath her, began to ride him. She had never wanted anyone more, and she was determined to take from him what she could. She ground herself down onto him, trying to merge with him as totally as possible, then lifted her hips until her tight muscles had stroked his entire length, then, once again, she would plunge down to be filled by him. Her thoughts captured by the moment, it didn't occur to her that it was the first time she had ever assumed the dominant role in lovemaking. On the contrary, her driving urge to consume him for her own pleasure seemed the most natural expression of womanhood she had ever experienced. She grasped his hands and placed them on her breasts, demanding that he knead them to heighten her pleasure. She bent to kiss him, thrusting her tongue into his mouth so she could taste again of his delicious masculinity. She pulled up on his buttocks, needing to know him even deeper inside her body. She bit into his shoulder, wanting to taste his blood.

The room resounded with carnal yells and ecstatic cries. She rode him faster and harder, pausing occasionally to swivel her hips erotically on his steely-rodlike extension. Her hunger devoured him as completely as was possible.

When she opened her eyes, the room seemed filled with billowing flames, but they didn't frighten her. She knew herself to be their source. She felt expansive, as if she were the universe stretching to contain within herself all life; the masculine force she was trying to merge with was the life she sought to engulf.

When the fusion reached the critical point and the explosion erupted, Leigh had a brief glimpse of infinity.

Afterward, when Marek lay spent beneath her, she glanced up to see the ethereal vision of a woman in the air a few feet away. The woman had long blond hair and green eyes, like her own, but she knew that this woman was the Goddess. And from the Goddess Leigh felt a measure of the force and power she had just experienced. She also felt love, in a stronger and more pure form than she had ever imagined possible. Tangible waves of unbearable tenderness, compassion, selflessness, and devotion filled the room. Leigh felt her heart tug painfully in response, and then she began to cry.

6

As Leigh's consciousness began to surface, she heard the gentle sound of the waterfall and smelled the sweet incense. She opened her eyes and discovered herself to be alone on the altar, her nudity covered by a large afghan. She lay for a time basking in the internal calm of fresh awakening, then her mind began to recall the events of her initiation. It had been a dynamic experience, there was no denying that. However, was she now different? Was she a witch? If so, what powers would she discover herself to possess? Would she become a healer like Craig and Kammi or a psychic like Adrian? She recalled the vision of the Goddess she had seen. Was it a hallucination? The profound emotions that had accompanied the vision washed over her in a renewed flood, and she felt a deep certainty that what she had seen had been real. It hadn't been an earth goddess, or a warrior goddess, or a goddess of wisdom or healing who had appeared to her. No, it had been a goddess of love. And that was a goddess she could feel comfortable in worshiping, she decided. As she continued to muse about the extraordinary events that had transpired, she got up and began to dress.

She found her way back upstairs to the kitchen, where she found Helena hard at work. The sun was shining brightly through the open window, and the clock on the microwave said 2:47. In her mind she calculated that it was Tuesday, Helena's day off from her duties at Hawthorne Manor. It was Marek's day off, too. She felt a catch in her throat as she thought of him and looked around, anxious to see him. Then she felt a pang of guilt. An initiation happened only once, she was sure. And despite her fears of last night, she doubted very much if the Janowskis had an open marriage; even if they did, she wouldn't find the situation acceptable. She didn't want to invite the pain of falling in love with someone else's husband.

"Hi," she said.

Helena turned from the stove to greet her. "Good morning. How was it?"

"Incredible."

Helena shook her head. "The incredible part's just beginning." She gestured to the Mr. Coffee on the counter. "Help yourself. I'm just finishing this up."

Leigh poured herself a cup, deciding to drink it black. She sat down at the kitchen table in the same chair where, just a little more than twelve hours ago, she had sat as an ordinary person. Now she sat in it as a witch. She mentally examined herself to see what was different and was aware only of a peaceful sense of well-being.

"Usually on my day off I don't do anything," Helena said as she added another touch of salt and pepper to the simmering pot. "We eat out, and the beds don't get made, and anybody who makes a mess is on their own. But today's a different matter." She raised the wooden spoon to her lips and tasted. "I imagine you must be hungry."

As if in response to her observation, Leigh's stomach made a loud growling noise, and she laughed. "Sounds like it."

"Yes, I heard. You have a long history of going without. History of trouble with Christians, too."

Leigh didn't understand Helena's meaning. True, she hadn't always eaten well as a child, but Helena couldn't have known that. And she had never had a bad encounter with a Christian until Cody. Her stomach captured her train of thought as a gnawing pain seized it. *Gods, I've never been so ravenous*, she thought, looking around frantically for something to stick in her mouth.

Helena poured herself a cup of coffee and sat down across from her where, Leigh noted, she had sat twelve hours earlier trying to decide whether to loan out her husband.

"Once someone initiates you, you're bound together forever in a very special way. However, I want you to know that although I gave my all to you last time, this time I'm not planning to be so selfless, particularly where my husband's concerned. Hope you'll understand."

Leigh was startled by her words. "I . . . I've got no designs on Marek. I understand—" She stopped herself short. What had she meant, *gave my all to you last time*? "What—" Suddenly Helena's face took on a shadow and darkened, and Leigh blinked her eyes in confusion. Helena's face came back into focus for just a minute, then once again it was a darker face, one more exotic, extremely beautiful.

"Could I have something to eat, Mirasaya?" Leigh asked, then paused. "What did I call you?"

"I don't know, Rebekah. What did you call me?" Helena's voice was deeper in timber, richer than usual. It seemed to match her new sultry appearance.

"What? Who?"

"You tell me. Try to remember, Rebekah."

Oh, the hunger's unbearable! "Don't you have a piece of fruit or something I can eat? Prissy gave me an apple last time Alida Van Carel brought fruit, and it was a piece of heaven." *What did I say*?

"You always fragile one, Rebekah. But you not anymore, are you?" Helena's new voice took on a different accent.

Leigh's cheeks flushed, and panic surged. Was she losing her mind? Could an initiation go sour and inflict madness? "What's happening?"

Helena's new face smiled its effervescent smile. "You just remembering. You not worry."

Something clicked, and in a startled moment of comprehension, Leigh remembered. "Mirasaya! You're alive!"

"Me no die. Nobody ever die for good."

Leigh lunged across the table to embrace her friend, tipping over both coffee cups in the process. Tears filled her eyes. "Oh, I knew somehow you'd get out of jail."

"I got out of jail when they carry my body away and put in ground."

"Oh, no . . . I'm so sorry."

"I choose. It best way. They never stole my spirit. I made them mad, being happy until the end."

Leigh smiled through her tears. "I bet they were."

"What happened to little ones?"

"Bridget lived to old age, but she was a spinster. Prissy ran off when she was fourteen and married an Indian. Phip grew up and went into business with Jansen

221

and Peter Van Carel. He married and had two children, but only one lived." The highlights of those years surfaced in her mind with ease.

"You?"

"I became Jansen's mistress. His wife was afraid of getting pregnant; she almost died birthing Peter. I had a good life." She paused. "I owe you."

"Interesting turn of events, don't you think?" Helena was back. "Now look at us. This time we really are witches. After what we went through last time, you'd think we'd have known better."

Leigh studied her friend, amazed at the revelations the past few minutes had brought. "Maybe this time we'll win."

"Well, at least we'll give them a hell of a fight."

7

Cody was not happy. The woman had managed to escape somehow, and in his prayers God had told him to let her go. She had made her choice. It was a shame, but by refusing God she had declared her allegiance.

And now she was destined to meet the same fate as the rest of them.

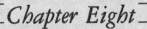
Chapter Eight

1895
Montvue, Colorado

1

It was autumn when Denver finally mounted the gold-lettered sign that read "Hawthorne Manor," on the tall wrought-iron fence. It had taken two years to complete construction of the mansion, and the grounds had yet to be landscaped, but he and his mother were finally moving in.

Denver had mixed emotions about the move. He had been raised in the small white-frame house just one block off Main Street, and it was a warm, cozy home. It seemed rather silly for just the two of them to be moving into a house so large and ostentatious, and he felt a nagging embarrassment about the whole affair. But it had been Rose's inspiration, and she had expressed her urgent wish that he would people the premises with lots of little Hawthornes in the not too distant future. He was, after all, already thirty-five years old and not getting any younger. He had assured her that he would be happy to oblige her, if and when he found the right woman to marry. So, with that motivation, Rose had approached the Hunters and the Winthrops—who, along with Rose, had founded the town of Montvue in the late 1860's—about a new town growth incentive program. Maybe with more young women to choose from, she had reasoned, she'd get those grandchildren before it was too late for her to enjoy them. Rose had always been industrious.

The Hawthornes, who had sunk much of the wealth garnered from their gold mine into fertile farmland, the Hunters, whose dairy was the top producer in the state, and the Winthrops, who owned the sprawling mercantile around which Montvue had been built, had decided to encourage development of their town by investing in small local businesses to be run by immigrant families. They had placed ads in newspapers in New York City, hoping to attract newly arrived foreigners and had so far sponsored the relocation of twenty different families. Detractors of their plan accused them of megalomaniacal dictatorship because of the fact that they were handpicking the new town residents and, through their monetary investments, were able to maintain control over most of the town's purse strings. But their motives weren't entirely self-serving, and the plan was proving to be successful.

More immigrants were scheduled to arrive in town that evening, and Denver had been elected to greet them and get them settled into their new homes. Rose had been responsible for choosing this particular group of newcomers and had promised Denver that there was a surprise package among the expected goods. He assumed she had finally managed to find a family of old blood among the applicants. The prospect evoked a mild curiosity in him, but for the moment his thoughts kept returning to more familiar—and exciting—territory. By the time he put away his tools, his desire had captured his mind completely. Leaving the rest of his chores incomplete, he headed for Anita's house.

2

Sylvan Sanfillipo, lulled into a gentle sleep by the rhythmic rocking of the train, had yet another dream about the rabbit. The soft, mottled fur felt comforting against her bosom as it pressed into her, eager for love and protection. Waves of maternal warmth filled her, and she guided the creature to a nipple, where it began to gently nurse. The pleasure that coursed through her body soon changed into a passion that was hot and incestuous. She felt the transformation come upon her, and it wasn't long before she changed into a rabbit herself, her fur black and silky. It was then that the mottled rabbit mounted her and they began to mate.

3

Anita Salazar and her two grown sons lived in a small cabin on the Snyder farm outside of town. The Snyders had recently hired the Salazar boys as farm hands and provided them their living quarters. Fresh from Mexico, Ramon and Enrique Salazar could speak only halting English, but Anita knew the language well. As a matter of fact, in Denver's mind Anita could do everything well.

He had first seen her at Winthrop's Mercantile and was taken by her seeming youth and beauty; he had been shocked to learn that she was old enough to have children his own age. That fact had initially deterred his impulse to pursue her, but he hadn't been able to resist her for long. He went to her home for the first time ostensibly to bring a bushel of sweet corn fresh from his fields and to welcome her and her family to town, and had remained there for more than a week—until his mother had come to claim him. Intoxicated by lust and peyote, Denver had left Anita's bed unwillingly, but Rose was formidable and the farm needed him. It was the farm more than Rose's will that caused him to allow her interference; he was more attached to the land than anything else in life.

But he had kept returning. Anita, it seemed, was a *bruja*—a witch—and knew the secrets of peyote and men's loins. For Denver, it proved an irresistible attraction. She opened the door to him and greeted him with smoky eyes that smoldered with passion. The cleavage of her plump breasts smiled up at him, and he bent down to take the top button of her blouse in his teeth. He ripped it off, and her bosom heaved free of its constraints. "I've come to eat buttons," he said with a grin.

"My buttons are your buttons," she said in her sultry way.

She ushered him inside and closed the front door, leaving the sunny afternoon outside.

4

The train pulled into the station at Montvue, and its weary passengers flooded out onto the platform. Sylvan helped her father, who was blind, from the train and got him settled on a rough-hewn bench. Then—slight as she was—she managed to unload all their luggage by herself. Finally, she stood anxiously awaiting the appearance of Mrs. Hawthorne's son, who the letter had informed her would be welcoming them. To every man who passed, she surreptitiously made the hand gesture that was a universal greeting among witches, but none recognized it or responded in kind. Others, who were also newcomers brought to Montvue by the Hawthornes—all outdwellers, or nonwitches, from what Sylvan had been able to determine—lingered nearby, murmuring nervously among themselves until, at last, the train pulled away, the stationmaster closed his doors, and the immigrants alone remained.

After an hour, the sun set behind the western mountains and the cold seized the night. Antonio Sanfillipo began to shiver and his daughter rummaged through baggage looking for something to wrap him up in.

"Rude, how inconceivably rude," Sylvan muttered. "I can't believe it . . . especially coming from our own."

"Now, maybe there's a reason," Antonio said. "Don't get worked up. It's not like you."

"Well, there's little about this country so far that brings out the best in me."

"Is this place beautiful?"

She glanced at the fading purple of mountains. "More beautiful than New York, less beautiful than Italy."

"That'll do," he said, satisfied.

She wrapped a quilt around Antonio, gently tucking it around him to keep him snugly encased. "You stay here. I'm going to find the Hawthornes and make them honor their agreement with us. I'm not going to tolerate this kind of treatment."

"But it must be almost dark."

"Don't worry. Wherever I go, you know I've got friends." She turned to the other two families nearby. "Stay here with him; I'll bring back a Hawthorne."

Under the cover of night, Sylvan, her anger righteous and intense, headed out to put things right. She pulled the hood of her black woolen cape up over her head and fastened the ornate hooks in front that held it closed. Used to traveling incognito at night to secret coven meetings, she had no problem adjusting to the dark. She walked out of sight of the station and then made the low whistle designed to summon help. Within a few minutes, she heard the telltale rustling in the bushes.

"Come on, it's all right," she urged.

Soon a soft glow of eyes appeared, and then a sleek gray cat leaped up into the air and landed at her feet.

"Ohhh," Sylvan cooed. "You sure are beautiful."

The cat, appreciating the compliment, rubbed itself up against her legs—sharing its scent—and allowed her to scratch it behind the ears.

"I need to find the Hawthornes," Sylvan told it. "Can you show me?" All the while scratching and petting, she mentally conveyed her need.

The cat rolled over onto its back and displayed its underside proudly.

"Yes, your belly is exceptionally pretty," Sylvan agreed, and stroked it accommodatingly.

Finally, when it decided it was ready, the cat leaped back onto its feet and headed into the shadows. Sylvan followed it easily.

She had been born with the gift of communication with animals.

It was a long hike, and more than once Sylvan had to

stop to gently coerce the cat to continue to guide her instead of following its natural instinct of stalking the small game that wandered into their path. But they eventually landed at the gate of Hawthorne Manor.

Sylvan gave the cat an ancient blessing that would ensure its future well-being, then pushed open the gate, made her way to the front door, and knocked furiously.

The heavy door swung wide, and Sylvan was greeted by an old, ugly woman wearing a dress that didn't quite fit her tall, gawky frame.

"May I please speak to your employers?" Sylvan asked. Her English was good, even though her accent was still strong.

Rose laughed. "Speaking."

"Excuse me?"

"I'm Rose Hawthorne. What may I do for you?"

"You can tell me why you're so rude."

Rose frowned. "Am I?"

"There are eleven people freezing to death at the train station waiting for someone to claim them. And you, or yours, are that someone."

"Oh, my. Oh, mercy." Rose grasped Sylvan's hand and unceremoniously yanked her inside. "My son was supposed to greet you. Oh, my." She pushed Sylvan toward the parlor. "Go, sit by the fire. I'll go get the stable boy to hitch up the wagon and get them. I'll have him bring them here for the night. I'll cook something for them myself and get them settled in their own places in the morning. Oh, my." Frantic, Rose scurried from the room.

Sylvan, a gentle soul, instantly forgave the woman. But her son was another matter.

Rose returned to claim her fifteen minutes later. "Come and join me in the kitchen while I fix the food. We'll get to know each other."

She followed Rose into the huge kitchen and sat down at the marble-topped table. "I'm Sylvan Sanfillipo."

Rose paused in her stoking of the cookstove to eye her with a look of penetrating appraisal. "Welcome to my home, Sylvan. It's always a joy to meet one of our own; the world is so big, and we are so few."

"I'm glad you recognized the symbols on our letterhead."

"Symbols are universal." Rose finished her task, then put a pot of coffee on the stove to reheat. "I'm anxious to meet your brother and sisters. It'll be a fresh infusion of old blood for all of us. Besides my son, my nephew Brady hasn't found a spouse, either. My niece, Laura, she went to school in Switzerland and met her husband, but the others—"

"My brother and sisters died last month. Dysentery. We weren't prepared for the dirty conditions in which we were forced to live in New York. I couldn't find the herbs I needed . . ." Her voice broke, and she shuddered.

Rose paused again. "Oh, I'm so sorry . . . for all of us."

Sylvan experienced a moment of fear. She had her father to take care of, after all. "It's true that my brother was the gardener and landscape artist, but I learned a lot from him. I'm sure I can do the work you wanted him to do. I'm also a sculptor; I work in wood and stone. My father and I can stay, can't we?"

"You're awfully small to do such manual tasks, aren't you?"

"I'm stronger than I look."

Rose shrugged. "Then you can start with my grounds. Make the statues over the winter and begin the landscaping come spring. You and your father can stay here with us." Rose hefted a huge pot of water onto the stove and added beans, pork rind, and spices to it. "If you prove yourself, then I can line up other projects for you. As I stated in my letter, in exchange for work and housing under my sponsorship, I get a share of your income for the first three years. Then it all reverts to you. Fair deal?"

"I think so."

"Good enough." A soft cloud of flour filled the air as Rose emptied a small sack into a mixing bowl. In a few minutes she had worked the bowl's ingredients into a stiff ball of dough.

Sylvan relaxed and began to look around more closely at her new home. "This is quite impressive. Who all lives here with you?"

"Just my son, the rude one."

Sylvan felt her feathers ruffle. "Why didn't he come, do you know?"

"There's a Mexican witch he's taken up with. She's a master of illusion. She's my age and, though not as ugly as me, she's no beauty, either. But try and tell him that. She feeds him alcohol and drugs. He's part Indian and part Irish, and neither does well with that stuff. She's used her sex on him like a weapon. She's ruining him." She wiped her eyes. "Excuse my old woman's tears."

"Why is she doing it?"

"Money. I'm sure she's working up to a marriage proposal."

"And you were hoping that I or my sisters . . ."

Rose began kneading the bread dough with a vengeance. "That was my hope."

There was an uncomfortable silence.

"Tell me about your tradition," Rose said at last. "I've never known an Italian witch."

"The women call themselves *strega*; the men are known as *stregone*. My tradition is from northern Italy, where it's called Fanarric. It deals with the earth mysteries. La Vecchia—the old ways—was reorganized in Italy during the persecutions into three separate traditions to help preserve its secrets. The other two—Janarra and Tanarra —safeguard the lunar and stellar lore."

Rose shook her head. "That sounds terribly structured. We've always worked loosely, autonomously."

"Yes, well, in Italy lies the Vatican, with all that implies. And by the fourteenth century those of our kind were becoming scarce. A great holy woman, her name was Aradia, chose that time to appear among the peasants, and she reestablished the old ways. She was the one who organized the triad traditions."

Rose set the bread near the oven to rise, then poured coffee for them both. "You were lucky to have had your Aradia."

"Yes, we think so."

"So, your gifts are earth-related?"

Sylvan nodded. "Nature, her creatures, the veins of energy that pass through her."

"Good. You and my son will work well together. His gifts are similar. Specifically, he can control the weather —an invaluable gift for a farmer. He inherited that ability from me and his father both."

Sylvan felt a knot of resistance take root in her stomach. She didn't want anything to do with Rose's son. "Where is his father?" she asked, changing the subject.

Rose waved her hand absently. "Out there. Or dead. I don't know. He was an Indian who killed my family and took me forcibly."

Sylvan felt compassion for Rose's history, but she knew that the gods invariably had their reasons. "You were lucky to have had your man of power."

Rose became momentarily pensive. Then she smiled, and the harshness of her features softened. "Yes, I think so."

"About your son—"

"Please save him from that woman! If you don't, he'll be ruined. He's more mystical than practical, and he'll not survive her, you understand. And there'll be no more Hawthornes. He's the last of the line. The Puritans didn't manage to wipe us out, nor did the Indians. Don't let one evil *bruja* do it to us."

Rose's passion took Sylvan aback, and she withheld her dissent. *The gods have their reasons*, she heard a voice in her head say. "I'll consider your request," she said softly.

5

Denver flew with the gods. Exhilaration filled him as he circled high above the earth in the company of black ravens, red hawks, golden eagles, and white condors. The birds weren't truly of the animal kingdom, however. They were, like Denver, in disguise. They spoke to him in Gaelic and Cheyenne and Incan—he assumed that the Incan was a distant ancestral link through his father— and he understood their words, which conveyed great mystical truths. His spirit soared as he began to comprehend the elusive nature of divine reality. He looked down and saw the world as a brilliant web of multicolored light woven together to create the illusion of substance. He felt the air beneath his wings as the potent mind supporting the tapestry that was life as he knew it. He felt the feathers of his body begin to slough off, then his skin, then his blood and organs, until there was nothing left but his essence, and his essence was one with the potent mind. It was then that he began to weave the tapestry of multicolored light. He designed the form of a great bird, complete with blood, organs, skin, and feathers. And once again, he was a bird flying high with the gods.

The sky darkened, and from the slate of clouds that shadowed him emerged a grotesque vulture. It was deformed and emitted the stench of death, and from its beak dripped a bloody drool that spoke of hapless victims. It flew straight at him with the speed of lightning and struck him with violence. Stunned, he fell from the sky. His body hit the earth with tremendous force, and his mind told him that he must surely have died, but he found himself inside the form of a small rabbit with mottled fur. He looked up and saw the swift descent of outstretched claws. Terrified, he scampered through the field in search of shelter, but he didn't find it soon enough. As he was swept back up into the air, he shrieked with despair and tried to wriggle free of the beast's grasp. He struggled—

"It's all right," he heard the insincere voice say.

—and struggled—

"Denver, come out of it. It's all right."

He opened his eyes to find himself in Anita's embrace. For a moment, she seemed repulsive and foul, but that image passed quickly.

She released him and offered an odd-tasting brew to drink. He sipped it without great relish, but it seemed to help dispel the sick feeling of dread that the peyote had inspired in him.

"Too many buttons this time," she said.

"Maybe," he agreed.

"We'll cut back next time."

"Yes." He felt as if the room were spinning, and his

stomach juices began to surge. He made it off the bed, through the cabin, and out the front door just in time to vomit all over his mother's shoes.

Her hands on her hips, she regarded his condition with disgust. "Having a good time, I see." Her tone was drier than her shoes.

He shielded his eyes from the bright light of morning. "Go home, Mother."

"I came to fetch you back with me. We have new-comers to settle in. We also have house guests." She raised her voice, throwing it into the depths of Anita's house through the open door. "We have a beautiful, young *strega*—that's an Italian witch—living with us now. I think she'd make you a wonderful wife."

Denver groaned. "Mother, don't."

"She's talented, her gifts are strong, and she's got wide hips . . . wide for bearing babies with ease."

Denver reached behind him and drew the door closed. "That's enough."

Rose grinned with self-satisfaction. "Yes, I think so, too. Coming?"

He sighed and wiped his mouth. "Sorry about your shoes."

"I can get more shoes. But I've only got one son. And I love him very much."

Denver felt remorse but covered it with an excuse. "I don't get sick on it very often. Most of the time I just visit the gods."

"There'll be time enough for that when you join them. But for now, you're in this world and have a destiny here to pursue. They would want you to do that. That's why they've given you a human birth."

"And what kind of destiny do you think I have?"

"I've always felt that your destiny lies in your unborn children. I have this sense of the future, of a time to come when the Hawthornes will have an important role to play in the survival of the old ways . . . kind of like Aradia did."

"Aradia? Who the hell is that? Mother, you're an old, babbling fool."

Rose winced.

Denver felt remorse again. He took her hand. "I'm sorry. Let's go home."

She nodded and forced a smile. "Yes, son, let's go home."

6

It didn't take long before Sylvan's soft heart forgave Denver his initial indiscretions. It was obvious that he had been bewitched by the *bruja*. But the *bruja*'s powers were strong, and he remained spellbound.

"So, is Denver handsome?" Antonio asked.

Sylvan placed a glass of wine in his hands. He had joined her in the basement room she was using as an art studio.

"Not very, but he's not ugly either. He has a gentleness I like."

Antonio made a sound of disapproval. "Are you sure that's not just plain weakness? You've always had a soft spot for the wounded and helpless. You're talking about a man here, not a stray animal."

Sylvan was momentarily touched by anger but admitted to herself the truth of his observations. "Weak isn't necessarily bad."

"According to the gods you worship, it is. Look at nature. Only the strong survive her tests."

"Well, I think it's important that Denver survive. Rose has a feeling about the destiny of his heirs. And I keep hearing a voice telling me that the gods brought me here for a higher purpose than the one we had in mind."

"Has he responded to you at all?"

Sylvan sighed. "No."

"Then it's time you start using your magic, woman." He paused to slurp his wine. "The gods always did enjoy a good fight."

It was near midnight, and the full moon threw a silver glow through Sylvan's uncurtained bedroom window. She sat naked on the floor and basked in the light for a time, drawing down the divine power that the beams

234

symbolized. She took up her ritual brush—the one that
had been passed down through her mother—and began
to brush her unbraided hair. She drew the stiff bristles
slowly from her scalp down to the ends of her long black
hair, and as she did so she sang the song she had
been taught. It wasn't long before she began to experience the magnetic energy that her act of magic was
raising. With each stroke of the brush, her hair began to
crackle and spit sparks. The hair on her arms and legs
rose up in response, and the air around her grew warm.
When the power was sufficient, she directed it in a spell.

"Blessed Diana, Queen of the Witches, hear my plea.
Bring that man's desire to me, so shall it be."

The words spoken, she closed her eyes and created
the vision.

Denver lay spread-eagled on Anita's bed while she,
kneeling between his legs, worked to consume his essence. Elated by the wine they had shared, he relaxed
and submitted to her ministrations. She took his entire
length into her mouth and down into her throat, where
she held it while she hummed. The vibration she created
sent shock waves through his organ that caused him to
gasp. She began to slide her mouth up and down on his
shaft while her tongue caressed its underside artfully.
All the while, she gently milked his testicles with her
soft fingertips. He fought the urge to grasp her head and
thrust himself into her, because he knew it would ruin
her carefully orchestrated performance. Instead he channeled his aggressive desires into attention to her breasts.
His hands massaged and his fingers pinched, and she
squirmed in delighted response.

As he floated on the sea of pleasure she had conjured
for him, he began to think of Sylvan. Disconcerted, he
tried to drive her image from his mind, but it refused to
leave. He saw her, for the first time, as a woman with
erotic possibilities. Up until now, he had viewed her only
as a wedge his mother was trying to drive between him
and Anita. He had virtually ignored her. But suddenly
he recognized how pretty her tiny face was and what a
nice curve she had to her hips. Her small breasts even

seemed inviting; he realized he could completely engulf them with his mouth, and he found that concept appealing for a change. He wondered what sexual secrets *stregas* possessed that *brujas* might not.

He pulled himself out of Anita's mouth, and she smiled and settled back on the bed with her legs spread. But, instead of mounting her, he got up and started to get dressed.

"What the hell are you doing?"

"I'm sorry, Anita, but I've got to go."

"You've got to what?"

"Go. I'm sorry, but I've got to get home. I . . . I forgot something."

She watched in disbelief as he tried to get his massive erection tucked into his pants. "You're going to go like that? Why don't you at least let me get rid of it for you first?"

"I appreciate it, but I can't wait." As he bolted out of the front door, he heard the empty wine bottle crash against the wall of Anita's bedroom.

Driven by his sudden, urgent need for Sylvan, he whipped his horse into a hard gallop and made it home in record time.

When he arrived, he quietly entered Sylvan's room and found her lying naked on her bed, the soft glow of moonlight through the window illuminating her form.

"I've been waiting for you," she said.

Wordlessly, he began taking off his clothes; his erection still full, it popped free of its restraints eagerly. He sat down on the edge of the bed, and his hands began to explore her body. Her skin was like satin to the touch, and he caressed it appreciatively. Her body hair, like that on her head, was silky and attractive, and he ran his fingers through all of it. He spread her legs and inserted a finger inside. A hot tightness greeted him, and he felt a thrill pass through his loins. He had never been with a woman who held the promise of encasing him so snugly. He bent to kiss her mouth and was aroused even more by the sweetness of her breath.

"Become one with me," she whispered, and he could resist no longer.

He moved onto her and was about to penetrate when he felt the blood leave his penis in a rush. In disbelief, his hand flew down to examine himself, and it discovered only limp flesh. Embarrassment flooded him, and he rolled off of her.

Her hand darted to explore, and she knew in an instant who had snatched his desire away from them. But she decided it would be wise to hold her tongue. Instead she snuggled up in the crook of his arm and pulled the covers over them. "Maybe the gods want us to wait."

"Maybe," he muttered.

"Hold me. Make me feel safe and loved," she asked.

After a moment's hesitation, he wrapped his arms around her, and together they fell asleep.

7

"Of all the luck, I have to come up against the Delilah of witchdom."

Rose sighed and began to pace the length of Sylvan's studio. "What are you going to do?"

"This for starters." Sylvan, who was standing at her workbench, held up a small wooden ball which she had carved and on which she was using a resin glue to paste small squares of silvered glass. "A witch ball. When it's done, we'll hang it in the front window, and it'll reflect away from us all negativity. Her spells will return to her and leave us untouched."

Rose nodded with approval. "Good. What else?"

Sylvan held up a small bottle filled with pins, needles, shards of glass, herbs, and wine. "A witch bottle. Once it's charged and sealed, it'll pierce and drown any evil that comes our way. I'll bury it out by the front gate of the grounds."

"Perfect." Rose grinned. "We'll show her, won't we?"

An uneasy feeling arose in Sylvan. She had never encountered anyone like Anita before, and her confidence was shaken by the events the night of the full moon. "Sure we will," she said anyway. It never hurt to be positive.

"For now, it's getting late and dinner's ready. Your father's already at the table with his napkin all tucked in. Chicken and dumplings tonight. Shall we?"

Sylvan's stomach growled in anticipation. "Denver?"

Rose shook her head. "He's still at the Hunters', planning the Samhain festivities." It was October 31, the witches' New Year. "We'll join them later. Maybe you can share with us some of the traditions Italian witches honor on Samhain."

"Shadowfest," Sylvan said. "We call it Shadowfest."

"See, we have so much to learn from one another." Rose put her long arms around the tiny woman and gave her a warm hug. "I'm so grateful you're here."

Hand in hand, they headed up the stairs to the kitchen, when Sylvan felt the sudden energy drain. Her knees buckled, and her head began to swim. She reached out to grasp the railing and lost her hold on Rose, who, in a condition akin to Sylvan's, fell down the stairs. Above her, Sylvan heard her father's chair overturn and her father's body slam against the floor with a resounding thud. Waves of nausea flooded Sylvan as she looked down to see Rose's twisted body in a heap at the bottom of the stairs. Slowly and carefully, Sylvan inched her way down.

"What?" Rose's voice was faint, and her eyelids fluttered only momentarily in a vain effort to stay open.

"We took a hit," Sylvan said, her tongue feeling swollen and lazy. She had never before realized a psychic attack could be so potent. "Anita."

"Hard. Hit hard," Rose said. "Can't move. Think I'm dying."

The spinning in Sylvan's head grew worse, and she felt a terrifying darkness rising to claim her. She was sure that if she succumbed to it she would be plunged into a dank labyrinth from which she would never emerge. Her hand snaked its way into her dress pocket, where it clutched her *nanta* bag, a small leather pouch that contained sacred items which linked her with the forces of the earth. "Janus, god of two faces, turn away from us your face of death and let your face of life shine upon us," she whispered passionately.

238

The room seemed to lighten a little.

"Rose."

"Still here."

"Where do the Hunters live?"

"Take Main Street east until it ends. Keep going. Another mile, you'll come to their farm."

Sylvan took her *nanta* bag and pressed it into Rose's hand, then she began to crawl up the stairs.

In the kitchen she found her father's body. For him, it was too late for prayers.

"No time to weep," she whispered as she gave him a farewell kiss and, still too weak to walk, crawled out of the back door toward the stable. The stable boy had also taken a measure of Anita's attack. He had fallen and struck his head on the anvil upon which he had been hammering horseshoes. His blood flowed freely, but Sylvan could stop only long enough to wrap a strip of her petticoat around his wound. She pulled herself up onto the back of a mare, all the while trying to communicate her need to it.

At first, the horse seemed to comply with Sylvan's wishes and got her as far as Main Street, but then it became possessed by a madness that caused it to buck and squeal with frenzy. Sylvan clutched its mane and tried to calm it down, but it didn't respond. Finally, as if its tail had been set afire, it bolted past the small group of curious bystanders that had gathered and headed west at a furious gallop. Within minutes, they had left the town behind and were out in the wilderness, headed toward the mountains.

Sylvan laid her body down, wrapped her arms tightly around her captor's neck, and pressed her knees into its side. Her mind swimming, she tried to find an anchor in prayer.

Around her the night shadows swirled. Vague images, gray against the slate of darkness, rushed past her as the crazed mare chased its demons. The sound of hoofs and two pounding hearts merged, and Sylvan realized that both hearts were galloping to their deaths. In desperation, she tried again to communicate with the beast, but the thoughts she sent were stolen by the wind that their ride had invoked. With an explosion of red, her mind witnessed the mare's heart as it reached its limit of endurance. The horse and its rider went tumbling into oblivion.

Sylvan's last thoughts were of Denver and the tragedy of what his life would now become.

8

Thunder Eagle's face looked like a stretch of sun-baked red clay desert, and his hair was like the gray dirt that blew in the wind. He knew this because he had seen his reflection in the round mirror he found alongside a wagon trail in Wyoming. He had picked it up and kept it because it reminded him of the shield that Red Fire Woman had owned. And Red Fire Woman and the son she had borne him had been foremost in his mind for the past thirty-five years.

His body, though tired, was still straight. And his mind was still good. It was for this fact, more than anything else, that he thanked the Grandfathers.

When as a young man he had pursued his first vision quest, he had seen that he would someday return life to a woman. The woman, however, wasn't his beloved Morning Star or the woman with whom his seed was linked, Red Fire Woman. It was the woman the Grandfathers had brought to him on a crazy horse, in the middle of the night, at the outskirts of the foothills camp he had made. His medicine gift of wind had breathed life back into her as his youthful vision had instructed him. Her own medicine soon took over, and the woman who had been dead was made alive again.

By the light of the fire in his tipi, he gently washed the dirt and blood off of her and wondered why her life was such a special one. He decided that he didn't need to understand.

Her large brown eyes opened with sudden alarm. "Are you one of Anita's demons?" she asked in greeting.

He had learned to speak the white man's language through his travels of the previous three decades, and her words took him by surprise. He laughed. "Am I that ugly?"

For a moment she seemed disconcerted. "Yes."

He sighed. "When I was young I was considered quite handsome."

"So?" she pressed.

"No, I am not a demon. I'm an old Indian who found a . . . a hurt white woman at my feet. And who is this Anita?"

"She's the evil *bruja* who killed my father, hurt Rose, and has Denver spellbound."

Rose, Denver. In his visions, Thunder Eagle had come to learn of their white names. "Do these people live in Montvue?"

Sylvan nodded.

Thunder Eagle's heart began to race. "And how do you fit in with them?"

She tried to sit up but grasped her ribs and lay back down with a moan. "I'd marry Denver if Anita would let him go."

"Bruja?" He thought he knew the word. "Isn't that a sorceress?"

Sylvan nodded. "Evil. Powerful."

"What about you? Are you powerful, too?" It was a rhetorical question. She had had her breath returned to her, after all.

"Not as powerful as Anita."

He dusted a gash on her head with a dried herb mixture. "I think you're mistaken."

"How would you know? Are you a—what they call it—medicine man?"

"I'm a man with strong medicine."

Sylvan grasped his arm with desperate fingers. "Then help me."

Thunder Eagle set aside the herbs and took her hand in his. "That's why I'm here." He now understood why she was so special and why their paths had been destined to cross. "That's why I'm here."

Thunder Eagle had always known strong protection. He lent it to Sylvan in the form of his shield. He also offered her strategical advice.

"It seems to me that if Anita's power over Denver is that of illusion, then you simply must strip her of it."

Sylvan stooped gingerly to turn the spit upon which the venison was roasting. She had been under Thunder Eagle's care for five days and was trying to repay his kindness by preparing dinner. "How do I do that?"

"Create an image of the way she really is and present it to him."

Sylvan eased herself back down onto the sleeping robes. "Like a photograph?"

Thunder Eagle shook his head. "No, even photographs can capture illusion."

"I've never seen Anita."

"Ah, but you know her well. She introduced herself to you with great force. Translate the nature of that force into an image. Then show it to Denver. It'll be enough."

"Rose said she wasn't really ugly. Yet I felt her to be totally repulsive."

"It's likely that not even Rose is seeing the true Anita. Trust what you feel."

Sylvan pursed her lips thoughtfully. "Why can't Denver see? He's not stupid. I guess he really is just weak."

"He's a man of vision. His world isn't ordinary. He doesn't deal well with this one, but that doesn't mean he's weak."

"How do you know so much about Denver?"

Thunder Eagle started packing the bowl of his red stone pipe with tobacco. "Because I'm his father."

Shock, then understanding, showed in Sylvan's expression. "I think Rose still loves you."

Thunder Eagle felt a moment of pleasure. "I never thought she loved me much at all."

"Come back with me?"

He shook his head. "I've tried the white world. It doesn't suit me."

"You could help Denver."

"I am helping Denver."

Sylvan sighed with exasperation. "You're stubborn."

"A trait which I'm sure Denver has inherited, so get used to it."

He lit the pipe and said a silent prayer to the Grandfathers for his son, his son's mother, and his son's wife-to-be. Then he passed it to Sylvan. "Let's make pipe for the Hawthorne family, as they are today and as they will be in the future."

Sylvan smoked the prayer with him.

Finally, Thunder Eagle produced a hunk of gnarled wood, a piece of the root of a tree that had died of disease. "You say you can carve art. Make an Anita out of this."

Sylvan took it, her distaste for its aesthetic appeal evident. "It's ugly enough to work."

"It's your power that'll make it work."

A week later, under the cover of night, Thunder Eagle rode Sylvan back to Montvue and dropped her off near Hawthorne Manor.

She was reluctant to let go of his hand. "Stay."

"Go. And tell Red Fire Woman that I will always carry her in my heart. Until I die, and beyond."

"My father is dead. I'd like my children to know you."

"Your children will know your father through you, and me through Denver."

"Thank you for everything."

"I take no credit. I had no choice. There are powers that decide these things, you understand."

Sylvan thought of her voices. She understood.

Thunder Eagle rode off and left Sylvan holding his shield and the ugly, misshapen wooden figure that was Anita's true image.

Quickly, she made her way to the manor. She let herself in and found Rose dozing on the sofa. She shook her awake.

Rose's face came to life at the sight of Sylvan, and she stretched to embrace her. "I was sure you were dead," she said. "Oh, thank the gods you're not." She looked around nervously, then lowered her voice to a whisper. "Be careful. Things have changed."

"What things?"

Voices, strange to Sylvan's ears, came from the depths of the house.

"What's going on, Rose?"

Rose's attention had been captured by the shield that Sylvan held. "What's this? This is Magic Man's. How . . ."

The voices were coming closer.

"What's happened, Rose?"

"Well, your father passed over, and I can't walk anymore—it's all numb from the waist down, you see. And, well . . . how did you get Magic Man's shield?" She pried it out of Sylvan's hand to examine it more closely.

"So, the little *strega* is tougher than she looks, huh?" The woman's harsh voice caused both Sylvan and Rose to jump.

Sylvan looked up to see the living image of that which she held in her hand.

"You didn't knock, little *strega*. If you had, I would've told you that you aren't welcome in my home."

"Your home?"

Denver and two Mexican men followed Anita into the room.

"Sylvan. I thought you were dead." Denver's voice was a monotone.

Sylvan's mind raced. She had to be cautious. "Have you decided to marry Anita after all?"

Denver nodded. His glazed eyes veiled the life within.

Sylvan forced a smile. "Well, then I made you an appropriate gift while I was gone." She held up the leather bag that held the image. "I'm a sculptor," she told Anita. She held the bag up to Denver. "It's a statue of your fiancée."

Slowly, like a zombie, Denver started toward where Sylvan stood. "How thoughtful of you," he said.

"What kind of trick is this?" Anita asked. "Get the bag," she ordered her sons.

In one swift movement, Sylvan opened the bag, pulled out the statue, and moved to hold it up in front of Denver's face. "This is Anita. Don't you think it's a wonderful likeness?"

Anita screamed. Her sons froze. Denver blinked.

"What?" Denver asked.

"This is what Anita really looks like. She's had you under a spell of illusion." Sylvan shook the statue under Denver's nose. "Look at it real good. This is what you plan to take as your bride."

"Grotesque. Hideous." Denver's eyes began to return to life as his expression changed to one of disgust.

Sylvan pushed at him. "Turn around. Look at her. See for yourself."

Silence seized the room as Denver slowly turned to face the woman of whom he had been enamored. When his eyes fell on her, he gagged, then lunged for the marble spittoon that stood by the fireplace, where he retched. "Gods," he mumbled, then retched again.

Relief flooded Sylvan.

"So, the little *strega* has won, has she?" Anita's voice seemed to shake the house. "We'll see who wins in the end." She took a few purposeful steps forward, then pointed her fingers at Sylvan's belly in the sign of a hex.

Sylvan thought too late of the shield; Rose still held it.

"I curse your womb, woman. You'll only have one child, and he will be a bane to those who love him. And all his children will die horrible deaths, as shall their children, too. Mark my words and live with the terror they invoke."

As Anita swept from the room and the house and their lives, Sylvan knew she would always remain with them.

For Sylvan's womb told her that the curse had taken.

Chapter Nine

July 1992

1

Melanie ordered her third Cherry Coke float, only momentarily giving thought to the awesome amount of calories she was consuming. It didn't matter anyway, she quickly decided. There was no way to stop the expansion of her belly, so why try?

Melanie and her best friend, Amber, were sitting in a small booth at Happy Daze, Montvue's only teenage hangout. It had an old-fashioned soda fountain, a drive-in hamburger stand, and an overall decor that was classic fifties, but it also had a pinball arcade, a computer game alcove, and a wide-screen television that was tuned to MTV.

"God, I can't believe you're preggers," Amber said as she picked at her banana split. "That's simply gruesome."

"Tell me about it."

"So, are you and Frankie going to, like, get married or anything?"

"Don't mention the emword. I've sworn off men."

Amber reached across the table to give Melanie a

consoling pat, and her long hair—streaked with a rainbow of colors in accordance with the latest fad—fell into the high mound of whipped cream that topped her breakfast. She stuck the errant strand into her mouth, and her tongue wiped it clean. "I've heard that before."

"This time I mean it."

"Well, I guess they are a lot of work. Since my sister got married she's *aged*. It's been less than a year, and she's already had to start dying her hair to hide the gray. And my mother . . . well, look how shitty she looks after putting up with one of *them* for almost twenty years."

"Shitty," Melanie agreed.

"Then, no matter how hard my sister tries to keep the place fixed up, you go to visit her and there's all this groady manslime—you know, stinky socks on the floor, greasy motorcycle parts in the kitchen sink, dirty car repair manuals on the TV. It's truly a pukey state of affairs."

"Pukey," Melanie agreed, wishing that particular word hadn't been brought up so early in the morning.

"So, like, are you going to have the baby Kirbyed or something?"

"Mine's a fertility religion. We don't just go and vacuum away babies. It's not a wonderful way to honor the Goddess, you know? Besides, when we do decide not to follow through with a pregnancy for some reason, there are herbs and things we use."

"Mmmm." Amber pensively began to smash her banana and then stir it together with the ice cream and toppings into an unsightly mess.

Melanie eyed her friend warily. "What's wrong?"

Amber didn't look up from her project. "My dad's being a shit about us."

"Us?"

"Me and you, the rainbow kid and the witch. I never told him, but with the preacher going on . . . he doesn't want us to hang out anymore. Even made me go to mass last Sunday—with my hair in a hat, of course."

Melanie's stomach turned over, and the nausea began to rise again. "Please don't let them take away my best friend, too," she said, her voice small.

Amber looked up and grinned. "Dad says the alternative is mass twice a week, and I gotta start going to confession."

"With your hair in a hat, of course."

Amber nodded, then shrugged. "I guess you're worth it."

"Thank you."

"What's it like at home these days?"

Melanie tensed. "The bitch-in-law is now a witch."

"Pardon me?"

"Leigh went away and came back one of us. Someone—I can't talk about who—changed her."

"You sound angry about it."

"My whole family—what's left of it, anyway—is. She had no right."

"I think it's kinda courageous of her. She chose to stand with you guys. I mean, face it, it's not the best time to be joining the ranks, you know?"

Melanie picked her glass up off the table and slammed it back down noisily. "Let's change the subject, okay?"

"As you wish," Amber said in her formal tone of disapproval.

"You said you had something for me to check out?"

The ice cracked, and Amber grinned again. "That new guy in town, Ryan. I got his watch." She fumbled in her purse to retrieve it, then dropped it in Melanie's hands.

"You're quite the rip-off artist these days."

"Oh, I'll give it back when we're done. Actually, returning lost stuff to these guys is a great gimmick. Makes them feel beholden."

"I'm sure." Melanie examined Amber's find. It was an old-fashioned wind-up watch with a round face and three hands. The second hand quickly swept by the Russian writing in the lower half of the dial. *Perestroika* had opened trade with the West, and the quaint Soviet watches had become all the rage. "Well, at first glance I'd say he's not poor."

"He drives a Testarossa."

"Even rich guys produce groady manslime."

Amber shrugged. "No big deal. I already dye my hair."

Melanie closed her eyes and felt the images from the watch pass to her mind; psychometry was her magical gift. She received the impressions both mentally, in a

visual fashion, and emotionally. She saw the Testarossa
—it was red—and she saw a home. It was of modern
design, like those in the well-to-do Blue Fox subdivision
up on the hill. "He lives in Blue Fox."

"Yeah, I know." Amber sounded greedy.

A kaleidoscope of colors and unique designs raced
through Melanie's mind, and she had to will them to
slow down so she could focus better. It took a few
moments for her to realize she was looking at art. In the
bottom left corner of one of the canvases, she saw the
initials *RT*. "What's his last name?"

"Turner."

"Your Ryan's an artist. Pretty good from what I can
see."

"Ohhh." Amber sounded orgasmic.

A feminine silver-gray tabby cat came to mind, and
Melanie felt waves of tender affection and selfless devotion. "He's got a cat named . . . Precious, I think. She'll
be powerful competition for control of his heartstrings."

"That's okay. I'd never—well, hardly ever—go for a
guy who doesn't like cats. I have a theory that if they
don't like cats, they deep down don't like women, either."

Women. The Ryan in Melanie's mind had an emotionally charged issue about women. Melanie tried to pursue
it. She saw a girl in the night shadows, leaning back in
the leather car seat, unbuttoning her blouse, a come-
hither expression on her face. She saw the plump breasts
straining at the seams of the bra; the well-manicured
hand reaching up to undo the hooks in the middle of the
cleavage; the white lace falling away to reveal the tight
nipples, straining to beg attention; and the utterly cold
reaction Ryan felt. Melanie frowned.

"What is it?"

Melanie ignored her; she didn't want to lose her concentration. She saw Ryan leave the car in distress and
make his way to the grimy men's room the drive-in
theater offered its patrons. Ryan splashed cold water on
his face and turned to see a young man. Mutual recognition. "I told you it wouldn't work. When are you going
to face facts?" the man asked, then opened a toilet stall
and stepped inside, leaving the door ajar. Melanie felt

Ryan's sexual quickening as he followed his lover and slid the latch shut behind them.

She quickly opened her eyes and shook her head to rid her mind of the images. She didn't want to see, or feel, what happened next.

"Forget him, he's gay."

"Oh, no." Amber's fist struck the table. "No!"

Melanie tossed the watch for her to catch. "Better you should know right off the bat."

"It might be worth a sex change."

"I leave that decision to you."

Amber sighed. "Well, fuck it. When I went to church Sunday, we sat next to the McKays. Brett's face has cleared up. I'll try and grab his rosary or something next Sunday. If we're lucky, maybe we'll discover him to be only a little kinky."

"You're such a fickle broad."

Amber grinned and licked her lips. "Healthy. And incredibly horny."

"Yeah, well, watch yourself. Look where that kind of mentality got me."

They flagged down the soda jerk and ordered another round.

"Speaking of sex, look at what just came in."

Melanie's eyes followed Amber's gaze, and she saw him. They called him Essex—just Essex—and he had moved to Montvue that past spring. Unsavory rumors of all sorts abounded about who and what he was, and the town had not extended a hand of welcome to the unusual newcomer. It had been said that he was a white slaver, a drug dealer, an undercover spy—although what he might find to spy on in Montvue was never discussed— a criminal on the lam, and an international playboy in hiding from an irate husband. Melanie had learned to ignore the small-town mentality and its rumor mill. All she knew for sure was what she could see for herself. He was in his early twenties, he seemed to be independently wealthy from all appearances, and he looked— and dressed—like a British rock star. He even had the smooth English accent. She heard it for the first time when he ordered a Coke at the counter.

"I heard he just bought the old Snyder farm," Amber whispered. "That's like a hundred and fifty acres. What do you think he does?"

"Well, if I have to take my pick of the available choices, I'd bet he's a dope dealer."

"No, the worst drugs I associate with are my stogies and mother's ruin," he said from his seat at the counter. He flashed them a winning smile.

Melanie was flustered. "My, what big ears you have."

"My, what gossipy natures you have."

His accent was nice to listen to. He didn't have the snooty tones with which Vivian and her family spoke. It was more raw, more *sexy*, Melanie thought with dismay.

"Join us?" Amber asked, and when Melanie kicked her, she covered admirably with a mere grunt and a forced smile.

"Thought you'd never ask, luv." He moved to take a seat at their table.

"So, should we be nervous about your use of stogies and . . . mother's what?

"Ruin." He pulled a half-pint of Beefeater's gin out of the inside pocket of his light leather jacket, opened the bottle, and splashed some of it into his Coke. Surreptitiously, he offered the bottle to his companions.

"Not with a float. Thanks anyway."

"Bananas and gin before noon? Putrid."

He stowed away the bottle and removed a slender brown cigar from the same pocket. "Stogie," he explained. "Mind?"

The girls shook their heads, and he lit up. The smoke carried the pleasant aroma of rum and cherries.

"I'm Amber Whittaker, and this is Melanie Hawthorne."

"Essex."

"Essex what?" Amber asked.

He ignored her. "So, Miss Melanie, I've been reading about you in the rags. Understand you're a witch."

There was no escape. "What of it?"

"Don't get your feathers ruffled, luv. I'm from England. Over there the witches have a bloody union. I've no problem with it."

"Essex what?" Amber repeated.

"Just Essex."

"If you're not a pusher, what are you?" Melanie asked.

"My family's veddy upper-crust. Didn't like my style and banished me to the colonies. Pay me to stay here where I can't embarrass them."

Melanie didn't believe him. She knew enough from Vivian's branch of the family to know that his accent didn't jibe with the story.

Amber, however, was impressed. She issued her second orgasmic noise of the morning.

"Me and my mates are having a party Friday night under the full moon. Out on my farm. A couple of pretty birds would lend the landscape some beauty. Want to come?"

"Ah, would we be the only birds to be caged?" Melanie asked coyly.

"No, just the rarest specimens."

Amber became pensive again and began another search-and-destroy mission inside her banana split.

"I know the town has some strange ideas concerning what I'm about," Essex said astutely. "I won't tell anyone you're coming if you don't. No need to stir up a hornet's nest."

Amber looked up and grinned. "Now, that's an idea."

"Besides," Essex said, "who knows what kind of trouble that bloody bloke Cody might make for me if he found out I was entertainin' a witch on the full moon."

2

Leigh had been a witch for less than a week, and already the nature of her power was beginning to make itself evident. She stood across the room from Adrian, who was standing with his hands buried deep in his pockets, looking out the ivy-covered window, and she could feel his longing. He was longing for his father with quiet desperation. His stance, along with the tiny golfing cap he had begun to wear angled over one eye, was a blatant mimicry of Craig, perhaps some strange form of sympathetic magic. *Act as if* . . . "Pacifically, I'd say it's going to rain," Adrian said with as much authority as he could muster. *Specifically* was his newest word, but he couldn't quite get the correct pronounciation.

"I think you're probably right," Leigh said gently, the tears of his pain brimming in her eyes. *Gods, is empathy going to be my gift?* she silently asked, appalled at the thought. Hadn't she suffered enough of her own emotional pain in life? Was she going to have to suffer everyone else's, too?

"Want you to know that we're right proud of you, Mom."

His tone was Craig's. It was more than she could bear. "I . . . I did it because I love you and Kammi. I wanted us to be a team."

"What the gods have joined together, let no preacher man put asunder."

Leigh caught her breath. Had those words come from Adrian? He tugged at the cap's brim, in a manner reminiscent of Craig. "That's pacifically speaking, of course."

"Of course."

3

Diane Fox, who had braved the torrential downpour to check her mailbox, was dismayed to find another one of those unwelcome letters waiting for her. She could tell by the sign of the fish that was in the upper lefthand corner of the envelope where the return address should have been. She considered tossing it away unopened, but her reporter's instinct for knowing the facts overcame her emotional discomfort, and she slid her razor-sharp letter opener along the top edge. She unfolded the enclosed sheet of white paper and read the typewritten message.

I see that you haven't yet recanted your earlier printed statements in defense of the Hawthorne witches. You are teetering precariously on the edge of the precipice, and if you're not careful, you're going to fall in. Of course, the Devil is most assuredly waiting for your descent, lurking beneath you with his pointed prick at attention, ready to spear your pussy and fill you with his demon filth. But, then, that might be something you'd enjoy. Because you are a witch-loving whore. The question remains, who—or what—really is the father of your bastard child? Act now, before it is too late.

Like the others, it was unsigned.

Trembling, Diane put it in her dresser drawer with the others. Up until the receipt of this one, the letters had been an unpleasant nuisance. Now it was worse. They had brought Tiffany into the battle, and that was something she couldn't leave unanswered.

Since she couldn't respond directly to those responsible, she'd make her reply a public one. She still held the power of the press in her hands.

4

Until now, Jason had never understood the nature of his power. It had always bothered him that everyone else in the family exhibited their own unique talents from the earliest of childhood years, and he had never demonstrated an inborn propensity toward doing anything unusual at all. However, it now seemed as if it had taken this crisis to stir the embers into flame. He now realized that he held the power of the warrior. And he was determined to use it to its fullest.

"I've never felt more exhilarated," he confessed to Gil as they sat together on Jason's bed, going over the last details of their battle plan. "This is what I was born to do."

Gil offered a weak smile. "Are you sure we're not taking this too far?"

"Fuck no. Look how far they've taken it, over and over again."

"Why don't we just hit Preacher Cody? Don't you think that would be the old 'nipping it in the bud' strategy?"

"Because this'll hurt more. And the plan is not to get mad but to get even."

"Well, we're certainly going to do that," Gil conceded, his regret evident. "And it's going to be done in spades."

5

Melanie hadn't decided that she would rather pursue Essex in lieu of Frank, but she thought the interest of another man might reawaken Frank's interest in her. However, before laying out the bait, she wanted to be sure the fish was there. So, she didn't tell Frank she was going to the party at Essex's farm. She didn't tell anyone.

The girls, decked out in their most hip finery, met at Happy Daze and, in Melanie's Porsche, drove out to the country to the old Snyder farm. It was almost dark when they pulled into the driveway at the secluded farmhouse.

The moon loomed low over the horizon, hugging the earth intimately—as a mother and daughter might do, Melanie thought as she paused to offer silent homage. Her hand slid down to her belly, and she patted it gently. *I promise you that I'll be there for you, even if your dad isn't,* her mind told her fetus. She was determined to give her baby more than she had grown up with. True, she had had a father, but he hadn't been there emotionally for her. No one had been there emotionally for her.

Essex came out from the house to greet them, and when Melanie rolled down the car window, his musky tobacco-tinged scent wafted in on the warm summer air. She shivered in response.

"Hiya, ducks. Have trouble getting away?"

"We did what you suggested," Amber said, winking at him. "We're on the QT tonight."

He winked back. "Well, I'm glad it worked out, luv. Do the old man a favor and pull in around back and park with the other cars."

Melanie did as she was instructed, and, following on foot, Essex helped them from the car. Offering each an arm, he gallantly escorted them into his home.

The back porch was screened and opened into a huge, country kitchen. A tall, shapely teenage girl with long, black, heavily ratted hair was removing a cookie sheet from the oven. She was dressed in skin-tight black jeans, a silver-sequined tube top, and what Frank liked to call CFM shoes. They were daggerlike spiked heels. Euphemistically, Frank told Melanie the initials stood for "Come fondle me." However, when she wore CFM shoes for Frank, he ended up doing much more to her than merely fondling. Melanie was dismayed to find herself thinking about Frank; she closed her eyes for a moment and willed him from her mind, then reopened them when Essex introduced the vixen cook.

"This here's my sis, Lilith."

"Charmed," Lilith said in a phony-sounding British accent.

Melanie's greeting caught in her throat when she noticed the necklace Lilith wore. It was a black inverted pentacle on a silver chain. She took a deep breath and tried not to jump to any conclusions. The satanic symbol had been adopted by many in the heavy metal music crowd as a badge of rebellion. It was probably nothing.

Essex grabbed a hot sugar cookie off the sheet and gestured for Melanie and Amber to follow him through the dutch doors that led into the living room, where they were met by a dozen teenagers.

Names like Drac, Pox, Judas, Jezebel, Salome, Pandora, and Jynx were thrown at Melanie, and the entire crowd dressed like bizarre refugees from a bad vampire movie. The ambience of the room was strictly horror. An open mahogany coffin lined with red satin stood in the middle of the room, and flickering red and black candles were scattered about anchored in holders designed like skulls. An entire wall was decorated with gruesome antique weapons: swords, maces, daggers, and iron collars. Saint-Saëns's *Danse Macabre* played from an unseen stereo system, and dusty volumes of Dante's *Inferno*, Marlowe's *Dr. Faustus*, and Stoker's *Dracula* were displayed on end tables. The room was heavy with the smell of basilica, the incense favored in Catholic masses. An upside-down cross hung on the wall over the fireplace.

"Totally," Amber said with awe.

"Yeah, but totally what?" Melanie asked. She wasn't comfortable. It was too strange.

A small fountain that resembled a coiled cobra spewed blood-red punch from its fangs, and Essex filled two goblets and handed them to the girls.

Melanie declined it. "I think we're leaving. This doesn't seem to be the kind of party we expected."

He grinned. "Oh, duckie, don't be a square. These are just our usual full-moon antics. We do Halloween once a month. It's fun." He urged the goblet on her again.

She ignored it.

"Oh, let's stay a little while," Amber said, then tasted the punch. "Mmmm. Jesus, this is good." She drank some more. "Mmmm. Never tasted anything like this. What's in it?"

"Exotic liqueurs and tropical juices." He took Melanie's hand, placed the goblet in it, and wrapped her fingers around the stem. "Don't be a square."

Melanie sighed and accepted the cup. She took a small, polite sip and resisted the urge to drain the delicious beverage, as Amber was doing. She felt a nagging need to be cautious.

"Ah, this is a little extravagant for a once-a-month deal," she said.

"I can afford to be extravagant. I'm loaded." He grinned again, and Melanie felt disarmed. He certainly was attractive.

"So, which of these interestingly named cuties is your number one?" Melanie asked.

"Actually, a bird named Belladonna was my pet until last month. She's gone now."

"Too bad," Melanie said. *Good,* she thought.

"Can I have some more?" Amber asked, thrusting the goblet at Essex. "Makes me feel oh so good."

"Help yourself," he said.

"Don't overdo it," Melanie warned, feeling like an old mother hen.

Amber made a face at her and moved to refill her goblet with the cobra's venom.

"So, tell me all about being a witch," Essex said.

Melanie took another small sip of ambrosia. "Not much to tell."

"So, you are one, then."

"Didn't say that."

"Didn't have to."

His magnetic eyes captured hers, and she had to force herself to break the link. She scanned the room. "Where'd you find all these weird people?" she asked.

"Boulder, mostly."

"Boulder does have a lot of oddballs."

"Are you insinuating that my mates are freaky?"

"Yes, I am. Every last one of them," she said, then giggled. The small amount of punch she had ingested was making her feel giddy. That thought was sobering, considering how much of it Amber had drunk. She looked around for her friend and discovered her to be leaning unsteadily against the wall, in seeming deep conversation with a suit of armor.

"Is there someone in that thing?" Melanie asked Essex. "No."

Melanie giggled again. "Oh, dear. Maybe we should get her a cup of coffee."

"Tea?"

"If that's what you've got."

"Right. Cuppa tea," he said agreeably, then made his way to the kitchen.

Lest she be tempted to drink any more punch, Melanie put her goblet down on the coffee table, then began to wander around the room in exploration.

On the mantel of the fireplace, there was a miniature nativity scene, only the infant in the manger wasn't the baby Jesus; it was some kind of barbarous, demonic monstrosity. The sight of it upset Melanie. Although not a Christian herself, she had respect for the religious beliefs of others—even though they had never been inclined to extend the same courtesy to her people. That Essex and his friends seemed to revel in such blasphemy increased her growing discomfort.

On the small table at the end of the leather couch was a statue. It was of a man and woman, wearing collars and leashes, kneeling behind a figure of the Devil. They were each kissing one of his buttocks. Melanie thought it was disgusting.

She moved to the wall that held the display of weapons and examined them. There were unusual markings scratched into the handle of one of the swords. Curious, she reached up to touch it, and when her fingers made contact with the cool metal, her mind was cruelly captured by it. The images came fast, and the emotions came hard. She saw ritual, but it wasn't like the kind she practiced. It was dark and ugly. Intense waves of blood lust, fear, greed, and pain coursed through her, and she began to tremble. Real blood poured from the fangs of the cobra fountain. Naked people smeared each other with the gray matter of brain.

The sword revealed those it had intimately known. A German Shepherd, a pig, a newborn human baby. She didn't want to see more, but morbid fascination kept her from releasing the sword.

She saw Belladonna, a young Asian girl of about sixteen. Her head, freed from her body by this sword, rolled onto the floor, its eyes frozen in horror. A large cast-iron pot caught the flow of blood.

"Oh, my gods, it's real. This is all real," she whispered. Her hand pulled away from the weapon and flew to her throat, where her pulse was throbbing hard with fear. She spun around on her heel and saw that Amber was now on the couch, sitting on the lap of someone Essex had called Adolf. She resisted the urge to race across the room and yank Amber into desperate motion, knowing that she would have to be more restrained about making an escape. Maybe if they assumed that the girls knew nothing, they would allow them to leave unharmed. If they knew that she knew, there would be no hope.

She forced a grin and made her way to the couch on jellyfish legs. "Come on, Amber. Time to go."

Amber looked at her with eyes that refused to focus. "Go? Already?"

"Yeah, I told Aunt Glynis I wouldn't be late."

"Your auntie, huh?" The voice of Essex came from behind.

Melanie tossed her head and giggled. "Yeah. The truth is, I told her I was coming here tonight—I can never fib to her—and I know she'll be worried and tell on me if I don't get back early. She's that way, you know."

Amber's eyes rolled, and she stood up. "You told? Shit, you said you wouldn't tell. Your grandma finds out, and she'll go to my folks. Shit, we gotta go."

Essex grinned and handed Amber the cup he held. "Drink the tea first, luv. You can't go home under the sheets . . . drunk. Come on, tip the cup."

Melanie couldn't let her drink it. There was no telling what he might have put in it. "No, Amber. We don't have time. We'll get you some coffee back at my place." She reached for the cup, but Essex grabbed her arm.

"Let her drink the tea, duckie. Meanwhile I'll give you the grand tour. An extra few minutes won't hurt."

She tried to break free of his grasp. "Yes, it will. We have to go *now*."

His grin disappeared and was replaced by a hard stare. "I don't think so." His fingers dug into her flesh, and he jerked her into motion. "*Now* we're going to take the tour."

"No!"

Amused eyes turned to stare. There was no sympathy in any of them.

Adolf eased Amber back down onto his lap.

Essex pulled Melanie from the room.

Melanie's head reeled as he forcibly led her up a flight of stairs and into a large bedroom. Locking the door behind them, he pushed her roughly onto the bed and began to tear at her clothes.

Panic flooded her. "What are you doing?"

"What do ya think?"

"You can't." Her mind raced. "I'm pregnant."

He grinned. "Oh, I like that."

"I told my aunt. She—"

A hard slap silenced her. "Don't give me that crap. You figured things out and made that up. I'm no fool, luv."

Within seconds, he had her jeans down and had his

rigid organ released from his pants. He flipped her over onto her belly.

"I like to take my women before we get down to more serious business. It makes things so much more intimate. Besides, you're the first real witch I'll have ever taken, and I can't wait to explore."

Melanie screamed as he pressed himself into her; she had never before been sodomized.

Excruciating pain tore through her, and her screams quickly turned to frenzied sobs.

"Stop! It hurts! My baby! Please stop!"

"It's the way the Devil does it, luv. Relax and enjoy."

She tried to twist and claw, but he only bore down harder and rougher.

"I've decided to call you Damiana," he whispered. "You incite me like a good aphrodisiac should."

"Please?" she whimpered.

"Oh, so you do like it. I thought you would once you tried it. As a matter of fact, there's a lot of kink we're going to get into together before you go under knife. Trust me, duckie. We're going to have a real good time."

6

Melanie had trouble walking when they returned to the party. Most of her bruises and swellings were hidden by the long black robe he had made her put on, but her face revealed some evidence of his violence against her.

The living room was darker than it had been before, and everyone else had donned robes similar to the one she wore. After her eyes adjusted to the dim light, she scanned to find Amber. It took a while before she realized that her friend was lying on top of the now closed casket. She was naked and tied down by leather straps.

Melanie raced to her side. Amber looked at her with eyes that were no longer fuzzy. They were wide and apprehensive.

"What are they doing, Melanie? What are they doing to me?"

Melanie fumbled with the restraints, and tears began to stream down her face. "You'll be okay. We're getting out of here."

Essex grabbed Melanie's hands and grinned. "Don't be silly, luv. You'll ruin all the fun." He shoved her into the arms of Judas, who held her in an iron grip.

Essex began to strip himself of clothes. "Like the sacrifice, the priest performs naked."

"Sacrifice?" Amber began to thrash about lamely. "Oh, sweet Jesus, he said sacrifice! What's going on? Melanie, help me!"

"Darlin', Melanie's not going to help you, she's going to help me," Essex said as he moved to claim a dagger from the arsenal on the wall. "I always wanted to work side by side with a witch. Might be I'll learn something, huh, luv?"

Melanie was frozen by Amber's horrified stare. "You're with them?" Amber asked, her voice a hoarse whisper. "I thought you were good. Oh, my God, the preacher, my dad, they were right about you."

"I . . . I'm *not* with them."

Essex laughed. "She's not only with us but has even been initiated by us. She's been butt-fucked by the Devil himself, little Amber."

"Oh, Melanie." Amber's voice was bitter with what she saw as her friend's betrayal.

Melanie's throat was tight. "Don't believe him, Amber."

But Amber's eyes told her that she did.

The others in the room began to chant, urging Essex into action.

When Amber saw the dagger in his hands, she emitted a scream more horrible than any Melanie had ever imagined. "Don't kill me! Don't hurt me! Please? Anything, I'll do anything, but *just don't kill me!*"

Melanie held her breath in disbelief as Essex taunted Amber with the sharp tip of the blade. "How should I do it?" He ran it lightly around her face. "Maybe dig out your eyes for starters, then ram it up your nose and into your brain as a fit ending?"

Amber, her eyes bulging with horror, began to hyperventilate.

He moved the blade to her chest. "Or how about a nipple slicing and then a quick plunge into the heart?"

Melanie wanted to plead and rage but was too stunned to utter a sound.

The knife moved to Amber's belly. "Or how about a simple gutting? What do you think, luv? Is that the way you want to go?"

The chanting stopped, and everyone waited in morbid anticipation.

"A gutting it is," Essex said. Laughing, he plunged the dagger into Amber's abdomen.

Amber moaned her agony while Melanie watched in disbelief as her friend was disemboweled.

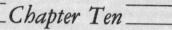

Chapter Ten

1941
Montvue, Colorado

1

The Hawthornes' celebration of the pagan Yuletide was comfortably camouflaged by the trappings of the Christian Christmas. A holly wreath, symbolic of the Holly King of the waning year, hung on the door. It represented the mourning of his passing away at midnight on the eve of the Winter Solstice. It was then that his six-month reign was surrendered to the Oak King of the waning year, whose presence was celebrated in the huge oak root that was laid in the fireplace as yule log and the sprigs of the sacred mistletoe that graced Hawthorne Manor's multitude of doorways.

However, the mood of the Hawthornes, like the mood of the country, wasn't entirely festive.

The head of the Hawthorne family was Tony, the son of Denver and Sylvan. Denver had been killed in a combine accident a decade earlier. Sylvan, declaring that Denver's death had been a blood sacrifice to Mother Earth, buried him and then simply lay down and died herself. With the passing of her husband, it seemed her own life work was completed.

Tony was a practical and dictatorial man. The mystical natures of his parents had caused him to rebel and become their opposite. He had married Beatrice MacDonald, of the Scottish MacDonald family of witches, and had two sons and a daughter. The children, like the father, were inclined toward rebellion.

After sundown on Midwinter's Eve, the family gathered together in the parlor and set a light to the yule log. Flickering candles combined with the flaming log to illumine the room, while a punchbowl full of brandy-laced eggnog warmed its inhabitants. In lieu of dinner, the maid, Natalia, had set out a spread of specially prepared foods—a cold tray of sliced ham and assorted cheeses, freshly baked poppy seed rolls, roasted chestnuts, pomegranate seeds, mincemeat pie, and plum pudding—upon which the family casually feasted.

Beatrice raised her glass to make the toast. "Blessed be the rebirth of the Sun God."

The others raised their glasses in response. "Blessed be the Oak King."

Beatrice downed her eggnog and made her way unsteadily to the punchbowl for a refill.

"Don't you think you should eat something, Mother?" Glynis asked.

"Eggs have lots of protein, dear."

Glynis, sitting on the floor in front of the fire, drew her knees to her chest and rested her chin on them. There was no reasoning with her mother about her drinking. And it seemed to be getting worse. She sighed in resignation and gave thought to her own plight. It reminded her of the plans she had made for later that evening. "When the log burns down, I'm going to take the ash and spread it over the fields. It's an old Yule fertility spell I've discovered."

"And from whom did you discover it?" The imperious tone belonged to her father. It always made her cringe.

"Dori's mother is a German witch. It's from her tradition," Glynis said, then braced herself.

"Dori again, is it? I thought I made myself clear on the subject of that damn sod farmer! You're too good for the likes of him. I had him investigated. His family *really* lives in a sod house, along the Platte River in Nebraska.''

"Father, I'm twenty-six years old, and I'd like to get married before I'm too feeble to care. I love Dori, and he's one of us. Why won't you give him a chance?''

Tony finished off his drink—he was drinking straight scotch—and poured another one from the decanter on the coffee table. "You're my daughter, and you'll obey me.''

"No, I—"

"I hear Dori's going to enlist right after the first of the year, so maybe the Japs'll kill him for you, Father,'' Alan, Glynis's twenty-year-old brother, said helpfully.

"Not a bad plan,'' Tony said, then settled back down to enjoy his drink.

Glynis stuck her tongue out at Alan, and he chomped his teeth at her playfully.

"I'm enlisting, too.'' Cliff's pronouncement gave birth to a fearful silence.

Glynis held her breath in wonderment. He was her twin brother, and yet he never ceased to amaze her. Well, if he could find the strength to openly defy their will, she should be able to as well. But so far she had lacked the courage to tell them what she had done.

"Excuse me?'' Tony said at last. His face held a tinge of purple.

"It's my country, and I care what happens to it. I know you're planning to buy draft deferments for Alan and me; I know you've got the bribable connections. But you never asked me about my feelings. You never ask anyone about their feelings.'' Cliff's voice was calm and sure. It sent a shiver through Glynis. She had never been more proud of him.

"But the curse,'' Beatrice said in a small, pathetic voice.

Cliff shook his head. "If the curse is going to get me, it'll get me wherever I am. I'll not live my whole life in fear.''

Beatrice refilled her glass, this time from the decanter. "We'll have to deliver the Corn Maiden to the Hunters this evening so they can add it to tomorrow's feed.'' The Corn Maiden was the last handful of corn reaped from their fields that year. It was a yule tradition to feed it to cattle so that they would thrive during the following year.

A change of subject didn't change the mood.

But Alan managed to add a little levity. He tossed a brightly wrapped present to Cliff. "Well, seems my present to you is by far the most appropriate of the bunch."

Cliff opened the package. It contained a roll of toilet paper which had a caricature of the German Führer drawn on it. The words written below said, "Wipe Out Hitler."

2

Glynis slipped away from the house shortly before midnight with the ashes from the yule log securely contained in an old, covered metal bucket. The night was cold and clear; the sky glittered with points of fire and the earth with patches of ice. The crisp crust of snow crunched beneath Glynis's feet as she walked beneath the veil of moonlight through the grounds of Hawthorne Manor, out the south gate, and toward the fields.

Melancholia filled her as she neared the edge of farmland that her family had nurtured for the previous seventy years. Her gift of foreknowledge told her that within a generation it would all be sold for commercial development. Even though she was sure of her facts, she didn't understand why they were going to become manifest. Cliff was committed to the land and would continue to operate the farm by their father's side. And if only Dori would be accepted by the family, they would find that his earth talents were exceptional. The only plausible explanation revolved around the possibility of something happening to prevent Cliff and Dori from carrying on the agricultural tradition Great-Grandma Rose had begun. The fact that both men were readying themselves to enter the war seemed the only answer, and it filled Glynis with anxiety and dread.

She came to rest at the fencepost on the corner of the northeasternmost corn field. As she waited, she looked up at the sky and studied the bright orb of the moon. Whenever she looked at it, she saw that in the not too distant future men would travel to it in ships similar to airplanes. She never analyzed the scientific improbability of such a vision but merely noted it. It made it hard for her to view the moon as something sacred, worthy of veneration, as the Hawthorne Book of Shadows had told her it was. There was a lot about the religion of her ancestors that she couldn't accept. However, the religious superstition aside, the magical knowledge of her people was profound. Her sight told her that science would someday acknowledge the supernatural principles she and her kind had always accepted.

Tonight the moon seemed to have an especially hypnotic effect on her, and she had trouble looking away from it. As she stared, the bright image became doubled, and soon she was looking at two round beams of light. Apprehension rose and quickly turned to fear as she felt the lights begin to bear down on her. She struggled to avert her eyes as the beams came closer. She uttered a cry of alarm and tried in vain to move out of their path—

"You okay, honey?"

The voice that broke the spell belonged to Dori.

The moon rode alone high in the sky, and Glynis felt an enormous wave of gratitude wash over her.

"Fine," she said, sticking her trembling hands deep into the pockets of her coat so that he wouldn't see. She had always been overly concerned with appearances and hadn't yet learned to let down her guard entirely with him.

"Did I startle you?"

"Yes."

He wrapped his long arms around her and embraced her tightly, then planted a hard kiss on her lips. "Oh, woman, how I want you." His voice was husky with need.

"I'm yours, body and soul."

He slipped his right hand out of his glove and fumbled with the large wooden buttons of her coat, then with the bulk of her sweater, and finally the hooks on her brassiere, until he completed the path to her breast.

She moaned with pleasure as her nipple responded to his caress.

"Did you tell them?" he asked.

How can I tell them I married the son of a sod farmer who has the illustrious position of porter at the local train station? "Not yet. Tonight wasn't the right time. Cliff . . . ah, he's . . . oh, what are you doing?"

His hand had snuck down to open the button on her trousers.

"I'm going to take you right here and now."

Glynis's knees grew weak at the sound of his words. He was so terribly sexy. "It's a little cold, don't you think?"

His mouth moved to her ear, and he breathed his warmth into her. "We just have to be creative."

He slid his hand down into her pants and into the moist folds between her legs, where he began to fondle her. Shocks of electric pleasure radiated from his touch, and it wasn't long before her whole body began to tremble. She clung to him tightly, sure she would otherwise collapse, and in the steam of their breath their tongues sought each other out.

He freed his engorged organ from his trousers and guided her hand to greet it. She ran her fingers lightly over the satiny smooth head and rigid length, enjoying the sensual feel of her husband's sex, then she took it into her closed palm and began to manipulate it. His own manipulation of her was heightening her pleasure, and she began to grind herself into him in response. He inserted two fingers up into her, and she moaned and bore down onto them while he started to thrust his hips to increase the speed of her attention to him. With his free hand, he pulled her sweater up to reveal her breasts and she gasped at the sudden shock of cold air against her skin, but he bent to bury his face in them, and the contrast of the winter chill and his warm mouth was the final impetus she needed to make her final surrender to the innovative sharing of pleasure they were enjoying. Her spasms were met by his sudden release of pleasure, and together their needs were fulfilled.

"Nice," she whispered breathlessly as she leaned into him for support.

"And we didn't freeze our asses off, either," he said in his good-natured way, giving her bottom an affectionate pat.

Laughing, they began to repair their dishevelment when

the harsh glare of two headlights fell upon them. A shot of panic entered Glynis's bloodstream, and in her fright she tried to bolt but was tripped up by the bucket of ashes. She and the ashes spilled onto the ground. Dori moved protectively between her and the car.

"Who's there?" he yelled. The car was only about a hundred feet away.

Too busy to hear it coming, Glynis thought as she floundered on a patch of ice in an attempt to get to her feet.

"I tol' you to stay 'way from that fuckin' sod farmer, and here I find ya fuckin' him!" The drunken voice belonged to Tony.

Blood began to pound in Glynis's ears. Her father tended to get mean when he drank. *We were only finger fucking*, she thought. "Daddy, don't get mad! I can explain!" Her right foot slipped again, and she fell down on her knee with a painful thud. "Get out of here, Dori," she whispered. "He gets crazy. He might hurt you."

Dori made a chortling sound. "Well, then I'm not going to leave you alone with him."

"He won't hurt me, but you're a different matter."

"We're going to have to tell him sometime."

"Not now. Not when he's drunk."

" 'Xplain?" Tony said. "How can you 'xplain a son betrayin' his own father? Cliff has no right . . . How can you 'xplain a daughter who defies? Tell me, girl!" The sound of his rage mixed with the sound of impending tears.

"Go, Dori! Believe me."

Dori turned and helped her to her feet, then began to edge away into the night.

"That's right, boy! Run away! Make like a rabbit!"

Dori speeded up his pace, and Glynis could sense his humiliation.

Shame filled her. *I don't have your courage, Cliff. Don't know how I'm going to tell him.*

"Don't wanna do it, but I gotta teach ya, girl! Must learn to obey . . . I'm the boss."

The engine revved, and before Glynis could respond,

the car lights—the two bright orbs of light—were quickly decending upon her. Disbelief flooded her. Her father couldn't really mean to hit her, could he? But as the car neared, she quickly accepted the harsh reality of his betrayal, and her limbs went into frantic action. She scrambled to dodge the oncoming vehicle and lost her footing on the ice. She fell to the frozen ground, where in terror, she tried to roll out of its path. When she realized that she wasn't going to succeed, she emitted a shrill scream of terror.

It was then that Dori threw himself in front of the car.

3

Katherine Winthrop had never been able to sleep well during the week right before Christmas; even at nineteen years old, the excitement of anticipation was simply too great to bear. This year, however, there was far more than the mystery of brightly wrapped presents keeping her awake. There was also the promise of seeing Alan Hawthorne—who had just arrived home for Christmas break—the following morning.

Her romance with Alan had begun two years earlier, right before he left for college, and they had pursued it during his brief visits home during semester breaks. Anxious to get on with law school—and avoid conscription —Alan had opted for a year-round program of under-graduate study, a fact that had frustrated Katherine. But she also knew that the sooner he graduated, the sooner they would marry. Although he hadn't officially pro-posed, she was sure it was only a matter of time.

Christmas had always been a season of wonder to Katherine. She never failed to be moved by the spirit of love and hope that it evoked. A devout Christian, she kept returning in her mind to the events the holiday was reserved to celebrate. Profound emotions welled up within her, and, unable to restrain herself any longer, she left her bed and crept through the sleeping house to the front room where the fragrant tree shone brightly.

"A beacon in the darkness," she whispered. She saw

the beautiful tree as symbolic of the light Christ had brought into the world. She knelt in front of the tree and rummaged through the packages until she found one that bore her name. She squeezed, sniffed, and shook it until, satisfied that it was the ballet slippers she had requested—they were the latest fashion in women's footwear—she returned it to the pile. She thought about Alan, and her breath grew short and her face became hot.

Katherine was a strange blend of mystic, child, and woman.

The shrill sound of the telephone's ring startled her. Glancing at the grandfather clock—it said it was two-fifteen—she crossed the room and picked up the receiver. Her father's sleepy voice preempted her own.

"It's two o'clock in the morning." Lloyd Winthrop always answered the phone with a statement of fact.

"Ah, yes, I know. Sorry, sir."

Katherine knew the caller's voice. Her heart began to pound.

"Ah, mayor, this is Alan Hawthorne. We need some help."

Lloyd's voice became concerned. "What is it, son?"

"There's been an accident. My . . . my brother-in-law's been hit by a car. My father was driving."

"Didn't know you had a brother-in-law."

Alan laughed humorlessly. "Yeah, well, neither did we." He paused. "Dad was . . . well, he was drunk. They've arrested him. I . . . we've never asked for any favors, mayor, but—"

"Where are you, boy?"

"We're all at the hospital. They're operating on Dori. My dad's getting stitched up—he cut open his head on the windshield."

"I'll be there shortly." Lloyd's line went dead.

Katherine started to say something to Alan, but he hung up too quickly. She put down the phone and scurried for her room so she could change. In a matter of minutes, she was ready and waiting for her father at the head of the stairs.

"I think you should stay out of this," he said as he brushed past her.

She followed on his heels. "I have a right to go. I plan to marry into that family."

Abruptly, he stopped and turned, and she unceremoniously bumped into him. He looked at her with a hint of anguish. "I think you should think twice about your desire to become a Hawthorne. Tony and Bea are honest-to-God lushes. And, speaking of God, I don't think there's ever been a Hawthorne who gave much thought to him. Why don't you try and find a good Christian boy to fall in love with?"

"Because it's too late. I've already fallen."

Lloyd sighed, started to say something, then turned and headed back down the stairs. "Well, come on then. If you're determined to be one of them, you might as well start getting used to their scandals."

4

Although his profound psychic abilities were labeled a gift by the Hawthorne clan, Cliff didn't enjoy them as such. He might have if his family had been of a different temperament. But the Montvue Hawthornes were a troubled lot, and for the sake of his own sanity, he had spent most of his life trying to shut them out of his mind. However, the tragedy that had befallen them that night was too extreme to turn off or tune out. As a result, he felt emotionally ravaged. As he paced the hospital's hallway awaiting final word on Dorian's condition, he contemplated how harsh his home front had become. The battle front that lay ahead of him couldn't be much worse, he reasoned. At least the war seemed to make more sense and have more inherent value than the battles fought by his own.

He plopped down wearily on a wooden bench and lit a cigarette. "Damn," he muttered to no one in particular. The Hawthorne ego trips and power plays had finally gone just too far for him to bear any longer. In a way, he was glad for the fact of the war. It gave him something to believe in, to stir his soul. He had been an empty shell for too long.

The elevator door slid open, and Lloyd and Katherine stepped off. Cliff sighed. Someone—probably Alan—had informed the mayor of their dilemma, no doubt in the hopes of soliciting a rescue. Cliff took a deep drag on his cigarette and tried to swallow his disappointment. He had hoped that his father would finally have to pay for his actions, but that had been an unrealistic expectation. The Hawthornes were powerful, in many ways.

Cliff was too tired to rise in greeting. Katherine, who rarely rested on formalities, plopped down next to him and regarded him with an anxious expression.

"The emergency room said that your father was up here on the ward," she said.

"They're holding him a while for observation. He hit his head." Cliff did little to hide the lack of sympathy he felt.

"What happened?" Lloyd asked.

Cliff met the older man's gaze and hesitated only for a moment. "Dad didn't approve of Dori . . . Dorian Wildes, my sister's beau. He got drunk and followed her when she went to meet him tonight. When he found them together, he tried to run her down, but Dori threw himself in the path of the car. Turns out that Dori and Glynis had got married on the sly. It's been three weeks now, I guess. Looks like Dori's going to lose his legs."

Katherine paled, and Lloyd's expression became dark.

Cliff dropped his cigarette butt on the floor and crushed it beneath his boot. "If you've been asked to bail Dad out of this, sir, I'd like to ask you to reconsider."

"Where's Alan?" Lloyd asked.

"With Glynis in the waiting room over by surgery. They're still working on Dori."

"Your mother?" Lloyd asked.

Cliff snickered. "Well, to be honest, she's passed out cold at home. We couldn't wake her up. She's . . . marinated."

Lloyd unbuttoned his wool overcoat and pulled off his leather gloves. His manner was brusque and business-like. "Katherine, you go see Alan and Glynis. Cliff, take me to your father."

Both young people responded to his orders.

Tony, despite the uniformed police officer who guarded the door, was comfortably ensconced in a private room. The guard didn't hesitate to allow the mayor and Cliff entry.

"Leave us," Lloyd told the nurse who was hovering over Tony's bed, taking his temperature and checking his pulse.

She started to protest but stopped herself, pulled the thermometer from Tony's mouth, then scurried from the room.

For an uncomfortably long time, Lloyd stood at the foot of the bed, regarding Tony with an unreadable expression. Cliff, leaning against the door, lit another cigarette and noted that he had never before seen his father appear more vulnerable. Forced to face the formidable Mayor Winthrop knowing that the secret of his personal ugliness had been laid bare, Tony looked—and felt, Cliff's gift informed him—scared.

The silence was finally broken by Tony's lunge for the bedpan that lay next to him and the sound of his violent retching. The room filled with the sour smell of used liquor. Cliff fought the urge to gag. Lloyd seemed unmoved.

"I'll get you out of this on two conditions," Lloyd said, his voice low.

Tony's trembling hand wiped the perspiration from his brow, and he looked up from the sight of his vomit with haunted eyes.

"First, you do right by that boy, Dorian Wildes. You've robbed him of a great deal, and you'll see to all his needs from now on."

Tony nodded slowly.

"And second, and most importantly to me, you'll not allow this romance to continue between my daughter and your son. There's no way in hell, after what I've learned here tonight, that she's ever to become a Hawthorne."

Tony's eyes turned away from Lloyd's before he nodded his assent.

Lloyd turned to leave, and Cliff stepped aside to allow him passage.

After the door shut behind him, Tony said to Cliff, "I wouldn't have let that bitch marry Alan anyway. After all, she's not one of us."

"In my opinion, that makes her an extremely lucky girl."

5

Along with the arrival of the new year came Vivian Eldon. The arrangement had been hastily made by her parents, but she wasn't entirely opposed to the plan. If nothing else, she was glad to be out of England. The war had become too much for her to bear any longer. Others of her kind had begun to devote their supernatural powers to the war effort in an attempt to influence Hitler's mind regarding his military strategy—as a devotee of things occult, he was well primed for psychic suggestion. But at eighteen, Vivian was more interested in exploring her own womanhood than in altering the course of world events. And if all went well, this arrangement should fulfill that need quite nicely.

The opulence of Hawthorne Manor impressed Vivian. The Hawthornes' lack of refinement did not.

She was greeted at the door by a sloppy, drunk woman who tried to smother her with an overly exuberant hug. "Oh, my dear Vivian! Welcome to our humble abode."

Vivian strained to catch her breath, then was sorry when she found it—the sloppy woman reeked of liquor. "It's not too humble, ma'am."

"I'm Alan's mother. Call me Bea."

Vivian disentangled herself from the other woman and tried to straighten her hat. "It's good of you to have me, Bea."

"Sorry we couldn't meet you at the station, but Tony— that's my husband—he's recovering from stitches, and, well, to be honest, our children are somewhat peeved with us at the moment and we just haven't got around to telling them about your arrival."

"That's all right. Your chauffeur and I got along just fine." She paused. "Am I then to understand that Alan doesn't know about me and why I've come?"

Bea giggled. "Alan always enjoyed surprises. We thought we'd indulge him."

Whatever have I got myself into? Vivian thought uncomfortably. "A Yuletide gift, fashionably late," she said lightly.

"Exactly!" Bea gushed, then giggled again. "Come on into the parlor and have some sangria with me."

Vivian followed Bea but declined the offering from the crystal pitcher. "I don't drink alcohol before noon."

Bea gave her a quizzical look. "But, my dear, it's got fruit juice in it, too." She took a few gulps from her glass and smacked her lips. "Good and nutritious."

Vivian's excitement gave way to weariness. "Actually, it's been a very long trip. What I'd really like right now is a strong cup of tea."

Bea shrugged her shoulders. "Well, it's up to you." She rang a loud bell, and it wasn't long before a uniformed maid responded.

"Bring tea," Bea said tersely.

Natalia curtsied and obediently left to fulfill her command.

Bea's treatment of her servant reminded Vivian of her last encounter with Johnny Bartlett, the Eldons' stable man. He had enlisted in the RAF, and Vivian had been indignant about his desertion of his equestrian duties. She had slapped him hard across the face when he came to the house to tender his resignation. Three months later, his plane had gone down in the English Channel. Her hand still burned at the memory of her last act of selfish cruelty toward him. "May I please sit down?" she asked as she began to remove her heavy wool coat and gloves.

"Our home is your home, my dear."

Vivian chose a chair to sit in so that Bea wouldn't sit next to her.

"So, what is your gift, Vivian?"

"Actually, I'm skilled at the Priestess arts."

Bea shook her head in confusion. "What?"

"The Priestess arts. I can channel the Lady. I preside over the religious festivals." Vivian was proud of her ability.

"Is that all?" Bea asked.

Vivian felt indignant. "Isn't that enough?"

Bea laughed. "Well, we don't go in for that religious stuff these days. We're more practically oriented."

Vivian didn't know how to respond. What would life be like without worship of the God and Goddess? She swallowed her disappointment and sudden sense of inadequacy. "What is your gift?" she asked politely.

"I'm a medium. Would you like to see?"

"I'm a little tired for a seance right now."

"No, no. It's okay. You just have to sit there." Bea put her glass on the coffee table and sat down on the ottoman in front of Vivian's chair. She grasped Vivian's hands in her sweaty palms and closed her eyes. "I can do it anytime, anywhere," she said proudly.

Vivian averted her head slightly in an attempt to avoid the noxious odor of oxydizing liquor that carried on Bea's breath. Soon she began to feel Bea's hands lose their heat. It wasn't long before she felt as if she were holding ice cubes.

"There's someone here who wants to say something to you." Bea's voice was several octaves lower than before.

Vivian could feel that the energy in the room had shifted and become more magnetic. The hair on her arms began to stand on end. "Who is it?"

Bea's voice went even lower and assumed a cockney accent. "It's me . . . Johnny. Just wanted you to know it's okay. Let it go. Okay, Tinkerbell?"

Vivian gasped with surprise. Only Johnny had ever called her that. She'd been to successful seances before in her life, but the ease with which Bea seemed to channel amazed her. "I'm sorry, Johnny."

"Being a bitch is just part of the human condition for you, luv. Use it to your advantage."

Vivian might easily have been offended, but instead she found herself accepting his advice. "Have a safe trip, Johnny," she whispered.

"You, too," he said.

Bea pulled her hands out of Vivian's and began to shiver uncontrollably. She wrapped her arms around herself and began to rock back and forth.

"Are you okay?" Vivian asked. "What can I do?"

"Scotch on the table there. Pour me a glass. Quickly."

Vivian did as she was told and threw her coat over Bea's shoulders for good measure.

Bea downed the glass of golden warmth and in a few minutes seemed back to normal. "Well, was it someone you wanted to connect with?" Her speech was starting to slur.

"Yes, actually, it was. Thank you."

"My, my, but you're a pretty girl," Bea said approvingly. She reached out and patted Vivian's cheek with her sweaty palm. "Your skin is just peaches and cream. And your hair's such a pretty color; that's called strawberry blond, isn't it? You and Alan will have beautiful children."

"About Alan and me . . ."

"Now, don't you worry about a thing. He thinks he's in love with that Katherine Winthrop, but that'll pass. You'll make him forget her. She's not one of us, you know. She's a Christian." She spit the word *Christian*.

Vivian's stomach lurched. The thought of competition was an unexpected hurdle to overcome. But more than that, she was appalled at the concept of a witch even considering taking an outlander—and particularly one who was Christian—as a spouse. "That's disgusting," she said.

"My sentiments exactly."

The two women had arrived at a common ground.

6

Vivian did not meet the rest of the family until dinner that evening. When she first saw Alan, she was captured by her own desire. He was the tall, dark, and handsome fantasy she had been entertaining since womanhood had first claimed her. She resolved to win him.

"This is our new house guest," Bea began when they were all seated. "Vivian Eldon, of the English Eldons."

Everyone greeted her warmly. She noticed that Alan regarded her with frank appreciation. If her gift wouldn't wow him, she felt certain that her beauty would have an effect.

"Vivian, this is my husband, Tony, and these are my twins, Cliff and Glynis—her husband, Dorian, is in the hospital right now—and Alan."

"It's a pleasure," she responded.

"What brings you to America?" Cliff asked.

"Your brother, actually."

All eyes fell on Alan.

His thick eyebrows knitted themselves together. "Ah, excuse me?"

"My parents and yours thought we should meet each other."

He squirmed and toyed with his fork. "What for?"

"To check out the chemistry, I imagine."

A red glow rose in Alan's face. "Well, that's nice of them, but I'm otherwise involved."

"Not any longer," Tony said, his voice as imperious as ever.

Alan's eyes flickered with fear as they moved to regard Glynis, whose face had paled.

Vivian didn't understand the significance of their reactions, but she instinctively knew that her task was going to be easier than she had expected.

7

Katherine spent another day waiting for Alan's call. When he had taken her home from the New Year's Eve party, he had promised that they would go out again before he had to leave for school, and that time was fast approaching. She had resisted the urge to phone him, as she was well aware of the problems his family was having. She didn't want to interfere or urge him away from pressing issues that might need his attention. But she missed him terribly, and his prolonged silence had begun to make her nervous. Finally, she gave in and called him.

Natalia answered the phone. "Hawthorne residence."

"May I please speak with Alan?"

"Who's calling?"

"Katherine."

There was a moment's hesitation. "I'm sorry, Miss Katherine, but Mr. Alan isn't home . . . to you."

Katherine laughed. "Don't be silly. This is Katherine Winthrop."

"Yes, miss, I know."

The solemnity in Natalia's voice began to sink in. Katherine's heart began to race.

"Is this coming from Mr. and Mrs. Hawthorne?" She had never felt as if they liked her much.

"No, miss, from Mr. Alan himself."

Katherine felt as if she'd been punched in the stomach. "Why? What did I do?"

"I'm sure I don't know, miss."

"Yes, well, thank you, Natalia," she murmured as she hung up the phone.

It didn't take long for shock to turn to despair.

Katherine had known Dorian Wildes only as the boldly sexy young porter at the local train station. Now she also knew him as the son-in-law Tony Hawthorne had crippled. Nevertheless, she felt that somehow she might find the answers she needed in his hospital room. She took him flowers.

He immediately began to sneeze and handed them back to her. "Thanks, but losing my legs has given me an allergy to things that pollinate."

Katherine didn't understand the analogy, but she politely removed the bouquet from the room and thrust it in the hands of a surprised but grateful passerby in the hallway. She returned to the foot of his bed.

"How are you feeling?" she asked.

"Emasculated. But otherwise just dandy."

"What you did was very"—she paused to grope for the right word—"gallant."

He laughed bitterly. "Yep. That's me. Just a regular Sir Walter Raleigh."

"What will you do now?"

"The next step, I suppose, is to get over my self-pity. Then . . ." He looked out the window at the gray winter

281

sky for a while. "Then I guess I'll learn a trade that doesn't require legs."

"Any ideas?"

He laughed again, but this time it was more mischievous than bitter. "What do you think about my becoming an accountant and taking over management of the Hawthorne finances? Would that get old Tony's goat or what?"

Katherine smiled. "I think it's perfect revenge."

He regarded her with keen eyes. "Why are you really here?"

Katherine blushed with embarrassment. "Am I so transparent?"

He nodded.

"Alan cut me off without explanation. Things were going so well for us, too. I tried to reach him, but my call was refused. I . . . I'm beside myself. I thought you might know something."

Dorian sighed and lit a cigarette. Katherine could tell he was planning his response carefully. Finally, he exhaled several rings of blue smoke and said, "It's my understanding there's another woman."

A small gasp escaped Katherine. Such a possibility had never occurred to her. "Who?"

"A friend of the family, from England. She came to visit, and, well . . ."

Katherine's head reeled in disbelief. "Why wouldn't he have told me? After all we've meant to each other?"

Dorian took a deep drag on the cigarette and chuckled. "The Hawthornes are a mighty unpredictable lot. Take it from an expert."

The door swung open behind her, and—thinking it might be Alan—Katherine's heart performed a small somersault. But she turned to find only Glynis. She smiled weakly. "Hi."

Glynis didn't return her greeting. Instead she fixed Katherine with a harsh stare. "What the hell are you doing here? Now that Alan's moved on to bigger and better things, you trying to hook my man?"

Katherine was stunned. "Of . . . of course not. I just came to—"

"Well, take your pathetic ass somewhere else. Just

because your dad did us a favor, we don't owe you anything."

"I never—"

"Get out!"

Trembling and fighting back tears of humiliation, Katherine did as she had been told.

Katherine wasn't too proud to beg, not when the love she felt for Alan was so profound. She rang the Hawthornes' bell and waited an eternity until the door swung wide.

"Hello, Natalia. I'm here to see Alan."

"No," she said, and began to close the door.

"Don't close the door in my face!" She tried to stop the maid's actions by sticking her foot in the way, but the door was heavy and Natalia was strong. As her foot became painfully lodged between the door and the jamb, Katherine emitted a shriek of pain. Then she heard the young Englishwoman's voice.

"If you break her foot, she won't be able to kick herself for having lost Alan."

A greater anger than Katherine had ever before known surged up within her like a wave of extraordinary strength. She pushed in the door and sent Natalia sprawling onto the floor. Oblivious to the pain in her foot, she stalked into the house and came face to face with Vivian.

"How dare you enter this house without invitation," Vivian said indignantly.

"And how dare you be so contemptibly rude."

"Get out!"

"I'm here to see Alan."

"Hasn't the situation been made clear enough for you yet? Or do you plan to stick around for the wedding festivities?"

"I have to hear it from Alan."

"Alan has nothing to say to you."

"What are you, his keeper?"

The smaller woman struck out with her hand and gave Katherine a hard slap across the face. Angered beyond reason, Katherine didn't hesitate to respond in kind. Within minutes, they were rolling on the floor, pulling hair, ripping clothes, and slashing at each other with their fingernails.

"I'll lay twenty dollars on Vivian," a man's voice said.

Katherine glanced up to see Tony and Bea standing in the parlor watching.

Bea shook her head. "I don't know. Katherine's bigger."

"Yeah, but Vivian's badder."

Bea giggled and raised her wine glass in toast to the frenzied tangle of enraged women. "Kick her when she's down, Vivian. No Marcus of Queensbury on this side of the great water."

Katherine balled up her fist and punched Vivian in the mouth. Vivian responded by ripping one of Katherine's pierced earrings out of her lobe. Blood sprayed, and Tony and Bea laughed.

"What the hell is going on here?" The booming voice belonged to Cliff. He rushed in the front door and quickly braved the maelstrom to separate the two women.

"How could you just stand there and watch?" he asked his parents, while struggling to keep Vivian and Katherine separated.

"It's not our fight, dear," Bea said.

"The hell it isn't," Cliff muttered. He pushed Vivian back out of the way and started to usher Katherine out the front door. "I apologize for my family, but it would be best for you if you just stay clear of them all from now on."

Tears of frustration began to flow down Katherine's bruised and scraped face. "But why?"

"For his own reasons and in his own chickenshit way, Alan's made his choice. Get on with your life, Katherine."

A sob of complete anguish escaped her. When she stooped down to retrieve her fallen purse, she glanced back toward the parlor and saw Alan standing behind the cherrywood pillar that supported the archway. From the look on his face, she knew that he had been standing there the whole time. She wanted to hurl her purse and her pain at him, to accuse him of cowardice and lack of honor, to call him a filthy bastard. But instead, she said, "I'll always love you."

8

Winter Solstice, 1944
Germany

A field commission shortly after D-Day had provided Cliff with his lieutenant bars, an event with which he hadn't been entirely pleased. As a matter of fact, his quick succession through the ranks since entering the Army in early 1942 had not been sought but rather imposed upon him. He had enjoyed his brief fling with the anonymity of a dogface GI. It had been the only normal thing life had ever brought him, and he reveled in having been lost in the mass of humanity. The problem was, however, he wasn't ordinary, and that was something he had been unable to hide for any length of time.

Once again, it was Yuletide, and Cliff was alone in his remembrance of the Earth and the mystery of her tides. He and his company had come to rest for the day in a barren tract of woodland. As he sat on the frozen ground under the gray, late-afternoon sky, he dug around in his K ration for something to offer the Earth as libation. There was a can of meat, some biscuits and crackers, caramel candy, dried coffee and lemon juice, bullion, fruit and chocolate bars, a stick of chewing gum, and a small pack containing four cigarettes. He knew he would need to eat the meat and biscuits for dinner in order to keep up his strength, the coffee and broth—if they were able to have a fire that night—would help to warm him, and the candy and cigarettes would bring him a small measure of pleasure. The fruit bar and lemon crystals were the most comfortably dispensable part of the ration. However, what good was a sacrifice, a spiritual offering, if it were easy? With reverence—and some regret—Cliff broke up the cigarettes and chocolate and, along with the caramel, threw it into some nearby bushes. *Thank you for the gift of life*, he said silently. *Sorry for all the life we've taken from you lately*.

Cliff had never before had religious sentiments. The

war—which had given him a taste of his own mortality—had given him that.

Bob Tucker, a friend of Cliff's from basic training days at Fort Benning, watched his actions with stunned dismay. "If you didn't want it, I would've taken it."

"Bugs got into it," Cliff explained.

"No shit?" Tucker slit open and peered into his own ration nervously.

Cliff tried to think of something to say to change the subject. "Warm enough, Bobby?" He had developed a strong paternal interest in the welfare of his men over the course of time. It helped the mostly younger infantrymen to deal with the situation better. It made his watching them die all that much more difficult.

"I got on a layer of cotton, a layer of wool, my fatigues, field jacket, overcoat, two pairs of socks, two pairs of gloves, boots, galoshes, a knitted hat from my girl—that was before my induction into the Dear John Club, of course—and my helmet. Can't move, but, yep, I'm okay warm."

The Dear John Club. All you needed to join was the all-too-common letter containing the morale-busting words, *I'm sorry, but I've met someone else.*

There were times when Cliff even felt jealous of the guys who received Dear John's. At least it was mail. He had never received any.

"So, why'd McTavish take his guys on ahead?" The question came from Guy Kibbodeaux, a newly assigned medic who insisted the men call him Kibby. A green recruit, his nervousness showed.

"Well, the sarge decided to scout ahead. Makes our journey in the morning that much safer," Cliff explained.

"I've heard you're one of those objectionables," Tucker said to Kibby. His tone carried scorn.

"I'm a conscientious objector."

"Goddamned chicken livers. Who the hell do you think you—"

"He's here, right beside you, facing the same enemy," Father Nolan, one of the company chaplains, said. The older man had a gruff voice that was nevertheless kind.

"Yeah, but you couldn't count on him to guard your back. It ain't fair, Father."

"Ah, but private, this young man would die trying to save your ass. Remember that."

Tucker sighed and dropped his attack.

Kibby sat up on his tree stump a little straighter.

Well done, Father, Cliff thought appreciatively.

"Are your reasons religious, son?" Father Nolan asked Kibby.

He nodded. "I'm . . . my family's Buddhist. My grandfather was French ambassador to Siam and took on their religion. It's been with the family ever since."

The priest nodded appreciatively. "I think it's a fine religion."

"Ain't Buddhism what the Japs do?" Tucker asked, his eyes narrowing with hostility.

"They practice a kind of Buddhism called Zen," Father Nolan explained. He paused and tugged gently on his priestly collar. "But I wouldn't follow where your mind's trying to lead you, son. A fair number of Germans happen to be Catholic, you see. And I'm just as Yankee Doodle as you."

Score two for the priest, Cliff thought with amusement. *Wonder what Bobby would think if he knew my religion?* He shrugged to himself. *Oh, well, it's not really much of a religion anymore. Something got lost along the way. Something's missing.*

A loud crash of thunder sounded in the distance, and a gust of wind carrying the fresh smell of snow assaulted the men. Cliff's train of thought was lost in the scramble to erect shelter before the storm hit.

The forest through which they had been traveling had seen battle, and many of the trees were broken and shattered. The dead wood provided the unit with the raw material to build lean-tos. And the lean-tos provided them with the privacy to build small fires in which they could heat their rations. Lately, as invaders into enemy territory, they had been too wary of revealing their position to risk the comfort of fire. When the storm finally came, it came as a harsh flow of freezing rain, punctuated by repeated rounds of thunder and lightning. The soldiers escaped all but the fury of the wind as they struggled to keep their small fires alive and heat their meager evening meal.

Cliff and Father Nolan ended up alone together in one of the hastily built shelters. They heated water and re-constituted the coffee, then put their tins of hash over the flames to warm.

"You're a good leader," Cliff said.

"So are you."

Cliff shrugged.

"You care about your men. And your command decisions have been amazingly . . . lucky. You have a magic genie or something?" The priest's bright blue eyes flickered with keen curiosity.

"Yeah, he's a family pet."

"Mmmm. He's priceless. Keep him well-fed."

"I try to."

Father Nolan slurped his coffee noisily. "I've noticed. Ain't many bugs around in the midst of winter."

Cliff looked at the priest with surprise. *How much have you figured out?* he wondered, but his mind chose not to probe. His war experience had taught him—for the most part—to respect the privacy of other men's thoughts. "Not many," he agreed.

"Your records don't list a preferred religion."

"I have my own beliefs."

"Do they include a god?"

Cliff nodded.

"Any particular kind of god?"

"One who is born, dies, and is resurrected."

"But not Christ."

Cliff shook his head.

"The myth of the dying god has surfaced in many of the religions man has practiced throughout time. But Christ was the only one I know of who actually played it out in the flesh. Kind of the living fulfillment of that concept."

Cliff had never thought about it like that.

"The Virgin Mary is kind of like an incarnation of the Mother Goddess the ancients used to worship, too," Father Nolan said casually.

Cliff grinned. Despite his best efforts to discipline himself, his mind couldn't resist the urge to invade the priest's.

Father Nolan had figured him out.

"You certainly know your ancient religions, Father."

288

"They were a special focus of mine in the seminary. A personal thing."

"Have you found that the knowledge has come in handy?"

"Oh, every once in a while. Every once in a while."

Cliff grinned again, and Father Nolan followed suit.

Cliff was finishing up the last of his hash when he heard the scream. It had the characteristic hollow sound that was the quality of his gift. The scream was lingering, and it belonged to Sergeant McTavish. Along with the internal flash of clairaudience, he also experienced a sensation that had only recently begun to manifest. He called it clair-malodorousness. This time it was the smell of burning flesh. He shuddered and dropped the tin and fork he was holding.

Father Nolan looked up from his meal. "What?"

"McTavish and his men are under attack. We've got to help them."

The priest set aside his food and immediately began to pack up his things. "Of course."

As the confused and weary company of men were rounded up and urged through the cutting sleet toward the site where Cliff knew the recon party to be trapped, Father Nolan fell in step beside the man with whom he had shared his dinner.

"You know, son, when all this is over, you should consider using the gift that God has given you to help your fellow man. You've got a lot to offer."

"I'm sorry, Father, but I'm not convinced that a well-fed genie is quite enough to change the world. Or even make much of a difference."

"My genie tells me that before all this is over, you'll have the stuff it takes to make it count."

9

McTavish and his ten-man squad had been trapped in a broad marsh which was bordered on both sides by a high embankment.

By the time Cliff's unit arrived, the night was advanced, and the storm had become more frenzied. McTavish's men were all down, either dead, dying, or hiding behind the bodies of their comrades. They were being fired upon by the illumination of every flash of lightning; the high ground on the other side of the marsh, with all of the muzzle flashes, looked like a cloud of blinking fireflies. The rumble and crash of thunder and weaponry drowned out most of the screams of the fallen men, but occasionally the sounds of agony and fear filtered through the cacophony of noise. Reluctantly, Cliff opened his mind to the men below, to try to determine their condition. Ironically, the first man to fall hadn't been struck by an enemy bullet. Rather, standing in the wet marsh, his rifle held high over his head, he had been struck by lightning. His was the flesh Cliff had smelled. The Germans had followed the lead of the hammer of their Thor and had then begun to fell the enemy. McTavish was dead, as were four others. Only five men were alive, and of those, only one was unscathed. Cliff shuddered from the intensity of desperation he felt coming from the survivors, then he directed his men to fire on the unseen enemy. Although he didn't anticipate that they would hit many marks, they would at least draw some fire away from the men below.

"Can we get them out?" Father Nolan asked.

Cliff looked to the sky. "Not until the storm relaxes. If the lightning would let up some . . . especially if it keeps on raining. Then their flares wouldn't do much good."

"I'll pray about it."

Cliff nodded. He thought about the wealth of information regarding weather magic that had been in the Hawthorne Book of Shadows and regretted that he had never applied himself to the mastery of it.

His mind swept the enemy line. He picked up a variety of thoughts—he had learned German in college—and most were of anger and hate and fear. There was a knowledge of impending doom for their fatherland and they seemed determined to take down every Allied soldier they could along with them. There was a notable exception, however, and Cliff was drawn to linger on that man. He was the ranking officer, and he was weary of the killing and dying. He was thinking about his wife and sons. He just wanted to go home.

"Can't go home 'til it's over, fella," Cliff muttered, then raised his own rifle to shoot. However, he aimed in a direction farther down the line than where the German officer lay thinking of Ilse, Max, and Karl Eberlein, Jr.

At four o'clock in the morning, the storm gave up. The enemy gunfire died off as suddenly as the thunder ceased. The moans from the wounded men echoed up from the marsh below.

"I'd like to request permission to go in to attend the men." The timid voice belonged to Kibby.

"No. They'll use their flares now."

"Maybe they'll take a nap. We're all tired, sir."

A smile at the young man's naiveté escaped Cliff's lips, and he was glad for the shroud of darkness. "That's unlikely. Besides, they won't see your red cross by the light of a flare. They won't hold their fire. I don't know if they would even if they could see you were a medic. It's kind of late in the game."

"I'd like to request permission to go in to attend the men." This time his voice was stronger.

Cliff sighed. The moans seemed to resonate louder and louder against the wall of night.

"Even if I can dole out some morphine. Anything . . ." Kibby's voice cracked. "They're suffering so."

The young medic's compassion overcame Cliff's reason. "If you want to try to help them, I won't stop you."

"Thank you, sir."

"God go with you, son," Father Nolan said.

"Well, I'll be damned," Tucker mumbled.

Cliff's mind followed Kibby's descent. He noted that the young man fought a growing terror with every step but that he never faltered. Kibby fueled his courage by a remembrance of the compassion of his Lord Buddha and a desire to emulate it. Cliff noted the greatest demonstration of bravery he had yet witnessed in the war.

There were only four of McTavish's men still alive. In the darkness, Kibby located the first patient by following the sounds of his anguish. In the darkness, he managed to give the wounded man a clumsy injection of morphine.

"My shoulder," the man mumbled.

"How long ago did you get it?" Kibby asked, his voice a whisper.

"Long time."

"Then I doubt if it hit anything important. You'll be okay."

There was a short, cynical laugh. "Yeah, right."

"Maybe you could try and crawl out."

"I'm staying right here behind Sanders and Joey. They've kept me alive so far."

Kibby felt around in the darkness and discovered that they were behind two bodies, one piled on top of the other. He fought back his revulsion. "Can you shove me in the direction of the next guy . . . who's still breathing?"

"Sure. Paul got it right before the lights went out. From the way he carried on, I'd say it's bad." He turned Kibby around to face another direction and gave him a push.

Kibby began blindly crawling through the thick mud. "Paul?" He kept his voice low, his tone urgent. "Paul, you out there?"

He heard a groan come from the direction in which he was traveling. Without warning, there was a loud hissing sound, and the night lit up as a parachute flare exploded in the sky above.

Kibby collapsed in the mud and lay still. Fear paralyzed him. He knew if he moved he would attract fire. He heard the groan for a second time. Slowly and carefully, he tilted his head and looked toward where Paul had fallen. The young face—whose age approximated Kibby's own—was deathly pale against the muck on which it rested. The boy stared at Kibby with pleading eyes. His hand was pressed tightly against his neck; blood seeped slowly from between his fingers.

"I'm dying," he said simply.

Don't move, Kibby's mind told himself. He closed his

eyes and tried to not think about the other man's condition. He felt himself consumed with a need to survive.

May all beings be happy and at their ease. The words of the *thera* who had been Kibby's religious teacher flashed through his mind. *Even as a mother watches over and protects her child, so with boundless mind should one cherish all living beings . . .*

A soft moan escaped Kibby. He didn't want to think about *metta* now. *Metta*, a deliberate and conscious direction of love and benevolence, was one of the keys of his faith. He knew that if he invoked such a state within himself, he would lose all ego consciousness and, with it, his animal instinct for survival. *No!* his human nature insisted. *Of course,* his Buddha nature replied.

He sighed in resignation and began the process of stilling his mind. He used the method of observation of his own inbreathing and outbreathing to quiet his internal turmoil before he turned his thoughts to the generation of love. First, he located within himself the center of love he had discovered through the years of religious practice. Then he applied it to his own being; he experienced compassionate forgiveness for his own cowardice. He extended the dynamic love he felt outward to embrace all the dead and dying who were lying with him in the marsh. Finally, he carried it further to include even the Germans who held them captive.

Another flare was launched, and the night became even brighter. Kibby opened his eyes and began to crawl toward Paul. A volley of gunfire rang out. Kibby took two bullets in the leg.

He paused only for a moment until the shock passed and he could catch his breath, then he continued his short trek.

Paul had built a low wall of mud behind which to hide. By the light of the flares, Kibby made a quick assessment of the man's injuries. He had made it just in time, he decided. A few more minutes and he would have been beyond saving. He wasted no time in giving him an injection and applying the necessary sutures.

"Your leg," Paul said weakly. "It's just pumping out the blood."

Kibby glanced down and saw the arterial wound. He grunted and continued his ministrations.

"Fella, take care of yourself."

Even as a mother watches over and protects her child . . . Kibby didn't miss a step in the first-aid procedure.

"You wanna die?" Paul asked in confusion.

Kibby was quickly growing weak. He needed to hurry if he was going to complete his work.

"Do ya hear what I'm saying?"

Kibby's heart felt as if it would overflow with love. He appreciated the concern of his patient. "It's my duty," he whispered, grateful that he was given such a compassionate job to perform.

Kibby looked at Paul's face, and, through the growing darkness of his own imminent death, he saw the tears form in the other man's eyes.

"Thank you," Paul whispered.

"Thank you," Kibby said.

"He just fell over," Father Nolan announced. They had been watching Kibby's progress since the flares had been launched.

"He's dead," Cliff said.

"You're sure?"

Cliff nodded. He had not only been watching, but his mind had been listening to both the internal and external dialogue of the last hour of Kibby's life.

Father Nolan began reciting the Lord's Prayer. The other men in Cliff's unit joined him. Cliff, however, didn't know the words.

It was a bitter dawn. Cliff's men were numb from the cold and the lingering tragedy of the night.

The wounded men continued to cry out for help while the Germans kept peppering the marsh with bullets.

"I can't take it anymore," Father Nolan announced. "I'm going to get them out of there. This is totally insane."

"War is insane, Father," Cliff said.

"Well, I'm not." He produced a long stick he had

found and began to affix the large Red Cross flag to it. "Who's coming with me?" he asked loudly. "Only medics and chaplains allowed."

Two seasoned medics and the Salvation Army chaplain joined the priest.

"You going to stop us?" he asked Cliff defiantly.

Cliff lit a cigarette and shook his head. "You're too mighty a force."

Father Nolan hoisted the large white flag with the bright red cross on it, and the four men emerged from hiding. The Germans' gunfire didn't die off immediately, but Cliff issued an order for his men to hold theirs. His mind sought out the German officer, Karl Eberlein.

Christ, my men aren't going to go for this, Eberlein, in his own language, was thinking. *If I order them to cease fire, they might take me out; they haven't gone through all of this just to let the poor bastards go. Ah, but it's all such a damn waste. Maybe I can show my support of the humanitarian effort and appeal to their higher instincts despite the anger and hate that fuels them.* A moment of fear for his own safety flooded him, then he chuckled. *Hell, if I don't try, I won't be able to live with myself, so what the hell?* Eberlein put his own gun aside and began to sing, in his loud baritone, the Christmas hymn "Silent Night."

Cliff's own shock at Eberlein's actions was echoed by the thoughts of the German soldiers. Cliff's mind swept theirs, and he could hear the resistance and, finally, the acceptance. The gunfire died off as, one by one, the members of the German line began to take up the song.

Cliff's men couldn't understand the words of the German song, but they knew the tune. Soon they began to sing the words as they knew them. Cliff, moved beyond words, couldn't join them. Instead, as the rescue party began to remove the fallen Americans from the marsh, he wept.

Cliff had been changed. Dori's self-sacrifice in his effort to save Glynis had impressed him, but he understood the power of human love and the courage it could lend. However, the selfless love and courage exhibited by Kibby, Father Nolan and his team, and Karl Eberlein toward others whom they didn't even know spoke of a higher love with which Cliff had been totally unfamiliar. It was a kind of love he now longed to know intimately. It was spiritual, and Cliff knew that his religion, as his family had come to practice it, couldn't provide such an experience. He set aside his prejudice and, with profound humility, asked Father Nolan for religious instruction.

10

Autumn, 1945
Montvue, Colorado

"A priest? You're going to become a damnable Catholic priest?" Bea's shock and obvious disapproval mirrored that of all the family.

"How could you?" Glynis asked. "I've always admired you so."

"I've found what I want to do in life," Cliff said calmly. He had expected a bad reaction.

"But the way they persecuted us . . ." Vivian, the new Mrs. Alan Hawthorne, said with disgust.

"The church has an inglorious history. And there are no excuses for the atrocities it has committed in the name of God. But through it all the church has preserved a spiritual gem that has remain unflawed. It's that beauty to which I've responded."

"But the persecutions," Vivian pressed.

"Well, as a member of the hierarchy, maybe I'll be able to help prevent that from recurring."

"How can you just forsake your beliefs like that?" Dori asked.

"I haven't. I've just added something."

"That's bullshit," Dori said, shaking his head in dismay. "Pure bullshit."

Alan shrugged. "Shucks, I guess we planned this welcome-home party for nothing."

Cliff sighed. "Because I'm not welcome now?"

Alan looked at Tony, whose face was glowing with rage.

Tony stood up and pointed at Cliff with a trembling finger. "This party was for my eldest son. My eldest son is dead."

Cliff swallowed his pain and tried to remain centered in his understanding of the greater Father. He put his hat and coat back on. "In that case, my condolences to you and your family. I'll pray for you."

"We don't need your prayers," Bea said.

"Madam, I have a feeling that you and yours are going to need them very much," Cliff said formally. He dodged her airborne sherry bottle as he let himself out the front door of Hawthorne Manor for what he supposed was the last time.

Before he left the grounds, he paused by the statue of Venus and reverently dropped a shiny new penny at her feet. "You need to help them find a higher kind of love," he told her. "You're the one they understand. Help them, somehow, at sometime before their mighty reign comes to an end, to regain what they've lost."

Chapter Eleven

July 1992

1

Friday Night

Melanie threw up into the cobra fountain.

"Oh, now you've ruined it," a gore-coated girl named Hemlock said petulantly. Essex's followers had all stripped themselves and were reveling in obscene orgy with Amber's entrails, while Essex had begun to surgically remove her various organs.

"This is just a nightmare," Melanie said dully, trying to convince herself.

"What a pussy," Hemlock said. "I thought you were a witch."

"Witches celebrate life. We don't destroy it."

"That sounds boring," Hemlock said. Seemingly unwilling to drink Melanie's vomit, the girl took her cup to a large bowl of Amber's blood and filled it.

Melanie kept her eyes averted from the desecration of Amber's body and crawled into a corner, where she huddled fearfully. She had never been too interested in the religion of her people, having been more entertained by the power. But now she felt an urgent need for spiritual solace. From the Hawthorne Book of Shadows entries made by her father's great-great-grandmother Sylvan, she had learned about the legend of Aradia, the holy woman who had appeared among the oppressed Italian peasants in the fourteenth century and helped them regain their lost power. Melanie found it easier to supplicate a great spirit who had once lived as a human being than a nebulous force of creation contained in the concept of Earth Goddess. So she prayed to Aradia and asked for protection.

2

Jason and Gil rendezvoused shortly before midnight at the appointed place, beneath one of the towering elm trees on the Hawthorne grounds.

"Did you bring it?" Jason asked anxiously.

Gil pulled a handkerchief from his pocket and unfolded it carefully. He removed a thick lock of pale blond hair.

"How'd you get it?"

"Gloria—the fat girl who tried to get in my pants all last spring—she works at the shop where Mrs. Cody gets her hair done."

The moonlight reflected off the hair as Jason examined it.

"Do you think we have the power to pull this off?" Gil asked.

Jason chuckled. "You sound as if you wish we didn't."

"I do."

Jason gave Gil a hard stare. "Wimps won't survive these times. And I, for one, am not a wimp."

Gil bristled. "Me either."

"Good, then let's get our revenge. Let's give them a reason to be afraid of us."

3

Leigh was dreaming about Craig. Since her initiation, her dreams were much more vivid than they had been before, and she had the sense that they were, at times, as real as the real world. She had begun to work on trying to remember them better, because she felt they had taken on such great significance. Craig was telling her something about someone named Tiffany—he was giving her a warning—when she felt her consciousness being insistently drawn back into her body.

"Mommy. Mommy, wake up."

Leigh opened her eyes to see the shadowy form of Adrian by her bedside. She pushed herself up onto her elbow and switched on the lamp beside her bed. The light fell on his tiny face, and Leigh gasped when she saw his pale, haunted expression.

"What's wrong?"

He swallowed hard. "I saw something."

She took his hand. "What?" She felt the dread he was feeling.

Tears filled his eyes and spilled over into the deep shadows that outlined them. "I don't wanna talk about it."

Leigh sat up and urged him onto her lap. "It might help to get it off your chest."

"I don't wanna tell you the pacifics."

"Mmmm. What about the generalities?"

"The what?"

"In general, what you saw."

"Lots of blood."

Leigh's heart seemed to skip a beat. "Anything else?"

"Melanie. Melanie needs help."

4

"So, are you going to kill me tonight, too?" Melanie asked Essex.

"No need. One at a time pleases the bloodthirsty bloke we serve well enough." He paused and ran a blood-encrusted fingernail along her cheek. "Actually, you hold the promise of two for one if we can keep you a secret long enough."

"What do you mean?"

"The old bloke just loves newborn babies."

Melanie's panic took on a new dimension. She quickly decided that she'd rather they just kill her with the baby inside her, loved and protected until the end, instead of as a separate entity with all the fear that held in and of itself. And they'd probably torture it, too. "You might as well just kill me now, because if you hold me they'll find me. You forget that we're witches. We have power."

Essex laughed. "Yes, I can see how far that power has gotten you, my little Damiana."

"The police will find me if my family doesn't."

"Your car's already been disposed of. And we have a hidden cellar in which we've held others before you. Face it, duckie, you're ours. You do have a choice, though. You could join us. I could dig havin' a priestess of your ancestry."

Melanie thought about it. Maybe she could buy time and get away.

"We could even start tonight," Essex said. "Pox brought along his collie. I'm sure he could be coerced into sacrificing it to the cause."

"Cause?"

"Your first ritual murder."

Melanie sighed. There was no way she could willfully destroy an innocent life.

Essex laughed again and began unbuttoning the black robe she still wore. "I thought not. Besides, you've got A-positive blood. Dead, you'll bring me a fortune. Big demand for organs with your blood type."

"What? I don't even know my blood type. How could you?"

"It's my business to know. I sell body parts on the black market—for transplant, you understand. Desperate rich people don't ask too many questions about how a new heart or kidney was obtained. I have a reputation for delivering quality stuff. I only kill young, healthy people. And I was a medical student for a time. Know how to handle the scalpel like a pro, and I'm a whiz at cross-matching tissue types.''

Melanie was too stunned by his revelations to give much attention to the fact that his British accent had faded to one more American.

"Adolf is a private pilot. We've got our own plane—the airport's close by. And he just left with the latest goods.''

"How industrious you young entrepreneurs are," she said wearily.

"Exactly. But we still find time for sport." He pulled her robe off and rolled her over onto her belly. "Tonight we play, for tomorrow we might die. Eh, luv?''

5

Saturday

It was dawn. Leigh sat beside Marek at the altar upon which she had been made a witch and tried to calm the pain, terror, and despair she felt. She was feeling Melanie.

After Adrian had told her that Melanie was in trouble, Leigh's thoughts had reached out for her, and she had linked empathically with the girl. It was a horrible experience for Leigh, but it did assure her that Melanie was still alive. Leigh had remembered that Marek said tracking was one of his gifts, and so she had wasted no time in seeking his assistance.

Marek had spread a county map across the altar and was scanning it with a crystal pendulum. Its swing had begun to center around a location east of the city limits.

"I'd say she's out on the old Snyder farm," he said at last. "Rumor has it that the man who owns it now is a drug dealer.''

"Adrian said he saw blood. And I feel the presence of quite a few people." Leigh paused. "Should we get the police to go with us?''

Marek nodded. "In this case, I'd say it would be a good idea."

"How do we explain ourselves to them?"

Marek chuckled mirthlessly. "Carefully. Witches always have to explain themselves with great care."

6

It was six-thirty in the morning when Sergeant Cosworth saw the Hawthorne woman enter the station in the company of the Polish gardener. He was just finishing his first cup of coffee of the morning, and the last swallow turned his stomach sour. He braced himself for another installment of the Hawthorne string of tragedies.

Leigh approached his desk. "Excuse me, I . . . we need help." Her face was anxious and drawn.

"Yep, Mrs. Hawthorne, what can I do for you?"

She was confused. "You know me?"

"I'm Cosworth."

"Oh, yes. Yes, I remember. Ah, thank you for your help with my husband's funeral." She stood awkwardly in front of his desk. "My niece, Melanie. I think she's being held against her will."

"By who?"

"I don't know . . ." She faltered. "By the drug dealers who live at the old Snyder farm."

"You say you know for a fact that Mr. Essex-whatever-his-name-is is a drug dealer?"

"Ah, no—"

Marek spoke up. "Miss Melanie was heard to say she was going out there last night, and she's not come home. We're worried about her."

"I see. Why did she go out there in the first place?"

"We aren't sure," Marek said.

Cosworth didn't usually light up a cigar this early in the day, but he found himself reaching for one. "Okay, let me get this straight. Your niece—how old is she?"

"Sixteen."

"Your sixteen-year-old niece went out to this maybe

drug dealer's house last night and hasn't come home yet, so you want us to go look-see, right?"

Leigh nodded.

"Why don't you two just drive out there yourself?"

"We're concerned because of the questionable nature of people involved," Marek said. "We thought it prudent to have some protection."

"Don't you think you may be overreacting a little? I've seen this Essex fellow about, and he's not bad-looking. Maybe she had a, you know, romantic interest and—"

"She's in trouble and needs help!"

The whole room quieted, and everyone looked at Leigh curiously.

"How do you know, ma'am?" Cosworth asked.

Leigh struggled to regain control. "I've got a feeling."

Cosworth sighed. Well, precedents had been set for woman's intuition. But, more likely, the woman was merely a little unbalanced from all she'd been through. Cosworth had come to feel a measure of responsibility toward the Hawthornes and their plight. "Okay, ma'am. I'll accompany you to go check on your niece."

"Just you? I mean, shouldn't we take some backup or something?"

Cosworth chuckled. "This is Montvue, not Miami. I don't think it'll take a whole squad to bring home one wayward little girl."

7

Cosworth led the way to Essex's house in an unmarked police car. At the last minute, he decided to take the back way into the property. When he was a teenager he had dated the overprotected Bessie Snyder; she had often snuck out that back way to meet him. Her father had quickly put the kibosh on that romance and even pulled Bessie out of school to keep them apart. Cosworth hadn't seen her again until, as a young police officer, he had discovered her body in the living room of her home, along with those of her mother and father. The old man had killed his women and then blew off his own head; no one had ever quite figured out why. As he pulled up alongside the seven cars parked behind the house, a feeling of unease overcame him. He had hoped the house would remain abandoned, as it had been from the time of the tragedy until this Essex fellow bought it and turned it into a—

"Party house," he mumbled disgustedly, taking note of all the vehicles.

Marek and Leigh parked behind Cosworth, then joined him as he walked around the house to the front door.

"Don't like people comin' to my back door," Cosworth explained. "Like them to come in the front. It's more respectful."

All the curtains were drawn, and the house looked sleepy. Cosworth knocked on the old screen door. He heard a dog bark and some muffled voices, but no one responded to him. He opened the screen and banged loudly on the inside door.

There was still no response.

He was becoming irritated. They should have had enough time to flush their drugs down the toilet by now. "Come on! I hear you, and I'm sure you hear me! Open up! I'm a cop!"

It was then that he thought he heard the muffled scream. Adrenaline surged into his bloodstream, and he pulled his gun from its holster. *Damn, I'm too old for this*, he thought to himself. "On the count of three, we're goin' through that door," he said to Marek.

Marek nodded his assent.

"One, two—"

The two men kicked in the door.

The scene that greeted them froze Cosworth in his tracks. The bloody, mutilated body, barely recognizable as a young woman, lay on display in the middle of the room. Cosworth's mind struggled with the memories its sight dredged up. One moment it was the body of Bessie, the next moment it was another, younger victim. Before he could completely get a grasp on the situation, he felt the hot searing of a bullet slamming into his shoulder. His gun flew from his hand as the force of the hit spun him around.

Shrieks filled the air as naked young people scattered.

A beautiful collie stood in the middle of the room and barked angrily.

A .357 Magnum, his mind informed him. *Shouldn't we take some backup . . . she had asked. How did she know?* he wondered.

Marek dove for Cosworth's gun. He recovered it, then rolled across the bloodstained floor as two shots were fired in his direction. He had hoped his military training would never have to be put to use again, but now he was grateful for it. Without hesitation, he aimed the gun at the man who held Melanie's naked body as a shield. He fired at his head, and it exploded against the wall behind him.

Melanie screamed as Essex was knocked back away from her. Her scream lingered as the full horror of the night finally sought release.

Cosworth scrambled to recover Essex's Magnum. He shot one bullet in the air to get the attention of the teenagers who were trying to escape. "I figure I've got two shots left in this gun, and I'll use them to stop anyone who tries to leave!"

Marek stood up. Brandishing Cosworth's gun, he recovered three of the teenagers who were trying to sneak out through the kitchen.

Leigh, who had been hovering anxiously at the front door, ran to Melanie, who was giving full vent to her hysterics. She picked a black robe off the floor and threw it around Melanie's shoulders, then took her in a comforting embrace. The girl clung to her in frantic desperation.

Cosworth felt a sharp pain in his chest. *Too old*, he thought again. "Who's the dead girl?"

Melanie tried to answer but couldn't control her sobbing long enough.

"That witch there brought her," Lilith said, pointing at Melanie. "We had a full-moon ritual last night."

Cosworth felt a different kind of pain in his chest. He glanced around at the satanic symbols that adorned the room, then he fixed a look of betrayal on Leigh and Melanie. "Damn," he muttered. The preacher had been right about them all along. He had been duped. He moved to Marek and took back his gun, then picked up the phone and dialed 911. He glanced at the mutilated body that lay on the coffin, then his angry eyes scanned his prisoners.

"If you ask me, burning's too good for the likes of you."

8

Diane Fox awoke and stretched sleepily, glancing at the clock. What a wonderful Saturday surprise: Tiffany had let her sleep in until nine o'clock.

She decided to lie there just a few more minutes and luxuriate in the afterglow of a good night's sleep. She had slept so well, she was sure, because she had finally found the guts to respond to the harassment she had been enduring. The article she had written was scathing and had included carefully chosen snippets of the actual letters that had been sent her. She was grateful to her editor for having had the balls to print it. Actually, he had been rather courageous about the whole damnable Preacher Cody/Hawthorne affair. She wondered when he and his family were going to start being attacked, too.

She sighed and decided to greet the day. She and Tiffany were planning to go to the pound that morning to pick out a new family member. Diane had decided it would be wise to have a dog around the house. Good companion, better protection.

She threw a bathrobe on over her negligee and slipped on her slippers, then padded out to the living room. She was again surprised to find the television wasn't on. *What is Tiffany doing with her morning?* she wondered. She made her way to Tiffany's room, and was stunned to see the window wide open, the ballerina-covered curtains dancing wildly in the wind.

Diane felt a shudder of weakness seize her as she saw the note pinned to the pillow. On rubber legs she somehow made her way across the terrifying expanse of room. She sank down onto the edge of the bed and, in disbelief, read the message.

You've now stepped over the line. You're not fit to be a mother any longer. Tiffany's better off with us.

A hideous feeling rose inside Diane and cut off her breath. She read and reread the words on the paper until she fainted.

9

Cody had had a late night. He had arranged for the relocation of the Fox girl and had stayed up until he received word that it had gone down successfully. So it was understandable that he had slept in. But why, he wondered as he rolled over in bed to see that the clock said 9:47 A.M., should Rachel have slept in so long? A woman had to be watchful of becoming slothful; it was the way of the sinner. Irritated, he shook her roughly, but she didn't respond. He shook her again, but she didn't budge.

"Rachel?" He felt the flutter of fear. "Rachel?" He pressed his hand against her neck and could barely discern a thready, weak pulse. "Oh, my God." In a panic-stricken moment he lifted her up and shook her, but she remained limp in his hands. He laid her back down and raced from the room. Eden's room, down the hall from Cody's, was raucous with her squalling. He peeked in at her in passing to be sure she was okay, then ran to the phone that rested on a stand at the end of the hall—he didn't like to have a phone in his own bedroom lest it disturb him at an inopportune moment. He reached for the receiver and began to dial for help when he noticed the message light blinking on his answering machine. Irrationally, he felt the urge to listen to it. He pressed the play button.

A muffled man's voice said, "Stop the witch hunt and we'll lift the spell that binds your wife."

10

By eleven o'clock, the Montvue police station was swarming with prisoners, their families, their lawyers, reserve police officers, and the press.

Leigh sat across from Lieutenant Brody and repeated the story that Melanie had told her.

"Melanie was invited with her friend, Amber Whittaker, to attend a party. Neither had ever been out to that house before or, indeed, had any prior relationship with those people. When they arrived, they were made prisoners, Amber was killed, and Melanie was raped . . . sodomized. When are you going to allow her to be examined by a doctor?"

Lieutenant Brody had a bald head which reflected the light in shiny fashion, and his perfectly manicured and buffed fingernails were equally bright. So were his capped teeth, his badge, his watch, and his two gold rings. Leigh could feel his vanity clearly enough; she wished it didn't advertise itself like a neon sign.

"The other teenagers who were arrested all, unanimously, implicated your niece as being Mr. Essex's accomplice."

"They all lied . . . unanimously."

"Where is her attorney?"

Leigh sighed. "We're trying to locate one in Denver. We've been unable to secure one locally."

"Mmmm. I see." He yawned and stretched. "If I were a small-town attorney, I'd be afraid to represent her, too."

"I'm sure you would." Leigh instantly regretted her sarcasm. "I asked you about a doctor. For Melanie."

"Lady, I've got a mutilated teenage corpse, a forensic expert on the scene who's already found evidence of more murders, a dead satanic priest, twelve little satanists in custody, a wounded cop, and a town that's probably going to riot when the news breaks. I can't worry about one little witch—"

Leigh jumped to her feet and leaned across Brody's desk until their faces were an inch apart. She had never felt such anger. "You get her some medical attention," she said, her voice low and menacing, "or I'll see to it that your ass is publicly bared and roasted."

Lieutenant Brody's glow faded, and, his disconcertment evident, he rolled his chair backward to get away from her. "Officer Hancock is due into the station at noon. I'll have her take your niece to the emergency room.''

Leigh turned and walked out of his office. "Score one," she mumbled.

"Judge Barker is going to hold a special arraignment hearing at three o'clock this afternoon for the prisoners arrested in the Whittaker murder," the loudspeaker announced.

Leigh found Marek waiting for her. "Special arraignment?" she asked.

"Most of those arrested were minors. And I don't think Montvue really has the facilities to keep so many minors in custody; they have to be kept segregated from the adult prisoners."

"How are we doing on getting a lawyer?"

"No luck. We may end up using a public defender, for today at least."

"Where do the Hawthornes keep their money?"

"Montvue First National."

"Is it open today?"

He nodded. "Until noon."

"Good. I'm not sure what a good risk a bail bondsman might find a Hawthorne right now. I think we should have the cash to be able to get her out ourselves."

"I just spoke to Helena. Mrs. Hawthorne's taken to her bed again."

"Well, we'll just have to get her out of it, won't we?"

As they were walking out, Leigh saw Diane. "Miss Fox?"

Diane looked at her but didn't seem to recognize her.

"Leigh Hawthorne," Leigh said.

Diane's eyes cleared. "Oh, yes." Her voice was dull.

"I wanted you to know that Melanie didn't do it. She and the Whittaker girl were both prisoners of the satanists."

Leigh began to feel Diane's confusion.

"What?" Diane asked.

"The murder of Amber Whittaker."

310

"Murder?"

"Are you okay?"

"They took my baby." Diane's eyes welled with tears. "God help me, they took my baby away."

Leigh felt the sudden assault of Diane's unbridled emotions, and she instantly understood. "Oh, no," she whispered. *Oh, how it hurts*, she thought. She put her arms around Diane and drew her to her. She tried to take into herself some of the other woman's pain; she felt a measure of responsibility for her plight.

"I should have bought a dog instead of a fire extinguisher," Diane said softly. "A dog would have been better."

11

"I'm sorry, Mrs. Hawthorne, but your account's been frozen," James Bradshaw, the president of First National, informed Vivian.

Vivian sputtered but didn't articulate anything of value.

"Why has it been frozen?" Leigh asked.

"Raymond Hunter obtained a court order to freeze it . . . ah, yesterday, I understand." He glanced over the top of his glasses at the two women. "Haven't you been notified?"

"Not a word," Leigh said, glancing at Vivian, who seemed more pale than she had just a moment before. "Vivian?"

"Ray's been calling. I . . . didn't return . . . I've been out of sorts . . ."

"It's my understanding it has something to do with questions of misappropriation of funds from Hawthorne and Hunter. The injunction is pending an investigation. I'm sorry I didn't notify you. I thought you surely knew."

Leigh sighed, then rose to shake Bradshaw's hand. "We'll be in touch, Mr.—" Upon touching his hand, she felt the smug satisfaction he was feeling. In a moment of comprehension, she realized that he was one of them! He was in Cody's camp. Had Ray actively sided with Cody, too? Her gift didn't give her that knowledge.

"Bradshaw," he offered, filling in the gap her startled reaction had left open.

"Bradshaw," she said coolly. "Yes, I won't forget again, Mr. Bradshaw."

12

Dr. Cole, the emergency room physician, was a young man. He had a simple and direct manner, and Leigh felt comfortable with him. She was glad that Melanie hadn't had to endure an examination by a doctor who might have treated her contemptuously.

"Miss Hawthone suffered no permanent damage as a result of her attack." He paused, then looked at Leigh with embarrassment. "Excuse me, I'm sorry. Physically, she's going to be okay. Unless . . . well, there's always the possibility of AIDS, of course. I've heard there's an AIDS semen test available, but we don't have access. She should probably be tested periodically, up to six months, for the antibodies." He cleared his throat. "The baby wasn't affected."

Leigh was startled. "Baby?"

"Why, yes. Miss Hawthorne's eight weeks pregnant. I'm sorry, did I let the cat of the bag?"

Leigh offered him a weak smile. "Yes, but it's a good thing you did." She felt his compassion for Melanie. "You've been very kind."

"The policewoman took her away as soon as we were done."

Leigh shook his hand. "Thank you."

"Witch!"

Leigh was well conditioned. She spun around to see Cody standing a few feet away, pointing at her.

"Witch!" He seemed frantic.

People stared.

Leigh couldn't restrain a smile. She found it ironic that, this time, she really was one. The last time he had confronted her, she hadn't been. "Why, Preacher Cody, what's your problem now?"

Her attitude seemed to disarm him. He dropped the accusing finger and inched toward her cautiously. "Which one of you Hawthorne witches cast the spell on my wife?"

Leigh laughed. He really was absurd. "Pardon me?"

"My wife . . . she's in there—" He gestured toward an examining room. "Dying. I received a message from a witch saying he'd let her live if I stopped God's work."

"God's work?"

"You know what I mean."

"Oh, yes, the persecution you've instigated."

He now stood less than a foot from her. For the first time, he didn't scare her. And for the first time, she threw up an invisible barrier of will to prevent an empathic connection. She didn't need to be inside the man to know how dark his inner world was. The saddest part was that he was so sincere. It was too bad he was so terribly, tragically wrong.

"Well, I'm not going to succumb to blackmail," he said. "Even if my beloved Rachel is sacrificed to the cause, you can tell whichever witch it was who did this that I won't relent."

Gil and me, we've got a plan . . . They want a war, they'll get a good one . . . They're the ones that started the trouble. Gil and me, we're just going to finish it. Jason's words came back to Leigh, but she didn't miss a beat in the dance she and Cody were performing. "You're really quite pathetic," she said, her condescension thick.

"I'm no longer going to maintain my national silence on the issue of the Hawthornes. Tomorrow night, I'm going to tell America what you people are and what you've done to my wife. And then I'll tell the world; I've just signed contracts for foreign distribution—thirty-one countries in all—of 'Preacher Cody.' The whole world is going to hear my message about witchcraft, and there won't be any place that'll be safe for the likes of you."

They're going to kill us all. All of us. Everywhere. It'll start here, but it'll spread. There will be no place that will be safe.

"You know something, Cody? I think you're truly insane." She gave him a consoling pat on the arm, which caused him to flinch and eye her warily. She laughed again, then winked at him. "Don't worry, I didn't hex you." She turned on her heel and walked away.

Cody stood gawking at her, openmouthed.

"Don't mind me, Preacher, I've just grown up since our last encounter," she whispered after she was on the other side of the emergency room doors.

Marek was waiting for her in his truck. As she slid into the seat beside him, she realized that she was not only older but wiser.

"We've got to get Melanie out of jail this afternoon so we can all get out of town," she said.

"Why?"

"Because dead's dead. Alive and in hiding, we have a chance to turn things around, form an underground network, fight to try and stop the madness."

"You think it's gone that far?"

Lieutenant Brody had told her the town would probably riot. Cody had been driven over the edge. "I know it has."

13

Leigh had never been a good decision maker. She had always been indecisive and diffident.

But that was before she became a witch.

Katherine Winthrop sat primly on the brocade love seat and sipped tea. Her house was elegant and tastefully decorated; it wasn't as blatant a statement of wealth as Hawthorne Manor, but the money it represented was on a par.

"I understand that you're very involved with the local Methodist charities," Leigh said.

Katherine nodded. She had said little in the fifteen minutes since Leigh had arrived. She seemed cautious.

"You never married?" Leigh asked.

Katherine shook her head.

"It's hard to be alone. I—"

"State your real business, Mrs. Hawthorne."

Leigh sighed. She could feel that Katherine's wariness

stemmed from the hurt she had been dealt by the Hawthornes. Leigh didn't blame her. "The Hawthornes need
your help."

Katherine giggled, a reaction that seemed incongruous
coming from someone as refined as she. "That's very
good." She giggled again.

"Melanie, who's pregnant, has been arrested for a
murder she didn't commit, and the family's bank account has been frozen pending some ludicrous investigation for fraud. We need to post bond—in an amount that
I'm sure will be quite substantial—for her this afternoon, and we don't have the means. We—"

"What about your money? I understand your husband
was a doctor."

"He . . ." Leigh faltered. She had never participated
in financial matters with Craig. He invested and donated
and carried patients and, in general, kept little of their
assets liquid. "There isn't enough."

"Why should I help them?"

"Because you once loved one of them." Craig had
told her the story.

"They treated me like a dog."

Leigh made an impulsive decision to take a chance on
the truth. "It was because you weren't a witch. Vivian
was."

Leigh could feel Katherine's shock, then understanding, and finally a sense of consolation. "Then he did
love me?"

"Very much. His family had other ideas. Tradition
and all. They've treated me much the same, I'm sure, as
they treated you."

Leigh felt Katherine relax, but just for a moment. Her
defenses came right back to attention. "All I really have
that's important to me is my reputation. If I put up the
money, the town would find out. That could implicate
me in your . . . ah, situation."

"That's unfortunately true."

There was a long silence.

"And you think I should put myself in that position?"

"I think that a sixteen-year-old girl is going to end up

a victim of a system guilty of temporary insanity. She's already been judged and will be convicted."

Katherine shook her head. "So, how will getting her out on bail prevent that eventuality?"

"If they never get to try her, she won't be convicted."

Katherine giggled. "So, you want me to put up bail, knowing she's going to run away?"

Leigh pulled a piece of paper from her pocket and handed it to her. "It's a quit-claim deed to Hawthorne Manor, made out from Vivian to you. It should more than cover your losses."

Katherine stared at the deed in disbelief.

"It's been signed and notarized; we went to a title company this afternoon. It's all legal. All you need do is get it recorded with the county."

"How did you ever get Vivian to do this?"

"I did, that's all that matters." Leigh didn't think it wise to tell her that Vivian was in such a state she really hadn't understood what she was signing. She'd deal with Vivian later. All that counted now was their escape.

"I told you what matters to me." Katherine handed the deed back to Leigh. "This wouldn't make up for a loss of reputation."

"I understand your bitterness, but—"

"Do you? I don't think so. Your man had the courage to defy the Hawthornes. Mine didn't."

The maid interrupted them. "Miss Winthrop, you have another guest. It's a priest."

"A priest? Whatever . . . Show him into the parlor, Maria. My visit with Mrs. Hawthorne is over."

14

Cliff stood at the parlor window and watched Leigh leave the Winthrop home. *She's the one God sent to them*, the feminine voice told him. In the past few years, the Holy Mother had begun an inner dialogue with him; it had seemed appropriate, given his roots.

"May I help you?" Katherine asked.

Cliff turned to see her looking at him without recognition.

"I'm Cliff Hawthorne."

Katherine looked startled, then she giggled. "Excuse me, but Cliff died in the war. Besides, it's unlikely that they'd spawn a Catholic priest. If this is a joke, it's hardly—"

"I am who I claim to be. I experienced my religious calling on the battlefield in Germany, and my family disowned me when they found out. Have I changed so much with time? You certainly haven't, Katherine."

She inched closer to him, and as his words seemed to sink in, so did her receptivity. "My God, it is you."

He held out his hand to her, and after a moment's hesitation, she took and squeezed it.

"I've come a long way. Would it be possible to have some refreshment?" he asked.

"Of course. Please have a seat." She summoned Maria and asked her to bring a tray, then sat down on the love seat next to him. "I assume you've heard?"

He nodded. "Father Shaw, at the local parish, tracked me down and filled me in. I got here as soon as I could."

"Where do they have you . . . stationed, or whatever it's called?"

"I've been in Rome for several years, at the Vatican. I've been working to effect some changes in the church. Kind of a personal crusade, you could say."

"I see. Ah, does this mean that you weren't born a, you know, witch?"

Cliff smiled. "No, I was born one, but I chose this instead." He didn't mention that even as a Catholic he couldn't escape his birthright. However, it complemented, rather than detracted from, his spiritual experience.

"Oh." She giggled. "I didn't know you could choose. Oh, good, here's the tea and biscuits. Do you like tea and biscuits?"

"Yes, thank you."

They ate and drank for a time in silence.

"Is this witchcraft evil, devil stuff?" she asked.

"Not what the Hawthornes do. Witches like the Hawthornes are gifted; God has given them extraordinary talents which they should be using for the betterment of humanity. Unfortunately, when the ego becomes involved, humanitarian concerns surrender to selfishness. That's the greatest sin the Hawthornes are guilty of."

"I see." She paused. "They want me to help them."

"And you don't want to."

"How they treated me."

"Resentments poison the soul."

She became defensive. "I'm a good, spiritual person. I work with the charities. I give to the poor."

"If it's easy, it isn't necessarily noble. True charity often involves some hard choices and measurable self-sacrifice."

"You're asking a lot."

"Where there's life, there's hope. I would like to believe that, for the Hawthornes, there's still a chance to hope."

15

"It is hereby ordered that bail in the case of the State of Colorado versus Linda Sue Florey—also known in these proceedings as Lilith—be set at one hundred thousand dollars," Judge Barker told the court. "Bailiff?"

"State of Colorado versus Melanie Hawthorne."

The district attorney, Braden Avery, stood up. His suit was wrinkled from the summer heat—the air conditioning had been shut down at the courthouse for the weekend—and rivulets of sweat issued from beneath his short gray bangs. His voice sounded weary. "Your honor, it is our understanding that Miss Hawthorne was one of the ringleaders of this little cult. She is known within the group as Damiana and was the apparent mistress of the late Mr. Essex, the alleged murderer of Amber Whittaker. Until recently her family has always held a prominent place in our community. As I'm sure you know, there have been allegations of witchcraft leveled against the Hawthornes, and the State does not consider—given the occult overtones of this case—that Miss Hawthorne, who is a minor, should be released into their custody at this time. The State therefore requests that bail be denied."

The courtroom, which was overflowing with people, began to murmur excitedly. The prosecution had not asked that bail be denied for any of the other defendants.

The judge gaveled the room to silence. "Ms. Dawes?"

Jeanne Dawes was the public defender assigned to Melanie. She was young and inexperienced, but she faced the court with confidence. "Your honor, Melanie Hawthorne is sixteen years old, and is an exemplary student and citizen. She has never before been in any legal trouble. All parties agree that Mr. Essex killed Amber Whittaker. My client is accused of aiding and abetting this murder because she took Miss Whittaker to the ritual last night. The truth is that she, herself, was a victim. The two girls were invited to a party by Essex, whom they both met for the first time just days ago. They both went willingly. They were both taken prisoner; Amber was murdered while my client was forced to watch. Now, on the issue of the Hawthornes supposedly being witches, well . . ." She laughed. "That's so ridiculous that I don't even know how to address it. I respectfully request that my client be released on bail compatible with that granted to the other defendants in this case."

Judge Barker's sigh was audible throughout the court. Leigh leaned forward in her chair and strained to feel his emotions, but the room was filled with such unseen chaos—fear, anger, grief, shock—that she could not discern his specific energies.

Finally, he cleared his throat. "I, for one, Ms. Dawes, cannot easily dismiss the recent public charges of witchcraft against the Hawthornes, most particularly because of the blatant evidence of satanism and the occult that surrounds this case. I'm not convinced there isn't some kind of link between the whole Hawthorne family and the satanic cult this unfortunate murder has uncovered. On the other hand, Mr. Avery, Miss Hawthorne apparently did not kill Amber Whittaker, and she is a minor, so I would be uncomfortable about denying bond altogether. Therefore, I'll allow bail, but it's to be in the amount of one million dollars.''

The courtroom exploded with commotion.

Melanie looked at Leigh with a silent plea of desperation.

Leigh had not noticed Katherine's presence. Without any preliminaries, she leaned over Leigh's chair and whispered in her ear, "If I couldn't have the man, I suppose the house'll do.''

16

As soon as they had Melanie home, Leigh called a family meeting. It was six o'clock. The Hawthornes, joined by the Janowskis, met together around the large dining room table at Hawthorne Manor.

"Okay, to begin with, let's hear from Jason and Gil about their special little spell." Leigh was rarely sarcastic, but she was beyond worrying about offending people.

Jason shrugged. "We figured it would put the brakes on the preacher."

"Well, you were wrong," Leigh said. She looked around the table. "For any who might not have yet heard, our little wizards here zapped Cody's wife. She's in a coma. The preacher figured us for the culprits, and he's vowed to go for the jugular."

"Oh, gods, how could you?" Vivian wailed at the boys.

Gil looked sheepish. Jason looked as if he didn't much care.

"Lift the spell," Marek said, his voice soft, his tone uncompromising.

"Yes, sir," Gil said.

"The way we set it up, we can't 'til midnight," Jason said sullenly.

Marek nodded. "Just do it."

Everyone jumped as Jason gave the underside of the table a loud kick.

"Now, to Melanie's mess," Leigh said. "We—"

"Why did Katherine pay the bail?" Vivian asked.

"Because she's a gutsy lady with a heart," Leigh said, her tone defying Vivian to argue with her.

Vivian sputtered, then fell silent.

"We know Melanie's innocent, but the events have tipped the scale against us all." Leigh paused. "And from what I learned today, if we stay here I don't believe we're going to survive. So we're leaving tonight."

"What are you talking about?" Glynis asked. "Where in the world would we go?"

"Who made you God?" Jason asked.

"I'm not leaving my home," Vivian said, shaking her head. "No, I'm staying right here."

Leigh threw up her invisible barrier for the second time. She couldn't allow their fear and foolish defiance to affect her resolve. "In hiding there's a chance we can fight the wave of hysteria that's swelling. Craig wanted to fight them. His way didn't work. Now we're going to try it my way."

Shocked silence filled the room. Even through her barrier, Leigh could feel their surprise at her arrogance . . . or maybe it was her own surprise she was feeling.

"We'll go with you, Mom," Kamelia said earnestly.

"Fur sure." It was Adrian's latest.

"I never wanted to run again," Marek said. "But if it's the only way to stay in the fight, I'll go."

Helena took his hand. "We're a team."

"I'm sure not staying here," Melanie said.

Frank shrugged. "Yeah, why not?"

"Well, if you all go . . ." Glynis sounded dismal.

"Fuck you," Jason said, then slammed his fist onto the table. But he didn't leave.

Vivian stood up. "I'm going to my room now. You do as you please. This is my home, and I shan't abandon it."

"You're going with us, Vivian," Leigh said evenly. "This isn't your house anymore. It's Katherine's. Melanie is going to skip bail, Katherine's going to be out a million dollars, and she gets the house as recompense."

Vivian sat back down. She stared at Leigh vacantly for a time while she processed the facts. Finally, her expression slowly began to change. As Leigh watched, she saw the glimmering of respect dawn in Vivian's eyes.

Vivian cleared her throat. "All right. We've always been an honorable family. I'll go with you."

"Where will we go? How will we live?" Tears began to stream down Glynis's cheeks.

"I don't know," Leigh said honestly. "To protect Melanie, as well as ourselves, we'll probably have to don disguises. It might be best if we split up somehow. We'll need to find others like ourselves. Do any of you know about other families?"

There were tentative nods around the table.

"We won't be able to risk trying to get our respective monies," Leigh continued. "I guess we're going to have to struggle in more ways than the obvious."

"I'd suggest that we pack up what valuables we can in our cars and drive to Denver," Marek said. "There we can sell or pawn what we have and use that money to catch a train or plane to some big city. It's easier to get lost in a city."

"Man, this could be fun. We're goin' underground." Jason was suddenly becoming animated.

"I'll hold on to my axe," Frank said. "Get on with a band. You know, help support us."

"I can always find a job as a domestic," Helena said. "And I know for a fact that Gil's a hell of a dishwasher when he wants to be."

"I can wait tables or something. At least 'til the baby comes," Melanie offered.

"Baby?" Vivian asked.

"Yes, didn't you know?" Leigh said. "Melanie and Frank are the proud soon-to-be parents of a new little baby witchlet."

Adrian dissolved into delighted laughter. "A witchlet?"

"Not if the preacher has anything to say about it," Jason said, his mood once again dark. "Haven't you heard the motto they're attributing to him these days? It's 'Burn, baby, burn.'"

17

Leigh was in her room packing when she noticed Vivian standing tentatively in the doorway.

"Are you all packed?" Leigh asked.

"Not quite. Ah, there's something I came across that, well . . ." She held up an old, worn carpet bag. "I think it's something . . ." She made a sound of distress.

"Come on in and sit down," Leigh offered gently.

Vivian accepted Leigh's invitation, sitting stiffly on the edge of the bed, the carpet bag resting in her lap. "Ah, I lied before when I said the Hawthornes have always been an honorable family."

Leigh sat down next to her. "How so?"

"Since I've been a member of this family—and before that—the Hawthornes have been rather . . . ah, arrogant, I guess, is the word I want. It's easy to get that way when you've got powers that set you apart. But we've hurt people, and I feel a certain regret."

Leigh could sense the terrible pain and remorse Vivian was hiding behind her formal bearing and tone. She could also feel a sense of foreboding, a foreknowledge . . .

"You are one of those we hurt, and I want to apologize for that. I also want you to know that I'm grateful for the manner in which you've handled this crisis. We're . . . lucky to have you in charge of things. It's been a long time since there's been a woman at the helm of the Hawthorne clan, and . . . with the times that are coming, I'm glad we have one. A woman has the power to channel the Goddess. A man can only worship Her. We're going to need that direct link to power, that inexorable strength, if the Hawthornes are going to survive.

"I . . . it's been a long time since I've given thought to spiritual issues. It's easy to get caught up in the powers, and the sensual indulgence—you know witches aren't sexual prudes, by any means—and the things that have always made us feel more special than the rest. It's easy to forget to love. I guess it took this . . ."

Leigh put her hand on Vivian's arm and tried to absorb a measure of her distress. "Are you okay?"

Vivian shook off Leigh's arm, and Leigh understood that she was trying to break the empathic connection. "You're not responsible for my regrets. But"—she thrust the carpet bag at her—"I do want you to take responsibility for this."

Leigh took the bag. "What is it?"

"It contains the Hawthorne magical heirlooms. They've been handed down for countless generations. It's time to pass them on."

With that said, Vivian stood and strode quickly from the room.

For reasons she couldn't quite comprehend, Leigh began to cry.

18

It was seven-fifteen, and the parlor was filled with suitcases, boxes of valuables, the Janowskis, and the Hawthornes.

"The Caddy, the Mercedes, Jason's Jag, and my truck all have enough gas to get us to Denver," Marek said. "I'll start bringing them around so we can load—"

A loud knock on the door interrupted him.

"Who could that be?" Marek wondered aloud. "I locked all the gates."

Helena quietly made her way into the foyer and to the front door, then peered through the peephole. "It's a priest."

"There was a priest at Katherine's earlier today," Leigh said.

"A priest?" Vivian followed Helena's lead. She inspected him for several moments, then drew back with a puzzled expression. "It's been so many years, I can't be sure, but I think it's Cliff."

"Cliff?" Leigh asked.

"My brother," Glynis said, beginning her slow shuffle toward the front door.

"A Catholic priest?" Leigh asked.

"And you thought Craig was a rebel," Helena said with an amused wink in her direction.

Glynis swung the door open to greet him. They stood looking at each other in silence for a moment, before Cliff smiled, then held up a key. "It still fits the gate, but I thought I should give you a choice here at the door."

Glynis's confusion was clear. "Why are you here?"

He shrugged. "The circumstances are rather ironic—given my present religious affiliation—but I came to see if I could help."

"There's been so much death."

"There'll probably be more."

"You're a part of the Salazar curse . . .the last grandson. You must go. Quickly."

Cliff stepped inside the door and bent to embrace her. "Thank you for caring."

Helena closed the door behind them.

Cliff saw all the suitcases and quickly assessed the situation. "If you're going, you must go quickly. On my way here, I saw crowds of people heading on foot in this direction. I also saw some people already at the back fence. I'll stay here and stall them all for as long as I can so you can get a head start."

Everyone looked at Leigh.

"Yes. Thank you."

"Jason, Gil, help me get the cars out of the garage," Marek said. He threw his keys to Frank. "My truck's parked just inside the south gate."

The men left to perform their duties.

Cliff approached Leigh and held out his hand. "Katherine tells me that you're the rebel leader. I'm pleased to meet you."

When Leigh took his hand, she felt a jolt of energy connect between them, and then an onrush of love passed through her. She held her breath as she savored the purity of the emotion that was . . . *Better than any drug rush, eh, babe?* Craig's voice was clear as a bell. She looked around the room, half expecting him to have resurrected or, perhaps, ectoplasmically manifested, but he wasn't visible. But she felt he was there in some form, and she was grateful.

"Your energy is quite intense, Father," she said.

His eyes narrowed to slits as he, in turn, sensed her inner quality. In the previous half-century, he had met several contemplatives who had embodied a high degree of divine energy. Leigh ranked among them, but he didn't think she knew it yet. He squeezed her hand.

Venus had finally answered his prayer.

19

Cody crouched behind the fence of the enemy compound and watched them—*fuckin' goddamn gooks*—as they snuck through the night toward the hut where they had their jeeps hidden. They were trying to escape, as he knew they would. But he didn't intend to allow them to get away this time. And he wouldn't let them hit him again with their napalm. No, he had finally learned how to outwit them. It was going to be a full-scale assault, and—even with the short notice—he had, through his weighty connections, secured for the job two of the best mercenaries Special Forces had ever produced: Nate Randall and Juan "Junkman" Martinez. They had rigged the bomb and had done it with readily handy materials so as not to identify the operation as military. They were clever and would do whatever he told them to. They had nothing to lose. Officially they were MIAs.

For some the war never seemed to end.

20

Marek hit the outside buttons, and three of the six garage doors began to rise. He and the two boys didn't proceed cautiously; they assumed that what they had to fear hadn't yet made its way onto the grounds. It was Jason's foot that found the trip wire.

The explosion shattered the glass in the overhead transom and knocked Leigh off her feet. She and the glass fell together.

"Mommy!" Adrian crawled into her arms.

Her adrenaline rush forestalled her immediate notice

of the jagged piece of crystal that was imbedded in her calf. Her mind didn't register the fact that Kamelia yanked it free. She struggled to her feet and followed the others into the dining room, where, through the terrace doors, they could see the burning wreckage of the garage.

"No!" Helena fumbled with the door latch. "Oh, gods, no!"

Cliff gently pushed her hand aside. "Stay here. I'll go see."

Leigh put a firm hand on Helena's shoulder to urge her to obey, and Cliff slipped out the door. Leigh could feel her grief and horror; the emotions were all too familiar. Leigh, knowing that she couldn't allow herself to be affected by it if she were to be able to effectively lead the survivors to safety, erected the invisible barrier once again.

The wind told Cliff what he needed to know; he had smelled the scent of burning flesh before. Still he proceeded in case there were survivors. His mind reached out for thoughts, but the mind he touched was that of the enemy. And this time the enemy wasn't gracious.

Got him in my sight. Good . . .

The bullet from the hunting rifle ripped through Cliff's chest like a searing fireball and threw him to the ground, where he quickly began to drown in his own blood.

"Into your hands I commend my spirit," he managed to whisper. But he didn't will himself into the waiting arms of the Father God. It was the Virgin Mother who appeared to accept his sacrifice.

21

Leigh watched in shock and horror as Cliff was killed. The men were dead. Now it was down to the women and children, and Leigh knew full well that the enemy would show no mercy.

"Do we have guns?" she asked.

Everyone was too stunned to reply.

"Guns! Now!"

That got their attention.

"Yeah, Jason packed all the hunting stuff," Melanie replied.

"Find it." Leigh drew the curtains across the terrace doors and urged everyone on ahead of her into the parlor.

Melanie used the fireplace poker to pry open the steamer trunk, which was full of firearms and ammunition.

"Does anyone know how to load these things?" Leigh asked.

Melanie nodded. "I hunted with Dad and . . . and Jason."

"Good, then you load them. I'm sure the rest of us can figure out how to squeeze triggers."

"I don't know if I can help," Glynis said. "My arm is numb." She was holding a limp left arm with her right hand.

"Kammi," Leigh said. It was an order.

Kamelia made Glynis sit down and examined her, then looked at Leigh with a puzzled expression. "I think her arm's okay, but there's something funny about her heart."

They're going to kill all of us . . . "One way or another," Leigh muttered. "Just take it easy, Glynis," she said.

Melanie began to hand out the guns. "I've turned off the safety on all of them so it'll be easier for you. Aiming isn't so important with the shotguns; just point and fire." She gave the shotguns to Kamelia and Vivian. "There's a .22 for Adrian," she said, then gave him the small handgun. "Don't touch the trigger until you're ready to fire for real," she explained as he took possession of it. "The deer rifles will be good for us," she said, giving Leigh and Helena the .308's and keeping the .243 for herself.

Leigh picked up the phone to call the police, but, as she had half expected, the line was dead.

It crossed her mind that the attack seemed professionally planned.

"Cody," she whispered.

22

Cody rendezvoused with the approaching crowd. His people had had no difficulty stirring up the locals, especially when the news of the Whittaker murder broke. Cody himself hadn't been surprised by the news; he'd known all along that he was right about the Hawthornes.

Nate and Junkman also found their way into the crowd and got lost among it.

When they came to the north gate of the manor, they stormed it, and, like a giant wave of self-righteousness flattening everything that resisted it, the crowd swarmed onto the grounds. In an orgy of destruction, the people trampled flower beds and toppled statues; the fallen gods and goddesses were attacked with rocks and tire irons for good measure.

As they surged toward the mansion, other guns besides those belonging to Nate and Junkman were drawn.

23

"Adrian, tell me quickly if Frank's still alive."

Leigh had never asked anything like this of her son, and he blinked for a moment with confusion. Then he closed his eyes. "Yes," he said with surprise. "I can see him hiding in Marek's truck."

"Can your mind talk to his?" Leigh asked.

Adrian hesitated, then nodded.

"Tell him to get ready. On your order, he's to drive the truck up to the kitchen door."

Adrian, his eyes still closed, scrunched his forehead with effort. Then he looked at Leigh. "Okey-doke."

"Good boy. Now—" She peeked out the front curtains at the approaching crowd. "I've got a plan that might work. If it doesn't, do whatever it takes to survive. *Whatever* it takes." She took the fireplace poker and began knocking small panes of glass from the front window, "I want them to see lots of deterrent; everybody get down low, stick your guns through the window, and point the barrels at them." She held Adrian back. "Not you, honey. You've got to stand right inside the door and wait for my signal to summon Frank. Melanie, I want you to shoot at the ground ahead of them; try and stop their approach."

Melanie aimed the rifle, and her bullet found its mark. The crowd stopped and fell silent.

"Now, cover me," Leigh said. Her gun firmly grasped in her hands, she walked through the foyer and out the front door.

She was greeted by close to a hundred people. They were an even mixture of men and women, a respectable-looking cross-section of Montvue society. Many were couples who stood hand in hand, facing their enemy together, *for better or worse, 'til death do us part*, Leigh thought with a touch of irony. She also took note of the fact that they were all adults; there was no chance of their children getting hurt. Only hers were expendable, it seemed. They stood in a large semicircle behind Cody, who was about twenty feet from the foot of the porch steps. For a moment, as she stared into the faces of the enraged intruders and felt their blood lust, fear threatened to overcome her. But she said a silent prayer to the Goddess whom she had met the night of her initiation, and she felt an uncanny peace settle upon her.

"There's been enough death," she said, her voice strong. "There's still time to turn this around and stop the madness."

Cody was momentarily startled. He had expected them to attack with more hexes, not defend themselves with mortal weapons. *Goddamn VC always were clever bastards.* He shook his head to clear the conflicting images that were assaulting him.

Melanie scanned the crowd through the scope; she had always had the best eye for game, she recalled absently. But Jason had been the better shot.

"The Bible says that 'thou shalt not suffer a witch to live,' " Cody said.

"The Bible also says that you should not judge or

330

condemn. And I seem to remember something about loving your enemies," Leigh replied.

Clever. Yes, they're clever. "What do you know about love, you witch bitch?" Cody asked.

"More than you," she replied calmly, becoming aware of a pulsing power arising within, growing stronger with each heartbeat.

"Your people put my wife into a coma!"

"And your people killed the only ones who could have reversed it," Leigh told him. There was a soft light beginning to fill the air around her. "See how your righteous anger can backfire, Preacher?"

Melanie stopped scanning. The Chicano man on the far edge of the crowd had thrown a rifle to his shoulder and aimed it at Leigh. Without hesitation, Melanie pulled the trigger, and the shot rang out.

The people began to panic as Junkman crumpled to the ground.

Melanie saw the other man's rifle as it turned toward the window. "Duck!" she yelled, but Vivian didn't respond fast enough. The second bullet fired in as many seconds caught Vivian in the throat. The hit knocked her backward, and she fell on the floor, where she frantically clawed at her neck for a few moments. Then she lay still.

Melanie tried to sight in Vivian's murderer, but he had disappeared in the crowd.

Neither Leigh nor Cody had moved. They stood facing each other, their mutual gaze unwavering.

Something within told Leigh to drop the gun she held. Without thought, she obeyed.

Her action served to momentarily defuse the situation. Others who had raised their guns stood hesitant.

"Don't you understand yet that love bears the fruit of love, but hate breeds only hate?" The voice was Leigh's, but the words weren't her own. She felt a sense of disassociation with herself. Something powerful had taken charge. "How much more suffering is it going to take before you learn?"

Cody's eyes smarted from the bright light. Was it the

rays from the setting sun? Or perhaps the gooks had some new secret weapon?

Leigh lost herself totally in the warm radiance of the Lady.

Adrian, his hands empty, his demeanor trancelike, appeared on the porch beside Her.

"Listen to the words of this child," Leigh's voice said. "See the visions he has to share."

"This is the beginning of the greatest of holocausts," Adrian said, his voice old and wise. "More will die than in any other battle ever fought. Fear, superstition, avarice, and hate will take man captive, and the darkest night of the human soul will fall like a smothering, putrid cloak. It will leave none of us untouched.

"Alexander Cody, your hatred has damned your wife to an endless sleep. The witch hunt you're instigating will cause your daughter to come to forever fear and resent you.

"Nate Randall, your sister will be stoned to death outside her home in Georgia. The accusations of witchcraft will come from her estranged husband; it'll be his way of gaining custody of their children.

"James Bradshaw, your brother will suffer a fatal stroke defending his daughter, Stephanie, who will find charges of witchcraft leveled against her for practicing transcendental meditation, working with crystals, and studying herbalism.

"Maggie Kolatch, your son and daughter-in-law are going to have you committed to an insane asylum for practicing witchcraft; and they'll thereby achieve their goal of obtaining control of your estate.

"John and Penny Denman, your daughter, Autumn—who has epilepsy—will be set on fire by her little friends, Shannon and Lisa. They'll just be imitating their parents, who were party to the deaths of Craig Hawthorne and Dorian Wildes. Shannon and Lisa have been told burning witches is a righteous thing to do."

Adrian paused. "If there's not enough love left in you to care about what happens to faceless millions of people, then maybe there's enough selfishness in you to make it stop before those you love fall victim to the evil that has been unleashed here. You stand at the turning point. After today there will be no reversing the tide. The time has come to make a choice.''

24

Both Leigh and Adrian came out of their trances while the people were still reeling from the revelations Adrian had made.

"How could he possibly have known about Autumn's condition? We've kept it a secret," Leigh heard one woman say.

"Stephanie's into that shit, too. Could she really be a witch?"

"Mark Kolatch has always been a greedy SOB."

"Cody, how'd the runt know my name and that my sis lives in Georgia?"

Leigh bent down and whispered, "Give Frank the signal." Then she took his hand and led him into the house, closing and bolting the door behind them.

Vivian's body lay wide-eyed in a pool of blood, and Glynis's body was slumped in a lifeless heap on the couch.

"Her heart stopped," Kamelia explained. She looked much older than she had only an hour before.

"Get to the back door. Quick."

Kamelia, Adrian, Melanie, and Helena all ran toward the kitchen. Leigh paused only for a moment to grab the old carpet bag full of the Hawthorne magical treasures. She gave a final, loving look at the forms Vivian and Glynis had left behind. "We're of the same blood now, ladies. We'll meet again," she whispered.

At that moment, with a rock heaved through the front window and a volley of wild gunfire, the crowd outside declared the choice they had made.

Epilogue

Winter

Leigh danced. Her bare breasts swung wildly as she undulated to the hard rock music that filled the smoky club. Craig had once dubbed her style hot-to-trot T-and-A sexery, and never had the label been more applicable than now.

As she danced, she tuned out the men who gawked and shouted lewd suggestions. She had long since overcome her stage fright. In her mind, she dedicated her dance to the Goddess; she was dancing in celebration of life and womanhood and beauty. It became her form of worship of the Lady in a world that sought only to defame Her. Leigh's creation linked her to the Creatrix, and she often wore an enigmatic smile that gave testimony to her secret.

Sometimes a man in the crowd would respond and find himself unconsciously a part of the ritual. Leigh would occasionally feel such a man lifted from a sensual reaction to her movement to a disconcerted awe that defied his own reason. Through Leigh, the Goddess would occasionally bless such a man, and that was good.

When her final set of the evening was complete, Leigh

went back to the dressing room to change. When she walked in, the new girl—Jack had said her name was Holly—was sitting on the couch massaging her feet. Holly looked up at her, and Leigh sensed the same familiarity that she had earlier in the evening. Leigh momentarily lowered her psychic defenses, and she knew.

Leigh and Holly lingered in the dressing room while other dancers retrieved their wraps.

" 'Night, Nicki," Janet said.

"Good night. Be careful going home," Leigh responded. In this town, in this club, she was Nicki.

"Good to have you aboard, Holly," Karen said. "Makes for shorter sets for me."

Soon they were alone.

Leigh sat down next to her. "Did you ever find your daughter?"

Diane Fox shook her head.

"We both chose red. Think that means something?" Leigh was referring to their dyed hair.

"Color of blood," Diane said.

"How long have you been on the run?"

"I was on your heels. You were right about the results of my stance." She paused and looked around. "Funny about the world today. This place is more respectable than a Buddhist temple. Sad commentary."

"This'll be my last night. There was a man in the audience. I think he recognized me."

"Pictures of you and yours have certainly gotten around. I think they've been shown in the media more than those of Kennedy's assassination." Diane sighed. "God, I'm sorry you're leaving so soon."

"What are your plans?"

"Just trying to survive. I'm compiling writings on the persecution. Some of my own, some from other renegades. When it's over, I'll publish it. Maybe it'll help keep it from happening again."

"I have a poem," Leigh said. "Maybe when we meet again I'll have a chance to give it to you."

Diane offered her hand. "Good luck."

Leigh shook it warmly. "Stay alive."

*   *   *

Leigh walked through the hushed, snowy night toward the seedy hotel that had sheltered them for the past six weeks. Six weeks had been a long stint . . . comparatively. But in their running they had made connections with others in the underground, and there was a slowly developing network. Leigh couldn't see the light at the end of the tunnel yet. But she knew it was there.

A man stepped out from the shadows of an alley and blocked her path. "Where ya goin' in such a hurry?" The steam of his breath carried the strong smell of gin.

Leigh wasn't afraid. She was angry. She could sense his lust and his need to violate the sanctity of her femininity, to inflate himself by degrading her, to feel good by hurting her. That's what they were doing to Her, too. Leigh was tired of always letting them win.

She made the sign with her hand and pointed it at his genitals. There were some spells she had learned to cast.

He doubled over and emitted an agonized scream.

Wordlessly, she stepped past him and continued her homeward journey.

She heard the names he yelled after her, but they didn't faze her. She had long become accustomed to being called a witch.

Quietly, she let herself into their rooms. The baby—Melanie and Frank had decided to call him Marek—was fretting in the large basket that served as his crib. Leigh gently checked the state of his diaper and then cuddled him until he settled down.

Then Leigh performed her early-morning ritual of accounting for everyone. Her children were sleeping together in their bed, Melanie and Frank were asleep in tender embrace, and Helena was restlessly tossing and turning. Leigh put a cool hand on the woman's forehead and tried to sooth the ugly dreams that taunted her. Soon she became more peaceful.

Leigh hung up her heavy wool coat, then made herself a cup of hot cocoa on the single-burner hot plate that served as their kitchen. As she sat down to drink it, she pulled from her hiding place the Hawthorne Book of Shadows. Her only contribution to it thus far had been the poem she had mentioned to Diane. It would probably be the only contribution she would make, too. She didn't believe there was a greater lesson she could share with the future than that which it contained.

She read it again, to remind herself.

Shadow Play

With his eyes fixed on Paradise,
   the haunted Christian
blames the shadow. Plagued

by his own demons,
   soul bitten and loveless,
he is bound in the sackcloth of pride,

in cobwebs and ashes.
   While there, thrilled to the wild,
dizzying ride of the flesh,

of phallus and womb, the fresh
   dew of this world, the red,
simple wing of original joy,

like the berrying spring of a child's
   renewal, the Witch slips out
of the black diaphanous robe

of our common sleep. Behind
   that half-curtain, lives with the sharp
knowledge of danger (Do not, whatever

else you may do, be discovered!).
   Out of that horn of magic, desire,
flesh at once richer and paler than ivory

is bathed—Look!—in original light!
   . . .Or are those only the elegant
ivory bars of the cage

in which both have been trapped:
   Earth-delighted no less than he
with his cross-obsessed pain?

While She-Without-Form,
    resurrected again and again,
cries out from the nailed thirst of this world

to our own resurrection, that single
    commandment: Love!—O heart's simple name!
O first and final salvation!